Life After Death
(For Beginners)

Michael Gerber Admits to the Following:

The Bull Street Journal (1996)
(with Jonathan Schwarz & Robert Weisberg)
Barry Trotter and the Shameless Parody (2002)
Barry Trotter and the Unnecessary Sequel (2003)
Barry Trotter and the Dead Horse (2004)
The Chronicles of Blarnia (2005)
Freshman (2006)
Our Kampf (2006)
(with Jonathan Schwarz)
Sophomore (2007)
By Jove (2007)
A Christmas Peril (2008)
This Book (now)

Life After Death (For Beginners)

A Singular Fantasy

by Michael Gerber

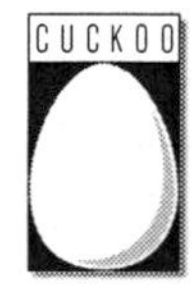

For Mary—who else?

• • •

This is a work of fiction. Any similarities to persons living or dead, without satiric intent, is purely coincidental.

• • •

ATTENZIONE! This book was self-published. There are no big, faceless corporations involved here; it's just me, the author, and you, the reader. I received no advance, and my only payment comes from readers paying for copies. **PLEASE DO NOT PIRATE THIS BOOK**. I have tried to keep the price low, so that anyone who wants one can purchase it legally. If you're broke, request a paper copy from your library. If you're *really* broke (and trust me, I've been there) write me directly at contactmike@mikegerber.com, and I will send you a copy if you help me promote it. This book represents three years' worth of hard work, and many years of research and thought before that. I hope you love it; please help it have a long, happy life in the world.—*MG, 2010*

• • •

 For information, write him c/o Cuckoo Books, 1122 Sixth St. #403, Santa Monica, CA 90403.
Cover and book design by El Gerberino.
First Edition / August 2010
ISBN: 1-890470-06-6
Why not visit www.mikegerber.com? Hm? *Why not?*

CONTENTS

"You sort of wonder when something like that happens, well, who stands to benefit? Who had the opportunity and the motive? You just kind of look at these basic things...I saw that the US government was going to benefit, and the White House people, the Republican administration to take the mind of the public off the crashing economy...And I have spent enough time on the inside of, well in the White House and campaigns and I've known enough people who do these things, think this way, to know that the public version of the news or whatever event, is never really what happened."

—Hunter S. Thompson

CHAPTER ONE

"The world gave you its friendship pin
But you wound up in the cutout bin
Pricked with holes and soaked in sin
Suckered in, suffering, trapped by what you've chosen…"

—unreleased Zimmerman parody
(taped 1979, found under my bed, 2009)

Let me tell you about the last day of my life.

Firstwise, if I had known it was going to be the last day of my life, I would've gotten up earlier. But I didn't, so I rolled out of bed at my usual time, around noon. Then I took a shower, which took about an hour. Most people hop in and out and never get really clean, but I read a book once that explained exactly how you're supposed to do it. As the steam massaged my pores, I thought about a show I'd seen on TV the night before, a documentary where these guys were making a catapult. Or was it a trebuchet? Trebuchet, catapult, the best shows are always on really late at night, why is that? It's like they don't *want* anybody to see them. That's one of the reasons I loved living in New York: fifty-two channels, A through ZZ, twenty-four hours a day. In 1980, that was more than *anybody*.

When I went down the hall to breakfast, Der Fraulein was sitting at the head of our big long black dining room table. Everything in our apartment was either black, or white, or clear, or gold. Very pure, you know? That was our aesthetic.

Everyone in the Western world knew what Katrinka looked like then, she was almost as big a star as I was. My wife was lanky and blonde, and liked to wear men's clothes. (Diane Keaton didn't invent anything.) When I walked in Katrinka was on the phone, chewing someone out in Russian. It's good for that.

My wife is the most beautiful woman in the world, but very misunderstood, because she's also a genius. It's very hard to be a genius on this plane of existence, and I know because I used to be one, too. Now I'm just a guy, and things are much easier. Well, sort of. You'll see what I mean soon enough.

I sat down at the other end of the table, about thirty feet away. Katrinka had insisted that it be this big when we got it, for the dinner parties we were going to have, for her "salon." I put it in quotes because we hadn't had a houseguest in two years. The table had been made from a single tree, at a druid monastery in Wales. It was somewhat magical; a lot of our things were. That's why they cost me so much. Nowdays, none of my things are magical, which is less convenient, but you cannot believe how much money I save.

The wife had these buttons drilled into the table which you could press for food. I pushed mine, and Bettina came scurrying out with my breakfast. Coffee *and* tea, as usual. If it's organic, you don't get addicted to the caffeine. Plus shredded wheat, to clean me out. Most rock stars don't get nearly enough fiber, that's why they're so full of shit.

Bettina put the tray down with a clatter. "What's your hurry? Trying to get back before the end of the commercial?"

"No, Mr. Tom."

She was lying, of course—I'd caught her watching soaps the week before and given her a talking-to. Oh, don't give me that look. I was no worse than the rest of humanity—we're all exactly as nice as we have to be. Back then, I didn't have to be nice, so I wasn't. Anyway, Bettina liked the attention. Otherwise why didn't she quit?

I'll tell you why: because she wanted to tell her friends she worked for Tom

Larkin. "This is the kind of deodorant crystal he uses; and this kind of jam; and can you imagine?—two days ago I heard him making an appointment at *Bosley Hair Clinic*." As recompense, I tortured her occasionally. Why should she have all the fun? Just because she was poor?

Fraulein always said that some people were natural slaves. I used to make a big deal out of treating everyone equal, but after getting screwed one too many times, I realized people don't want to be equal. They resented it, it made them nervous. So then I treated everyone appropriately, but sometimes I made mistakes and thought someone was higher than they were. My wife was better at telling people's *true* level, so I followed her lead.

"Hello, Tom," Fraulein said, hanging up the phone and finishing a glass of champagne. She lived on champagne, and black coffee. Der Fraulein wore an amulet that allowed her to survive on precisely 100 calories a day. Bettina hid pizza boxes in her office trash, out of spite. See what I mean about the resentment?

"Hello, Katrinka," I said through a mouthful of shreddly wheat. I didn't have an amulet, but lived on health foods. Mostly. "What's my schedule for today? Where's Jasper?"

"Daycamp. Today's museum day."

I imagined our son as part of a massive herd of five-year-olds, shrieking spastically and knocking over priceless objects. What a great kid. "Think I'll be able to see him?"

"Doubtful." Der Fraulein made a sour face. "Where is Bettina? She saw my glass was empty." She pressed the button savagely. "This is really too much."

"She probably thinks you're a lush."

"People like her can't afford opinions. We should fire her."

Bettina emerged holding a bottle, and quick-stepped over to the far end of the room. She filled Fraulein's glass with champagne, and her ear with apologies. After she left, Fraulein said, "Do you see how quickly she came after I complained? She was listening to our conversation. *Spying.*"

My wife had that Russian thing about spying. Being English, I didn't. "If she was, she's probably even more bored than I am."

"You're only bored because I do everything. Anyway, don't stick up for her. That's why none of our people do their jobs, because you're too kind to them."

"No, it's because this is 1980 Manhattan, and not Hitler's Russia."

"Idiot." Jokes like that let me have a laugh and Fraulein think I was stupid, so we both won. It cost me nothing to make her happy. "Traitors," she muttered happily. "Surrounded..."

Even though my wife was born in Berlin and went to college in California, her great-grandmother was the Czar's girlfriend, and this makes her White Russian nobility. Right? Don't ask me, we didn't have nobility where I grew up. You were lucky if you had a television. My mates and I dubbed Greasby "Yesterday's City Tomorrow," and it was.

"Have you noticed we often fight when you first wake up?" my wife said. "I think you have a glandular problem. I'll make an appointment for you with Sven."

"Oh, don't. Sven makes me damp." Sven was our acupuncturist, but instead of needles, he used ice cubes. Fraulein thought he was a genius, but that's only because she was afraid of needles. "That's the third appointment this month," I said. "I think Bettina should move out, and Sven should move in."

"What do you care? You can afford it."

"That's true." Back then, I could afford almost anything. I'd made an immense pile in the Sixties—though rather less than I ought to have done, thanks to an overmatched manager. Who was replaced by a typical show-biz sharpie. Who was replaced by Der Fraulein. "If you can keep from suing people, dear."

"I only sue people who deserve it," Fraulein said, but she went to court like other people went to the dry cleaners. She'd use a Oujia board to contact Adolf Hitler, and they would strategize together. "You have a haircut today. Have you been using the placenta mixture?"

"Yes," I lied.

"Tom, don't lie to me. How can we have a healthy marriage when you always lie? I can tell you haven't been using it, your scalp looks dead."

"I can't help it. I've been anxious."

"What about?"

"Oh, nothing," I said, "just my first album in five bloody years. Which ain't selling!"

"Give it time. And don't swear."

"I hate the bloody placenta mixture. It's fucking foul."

"Well," Fraulein sniffed, "I never knew you hated women's bodies so much."

"It's not human, Katrinka! It's from cows. I called the number on the bottle."

"Why did you have to do that? I wish you'd just trust me."

"Don't care about my bloody hair..." I pushed away my forage. "Lost my appetite."

"Go on, eat the rest."

It wasn't worth fighting over, so I picked up my spoon and finished. Slowly, though, just to show her who was boss.

"Tom, you must take better care of yourself. I *forbid* you to get old. If you look old, the fans will stop loving you—"

"I know, you keep telling me."

"If it weren't for my publicity work, they would've stopped years ago."

"I wish they had." It was humiliating, owing everything a mob of mad strangers. "I don't need all this stuff. Happiest times of my life were when I was living out of a duffel bag."

"Oh, that's good," Fraulein said, making a note. "Remember to say that to the man from *Roogalator*."

"Christ, that's today? I haven't even thought about what I'm going to say."

"*We're* going to say, Tom. It should be fine, I've vetted him thoroughly. His chart looks clean"—that's astrological chart, folks—"and Warren has assured me that he's friendly. So don't be worried."

"I'm not worried, Fraulein. I've been giving interviews for twenty years.

You're worried."

Fraulein denied it, then coped with her nerves the way she always did: planning my life obsessively. Just like that, every moment from then until midnight was spoken for, right down to picking my nose and shitting.

"Come on, der Fraulein, this is worse than the Army." I wanted her to think I hated it—it would give her more pleasure. Secretly I loved it. I considered it a luxury, the ultimate time-saving device. She could think about all that, which would free me up to think about...nothing.

As she talked, I remembered last night's documentary again, and wondered if we could put one of those catapult-trebuchet things up on the roof. Of course the other tenants in the Oneida would stamp their little feet, Gloria Swanson and Capote and whichever Auchincloss was bunking here now. But we were much bigger stars than they were and that should count for something. I ask you: what's the fucking point of living next to Central Park if you can't take advantage of it? I wondered if we could hit the reservoir.

The first step was getting the wife on board. "Do you know anyone in Zoning?" I asked, trying to act casual.

"Whatever you're planning, stop it," Fraulein said. "This is much too delicate a time for us." She knew that the intersection of me and reality meant trouble. She looked at her watch. "I have to go take a meeting. I'll call the car. Be ready for your haircut in two hours."

I was ready, but only just. Going out was quite stressful when you were as famous as I was. People expected me to look a certain way, so I had to dress carefully. Did you know President Callaway changed shirts six times a day? A lot of celebs have little quirks like that, it's how we remind everyone we're special.

And I got touched a lot, so I had to take certain precautions—"normal" people usually don't have a very high level of hygiene. Sure, they looked clean, but two weeks later, you'd be sick as a dog and wondering why. I had a pack, a sort of kit that I always took around with me. It was nothing you'd notice, just stuff like wipes and rubbing alcohol, and some gel that Fraulein got from one of her friends who was a plastic surgeon. The funny thing was, it smelled exactly like toothpaste. I was going to taste it once, but Fraulein saw me. "Stop! That's poisonous!" She said it was a very powerful experimental antibiotic.

Fraulein didn't say goodbye to me when I left; she was in her office, on the phone, buying up water somewhere. She always said to me, "Tom, someday water is going to be huge." I was happy to let her take care of all those things, and signed the papers to prove it. I hadn't written a check in two years.

That threatened some people, some so-called friends. When Fraulein began taking my place for all the Ravins meetings (and believe me, there were plenty, even ten years after we split) my one-time songwriting partner wrote me a little note. In it, my old buddy old pal Oliver said that he was worried about Katrinka "working things to her advantage." I-fucking-e, screwing me over somehow.

"The jealousy in your note was unmistakable," I wrote back. "I'm sorry you don't have a very close relationship with your own wife, but that's no reason to criticize mine. Katrinka can't be after my money, because it's already hers. CAN *YOUR* WIFE SAY THE SAME?" Then I signed it with a smiley face. Ollie would recognize the handwriting.

I'd always liked getting my hair cut, which is amusing given that I'd done more to bankrupt barbers than anyone else in history. (Ollie, Harry, and Buck were just coattailing.) I particularly liked going to this guy, Mr. Fong, because he didn't cut my hair as much as fondle it. He believed that violence in the outside world kept hair "hiding in the cranial reservoir," and that by petting it and pulling it very gently, wooing the follicles, you could make it grow.

I hoped he was right, because a tangelo crop circle was taking shape on the back of my head. Fraulein's opinions about my fans were bullshit most of the time—strangely enough, whatever they wanted aligned precisely with *her* wishes on any given matter—but thanks to the centrality of hair to my myth, I didn't think it wise to take chances.

The fans. Fickle, selfish, impossible to predict; givers of all that we had; drivers of our gravy train. Naturally we hated them. Who wouldn't? We lived at the whim of a bunch of unpredictable psychotics living in a fantasy world. I don't know what I'd have done without Fraulein to keep it all in perspective. We used to fantasize about running away, chucking the whole game. "Someday we'll be free, we won't have to do what anyone says. Won't that be wonderful?" "Only if we could keep the money."

After my haircut I planned to stop at a bookstore down in the Village, one of my favorite haunts. Gnomon's Attic was quiet, private, and had a good section on esoterica. Plus, the cashier was far too old to care who I was, and would throw anyone out who made a fuss. Last time, he told me about playing croquet with Alistair Crowley.

I was interested in Rosicrucianism. You gotta respect any religion with the balls to advertise in comic books. But Fraulein called me right as the car was dropping me off. It's uncanny how she always knew where I was; I think she had second sight.

"You have enough religions," she said. "You have to come back uptown, so we can prepare for the interview." I knew what "preparing" was: spending an hour sitting at the kitchen table getting our stories straight. I had this habit of spouting off which drove Fraulein crazy. "It muddies the picture. We can't allow that. We must provide something clear and simple for people to believe in."

"Dear, your Prussian is showing."

"I'm not Prussian, I'm Russian," she said. "My grandmother was mistress to…"

"'Czar Nicholas the Second," I chimed in. "And *my* grandfather followed behind his horse with a scoop."

Not really, but grandpa might as well have been. I think it bothered her that I was so rich, given that I'd come from drunken illiterates. Fraulein didn't understand the concept of upward mobility. She took it personally.

First, the photographer came, and then the interviewer. He'd tried to dress up, but I could see he was broke, a nobody. You can always tell by the shoes. His name was Dave or Gabe or something, I don't recall, but what I remember for sure was how aggressive he was.

Fraulein hated him. I think he wanted her to hate him, because he asked questions designed to insult her. "Tom, what do you say to people who think Katrinka controls you?"

"I'd say that they have no idea how we live. Our private selves are very different than what you see in public."

"Weak men are often threatened by strong women," Fraulein said. "It's a sign of Tom's strength that we are equals."

"Uh-huh." You'd think that would be outrageous enough, but then the guy starts basically calling us hypocrites, looking around at our apartment and saying, "Speaking of how you live, doesn't that contradict what you, Tom, have said in your songs?"

"What are we supposed to do, starve?" I was really annoyed, so Fraulein jumped in. She was great at PR, just as good as my old bandmate Oliver, only with Katrinka, she wouldn't lie to you. She has a great commitment to the truth. That comes from her scientific work. She shot straight with the guy, even though he didn't deserve it.

"People like us play a role in society. We can't live like we might want to, because—I mean, Tom and I both grew up doing without, we don't need any possessions because we have each other."

"Happiest times of my life have been when I was living out of a duffel bag."

"He said that just this morning," Fraulein said. "But he can't, you see? People want us to be rich, to be stars—"

"To fulfill *their* fantasies," I said. "So you've caught us red-handed: we're comfortable. We never said we weren't."

"You're more than comfortable, though, right? You're rich."

"Our money is clean," Fraulein said. "Not like some businessman's."

"I'm just trying to understand…"

Bullshit. He was trying to stir up shit to further his own career—and we knew this because he immediately went into detail about Fraulein's business things, like he'd been saving it. "You're buying up forests, arable land, water rights in Africa...This from a guy who famously sang, 'Possessions aren't reality.' Don't you see any contradiction in that?"

"No," I said.

"It's just how the game is played," Fraulein said. "We didn't make the game."

"We're good people," I said.

"But you're on *Forbes'* list of the richest entertainers, and yet you refuse to perform for charity."

"I'm sorry, I can't handle this any more." Eyes wet, Fraulein got up and walked out of the room. She played that chump like a violin. Like she was really about to cry. Like someone like him—a nobody—could affect her in any way!

"Oh, now you've done it," I said, genuinely angry. I reached over and snapped off the tape recorder. "Is this how you treat people who invite you into their home?"

"Come off it, Tom," the interviewer said. "You've got an album to sell."

"So let me sell it! What do you think this is, Watergate? We have money, we try to make more. Everybody does. Just because I write something in a song...When you interview Mick, do you expect him to be Satan?"

"But people take you more seriously than Mick. Your image—"

"That's about them!" I yelled, then realized that yelling was playing *his* game. "Look, I'm sorry. I want that person to exist, too. I want to be the guy in that song—that's why I wrote it. But I have to make do with who I really am, just like everybody else. And if it's a choice between saying good things and not always living up to them, or not saying them at all, I choose the former. Wouldn't you?"

"But I'm just a guy, and you're—"

"—just another guy, whom people think they can judge, because they think they know me. They don't. The readers of *Roogalator* don't know the 'real me.' I'm not sure such a creature exists. We're just pretending, you and

I. Pretending for money. So either play nice, or get the hell out."

Maybe I was a little rough on him, but I have a thing about total honesty. Then and now. I *crave* it. That's why I left The Ravins, 'way back when—I couldn't stand it anymore. My life had become a series of little deceptions, all to please other people.

Since Katrinka wasn't around, I tore open a packet of Raisinets. I lived on those fucking things. Every jacket I owned had a secret pocket in it, so I could sneak 'em without Fraulein knowing.

I chewed in silence as the interviewer went through his notes, crossing out questions. There were pages of 'em. Total hatchet job. I listened to the LP playing over the apartment's sound system. I wondered why people weren't buying it—I guess they didn't like hearing me happy.

I'd given him the sour, now it was time for the sweet. "Listen, Dave, I'm not trying to be a prick, it's just...I'll give you what you want. We can talk about The Ravins until der Fraulein comes back. That'll make Warren cream his chinos." Warren Darden was the publisher of *Roogalator*, a fan, and a personal friend. Every Christmas, he sent us socks, which he'd knitted himself.

"Actually," the interviewer said, "Warren's big question didn't have to do with The Ravins. He wants to know if you're gonna get political again."

"Same old Warren. Trying to make the tunes *mean* something."

"So what's your answer?"

I raised a fist. "Power to the people... who buy my record!"

"But you said he was *friendly*," I heard Fraulein shouting at Warren several hours later. As usual, I'd gone off script and said some things I shouldn't've. Mainly that I still got high on occasion, and felt drugs had been mostly positive for me. Whenever people asked (and they always did) I said that drugs weren't nearly as bad as what we did to stop people from taking them. When the interviewer asked how I'd feel if Jasper took drugs, I laughed it off. "The new President is a much bigger threat to my son's well-being, and that's a fact."

"Honesty isn't the point," Fraulein said, "I'm trying to sell records. There's a major shift happening out there, and Warren, we both know what my husband is like. He'll 'honest' us all right into the poorhouse. We must protect Tom from himself."

She kept motioning for me to get on the extension so we could tag-team the publisher, but I didn't have time. I'd finished my cartoon for the day—I was doing a history of the world for Jasper, the *true* history, not that shit they force-feed you in school—and now was heading over to the East Side to shoot a commercial. "Thank him for the socks," I whispered as I walked out.

Der Fraulein didn't answer; she was in full throat. "I don't care, I don't care, I don't care! You will give us editorial approval or I will see you in fucking court!"

Ah. The Voice of Command, I knew it well. I smiled as I rode the elevator down to the lobby. I didn't envy Warren. He might have been just as rich as we were, but one of Katrinka's tirades would make him feel like he was back on the *Berkeley Barb*.

"My car here?" I asked the concierge.

"Yes, Mr. Larkin." Bow, bow, scrape, scrape.

"*Que pasa*, Mr. Larkin?" The doorman stuck out his palm for me to slap. Ever since we'd shared a joint, he thought we were best buddies. "Nice warm evening for December."

"Must be the end of the world." I smiled, keeping the illusion alive. It was useful. "Do you have my Raisinets?"

"Of course." He knew that whenever I left alone, I wanted a box of "walking candy." I opened the box and tipped some back, for courage. "Ready?"

He nodded, and we headed out into the scrum. "Stay back. Back please, Mr. Larkin's late for an appointment…"

Speed and focus are the key—you must never give the fans control. Somebody approached me, I'd look them dead in the eye. They'd stop, and I'd keep walking, no matter what. Stopping, that's when bad things happen.

"Kid, get back! KID!"

Anorak, pimples, an LP. I signed it without looking: "Milton Crouk 1980." Signing the same name was boring, and by the time he read it, I'd be gone. A flash popped. I kept walking. Were 99% of them harmless? Sure. Did they still frighten me? Fuck yes. I wasn't a person to them, I was their dolly, and sooner or later, dollies get broken.

Finally I was in, and safe, but the limo door wouldn't shut properly. I looked down and there was a striped scarf sticking out by the rocker panel. A smiling curly-haired woman tapped on the dark glass; the other end of the scarf was around her neck.

I opened the door a bit, and she pulled it free. "Thank you."

She looked normal, so I rolled the window down a crack. "You better be more careful, Isadora Duncan."

Laughing, she stuck a small, flat package through the crack. "These are for Jasper. The markers he's using are toxic."

"Really?" I guess that puff piece Katrinka wrangled out of the *Times* wasn't totally useless.

"Really. I won't let my kid use 'em. The 'banana' one causes brain damage."

Genuinely grateful, I rolled down the window a bit more. "Look, if you're here around ten, I'll bring you a souvenir from the studio."

"Mr. Larkin…" the driver said.

"I know, I know." That's the other thing about fans: If you wait too long, they'll surround the car and you'll be stuck. Then maybe they'll start climbing on the roof, which can give way and crush you to death. That's something I do *not* miss. "Hit it."

The ride down to the soundstage was okay; I could still smell the alcohol, which meant that the driver had wiped down the backseat like we'd asked. People were always having sex in the backs of limos; God knows I had. If it was the difference between appearing a little strange, and sitting in a pool of baby batter, I'd take strange.

On the set, more arse-kissing. I didn't usually do commercials, but it was ridiculously lucrative, and for the Japanese market, so no one over here would ever see it. It was for a brand of shrimp-flavored condoms.

"Shrimp-flavored condoms?" I said when Fraulein had told me about it. "Back in Greasby, we called those 'used.'"

"Don't be vulgar," she said, then told me the fee. The experience was just as demeaning as I had expected it to be—the script was pitiful, canned Larkinisms circa 1964, that old gobbledygook—but I got through it by concentrating on the money.

After that, I went to the recording studio. I was doing some overdubs on a song of Fraulein's. The month before, my wife the scientist, seer, and financial wiz, had decided she wanted to be a pop star.

"It can't be hard if you can do it," she said. "You can't even make oatmeal."

The thing is, folks: I didn't want to make oatmeal. Why should I? That's what other people are for. I had to preserve my vital energy—I never knew when I might need it.

That's why I was napping under the soundboard when Fraulein arrived.

"What are you doing sleeping?" she said. "I want my song out next week."

"I was waiting for you."

"Well, I can't sing right now, I'm too upset."

"What about?"

"What do you think?" High color, jerky movements, chain-smoking; Fraulein was exhibiting "attack posture." I'd better be careful. "That interviewer. Did you hear how he was insulting us? In our own house, where our child sleeps!" She puffed a Benson and Hedges. "Warren promised he was a friendly. Instead we got the fucking Spanish Inquisition."

"And nobody expects that."

"What? What's that supposed to mean?"

"It's just a joke," I said, realizing I'd stepped in it. "From a TV show."

"Tom, we've talked about this. You know I don't like it when you say things I don't understand. Please stop."

"Okay, Fraulein."

"All the TV you watch is bad for you. I think you ought to stop."

"Oh come on, Katrinka!" TV was my number one hobby!

"No, no, don't argue. Whenever you argue, I know that I'm right."

I didn't say anything for a while. Instead, I fiddled with a knob to show her how angry I was, how unfair she was being.

"I'm just trying to help you, Tom. I only want what's best for you."

I didn't say anything.

"Do you have any idea what your life would be like if I wasn't here, helping? I spend my whole life taking care of you, and do you thank me for it? No, you resent me. You fight me. You're always fighting me. Isn't that right, Tom? Isn't that true?"

I didn't say anything. Maybe she'd still let me watch videotapes.

A gofer named Gabe or Dave or something opened the door. Fraulein and I turned as one, fixing him with identical icy stares, and there was a squeaking sound as his testicles shot up into his body. "Sorry," he spurted, and left.

The interruption made Fraulein even angrier, though of course her tone of voice never changed. "Let's go home," she said. "I have a migraine."

Back in the limo, the onslaught continued. "I've given up everything for you. Everything! Even my experiments! Before I met you, I had a career. I was a *respected scientist*."

"I know." In fact, Katrinka had never finished college—she hadn't needed to. In her early 20s, she'd began conducting experiments on people, hooking them up to EEGs, seeing their reactions to fear, stress, pain. She'd invite people to a lecture, then lock the doors and announce that the hall was on fire. Or she'd crash a wedding, and halfway through the ceremony, release spiders and eels from the ceiling. Or she'd wire someone up, to monitor their heart rate, breathing and stuff, and then hit their fingers with a hammer. Nobody taught her how to do any of this, it just came naturally. Needless to say, I found her fascinating.

"*Tremendously* respected."

"I know," I said.

"Lots of governments were interested in my work. Really big ones."

"I know. *Jesus*."

"Remember how you asked me to stop my career? 'I need you,' you said. 'I need you to take care of me.' Do you remember that? You begged me. 'I'll do whatever you say,' you said."

It was all true, and we both knew it. Of course, I'd been fucked up on heroin, but still.

"I can see now what a fool I was to believe you...Are you listening?"

"I am," I said. "Whatever I say will only make you angrier. So I'm—"

"Stop playing with that when I'm talking to you!"

I had gotten out a Rubik's Cube. It was a prototype, one of the perks of stardom.

Fraulein grabbed the cube. Before I could grab it back, she'd opened the car window and thrown it out into the street. I watched it skitter across Broadway, then get hit by a mail truck.

Fraulein saw my expression and softened; she's really quite tender-hearted, you know.

"I did that for your own good," she said. "That interviewer? When you got up to get some tea, he had it in his hands."

"Oh shit, why didn't you tell me?" I frantically searched for my kit.

"Then he *licked* it."

I gave a full-body shudder.

"It was some sexual thing, I bet," she said. "You know how people are, how they develop all sorts of fetishes about celebrities. Your whole career is based on that, if you ask me."

I stuck my head out the window and gave a dry-heave or two.

"He might've been clean, but I wouldn't take any chances," she said. "I'd do your fingers as soon as we get home."

"Doing my fingers" was dipping my fingertips in very hot water. Painful, but necessary. "I should just wear latex gloves," I said glumly.

"We've been over this," Fraulein said. "You can't. People will think you're strange."

"Fuck 'em, it's my health."

"The fans don't care. They don't want you to be healthy. They hate you. Deep down they hate you, because you show them just how insignificant their lives are. They'd be happy if you died, so they could go all the way and worship you. People always worship what they hate. I did an experiment once..."

I'd heard the story before, so I zoned out. Fraulein eventually burbled to a stop. After a decent interval, I reached over and turned on the TV.

"Tom! We just talked about that!"

"Sorry, I forgot."

"You seem to be forgetting a lot of things lately. You're a very forgetful person. I never forget anything," Katrinka said. "I think it's the TV. You know I read something last week. It said that TV causes your brain to develop tumors. They're like little pockets of sand."

"I'd like to read that," I said. "Do you remember where you saw it?"

"I forget," Fraulein said.

I lay back in the seat, and stuck my Walkman in my ears. The woman on the tape was telling me "You can have a perfect marriage!" Doubting that, I felt a million trickles of sand rushing down into my neck. Wouldn't be long now.

We got to the Oneida, and the doorman opened the limo door.

I didn't recognize him. "Where's Sleepy?"

"He's off for the next couple of days."

Great, a whole new person to train in the ways of walking candy.

At least the new guy didn't have to run interference; the sidewalk was nearly empty. It was snowing, and close enough to Christmas that people probably had more sensible things to do than harass rock stars. Still, if the album had been *selling*...Marker Lady was nowhere to be seen. Shame; I'd brought her a pick.

"You go on ahead," I said to Fraulein, "I'm going to the bodega, we're out of shreddly wheat." We both knew I was going to get Raisinets, but fuck her. She threw away my Rubik's Cube. She owed me.

"Come on, Tom. Stop this nonsense, and come upstairs."

"You stop your nonsense," I said, walking a few steps.

"You're lying, I hate when you lie!"

"I'll only be a minute. Don't let's fight in front of the new doorman."

"You're ridiculous!" Fraulein shouted. She walked towards the gate, hoping I would follow. I didn't. A woman walking a poodle stared.

"What's the matter, never seen married people before?"

"No, I'm waiting for my dog to shit."

Katrinka turned back, pouring on the guilt. "I hate it when Jasper sees you killing yourself with junk food. You ruined one child, but I won't let you ruin another."

Bringing up my first marriage was dirty pool. I was about to respond in kind when Marker Lady appeared out of the gloom. "Oh thank God."

"This seems like a bad time."

"No, no, you're saving my marriage," I unzipped my leather jacket and extracted the markers. "How many autographs do you want? Forty? Fifty?" I grabbed her *New Yorker* and began scribbling on it. "Keep me signing until the love of my life goes inside."

I sneaked a peek at my wife. Katrinka was standing thirty feet away under the archway, next to the doorman's post. Next to her was an ex-security guy of ours, Sam Wisnewski. What was he doing here? Two weeks ago, we'd fired him for being "too paranoid."

"I bet she stiffed him," I mumbled.

"What?"

My neck prickled. I should really get moving, either towards the bodega, or inside. I looked around; the street seemed quiet. "Roll up your sleeves, I'll sign your arms, too."

Marker Lady laughed. I remember when I made Katrinka laugh. Now she was screaming at me on the street.

"Tom, you drive me insane! I'm going inside!"

Luckily we lived in New York City, where no one would notice. Sam started walking towards me, looking even more purposeful than usual.

"Uh oh, you better go. Disgruntled ex-employee."

Marker Lady shook my hand. "Thanks so much. I'll put this up in my class."

"And I'll make Jasper write you a thank-you note..." Then I yelled over her shoulder at Wisnewski, "Don't take it personally, Crimestopper. I'll double it, and we'll call it a Christmas bonus."

Before Sam could answer, a scruffy blonde kid emerged from a doorway. It was the anorak from earlier. "All right, I'll give you a real one this time. But quickly." It had gotten cold.

The kid didn't care about the cold, or the autograph. "I want you to hear my song," he said, voice strangely hollow. The tape-deck next to him began playing a circular tune.

"Not now, okay?" I gave the kid a glare, but he didn't flinch. Something wasn't right. "Uh... Wisnewski? You're re-hired."

Wisnewski was still ten feet away, so I began to move. "Kid, now is *really not* the time."

"No, now's the perfect time."

The flashes came before I could react, one-two-three. I didn't feel any pain; must've been the adrenaline. I hunched down, and Wisnewski tackled me, a few seconds too late. The sidewalk was freezing, and the markers spilled all over.

"Stay down," Wisnewski growled. There was another shot, and this time, I felt it, first a fire in my chest, then the wetness, then the fear. "Get his gun! Why won't someone—" That was all I got out before my throat filled with blood.

Wisnewski and another cop loaded me into the backseat of a patrol car even before Katrinka had made it back out to the street. I saw her run up to the car. She pounded on the window. "Let me in! *What happened?*"

I heard Wisnewski shout that there was no time, that she should follow us to the hospital, but she kept pounding and asking that question, over and over. Maybe that's why I wrote this book, I don't know. I know that there were men yelling and women screaming and poodles barking and as we pulled away, before I passed out I remember thinking: this was how I always thought it would end…so why was I so surprised?

CHAPTER TWO

An hour later, the whole world knew what had happened; nothing travels faster than Official Truth. Not that I had any reason to doubt the story, not then at least. A deranged fan named Eric Curtis Thigg had Greyhounded from Atlanta to Manhattan with a cheap .22 and a dream. Twenty-four hours later, he was in custody and I was bleeding out.

But why? The obvious answer was that Thigg was crazy, but if a crazy fan were all it took, there'd be more tombstones than stars on Hollywood Boulevard. Even *he* didn't seem to know why he'd shot me. Sometimes he said God made him do it, other times Satan. Or he wanted to get famous. Or I was a hypocrite. Or he wanted to increase the circulation of the *Reader's Digest*. Thigg gave so many motives, it became obvious he didn't have a real reason at all. The one that sold the most newspapers was that Thigg thought he was my illegitimate son. Now, I admit I'd spread the seed, but there's no way I'd produced *that*, a chubby pasty virgin with a Kubrickian million-yard stare.

That was unsettling, too, how much Thigg looked the part. It was like somebody'd fed in photos of every high-profile creep from Lee Oswald to David Berkowitz, and that's what the computer spat back. He was certainly nobody you'd ever help get a gun, much less dum-dum bullets...unless you were some low-normal security guard from his shit-kicking hometown: "Yuh cain't go to New York City without protection. Them blacks is *dangerous*."

Our planet is a fucked-up place, thanks to all the fucked-up people crawling all over it, and it would've been totally typical for me to shuffle off at the hands of a cypherous psycho. Like I said earlier, it's what I expected. But maybe that's what saved me. My life has been many things, but never for a moment has it been predictable. You can deny everything I'm about to tell you, the whole story. You can even say this isn't Tom Larkin at all, just another crazy fan indulging in macabre hero-worship. But if you know my life, you know that the unexpected has been the only constant. Believe it.

And believe another thing while you're at it: the shooting was real. I never turned to Fraulein and said, "Dear, if *Romance, Redux* doesn't sell, let's fake my death." We weren't that cynical. Okay, we were, but it's important that you know my getting shot wasn't some bit of theater, or a statement, or a joke. And it certainly wasn't one of Fraulein's experiments. She always followed the Geneva Convention, more or less.

The scene at the hospital was entirely appropriate for a star of my magnitude. Apart from the medical emergency—apart from that trifling matter—there were all these bloody fans underfoot. I was used to it, but it bothered the doctors. Especially after someone's incense set off the sprinklers.

Mary the Magic Fairy was there, in costume as usual, and Drummer Dan, too. He was a freak that used to hang out across the street from my apartment, yodeling and hitting his bongos. He was always trying to turn me on to joints sprayed with oven-cleaner. Just the kind of dude you want visiting you in the hospital, right? Other people get relatives bearing grapes, I get Drummer Dan and Easy-Off bombers.

The weird thing was how quickly the fans knew. They always knew things ahead of time. Back in the Ravins days, we'd call a secret meeting and they'd get there ahead of us. Our lead guitarist Harry called them "the collective unconscious." He was bitter about the fans; he felt the loss of privacy most, I think. But then Harry turned around wrote a song about them. Clearly, it was a love-hate relationship.

Somebody tried to take away Drummer Dan's bongos, and there was a scuffle. After that, the head of hospital went to my wife. "We need to clear everyone out of here," he said, blotting a bloody nose. "I want to announce your husband was DOA. We can always correct it later. Will you go along?"

Of course Fraulein agreed; in a situation like that, your first impulse is to do whatever Dr. Doctor says. So while I was elsewhere, they made the announcement: "Tom Dunkirk Van Weltanshauung Larkin died at 11:15 pm Eastern Standard Time. Every effort was made to resuscitate him, but blood loss from multiple gunshot wounds sent him into severe shock, and he was dead upon arrival. He was 40 years old."

They took a body from the morgue, put it under a sheet, and rolled it past the reporters. Who was it under there? A nobody, some bum, the man I would've been if The Ravins had never happened. Fraulein found out who it was, and paid for his burial, a proper burial. It was the least we could do for my Karmic twin.

Katrinka finally went home around 2 a.m., after they'd gotten me stable. She was supposed to sleep, but our apartment building was completely overrun. It must have been hell for her, lying there in bed, smoking, worrying, listening to all those people singing. Would one of them try to kill her? I'm sure she thought of that. A lot of Ravins fans are loony when it comes to Fraulein.

That was my fault—I'd used her to break up the group. She was as guiltless as a gravedigger's shovel, but the fans, they always blamed her. They never saw how wonderful she was. But that's on them; great souls are often misunderstood. Buddha, Gandhi, Christ. Being one myself back then, I knew that instinctively, but Katrinka taught me the rest of it, how to listen to no one, how being liked is common. She taught me *everything.*

It was very romantic, how we got together. I'm sure Katrinka was thinking of it that night. The crowds out there were just like the ones in '68.

It was May, and Paris was full of riots. Terribly exciting. Everywhere the old order was collapsing. There were rumors of secret meetings, assassinations, Godard sightings, new sexual positions…The kids, the artists, even the cops—everybody seemed so *alive*. Which was the exact opposite of how I felt.

For going on two years, I'd been holed up in boring old England, fighting with the wife and kid, taking drugs and wondering how my teenage dream had turned into an adult nightmare. I was questioning everything. Our manager had died, and I'd just sacked my guru after catching him scarfing a Whopper. Plus, if you believe in numerology—and why shouldn't you?—I was twenty-seven, *the* dangerous age for rock stars. There was nothing to say I had to keep existing. I certainly felt old; I was living on Thai Stick and the horrible suburban-London version of pizza my then-wife slipped under the door. Then I started watching the riots. They were like a newsreel from inside my heart. After three days, I ripped the TV off the stand and tossed it out the window. "Fuck it! I'm going over there!"

I called up the other three, more out of habit than anything. "The future is *happening!* Let's go record in Paris, and get it into the music!" Harold would've done it—he was still hero-worshipping me—but Oliver said no, and Buck wouldn't go anywhere he couldn't get Bovril. "Well, fuck you, I'm going over anyway."

Ever *la scientress*, der Fraulein was already in Paris, using the situation to run some very interesting experiments. For example, she kidnapped a policeman and a demonstrator, drugged them, switched their clothes, and then released them back into the crowd. What happened next was very interesting. Out of all the thousands in the streets, somehow those two found each other. They embraced…then beat each other to a pulp. Just try and explain *that*.

We had corresponded a bit when I was in India—back then, Katrinka was always looking for funding—but this was the first time we'd ever physically met. Instantaneous attraction. On our first date, she showed me how to throw a Molotov cocktail, to this day the only sport I've ever loved. (Unless you count boosting coinboxes, but that was more of a hobby.)

Fraulein and I, we complimented each other beautifully. Alone of an evening, I might think, "I'll take PCP," and she might think, "I should do an experiment on old people." But together we would think, "Hey! Let's slip PCP in Aunt Harriet's pudding!" That was quite an experience. Harriet put her fist through a car door, but calmed down once we explained it was all for Science.

Where was I? Right, breaking up The Ravins. None of those fuckers ever gave her a chance. They were trapped in their macho bullshit rock-star worlds. Buck was all right, but Ollie and Harry were shitty right from the start. Harry told *Roogalator*, "When Katrinka says 'peace,' she means 'the absence of disagreement. With her.'" He said that, can you believe it? Here she was, busting arse on experiments to end all global conflict forever, and he had the gall to...They were forcing me to choose, because they were so certain I would choose the group. I still remember the look on their faces when I didn't! It was either me or the band, The Ravins had to die if I was to live. Or so I believed. It's hard to think straight when you're young and dodging car doors and surrounded by sycophants snorting powdered Bovril. I used my relationship with Katrinka to do all the nasty, hurtful shit that was necessary, and did it under cover of romance so nobody could criticize without feeling square. "Don't blame us, we're in love! And scientists!"

Anyway, what I am trying to say if you'd let me get a verb in edgelike, is that none of this was Fraulein's fault. She simply followed my lead, but I didn't realize the price she would pay. That was why I could never re-form the band; I had to honor my wife's sacrifice. And her sacrifice was never greater than the night I got shot.

Katrinka explained it all to me later. "Because I couldn't sleep, I started to think. Your safety was at risk. You had to be moved someplace secret, someplace safe. Once that was taken care of, we could decide what to do next." So before dawn, a helicopter landed on the roof of the hospital, and ferried me to where I was to live for the next six months.

Lazarus Memorial (not its real name, obviously) is a small, private hospital in northern New Jersey. Lazarus specializes in all of life's little necessities: abortions, vaginoplasties, stuff like that.

For the first three months after the attack, I was in a coma. It's rare for someone to be out that long, but I've always been good at vegging. Comas have gotten a bad rap. People take care of you, you don't have to chew. Show me a spa that offers that kind of service. Besides, it cleared all the drugs out of my system; I hadn't been in that state of grace since Uncle Philip gave me my first sip of lager. Thirty-five years later, I was finally clean again, and I've stayed that way ever since, more or less.

I woke up on the Ides of March, March 15th. A chunky nurse was explaining something to Fraulein, something her tone suggested she'd explained many times before. "I told you, there's no way. All these machines would know if he was faking."

"What about that light? The one that just went on?"

"Holy cow! Dr. Dillon, the patient in 24 is awake!"

Fraulein sprang to my side so swiftly my IVs swayed. "Thank God you're alive! Tell the doctors it's okay for me to smoke!" Katrinka has a slightly different genetic structure.

"My wife is cancer-proof," I whispered to the nurse, who paid no attention. Fool. Second-hand smoke isn't nearly as dangerous as first-hand Fraulein.

"My God," I heard a male blur say (I wasn't wearing my specs). "I thought we'd lost him."

Fraulein handed me sunglasses, "Your regular ones broke. Arnold, this is Doctor Dillon."

"Thanks. Who the fuck is Arnold?"

"Hello Mr. Sandusky," Dr. Dillon said. "How do you feel?"

"Hello Dr. Zimmerman." If he wouldn't call me by my name, I wouldn't call him by his. "Can I have a glass of water?" My throat was scratchy, and I could barely talk. "Where am I? Who's Mr. Sandusky?"

"Try not to speak." Dr. Dillon looked a bit like Spencer Tracy. All the doctors at Lazarus looked like famous actors, it was just part of the package. "Disorientation is normal."

"Especially for him," Katrinka said. "You were shot."

"It was fucking O'Connell, wasn't it?" The week before I died, my ex-partner had gotten busted at Orly for carrying a dealable quantity of Nicorette in his carry-on. Ollie was convinced we were behind it. Fraulein's experiments made people a little paranoid, especially if they were control freaks to begin with, like Oliver.

"That's what I thought too. But Wisnewski checked into it. He says Oliver was in Montserrat making an album. It was a nut with a gun, simple as that," my wife said. "But you're safe now. You're in New Jersey."

"Oh no."

"What's wrong with that?" Dr. Dillon asked.

"Jeanne Dixon predicted all four of us would die in New Jersey."

"Four of you?"

Katrinka leapt in. "May I have a few moments with him? As man and wife?"

Katrinka doesn't have a great command of idiom, and Dr. Dillon was thrown momentarily. ""I really don't think he's up to—oh, just to talk? Sure."

After everyone else had left the room, Fraulein sat on the bed. "Tom, did you see the other side? What was it like?"

"Dark."

"That's all?"

"That's all."

"That's so like you, to waste the experience." Fraulein's voice dropped: "Now don't interrupt, because I have a lot to cover. It's March. You've been in a coma since December, faking probably, but we'll leave that for now. This is a very exclusive, very expensive hospital called Lazarus Memorial. Your name is Arnold Sandusky, and you're an architect."

"What happened to Tom Larkin, the musician?"

"As far as the world knows, that man is dead."

"Too bad," I said, half-there. "I liked him. Did they catch whoever did it?"

"Yes," Katrinka said. "Do you know, he didn't even run? Crazy as hell. And crazy people are like roaches, where there's one, there're usually others.

That's why we're taking precautions, with the fake name and all that."

"Sounds Jewish. You know I'm not circumcised."

"Well, sorry, Tom. Sorry I couldn't think of *everything*. Next time, we'll use 'Marvin Gina." (That was an alias I'd used during the Ravins days, to check into hotels.)

"It's all right." Actually it wasn't; it was totally depressing. I'd liked who I was. Well, no I hadn't, but there had been lots of advantages to being the old me, and I resented losing those, even temporarily. I'd give Katrinka a piece of my mind…later. My head itched, and I scratched it.

It was totally smooth.

"Ahhh!" I recoiled weakly. "Ahhh!"

"Calm down. Your thing is beeping."

"Fraulein, where's all my hair? *What did you do?*"

"Oh, take it easy, it'll grow back. They asked me if they could do it, and I said sure."

I gave her a black look.

"You said you didn't care about your hair! You said!"

"Fine." Another fight for later. Our schedule was really filling up.

"I put all the hair in a safety deposit box at a Chemical Bank in Long Island City. We'll wait for it to appreciate, then we'll auction it off," my wife said. "We have to pay for all this somehow."

That was slick, I had to admit. I gathered up all my energy for one last question. "When can I be myself again?"

"When it's safe. In the meantime, be good. Clean your plate, be nice to the staff, and for God's sake, don't tell anyone who you really are."

I have to admit I wasn't a very popular patient; in fact, I think the staff hated me. But feng shui is feng shui, and if my bed had to stick out into the hall to align with the healing energies, well, everybody would just have to deal. And Fraulein was right; the walls were "baby-poop green." Nobody could get well looking at that. So naturally we brought in the monkeys. They were very cheerful. The staff bitched constantly, but Fraulein had their number: "I will sue you so hard!" she yelled. "Me *and* Hitler!"

For the next three months, I lived more or less like I had before that last album: Lots of sleeping, lots of TV. Around 1975 I'd made my mind up about the Seventies, and refused to participate. People were puzzled, but it was an act of conscience. Also I look very bad in nuthugger shorts.

Fraulein was envious of all the weight I'd lost, but I couldn't get over my hair. It wasn't growing back. What did return was just on the sides, and whitish-gray instead of reddish-brown. I looked *ten years older!* The nurses called me Ebenezer Scrooge.

Then there were my wounds. "Lift up your shirt, I want to see what getting shot looks like."

"No you don't, Katrinka. You'll pass out." My wife had to be anesthetized just to get blood drawn.

"C'mon. I've never seen it before. Do it for science."

"All right..."

I'd barely passed my belly-button when she fell over. When she came to, Fraulein whispered, "You look like steak tartare with legs."

So Muscle Beach was out, but I felt surprisingly good, thanks to the industrial-strength painkillers they were pumping into me. (When I said I was clean, I meant recreational drugs; the mandatory kind don't count.) The staff considered me a medical marvel. "I've never seen a patient need this high a dose," one doc said. "Just between us, Mr. Sandusky, have you ever used narcotics?"

"Of course not," I lied huffily. She had no right to ask such personal information. That's what the tabloids are for.

When I got strong enough, I started doing some more drawings for Jasper's Codex of All Human Knowledge, trying to put the experience into crayons. I also took another crack at learning Latin, which was a bloody nightmare. I have a load of respect for sorcerers. Halfway through the vocative case, I realized why rich people are so stupid: it's difficult to learn anything new when you know you can simply hire someone to do it for you.

Occasionally I'd see someone I recognized. I went in the wrong door and saw Andy Warthog passed out, post-wigectomy. One day at lunch, I sat with the guy from Studio 54, Gabe or Dave or something; he was getting a new partition put in his nose. He and I pretended we didn't know each other, which was fine. That was the way Lazarus was, we all had secrets to hide. Plastic surgery is only cool if it's secret.

Der Fraulein called regularly, and I was happy to lend a sympathetic ear. After all, things were very hard for her. "There's a mound of crap two feet high on the sidewalk."

"*Still?* Anything good?" Fraulein always went through my fan mail, looking for stuff to re-gift. She was always so smart about money, unlike me. If someone's birthday rolls around, I just buy them something. Not Fraulein, she works the angles. That's why I never have any money, and she's always got plenty.

"From your fans? Are you kidding? Nothing but poems and candles and crap! Now you see just how much people cared about you, Tom. You *died*, and they wouldn't even go to the store and buy you something nice. If I had fans like that," she said, "I'd kill myself."

"If you did, they'd do it for you."

"I don't find that funny, Tom. This whole thing has been very difficult for me."

"I know, dear. Tell me how I can make it up to you."

"I'm thinking."

For weeks, I'd been hatching plans for my big comeback. I was leaning towards classy, understated, just a three-day worldwide all-star concert, with me appearing in the last thirty minutes. They'd roll away the rock, and there I'd be, sitting humbly behind an all-white piano. I didn't realize it, but I was inventing Live Aid. Reg and David were a lock, could I get Mick to do it? I'd invite Harry and Buck, but not Oliver. He'd try to upstage me. He always did.

Or Fraulein and I could make it political. Too bad Vietnam was over;

there had to be another war somewhere. Or we could pick some little shitty country, some incontinent bit of the subcontinent—Harry'd know a good one, he was always going over, collecting weird diseases. What would get maximum publicity? What would Jesus do, if he had an album to sell? The details would sort themselves, but one thing was for sure: my resurrection was going to be the most important international event since our Bathe-In.

I was too excited to notice that Katrinka wasn't offering any suggestions. Fraulein has ideas about everything, so I should've realized this was a warning sign. But I didn't, so it took me by surprise when she said I should stay dead forever. That's the only reason I ripped the phone out of the wall. (I threw it out the window because holding it felt foolish.)

Obviously, if it had been anybody else, I would've told them to fuck off. However, when you're dealing with a rogue genius like Fraulein, you gotta stay flexible—she always says, "The best ideas come when you're angry." So when she came for her next visit, I was perfectly willing to listen. The Plexiglas barrier was completely unnecessary.

"Staying dead, I never thought of that," I said. "Interesting angle. Are you thinking some kind of alter-ego thing?"

"No, I was thinking more of a no-ego thing."

"I don't understand."

"It's simple. You stay Arnold Sandusky. Forever."

"No way, no fucking way. I will not live a lie! Especially if it's boring!" I was hurt. "Oh, I know what this is about: You're punishing me for that time I cheated on you with Bella Abzug. For fuck's sake, Katrinka, that was 1974!"

"I'm not punishing you, Tom. I'm just telling you what our people are saying."

"Our people." Those were all the lawyers and advisors and assorted miracle-workers that Fraulein and I kept on retainer. It could be anybody from ex-KGB, to Sammy Davis Jr.'s Satanic accountant, to a gargling freak I met on the subway. "Who's saying that? Dr. Wang the genitomancer?"

"Wisnewski." Fraulein loved the ex-narc, probably because he made me nervous. Once a junkie, always a junkie, I guess. But Wisnewski was tough and smart, and you didn't take his opinion lightly. Except when it came to music. He was the only person I'd ever met who actually liked Muzak.

"He's convinced that it's never going to be safe for you. A boundary has been crossed."

"What does that mean?"

"Now there's been one, there will be others."

"Yeah, well, you tell Wisnewski I've been getting death threats since I was 20." Younger, actually, if you count the gangsters in Marseille. "Everybody's just keyed up. That's understandable, given what happened. I'll be fine."

Fraulein didn't say anything. She just lit another Benson and Hedges.

"Where was all this paranoia before I got shot? Who was the one that fired Sam in the first place?"

"You were," Katrinka said coolly.

"No, I wasn't!"

"Yes you were."

It's difficult arguing with a genius. They remember everything. "Okay, but I only did it because you said bodyguards were for shirt-lifters." That statement stuck in my mind, because Katrinka doesn't usually use slang. She considers it beneath her.

"Don't blame me for your macho bullshit. I'm not even going to tell you what the Tarot person said."

"Tell me, I paid for it."

"He said that to remain alive, you must give up your most prized possession."

"I'm not giving up our apartment, Fraulein. It's rent-controlled."

"Is that supposed to be a joke, Tom? Is it?" She was honestly asking. "I have to say, your reaction surprises me."

"That I don't want to give up everything I've worked for?"

"No, at how little you care about Jasper and me. Putting us in danger for your silly macho fantasy…"

"What do you two have to do with it? Why would anybody want to bother you?"

"That's very hurtful, Tom. I have fans, too, you know."

"Okay, then you can be Sylvia Sandusky." I scooted over. "I'll make room."

"You're being impossible."

"No, you said you're worried about fans shooting you, so I said—"

"My fans are scientists! Intellectuals!" she said hotly. "We don't have to worry about my fans, or Jasper's."

"Jasper has fans?"

"Of course he has fans. I started a fan club for him when he was born. The tax advantages are—"

Talking about our son calmed me. I missed him. I still do. "Spare me the gory details," I said. "I see your point. So we get bodyguards."

"Wisnewski says that next time it could be a bomb or something."

"Where is somebody going to get a bomb? Gristede's?" (Yes, I know. But this was years before Unabomber.)

"Or they could use a virus. Someone could spray it in the air," my wife said. "There's a new one from Africa that *dissolves* you."

"Oh fuck." Where was my kit?

"Three hours after you get it, they have to bury you in a kettle."

"All right, all right! I get the picture! I'll adopt a new identity."

"Identities," Katrinka corrected me. "Wisnewski says you should change them frequently. But always non-famous, average people."

I couldn't believe this was happening. "I'll be as many people as you want. I'll even be a chick." I said. "Tell Jasper not to worry. Is he asking about me?"

"Well..." Fraulein paused. "Tom, don't get angry."

"Why? Why should I be angry?"

"I told Jasper you died."

"YOU WHAT?"

"I told him you died! It was for your own good, both of you! We can't have him blabbing our secret all over the world."

I couldn't believe it. "You told our son that I'm dead?"

"Just temporarily," Fraulein said. "We'll tell him the truth when he's older. Plus, it's extremely interesting, from a scientific perspective."

"Okay," I sighed. What else could I do?

"I'll talk to Wisnewski today. He'll get you new ID, birth certificate, everything. You just stay here, healing. We're all very worried about you, Tom. We want you to get well, and have a nice, normal, safe life."

Normal? I'd always *hated* normal. "Normal" was two-parent families, and hairy blokes who liked football. Normal was chartered accountancy and civil service and dental college, and my Aunt Harriet putting my dog to sleep because it "didn't bark properly." Normal was "God Save the Queen," no matter what she did. It was all the posh birds who I'd pined for all through school, and their dads who never ran off or got drunk or got fired, and their icy little minges with the "Do Not Enter" signs, which sprang open the moment I got famous. Normal? Christ. Somebody shoot me.

The people at Lazarus didn't make things easier. They treated me like I was merely another well-heeled middleman from Manhattan, getting experimental penis extensions. Sooner or later, I was bound to snap.

I don't know if you've ever been on heavy opiates for any length of time, but they constipate the hell out of you. (Eric Clapton called it "the price of stardom.") I was having to get these epic clean-outs every couple of days. The same nurse always did my "work," a real beautiful young chick, who I was totally in love with. But I could tell that whenever she looked at me, all she saw was a stopped-up tube of ca-ca. My male ego was killing me.

One morning I called up Fraulein. "I can't take it anymore. I need you to pull some strings. Get me a different nurse."

Fraulein shocked me by refusing. "You may not be famous anymore Tom, but I still am. The more I, Katrinka Von Weltanschauung, help you, a supposed nobody who just happened to be admitted the day after my ex-husband was brutally and tragically murdered...There might be questions."

"Could you make an anonymous phone call?" I begged. "A police tip-line? Do I qualify for elder abuse yet?"

"What's the problem with this nurse? "

"I'm attracted to her, and—"

"You groped her, didn't you? You *fingered* her."

"Don't get hysterical," I said. "I just want her to like me."

"Oh, for God's sake. Men are such babies. Do you want me to get you a prostitute? That place is crawling with them."

In addition to spies, Katrinka saw prostitutes everywhere. "I think those are called 'candy-stripers.'"

"Whatever. I have to go. Promise me you won't do anything stupid."

"I promise."

I know Fraulein was just trying to look out for me, but the message I got was that I was a nobody now, so why would she help me? And why would a cute young girl dig me? I was old, and bald, and from tits to cock looked like a plate of spaghetti. My lot was the brush-off, and I'd better get used to it.

But I didn't want to get used to it, so two hours later, I raised myself up on my elbows. It's difficult to look seductive mid-enema, but I tried. "Monique, I don't know how to tell you this, but I'm Tom Larkin."

"I'll tell my mother," she said.

"You don't believe me. "

"I believe you."

"Go look on the cover of my *Naked Album*. Same bum." She kept fiddling. "So…what do you say? The supply closet in an hour?" I gave her my A-1 Come Hither look.

She shrugged. "No offense, but to me you're just another asshole."

We never discovered who ratted me out to the tabloids. I'd like to think it wasn't Monique, but my level of stardom has strange effects on people.

The morning it happened—sometime in mid-June—I was sitting in a chair watching "Hart to Hart," you know that old show with Bob Wagner, the one with the rich couple that solves crimes? I always used to watch it, and take notes, because we were going to take them to court.

See, der Fraulein and I had an idea exactly like that, which we pitched to Dick Cavett in 1971. We were going to be the stars, and solve crimes as ourselves. It was going to be half-TV show, half platform for really important new concepts like trepanning and orgasmic birth, all the stuff we were interested in. But you know, once an idea is out there...We were convinced somebody at the network pinched it. *C'est la (T)vie.*

The Harts had just been sealed up in their own secret vault when the phone rang. Normally I don't pick up mid-mystery, but this time I did, thinking it was my psychiatrist. Every other day he and I would work on my old fears (germs, crowds, writer's block) so we could eventually get to my new ones (flashes, loud noises, the smell of cordite). But it wasn't Dr. Deep Breathing; it was my wife. She didn't even say "hello."

"Tom, you've got to get out of there."

"Good morning."

"Somebody talked. There's an article in that paper you read."

"It's called *The World-Wide News*, Fraulein, and nobody will believe it."

"Jerry Rivers did. He just called for a statement. He's on his way out there with a van." When we knew him, he was just Jerry Rivers, but by that time he was on the way to becoming Geraldo. He was a friend, but a scoop is a scoop, right? "There's a cab waiting for you outside. It'll take you to the airport."

"Where am I going?"

"It's better that you don't know, in case you get tortured."

"But dear, if they have me, why would they care where—"

"DO NOT ARGUE!" She used the Voice of Command. "I'm sending you someplace you'll be safe until people completely forget about you."

"How about if they forget just enough to stop shooting?" There was a commotion in the hall. "Whoops. Gotta go."

I shimmied into some jeans, and threw on the Members Only jacket my P.T. guy had forgotten last appointment. Thank God I was on the first floor; I hauled my fragile body out the window and hid behind a bush until the coast was clear.

"That bloody car had better be here, Fraulein." I couldn't run or hide, or anything. I was wearing those stupid hospital booties, and was still quite delicate. All the muscles in my trunk had been severed, and—let's put it this way, I was in no condition to reenact *Daze and Nights*, running down the street in front of a mob. I'd run five steps, wheeze "You got me," then puke.

In the circular driveway, behind Jerry's news van, there were two cars: a taxi, and a limousine. Katrinka had said "taxi," but she knew I hadn't been in a taxi for years. Whenever I sat in one, I could feel venereal diseases crawling up my arsehole. So I ducked down, crept the five feet to the limo door, and sneaked in.

I found myself staring at a man's knee. By the time I got up to the face, it was shouting at me. "You're alive!"

"That's my line," I croaked.

Then the driver flexed his ankle, and we were gone.

CHAPTER THREE

If anybody invented The Ravins (besides yours truly), it was our manager, Clive Solomon. Where everybody else saw *nothing*, he saw "something splendid." We called him manager, but he was actually a prophet, inspired, insane. Religions need both, you know. Just for the record, that's what I was getting at back in '65 when I said Christ was antwacky. I wasn't knocking him. I also said he was beautiful, but nobody remembers that part. You get used to it, them twisting your words. Clive got me out of that. The man could get anyone out of anything.

Let me give you a week in the life of The Ravins, circa 1964: On Monday, I would say something outrageous. Tuesday, Oliver would knock up a chick. Wednesday, Harry would slug an eight-year-old. Thursday, Buck would stumble into a taping drunk. And by Friday—Saturday if he himself was hung over—we'd be everybody's lovable longhairs again, thanks to Clive.

After I started eating loads of acid, I wondered if Clive was the Devil—that was the kind of juju he threw down. Some promoter would call up, shitting mad at how short our show was, or how I'd bit some Mayor's wife—then Clive would whisper into the phone for two minutes, tossing "splendid"s, and the man would become our greatest friend. I saw him do it to Charles DeGaulle. By the end of that convo, he was "Chuck."

The Ravins were me, Oliver O'Connell, Harold Thompson and Bucky Rich, in roughly that order, but Clive was more essential than anybody realized, including us. After Clive topped himself in '67, we made some good music, but it was all me and a backing group, or Oliver and a backing group. Listen to the records: The Ravins were buried with Clive Solomon.

The story was that Clive died accidentally, from sleeping pills. Those of us who knew Clive well—or, more accurately, knew his taste for getting choked during sex—suspected otherwise. In fact, that first weekend the four of us spent with Swami Roger was simply a way to get out of London, in case the press unearthed something. That they didn't was Clive's last great coup. His power to charm was literally stronger than death.

I of all people shouldn't have been surprised to see Clive sitting in the back of that limo, but I was. That made him laugh.

"Me, overdose? Would Annie Oakley shoot herself? I never thought any friends would believe that. I'd rather hoped one of you would come looking."

"Sorry, mate. Things piled up."

It was a lame excuse, but Clive was a gentleman and let it stand. "We've found each other now, that's all that matters. It gets lonely, life after death. You'll see." He took a cigarette from his silver case, the one I'd seen him wager tens of times at the casino. "Surprised I still have this? I don't gamble any more."

"Yes, but you still smoke. You should try self-hypnosis tapes. I've totally quit."

"Then why are you…?"

"Why am I what?" I snapped my fingers impatiently.

Clive leaned forward with his lighter. "I've forgotten how strange your sense of humor is."

Things seemed a lot less dire all of the sudden. I guess it was being with Clive. "Where am I taking you?" he asked.

"JFC," I said. "How did you know I was alive?"

"I didn't. I merely thought, 'It would be just like Tom to take the piss.' So I began pondering how I'd do it, if I were you. It wasn't that difficult."

"I don't like to hear that."

"Don't worry. I'm an uncommonly devious sort." The years had been kind to Clive. He was a little grayer, and a little thicker, but still handsome. He had always been nice looking, but nobody you'd do a double-take over—like a movie star's son, but from his first marriage. I thought I spied a surgeon's touch around the eyes. "Who's been seeing Dr. O'Plasty, then?"

"That's how I really found you. My man splits time between Lazarus and a hospital in Monaco," Clive said. "So. Was it gratifying, to see how sad everyone was?"

"Dunno," I shrugged. "I was in a coma until March."

"A coma? Whatever for? You mean to tell me you actually got shot?"

"Three times. Or was it four? I lost count…I'm all right now," I said. "I mean, I'll make it to the airport. Probably."

Clive exhaled. "Bloody hell. Do you think anybody was behind it?"

I shook my head no.

"But your political activities—"

Clive was referring to, among other things, the time I'd declared war on the United States "so they could see how it felt." 1969 was like that.

"I doubt they'd go that far," I said, "unless they're totally insane. Why not just smear me? Pay our housekeeper five grand to say I molested her kid. I think it was just some malicious bastard. You know all the death threats I used to get."

"More than the other three combined, as I recall."

"Even the hospital was crawling with fans. My wife made an executive decision: die now, live later."

"I've always longed to meet Katrinka. I was this close to sending a wedding present, but it was just too risky…"

"Cheap Jew bastard." I always teased Clive like that, back in the old days, but now it seemed wrong. "Sorry."

He waved it off. "I always wanted to reconnect, but it never seemed like the right time." Outside, it began to spit. "I suppose I felt a bit…guilty," Clive said carefully, choosing his words. "Guilty for leaving you, all those years ago."

"I'm used to it."

"I know," he said. "That's why I came back."

"Awww. Big hug, music swells, the end." A sign flashed by. We were out of New Jersey, thank God and fuck Jeanne Dixon.

"When's the Resurrection?"

"Never," I said glumly. "I'm staying dead. Katrinka thinks somebody else would attack me, which I don't entirely believe. But if someone did, they might hurt her and Jasper as well, so..."

"Oh, Jasper. I've always wanted to meet him. Who does he take after? You?"

"Can we not talk about him?"

"Sorry. Does Carol know? Or Helen?"

That was my first wife and daughter. "Nah. Katrinka asked me not to tell them. She vaguely resents that I had a life before we met." I ran my thumbnail back and forth along the stitching on the seat. "What do you think? Would there be other attempts?"

Clive knitted his brows, like he was adding a column of figures. "It's possible. How are you now?"

"Jumpy as a fucking cat."

"Understandable. But I meant physically."

I counted it off on my fingers. "I lost four of my ribs on this side and five on the other, a kidney, most of my spleen, and two-thirds of my left lung. They also took out my appendix while they were at it. On the other hand," I said, "I weigh the same as when you and I met."

My old friend was appalled. "That settles it. You must come home with me. I'm taking care of you myself."

"I don't think der Fraulein would like that. I've got a ticket waiting at the airport."

"Where to?"

"I don't know."

"*No*," Clive said angrily, proprietarily. "Completely unacceptable. You're not fit to walk unprotected in public, not in your condition. You need round-the-clock care, and since you can't get that in a hospital anymore, you'll have to take it from me. I have plenty of room. We'll get doctors, any kind you need. And you'll enjoy my other houseguests."

"What, are you running a bed and breakfast?"

"-Ish. Remember that island off the coast of Greece, the one you four were thinking of buying?"

"Vaguely," I said. Nineteen sixty-seven was even blurrier than '66, which was blurrier than '65. Nineteen sixty-eight was blurriest of all.

"That's where I live now, completely private, and completely safe. And the Aegean sun has marvelous healing properties."

"But what about these other people? Won't they—"

"Trust me, you'll fit right in."

I looked out the window at the gray and grimy chunk of Creation rolling past. A Greek island was tempting. Then I imagined the customized hell I'd get from Fraulein. "Clive, I really appreciate it, but I think I better just—"

"Do you know who tipped off the press?"

"No."

"Have you considered the possibility that the leak is inside your wife's operation?"

"Come on, I don't—"

"How well do you pay your people?"

"Fraulein says they should be honored to work for us."

"Oh shit!" Clive seemed genuinely alarmed, which alarmed me. "Tom, I think it's highly possible that you're walking into a trap. You're in no condition to face the world press—which is the best case scenario. The worst one is another gun."

I broke out in a cold sweat. "Do you have any antibacterial wipes?"

"We haven't time for that nonsense. Do you have any ID? Show it to me. I need to know if we'll have to smuggle you on."

I dug out my passport, and handed it over.

Clive flipped through, pausing occasionally to check a detail, then handed it back. "Solid work. If Katrinka's worried enough to pay what that cost, she'd want you to take every precaution."

"You don't know her. She's like my parole officer."

"Play it safe, Tom. Come home with me. I can protect you until you're well. Then you can do whatever you like."

I felt the old sensation of being charmed, and I still liked it.

"Ahh, what the hell," I said. "Gotta live my own life, right?"

"Splendid!"

During the flight to Athens, Clive and I chattered away, trying to cram fourteen years into as many hours. "Overdose is the ideal method," he explained, "since there's no damage to the body. The trick is finding a friendly coroner, and that's not much of a trick at all. Provided you have the filthy lucre."

"So you weren't suicidal? I still remember you crying backstage—"

"Oh, you know how dramatic I can get, especially after I've had a few."

"Could've used a fucking hand with Oliver, y'know." Keeping my bandmate from taking over The Ravins was like holding back the ocean, and as soon as Clive was gone, the tide rolled in.

"I know, and I'm sorry. First my father died, and there was that whole terrible thing with Jon—"

"I *knew* that seemed fishy. Okay, Solomon. Spill it."

A month before his death, or supposed death, Clive had commissioned the playwright Jon Bolton to write us a movie. Jon was the current fave-rave of the West End, but anybody who'd seen his earlier stuff knew that this was madness, like asking Jean Genet to write for Disney. All of us suspected it was top-to-toe a romantic gambit of Clive's, not that we begrudged him that. For an attractive guy, Clive had an almost pathological fear of rejection. That's why he hired Jon, instead of merely bedding him.

For what it's worth, I liked Jon's script. The working title was "120 Days of Sodom"—Pasolini pinched it later for that film of his. I don't blame him, it did stick in the mind. The title alone was enough to do the movie in my opinion. "120 Days of Sodom," and our four cherubic faces high above Piccadilly? Priceless. And *honest*, for once. The part I remember had a hunchback (me) whipping a nun (Penelope Tree) with an ornamental dildo.

But it wasn't all swearing and fucking. There were also some really perceptive comments about England's class system. I think that's what got up Ollie's nose. He said it was the sex, but I think he didn't want to insult his posh friends. By then, he was hanging out with Snowdon and all that lot.

"But the *fans*," Ollie whined. "Think of the kids."

Likely story. This was nineteen-sixty-seven—as if kids didn't already know about frottage and toe-jobs and Viennese Oysters. What kind of bourgie fantasy was Ollie living in? But I didn't confront him; you can't fight that sort of narrow-mindedness. You can only ignore it, and pray God it doesn't reproduce.

Getting back to Clive: our manager didn't care whether we did the film or not. That screenplay bought him a week of romance. Then Jon's lover came home early.

"Jon and I had smoked some Lebanese hash, titanically strong stuff," Clive said. "We had both been overcome by its effects. He lay in his bed, dozing, while I was one room away, in the bathtub. I'd gotten up to get a glass of water and never made it back; rather undignified, but it ended up saving my life. Jon's lover arrived and found some gifts that I'd given Jon, a lighter, some cufflinks—Jon always used to hide them, but in this case he'd passed out first. Suspicions confirmed, the lover went mad. He bludgeoned Jon to death with a tack hammer, then killed himself with pills. Thank God he didn't wash up before retiring, or I would've died, too.

"Several hours later, I stumbled out to the most horrible tableau. It's impossible to know what to do in those kinds of circumstances. One simply reacts. After checking to make sure that both men were dead, I collected what little gifts I could see. Then I read the lover's suicide note, which said that 'Jon's diary would explain everything.' I searched Jon's desk until I found it, then tore out the last eight days' worth of pages. That was when Jon and I had begun our affair. I stuffed them in my pocket and left."

"As I was closing Jon's door, his landlady came out of her apartment. She saw me on the stairs, and I could tell by her face she recognized me. That's when I went home and started planning my own demise."

"Why? You hadn't done anything."

"The police investigation was sure to involve me."

"You were friends, working on a project together. All the scrapes you'd gotten us out of, I can't believe you couldn't talk—"

"Not this time, Tom. I'd be cleared, but everything would come out in the trial, all my various pastimes. It would be like getting kicked out of the Army again. There were a lot of people who would've taken positive relish in my humiliation, people whose toes I'd trodden on, on our way up." Clive paused, looking as tired as I felt. "Some Summer of Love, eh? I'm having another, would you like one?"

I waved him off.

"To be honest, it wasn't *just* Jon. The way I liked to live—the only way I've ever enjoyed—was disappearing."

"I don't follow," I said. "They repealed the sodomy laws that very summer. You could've lived a normal life."

"Oh, save me," Clive said. "If I'd wanted a normal life, I would've stayed on at the rug shop. We all get into showbiz to live special lives, in that delicious little space between image and reality."

The flight attendant wordlessly provided a fresh drink. Everybody worked for Clive; his genius was getting you to like doing it.

"A special life, a secret life. On screen, she's America's sweetheart; off it, she's the biggest tramp since Christine Keeler. All the hunks are queer, and the King of England is played by a Jew. Public/private, open/hidden, light/dark, each side sharpening the other. That's the *sweetness* of it—the hiding, the secret. That's how show biz has always been. That's how it should be."

"But it's dishonest," I said.

"So is fame. The guy who shot you thought you were some kind of god."

"He was insane."

"Was he? Or merely a little less sane than the rest of us? He thought he could judge you—since you were being so honest with everybody. How was he to know that was just another persona?" Clive said. "Back in '67, I saw where things were going. I couldn't live like that. As long as there was a gap between normal life and what people like you and I did, I could function. But the more open things got, the more reckless I had to become, to get the same thrill. I saw where things was going, all that false democracy, and it was going to kill me. It killed a lot of people. It damn near killed you."

"I still think it's better to be honest. People should be seen for what they are."

"Oh, come on. Most people don't know the truth about themselves, much less a pop star. They're just following fashion. The fashion became to wallow in the mud and call it 'honesty.' Is it any wonder the whole culture's gone into the toilet? Decadence simply doesn't work when it's got nothing to push against. I'm no prude, God knows, but where is the grace? Where is the beauty?"

"Clive, just tell me you voted for Thatcher and be done with it."

"Everybody needs boundaries, Tom. Even you."

"You sound like Harriet."

"Boundaries are why you became a recluse. They're why you married Katrinka."

"Now you sound like my shrink."

Clive laughed. "You know why we've always gotten along, from the very first time we met?"

"Because you fancy me bum?"

"We're both sin-eaters. We both live crazy, sinful lives, then turn it into harmless pleasures for others. When there are no longer any sins, we're out of a job. We might as well be dead."

"Tried that," I said, stifling a yawn. "I prefer napping."

"Oh, what am I thinking?" Clive stood up and dug out a pillow and blanket. "I didn't mean to overtire you. Words don't do any good anyway. I'm afraid we're all secrets, even to ourselves. That's what makes people so wonderful. It makes life worth living."

The rest of the flight was uneventful. One connection, a small plane and a chartered boat later, I finally ran out of news.

"Don't worry," Clive said, "we're nearly there."

"Where?"

"Come up to the flying bridge, I'll show you."

I like the sea, love it in fact, but it was noisy and windy up there, and as we bounced through the choppy waves, I clung to the railing like a nervous kid. I was still so bloody weak, I was afraid I'd get thrown in and be lost forever. Loving the ocean is one thing, but drowning in it is another.

Clive pointed to a greenish pimple clinging to the horizon. "There. Home."

"Looks small."

"Don't worry, it grows."

"Okay, but if you ask me to touch it, I'm leaving."

Clive laughed. As we approached, I saw that the island had a small mountain in the middle. Clive said there was a local legend about that. "When you die, this is where you come to walk up to Heaven."

"Don't mention Heaven. Bastards wouldn't let me in."

"Next time I'll make a few phone calls."

I began to make out houses peeking through the treeline. "Which place is yours?" I asked.

"All of it. The locals call it Oneiros, meaning 'Land of the Dead.' Appropriate, no?"

"Yeah, but marketing poison."

"I agree. I call it Brigadoon."

"Oh, that's not gay *at all*."

"Well, what would you call it then?"

I thought. "Clive's Last Resort."

Brigadoon was beautiful. What's more I felt truly safe there, surrounded by water, an electric fence, and a few unobtrusive security types who looked like they could make Bigfoot cry. What's more, Clive was as good as his word, monitoring every facet of my rehabilitation. Doctors were brought in, devices, special foods…I slid back into an old, very familiar groove. Clive had always taken care of me; next to Fraulein, he had been my closest friend. There haven't been a lot of those in my life, certainly not since I hit the big time. As my wife always says, "Friends are what poor people have instead of money."

Our voyage had worn me out. For the first four days, I didn't leave my condo. Tidy and secluded, it was situated right next to Clive's, and had everything a recuperating rock star might need. Except, of course, American television. SkyTV was still a few years away, and I didn't understand Greek, so I turned down the sound and made up the stories myself.

As soon as my pilot light was re-lit, Clive showed me around the grounds, which occupied the western half of the 80-acre island. In my condition, hiking was out of the question, so we used a golf cart. It sounded like a magic carpet made of sleepy bees. Once a mile or so, Clive would wave at some leathery Hellenic nabob, but overall I was shocked at how few people we saw.

"They're all crammed into the town on the East end," Clive explained. "We discourage them from coming over here."

"Why?"

"My guests crave privacy. That's why they choose Brigadoon instead of Sardinia or Ibiza."

"Who are these guests?" I asked, squirming a bit at the thought of other people.

"High net-worth individuals, looking for a place where they can really relax."

I squirmed more. "Like film stars, that lot?"

Clive laughed. "More boring than that, I'm afraid. Brigadoon caters to people who've made it in business, or inherited it. Really wealthy people need a place where they won't require bodyguards. It's a relief to be somewhere where everybody has the mansion and the jet and the yacht.

They can get a suntan anywhere. Here, they can feel *normal*."

"You're an innkeeper?"

"Not really. More like First Citizen. Members build their own units, which they can use or lease to other members. I keep an eye on the infrastructure, and monitor the staff, but mostly I just charge dues for the use of the island. Two hundred people paying a hundred thousand pounds a year, it adds up."

I whistled. "I was in the wrong business. Where is everyone now?"

"It's always slow during the hot season."

With that kind of money behind it, no wonder the compound was quite large. I saw at least thirty cheerily painted houses of varying size, some of them multiunits. Clive said they were planning more "as soon as we can upgrade the electrical grid." There was an infirmary, a central dining hall with a kitchen, and next to that a recreation area with golf, tennis, and a pool—a necessity because the beaches were rocky. There were all the comforts of home, and anything we needed, we could order from the mainland. Four days later, it would be waiting in the town at the other end of the island, a fishing village maintained more out of habit than commerce. Clive was their benefactor and unofficial mayor.

"The village school is named after you," he told me. "We did it the week after."

"I should hope so," I said, affecting mock-dudgeon. "I probably paid for it." I always pretended to begrudge Clive his commission. Deep down I'd like to think he knew I was touched. Yes, I'm sure he knew.

The next day—or maybe it was a week, who can tell on Brigadoon?—Clive and I were sitting on the patio off his living room, having just finished dinner. I was enjoying one of those bittersweet postcard moments where you stop and think, "I will never forget this." Realizing that you will forget it makes the experience even more pleasant, almost unbearable.

"Would you mind if I leapt over the railing?" I asked brightly.

"After I took the trouble to—*good one!*" Clive clapped at a bird which had snatched a bit of bread out of the air. He was a great one for encouragement, spraying it about like froth from champagne, and it flowed regardless of species.

"They definitely like bread," I said. Clive and I were running a small experiment on the dietary habits of seagulls. Bread and pastry, yes; broiled octopus, occasionally; vegetables, definitely not.

The green sea gnashed against the rocks with the fierceness of a lover. I tossed, then watched a bit of grilled squash plummet unmolested. "They never eat what I throw. It's beginning to hurt my feelings."

"Imagine how cook would feel; he's Cordon Bleu. May I ask you a question?"

"You can ask."

"Why did you break up the group? Whenever I heard you talk about it, it sounded like you were lying."

"I thought this was where the world's hounded rich-o's come to feel normal."

"Come on, Tom. Is it still that painful to talk about?"

"I quit because Ollie beat me. Not that I'd ever give him the satisfaction of knowing."

"Beat you? In what sense?"

I continued to hurl bits of food; the slight distraction allowed me to be more honest. "Ollie was a better Ravin than I was."

"You're the only one who thought so."

"I'm only one that matters." A bird caught something, then dropped it. "We set out to be pop stars. Those were the rules of the game and I accepted them. His songs sold more."

"But your songs were more unique."

"I bet you say that to all the supposedly deceased rockers. Any of those here, by the way? I'm not going to run into Elvis down by the tanning beds, am I?"

"Unfortunately not."

"Nothing unfortunate about it. You never had to talk to him, the flatulent old git." I try to speak ill of the dead whenever possible, just to show Fate who's boss. "By the time you died, watching Ollie succeed was really eating me up. I needed out. That's what all the lysergic was about."

"Yes, I rather suspected you weren't having any fun."

"For months I went around asking, 'What should I be? What does the world need?'"

"Send your answer, plus ten box tops to 'Miserable Rock Star, Surrey, England."

"Katrinka won the grand prize. Which was me, obviously."

"What was her answer?"

"Be Gandhi on acid."

Clive smirked.

"Smirk all you want, as soon as I started doing it, I saw the effect it had on people. There's a hole in life where all the heroes used to be. The old authority figures, we'd shown them for what they were. George Washington, who the hell is he to some kid living now? Or Buddha, or even Christ? People like that aren't people anyway, they're ideograms: "Honesty." "Charity." "Compassion." I gave people a modern alternative, that's all. Never mind that my own life was a mess, or that nobody could possibly live up to the standards I'd set, I didn't care about that."

"Why not? Didn't that hurt the message?"

"The message wasn't really my purpose. My purpose was to put Oliver in his place. And I did it. The demise of The Ravins was a mere side-effect. What do Katrinka's spook friends call it? Collateral damage."

"Spooks as in spies?"

"Yeah. Spies, ex-cops, stuff like that. They help us do stuff."

"I shouldn't like to have people like that around me, I would think."

"Oh, they're all right. You just have to show them who's boss."

The tidbits were gone, so we sipped our drinks and watched the sun set. Every so often a gull would knife by, giving the patio a final twilight once-over. "I admire seagulls," I said. "They're blatantly themselves."

"They also shit everywhere."

"Precisely." I wiped my hands on a napkin and sighed. "I won the battle but Oliver won the war. I've dried up, Clive. I talked big in the press, but that comeback album took me five years, and half of it was Fraulein's songs."

Clive cleared his throat.

"All right, 'songs' is a bit much." My wife had a theory that violent crime was caused by irritating noises. So after each one of my songs, we'd put two minutes of oscillating white noise. That's why we had such a hard time getting a record deal. But we had the last laugh: After we released the album, homicides went up.

"Well," Clive said, "maybe you'll find the muse here."

"Oh no," I said. "I'm done with that. Music's what got me shot."

"Bit of an excessive reaction."

"I am an excessive man."

"Still, Tom, I can no more imagine you not writing music than I can imagine that gull not flying."

"I thought you were going to say 'shitting.'"

Clive laughed. "What are your plans, Tom? Other than not making music?"

"Haven't any," I said, "and it feels *wonderful*."

I stayed on Brigadoon for nearly four years. There are a lot of things about the island that I'm not allowed to say, stuff like its actual name, or precise location, not to mention who slept with whom. There was a lot of that. Clive's little campers used it as a prime trysting-ground, creeping furtively from one condo to the next, combining fortunes in the dead of night. Thanks to the magic of mail-order, I obtained a motion-detector and a camera with a powerful flash. Every evening, I'd point it at the path in front of my door, and every morning I'd see who I'd caught. It was good fun—until one couple (a Peugeot and a Rothschild if memory serves) turned out to be exhibitionists. That bloody flash kept me up all night.

I didn't play around myself. Fraulein had a magic teakettle that whistled whenever I was unfaithful. But I was in no condition, even if I'd wanted to.

On Brigadoon, I did nothing but heal, and it kept me plenty busy; that's how near death I'd been. Every morning I'd get up early, meditate, and eat a bit, then I'd drive down to the town, to see if any of the stuff I'd ordered had arrived. When I got back, it would be time for physical therapy, acupuncture, and aura work. Then lunch, followed by a nap on the beach or by the pool. Finally I'd read and paint and stroll until dinner, sometimes alone, sometimes with Clive or the occasional non-boring rich-o.

Did anyone recognize me? I'm sure they did, even thinner and sans hair. But no one said a word. Clive invariably introduced me as "my friend Simon, he's in electronics." For the few that asked further, I told them I'd invented the Betamax. But it was not a problem. Just as at the hospital, everybody on the island had their own secrets to keep, if not ones as dramatic as mine, secrets nevertheless. In addition to that, I don't think anyone was surprised that I had survived. With wealth comes knowledge of Man's infinite deviousness, as well as a belief that money can do almost anything, including resurrect the dead.

Meals were the only time everybody came together, in the Minoan-themed great dining hall at the center of the complex. The food was as good as you'd expect, and after dinner, members would sit and talk, which was fascinating, but could get tense. These were powerful individuals, unaccustomed to disagreement, and everybody had a different philosophy on diet and politics and religion. Clive tried to stay out of it, but occasionally he'd have break up a fistfight. We had terrorism, too; one of the BMW heirs was a vegan, and she kept pouring sand in the scrambled eggs. Took the enamel right off my teeth.

People learned never to argue with me. Wrong or right, I'd simply keep talking until they gave in. One evening, a minor Agnelli and I were debating whether or not organic coffee was addictive. "...and that's not me talking," I said, "that's Roger Bacon, the famous alchemist. And I haven't even told you about the ancient Aztecs who, according to their calendar—"

The poor little rich man clapped his hands over his ears. "Clive! *Per favore!* Make Simon shut up."

Clive smiled sadly. "Been trying since 1961."

An eavesdropper, a former official in the US government, piped up. "Your argument is absurd," he rumbled. "The 'organic' designation—"

"Ahh, go fuck Cher," I shot back. People laughed, which egged me on. "Now I know what Dr. Doom looks like with his mask off." It was rude, but I have a thing about war criminals.

Red-faced, the man threw down his napkin and stood up, like he was going to take a swing at me. Before things could escalate, Clive stood up himself, and announced that there were a few extra pastries left in the fridge, "first come, first served." My adversary retired. There were certain things more important than his honor.

Clive leaned over and whispered. "Come with me. I have an early birthday present for you." The way he gripped my shoulder told me it wasn't optional.

As we walked to his condo, Clive said, "Can you tell me what you were thinking, purposely insulting Henry?"

"What can I say? I'm a sucker for an audience, you know that. At least I didn't call him 'Jew-boy,' like they did in the tapes. Besides, Clive, he's a war criminal."

"He's also a member, Tom." Point made, Clive changed the subject. "Have I ever told you how I got this place?"

"Card game between closeted peers, St. John's Wood, 1966."

Clive smiled. "Not quite. There's some Roman ruins on the cove, but for practical purposes this island was uninhabited until the 40s, when the Greeks turned it into a Club Med for their secret police," Clive said. "At some point the government became strapped for foreign currency, and they auctioned it off to the highest bidder."

"Which was you."

"Correct. It was a real tip. For the first year, I did nothing but supervise workmen—"

"Tanned, well-muscled, barely literate workmen..."

"There was no electricity over vast swaths, I needed to dig new wells, the whole place needed paint. Then there was the decorating—God did most of it, I just added a touch here and there."

"Quit being modest. Everybody knows you've got great taste," I said. "If you didn't, they'd kick you out of the union."

"It's a work in progress."

Someone was coming towards us on the path. It was Maria Something-Spanish, I think she owned most of the air in Madrid.

"Hello, Clive, Simon. Either of you want to come with me to book club? We're reading *The World According to Garp*."

"No thanks," I said.

"Bit tired," Clive said. "Next time, perhaps."

Evenings on Brigadoon were filled with events like that, yoga, discussions of the news (big topics: herpes and cocaine), Scrabble. Occasionally people would demonstrate skills, like the secrets of white-wine cookery, or how to restring a tennis racket behind your back. I even gave a talk on the evils of refined sugar. All pleasant enough, but one thing did have an impact on me. The few Americans—being Americans—started chapters of AA and NA, and held meetings. This amused the Europeans, with their generally wait-and-see attitude towards religion. The Brits, Clive included, thought it was all twaddle. I, as a transplant, was somewhere in the middle.

Around '71 or so, Fraulein had given me some tapes to kick heroin, and I did, then a couple years later went on to eliminate cigarettes and booze for good measure. People never believed that I'd really given it up, though—that's how powerful their image of me was. They absolutely would not believe, regardless of the reality in front of them. I went to meetings for a while, as much for the baklava as the twelve-stepping. I could see the benefit of it, but some of them came on so strong, it turned me off. A few even accused me of using, and wouldn't believe me when I'd said I'd kicked. But I didn't confuse the good message with the less-good messengers. Put it this way: I've read all the books, but I don't go to meetings. I don't drink or drug anymore for the simple reason that whenever I did, crazy shit would happen. And that is no longer a luxury I can afford.

We got to Clive's condo. "Wait here." he said. Moments later he presented me with a box wrapped in colored paper.

"Ooh, it's heavy," I said, pleased.

"Go on, open it."

I knew what it was after two tears: a carton of Raisinets, airmailed from America. "Aw, Clive, you shouldn't have." I looked around. "...especially after I gave that talk. "

"What's the harm in a little sweet? I'm a Cadbury Flake man myself," Clive said. "Happy 41st birthday, Tom. May we spend many more of them together."

"Yeah, Clive, about that. I've been meaning to ask. Can I ever leave?"

Clive laughed. "Of course you can! This isn't Kolditz."

"Do you think it would be safe?"

"I think so. Every day, people get more used to a world without you. Soon, they'll be so used to it that nothing could convince them that you were still alive. You could stand in Hyde Park warbling all your hits, and they still wouldn't believe it. Because everybody knows Tom Larkin is dead. 'Everybody knows.' That's powerful magic."

"So that's it then? I could leave tomorrow?"

"You could, but I wish you wouldn't. I'd like to teach you a few things, extra precautions. I've been dead nearly twenty years. I'm an expert."

"Don't worry, I'll be here a while yet. Marcia says my aura's still quite dingy."

"That's what happens when you pay them by the hour. I'll expect you to come back regularly; this is a lovely place to grow senile. When you want to leave," Clive said, "just say the word. We'll teach you how it's done. Properly."

After years of trying, I've come to the sad conclusion that living *la dolce vita* drives me insane—I mean that literally. There's simply not enough conflict in it to keep me interested, so first I get paranoid, then the compulsions take over.

Before, they'd settled on germs and sugar, but those had receded a bit. Now I became obsessed with tidiness. Things started off harmlessly enough, staying behind in my condo to supervise the maids on their daily visit. Then I began going with them to other condos. Then I began breaking into other condos, so "things could be seen to properly."

One day in February '83, Clive knocked on my door.

"Who is it?" I called without opening.

"Hello Tom. Haven't seen you outside lately, everything okay?"

I opened the door a crack. "What do you want?"

"I was wondering if I might have a word. Privately."

I turned and walked back into the dark. Clive took that as a "yes," but kept his distance, as if I were an aging family pet with a newfound tendency to bite. After closing the door he asked, "Were you in Jack Valenti's unit again?"

"No," I lied.

"He says he caught you ironing his towels."

"That's absurd."

"Someone smashed the locks on his linen closet."

"Have you considered pixies?"

"Here's a picture of you sneaking out the bathroom window. Do you deny that's your trainer?"

I moved the broom to hide my shoes. "It's faked."

"And here's the note you wrote him. 'Dear slovenly twat—'"

"Okay, Clive, I wasn't going to tell you this, but I think he's a druggie."

"All right…Tom, I think it's time for you to go back to civilization."

"That's beautiful," I said. "One bloke complains, and you want to throw me out. But I guess pill-freaks have to stick together, right?"

"It wasn't one person, and you know it, but that's not the point. You don't seem happy, Tom. In fact, you seem to be regressing."

"I don't know what you mean. Now if you'll excuse me, I have to sweep the walk before sand gets into the pool."

He reached up and grabbed the broom. "Five times a morning is enough."

"So you've been spying on me too, eh?"

"Hardly. Every time I go out on the patio I see you doing it."

I stood there silent, defiant, wondering if I had another broom.

"If you leave now," Clive said, "you can always come back, but if it gets any worse…Tom, what if someone claims you've stolen something? I'd have to ban you."

I saw his point. The people here were just crazy enough to do that. "All right, I'll go," I said. "Give me a week to pack my stuff. Place is a health hazard, anyway."

"There's no rush," Clive said.

"Yeah, yeah, yeah."

After I pushed Clive out the door, I placed a call to New York. I guess I had a vague idea I'd live near my wife and kid; I mean, if Clive was right about people forgetting…An assistant said Katrinka couldn't come to the phone, which was no surprise. Deeply sensitive and easily hurt, my wife had never forgiven me for going to Brigadoon in the first place. I told her that she was welcome, that she'd like it, that Clive wanted to meet her, but Fraulein wasn't budging. I didn't take it personally. Strong-mindedness is only natural when you're an island of genius floating in a sea of idiocy.

A week later, she delivered the bad news. "You can't stay here."

"Why not? I'll put on a disguise."

"I just turned the downstairs apartment into a museum."

"But my bedroom! All my stuff!" The idea of strangers milling about in my personal space, scuffing the floor, putting things out of order—it took effort not to vomit. "You can't *do* that."

"Oh yes I can," Fraulein said. "I spent six months lobbying the board. Fucking Swanson, I'll throw a party when she croaks. Whore made me fork over 50% to a building maintenance fund, but I'll get it back in tax-deductions."

"Tell them you've changed your mind!"

"I can't back out now, they'll know something is up. What's Plan B?"

I was speechless. I said the first thing that popped into my head. "It's a surprise."

"Okay. Call me when you get settled and we'll set up an allowance."

"But Fraulein, don't you *care*?"

"Of course I care, as long as it's not here and you stay dead." The undersea line crackled. "By the way, aren't you afraid of getting shot?"

Getting shot again couldn't hurt any more than this. I hung up, feeling afraid, unsure, and very much alone.

As the date of my departure approached, the romantic and practical sides of my nature could not agree. One possible future involved stowing away on the Orient Express, boarding a tramp steamer at Le Havre, and ending up somewhere in the Congo. The other was to go to Athens, stay in the ritziest hotel I could find, then eventually wander over to the airport and hop on the next flight that had a first-class seat. In the end, I decided to do the latter. *La dolce vita* may be bad for me, but it's a hard habit to kick.

The day I was due to catch the ferry to the mainland, my phone rang. "Come next door," Clive said. "There are some people I'd like you to meet."

"Bit busy at the moment, sorry." This was a lie; the books I'd accumulated had all been boxed, and I was taking only a duffel bag's worth of clothes. (Clive had convinced me to leave the rest for my next visit.) My feelings weren't even hurt anymore. To be honest, in the moments between spikes of anxiety, I found I liked the idea of returning to civilization. But playing hard to get with Clive, that's just how our friendship worked.

"Do come over, it won't take long. I'm sitting with a few members who've lived incognito. I thought perhaps they might have some tips."

"Oh, all right," I said in a put-upon voice. Clive liked to feel guilty. I was doing him a favor.

My host greeted me at the door in his usual get-up, a linen suit and pastel shirt. In all the many months I lived on the island, I never once saw Clive in shorts. English reserve, I guess, or skinny legs.

We walked through the house, which like all of them, was kept dark during the day to reduce the heat. At the entrance to the patio, one of the compound's security men shuffled bulkily to one side.

"Thank you, Dimitris." Clive stepped over the metal tracks of the sliding door into the sunlight. "Forgive the security, Tom, but this meeting has to be private. Obviously." We walked around the corner. It was quieter there because you weren't directly above the surf. "I'm glad you changed your mind," Clive said, putting on his sunglasses. "I think you'll—bloody hell! Look at that fool down there!"

I peered over the railing, and saw a small brown figure rappelling down the crags. "What the hell's he doing?"

"'Training,'" Clive said, crooking his fingertips. "Back and forth, climbing and rappelling, he'll be at it all afternoon. I invited Ramón over to talk to you. I should've known he'd be too compulsive to resist."

I turned and saw two members, one of each gender. They sat underneath an awning, next to a low table with cool drinks and finger foods on it. When they saw us, the man in the chair got up; the woman on the sofa stayed seated.

"Tom, I've told these two a little about your situation, and they've been gracious enough to offer their advice. This is Parquet Trobriand."

"Gracious nothing," the man said. He looked like a cross between Allen Ginsberg and Clark Kent. "I've wanted to meet you forever."

"I'd better enjoy hearing that while I still can." Smiling, we shook hands.

"And this is Evelyn Brown. She's one of our original members."

"Ah. The lady with the Luger."

"It is my custom to greet intruders that way," she said contemptuously, touching my hand as little as possible.

"Well you should make your bed." I looked at Trobriand. "She just pulls the sheets up."

Mrs. Brown colored under her makeup. "Really, Mr. Larkin, my housekeeping is none—"

"I bet most days she doesn't even do that."

"Yes, well…" Clive coughed. Then he said, "Mr. Trobriand's been incognito for—how long?"

"Twenty-three years."

"And you, Mrs. Brown?"

"Thirty-nine," she said icily.

I looked Brown over and determined she'd been cute, once; it's always such a shame when beauty is wasted on a bitch. From her marcelled hair to her flowered frock to the pearls strategically placed around her person, this birdlike bint was the epitome of what my Aunt Harriet longed to be. Maybe that's why I didn't like her.

"Your accent doesn't sound English," I asked. "Where are you from originally?"

"Lesson one, Mr. Larkin, is never divulge anything you don't have to."

"I wasn't aware we were playing yet."

"Lesson two is you are always playing. Simple rules, but ones that have saved my life."

"What, are you a secret agent?"

"Of a sort," the woman said. "More a refugee."

"Personally, I think it's going to be a piece of cake," Trobriand said. "All you have to do, Tom, is know people's expectations. Then act the opposite."

"So what's your story?" I asked. "Can you say?"

"My family's loaded. That meant I could do anything, and accomplish nothing. If I'd been a normal kid, I would've just split for the Village. But that wasn't possible, not when my Dad might run for President in '64. So I hooked up with an old instructor of mine from Yale, an ethnosexologist. I didn't give two shits about the circumcision rites of the Dindi tribe; all I cared about was getting on that expedition, then getting deep enough into the jungle to sneak away. They thought I'd been kidnapped, or wandered off into the swamps and starved. There were a thousand ways to die out there, that's why I'd picked it."

"I still say pills are better," Clive said.

"But so pedestrian," Trobriand said. "Anyway, as my father dispatched Pharaoh's armies to look for me, I was on a cargo ship, heading for Hawaii. From there, I flew to Seattle. I lived there for a while, then hit had my first hit of Owsley acid. Two weeks later, I was in San Francisco, just in time for The Sixties. The reason nobody ever found me was because they were looking for the guy I was in '61, a square-looking doof in horn-rims and a crew cut. The moment I became a hippie, I was safe as houses. You'll be fine," Trobriand said, "as long as you play against your image."

"Do you have anything to add, Mrs. Brown?"

"For me, it has been a matter of location. I live thousands of miles away from my original home, and in an area with many people like me. Bolivia has many Europeans. I do not cause any attention."

I chewed a canapé. "You're saying, 'blend in'?"

"And control your context, as Mr. Trobriand says."

"Have either of you had any close calls?" Clive asked.

"Yeah," Trobriand said. "I used to protest a lot—CND, Free Speech, Vietnam—until I realized that getting arrested was probably the one way I could get caught. I know you like to stir things up, Tom, but I'd strongly advise you not to. Stay out of trouble. Don't give anybody an excuse to dig. Politics is a luxury people like us can't afford."

"I have been fortunate in that I have always been apolitical," Mrs. Brown said.

"Uh-huh," I said.

"My worst moments came right after the War, when I was in the company of others like me. Alone, we could pass undetected, but in a group—each of us indicted the others. And stay in plain sight. As long as I was in hiding, Mr. Larkin, there was a chance that I would be captured. Once I returned aboveground, I was safe again. When you are out in the open, people assume you have nothing to hide."

"Do you have any questions, Tom?"

"Just one," I said. "Mrs. Brown, when you watch *The Sound of Music*, how does it feel to root against Julie Andrews?"

Trobriand laughed out loud, and even Clive had to bite his lip. Mrs. Brown, however, didn't see the humor in it. She got up. "Mr. Solomon, I have done as you asked. I will expect the agreed-upon adjustment to my fees."

"I promised myself I wouldn't cry," Clive sniffed when we were alone in his office. Before my mood shifted, I used to go there all the time to steal chocs and fool around on his Commodore 64. "Promise me you'll come back, if things ever get sticky."

"Sticky? You're the one who told me I'll be fine."

"You will be. If you keep your head down." Clive whirled in his desk chair, and removed a framed photo from the wall. "Here, take this," he said. "You always said you liked it."

"Are you sure?" It was a snap of Clive taken during his brief, unhappy stint in the Army. The boys used to swoon over his Brigadier General's uniform. Problem was, Clive was a Lieutenant at the time.

"I know how you adore taking the piss, but don't go around impersonating. If you ever weaken look at that photo. Now turn it over."

I expected to find a sentimental couplet written on the brown paper backing, but instead Clive had taped a key. "Aw, look. The key to 'is 'eart."

"Not quite. One of my many *pied a terre*. That one's in California."

"Clive, I can't take this."

"Yes you can. In fact, you already have," he smiled. "The lease has been transferred and there's nothing you can do about it."

"Aren't you afraid of someone connecting the dots?"

"No. It's a suite in a hotel, the Casa Marisol, in Santa Monica, outside of Los Angeles. You like it there, as I recall."

I did, what portions I could remember. Santa Monica had been the setting of a protracted public debauch, after my post-Abzug curb-booting. "Clive, I don't know what to say."

"I couldn't have you wandering the earth, could I? What you're about to do will take a kind of discipline you haven't had to show before. But I think you can pull it off. The stakes are high enough. Life and death, perhaps."

For the second time in the conversation, I wondered whether it was wise to leave Brigadoon at all. I resisted the urge to ask if I could stay on; I was indebted enough to Clive already. "Life and death...do you really think that?"

"I don't know—but I suggest you ought to. Otherwise you won't last a week. Oh, I will miss you!"

With that, Clive really began to blubber. He asked if I minded terribly if he didn't see me off at the ferry, and I thought it only kind to let him off the hook.

"All right. Thank you. Now you'd better go before I start flooding again."

I had a bit of time before the ferry arrived, so I slung my duffel over my shoulder and went for a final walk around the compound. The island wasn't beautiful in an English way, brown and frequently burnt, with a scrubbly and rocky terrain only a native could love, but all the same it had been my home, and sheltered me, and I was going to miss it.

Walking vaguely towards the ferry dock, I came upon a small copse of trees. One had been struck by lightning and cut away about chair-height. That seemed like an invitation, so I swung down my duffel and sat. It was so pleasant there. I smelled eucalyptus and hot dirt. I heard the wind, and the far-off hiss of the surf. Another postcard moment—I had to close my eyes to blunt the emotion.

I had only been meditating a short time when I sensed someone else near me. Staying still, I began sneak-looking through my eyelashes, like we all used to do back when we were trying to catch Swami Roger feeling up Mia Farrow. I saw a bit of movement in the bushes to my left; then an entire man emerged. I recognized him as Ramón, the climber of the cliffs under Clive's patio. His wiry shirtless body had been daubed with camouflage paint. There were even some branches tied to his head. He walked towards me and sat down.

"Hello," I said.

"Sorry I missed the coffee-klatsch," he said. "I can't stand that Nazi bitch. Clive says he doesn't make moral judgments, but I fucking do…So you're going back in?"

"Yeah."

"Scared?"

“A bit. Actually more than a bit.”

“Understandable,” he said. “But you’ll be fine.”

“Easy for you to say,” I said, letting my legs flop to normal position. “You’ve never been shot.”

“Yes I have. Two bullets, one of ‘em still in me.”

“Let’s never go to the airport together.”

“Back in the world I was a public defender. Did a lot of good, but I had a taste for *las drogas* and—you lay with dogs, man, you get fleas.”

I made a face that told him I related to that.

“My big mouth pissed off some coke dealers,” Ramón said. “They suckered me out onto a boat, then when we were out there they popped me a couple of times, and dumped me into the Gulf of Mexico. They thought I was dead. I should’ve been. Lucky for me, makos don’t prefer Chicano.”

“Are they still after you?”

“Would be, if they knew I was alive. But you won’t have to worry about that, everybody knows you’re dead. How long’s it been?”

I ticked it off. “Four years, four months, and seventeen days. But who’s counting?”

“And the guy who did it’s in prison, right?”

“Right.”

“You got it made, *ese*. With a man, you can hide, wait for him to die. A group is different. With a group after you, you’re the one waiting to die. That’s no way to be. With a group, you identify the man behind everything, the man at the top, then you take your shot. That’s your only chance; they won’t be expecting that.”

“That’s why you’re ‘training’?”

“Shit, man, Clive’s got to learn to keep his fucking mouth shut,” Ramón said. “Some of these rich fuckers associate with low people.”

“You think there’s a difference?”

Ramón smiled ruefully, then said, “You’re lucky, Tom. You’ve got a golden opportunity.”

“For revenge, you mean? Not really interested.”

"This isn't revenge for me, it's survival. But you—all the things that fuck people up, you're past that. You're already dead. That's a gift. You don't need to worry; you got no obligations. The only fears you have are the ones you choose. You can do what's right, be a free man. Me, I gotta be something else."

"What?"

"A weapon."

Ramon was pawing around in the grass. "What are you doing?"

He held up something wriggling and many-legged. "Lunch," he said, popping it into his mouth. "Ugh."

I was about to question the wisdom of taking life advice from a man who eats bugs when I heard the ferry's horn as it pulled into the harbor.

"My ship's come in," I said.

"I hope so, brother. I hope so."

CHAPTER FOUR

I didn't hurry off to California. After a leisurely stay at the five-star Grand Bretagne, I sauntered over to Athens Airport to begin my new life. Nowdays, a single man with almost no luggage buying a one-way ticket would raise all sorts of questions, but in '85 nobody said a word. The first place I went was London, which I thought would ease my transition. That too went perfectly; after all, I was four years dead and hadn't lived there for twenty. I was tempted to head north and visit Aunt Harriet, but decided against it. She had a weak heart, and Christ knew what might happen when she clapped eyes on me. She'd probably clench shut her aorta out of pure spite. "That'll do you, Larkin..." Harriet always had to have the last word.

Like I said, I'd discovered Santa Monica in 1974, when Katrinka decided to run an experiment on the effect of separation anxiety on rock stars. Creatures too fragile for New York inevitably wander west to LA; and those for whom Los Angeles is too much, end up in Santa Monica. Plus there were a lot of other ex-pats, so I could get teas and foods from when I was a kid. It was a perfect location, then as now one of the few places I actually felt normal.

Far from being a danger, my new city made me safer. When I dressed down, I was another scuttling Sixties casualty, waiting for a revolution that would never arrive. When I spiffed up, I disappeared into the mass of polished Westsiders, well-heeled, socially conscious demi-celebrities who'd made their money manufacturing things you can't touch. And Santa

Monica was far from Fraulein and Jasper, as far as I could get without getting wet.

I didn't feel strong enough to resist that temptation, so I appreciated the three thousand miles of dirt between us. Katrinka did too; she (and Hitler) agreed to my financial terms, a generous biweekly stipend in exchange for my not making a triumphant return, which I wanted less and less anyway. On the first and fifteenth I received a large wodge of cash from a subsidiary of a subsidiary of our shell corporation owned by our accountant.

Even though I didn't need a job, I was tempted to get one just to see what all the fuss was about. Nothing corporate, obviously, or too hierarchical, or too early in the morning. I remember applying to be a docent at LACMA, and bursting out laughing at the ridiculousness of the process. Applications, interviews, it's all so arbitrary and absurd. How does anyone stand it? The answer is, most don't. The vast majority of things that kill people—alcohol, tobacco, refined sugar, drugs—they're all slow forms of suicide.

I worked for a while collecting signatures for various left-wing causes; nuclear freeze, El Salvador, table grapes, stuff like that. Then the twenty-year-old girl I was ringing doorbells with (as Gandhi said, "it always helps to have a pair of tits") told me I looked a little like Tom Larkin. "Only older," she said.

That summed up the Eighties for me. The young people; they all seemed like robots. The problem with kids today is that you can fill a hotel room full of spaghetti and they won't even *perceive* the political significance. They just look at you like you're some sort of freak. How can I possibly relate to that? But it wasn't their fault. The truth was, I didn't care anymore. I was a forty-four year old man. At that age, the only kid I gave a shit about was Jasper, and the only point of genuine pain in my life was my relationship with him. Or, more accurately, the complete lack of one.

As far as Jasper knew, I was dead. At first Katrinka claimed this was for security purposes, but as the years rolled along, it became clear she simply didn't want to share. I tried to remain understanding; applying conventional morality to someone like Fraulein is simply not fair.

"I'm the one that has to raise him," she said whenever the topic came up.

"And by 'raise him,' you mean write a big check twice a year." I'd been strongly against sending Jasper to boarding school, and especially not the one Katrinka picked, which was packed full of World-Ruiners: The Next Generation. I'd despised those kind of fuckers my entire life, and the pleasure of my genetic code being allowed in their enclave was nothing compared to my fear that Jasper would come out more like them than us.

"Oh, stop complaining. I let you win on circumcision," Katrinka said. "It's hard enough to raise a child alone these days without you constantly questioning every little decision. It's not fair for you to get to be his father, but not have to put up with his bullshit."

"He's 10, how much bullshit can there be?"

"Oh, you know," Fraulein said. "There's his clothes, and his friends, and all the little things he says. He thinks he's so amusing. Just like you."

Hearing that made my day. No, year.

I came up with other ways to stay in touch, stay involved. I created elaborate pieces of junk mail, credit card offers and appeals from worthy causes, just so he'd read something from me. For Jasper's birthday he was always a "lottery winner" and at Christmas, cashing in some sweepstakes that didn't exist.

Six months after I moved to Santa Monica, I saw a show on *Nightline* about the "father's rights" movement. As soon as it was over, I called Fraulein and told her to go to hell. "He's my son, too! I can talk to him if I want!"

"Go ahead and try," she said. "He'll think you're a kook."

"He won't think I'm a kook."

"Oh yes he will. He'll say, 'You're a kook, just like the one who killed my father.' You know what he calls Ravins fans? 'Dad's zombie army.'"

"I wonder who taught him that?"

"You better not contact him, Tom. I'm warning you."

"You're warning me?" I laughed. "What can you do, kill me? I've got news for you, baby! I'm already dead!...Already dead...already dead..."

"You are immature and annoying," Katrinka declared, then hung up.

I couldn't help it; I didn't listen. I wrote Jasper, then counted the days until a letter came back. "Dear Kook," it began. I didn't have the heart to read the rest.

I wanted my son to know me, was desperate for it, in fact. But what could I do, send him a biography with the true parts underlined? By that time a whole raft of them had come out. Of course I'd read them, and found that the person they described wasn't like me at all. He was at best a myth, at worst a warning, but always a product.

The plain fact was that the best part of me—the only place I ever really made sense—was in my songs. So that's what I sent to my son. I went through all my tapes, Ravins and after, collecting the best stuff and mixing it down. Then I started bootlegging it, because Fraulein said I couldn't. I guess that's what they mean by "an oppositional personality,"

Apart from Jasper, though, I was happy with my new life. I was bruised but unbroken, tanned from the sun and tousled by ocean breezes, bossed about by my cats Glucosamine and Chondroitin, working on my painting and my cholesterol. Things weren't perfect—it could be a bit boring—but I had one hell of a lot to be thankful for. Which means, I had one hell of a lot to lose.

It was a Saturday afternoon in September 1985, and I was floating in my sensory-deprivation tank. This was a metal box half-filled with saline, one of the few holdovers from my old rock-star life. I found it soothed me, and gave me the kind of high-quality, truly entertaining hallucinations otherwise only achievable via heavy drugs. Sometimes, when I was really down about Jasper, the tank was the only thing that helped.

So there I floated, getting high on the absence of life, when I heard a noise—the creak of my front door? Then, perhaps, footsteps? I fought the impulse to call out, get up, investigate. As with meditation, part of the trick is learning to ignore external stimuli, and not feel anxious about the stories your brain compulsively weaves out of them. Besides, I was in a good groove and wanted to stay there.

Then I heard another noise, a closer one, something small and hard scraping against the tank's metal skin, and my Zen *sang-froid* collapsed.

"Is anybody there?" No answer. Then I heard a cough and peed my tank a little.

"Okay, whoever's—"

The hatch wouldn't open.

"Hey! I don't know what the fuck you're playing at, but"—I shoved the hatch hard, then harder—"you're about to see a very angry, very naked man!"

The hatch still wouldn't give.

"Help!" I shouted, voice echoing. "HELP!"

"Simmer down, simmer down," a deep male voice said. "You're perfectly safe."

I recognized it instantly—anyone my age would. "Is that Milton bloody Crouk?"

"No, it's Rich bloody Little."

"I want you out of my suite right now!"

"Or you'll what?" the ex-President taunted. "Anyway, I think you'll be interested in what I have to say."

"I doubt that." Milton Crouk had spent his entire second term trying to get me kicked out of the country. Him being near me was bad enough, him knowing I was alive was about the worst thing I could imagine. I banged on the side of the tank.

"Stop hurting yourself and listen. Why did you paint all this stuff on here? 'Next Stop: Nirvana', 'Enola Gay', 'Contents Under Pressure'—it's like a flivver."

"Ask Elton John." Reg had sneaked into The Oneida and done that before playing Central Park in 1978.

"What are you doing in there? Jacking off?"

"Wouldn't you like to know."

Crouk cleared his throat, which sounded thick and mucousy. "When a man gets older, Tom, he begins to reflect on a lot of things. The course of his life, what he's done. Who he was, and who he's become. Sometimes, he isn't too pleased with the picture. When that happens, my friend—"

"I'm not your friend."

"When that happens, a man only has two choices, to give up, or to try, as fruitless as that task might seem, to make things right. I'm here to make things right."

"You can start by letting me the fuck out of this box."

"Don't think I'll do that," Crouk said, chuckling. "I know you're not the peacenik everybody thinks you are. I've read the files. Or, my people have. I just read the synopses. Tom, I've just been to the doctor," Crouk said. "I haven't got a lot of time."

"Good. I hope you rot in Hell."

"I can understand why you'd say that. I understand that perfectly. I did you wrong back in the old days, I should've never listened to that idiot Elvis. Erlichman told me he was a druggie. But I let the paranoia get the best of me. You know about paranoia, don't you, Tom?"

"You should get one of these tanks."

"Maybe I will," Crouk said. "Can I wear swimming trunks?"

"I guess so."

"I tapped your phones. I tried to get you deported. You have every right to hate me. But now I'm asking your forgiveness."

"Ah, fuck you," I said, then banged on the lid again. "Lemme out."

"Do you want me to beg? Would that help?" Crouk said. "Would that speed things up? I don't mean to hurry you, it's just that I've got thirty of these scheduled for today. So I'm begging you Tom, as a man and a Quaker—"

"You can go fuck yourself!"

Crouk sighed. "I thought you might react this way, no self-control. I can't make you forgive me, but I can prove to you that my motives are pure, that I'm sincere."

"Yeah? How's that, Tricky?"

"By telling you something very important relating to your life. Your murder," he said, "wasn't what it seemed. It wasn't just some crazy fan."

"Uh-huh. The FBI, right?"

"They might've been involved."

"So know we're playing Twenty Questions?" My fingers were pruning. "Fuck!"

"I'm not holding out on you, Tom. I'm not sure. I only know a few things," Crouk said. "I don't have the access I used to—I have many enemies. As do you. You know, we're a lot alike, you and I…"

"Oh, spare me that bullshit!"

"If I were investigating it, I'd suspect everyone. And I'd be guided by one simple phrase: *cui bono*."

I gave another shove. Thank Christ, the hatch began to move.

Crouk saw it and muttered a profanity. I heard the chair scrape as he lumbered to his feet, then the clop of his wingtips as he quick-stepped towards the door. "It was someone who used to be close to you," he said over his shoulder. "Someone you trusted. I'd find them, before they try again!"

I walloped the hatch; it swung free, and the soup spoon Crouk had wedged between the handles fell to the floor. I took one step out of the tank, warm salt water dripping from every crevice. Twenty feet ahead of me was the dark-suited arse-side of the 36th President. "Stop, Milton!"

In my haste, I caught my foot on the lip of the tank, and my trick knee locked, sending me to the ground. I howled in pain; it hadn't been right since I'd fallen off the stage at the Litherland Town Hall in 1961. Maimed for life, and for a lousy fifty quid.

I hobbled after him, shouting profanities.

"*Cui bono*, Larkin! *Cui bono*!"

The fucker was faster than you'd expect; in college, he used to run track. A tourist got off the elevator drinking a bottled water. She dropped it, and when she bent to pick it up, Crouk hurdled her cleanly, without breaking stride.

"That's Milton Crouk!" I yelled to her. "Grab him!" There was no catching him; in my condition, I couldn't have caught FDR.

As the elevator doors closed, my only chance was to use the stairs. Between Three and Four I got a stitch and had to stop for a moment. Just as I got down to the lobby, I saw Crouk striding through the open front door, mopping his upper lip. A man let him into a limousine. "Shitbird refused to forgive me," he muttered.

"His loss, sir," the man said, and closed the car door.

I sprinted past the doorman, who was so fascinated by the celebrity that he didn't notice my 44-year-old sac swinging lowly in the breeze. I grabbed the car door and yanked the handle.

"Open up, you bastard!" I pounded on the window with my palm. "Tell me what happened!"

The tinted glass rolled down an inch. "*Cui bono*, Mr. Larkin. Remember that."

The limo began to glide away. I jammed my fingertips into the gap; then Crouk rolled up the window. I whipped my hands out of harm's way, then had to leap back a fraction to avoid having my toes run over.

"FUCKER!" I yelled at the limo. "I REMEMBER CAMBODIA!"

"Dude, I think that was just Milton Crouk," the doorman said, then noticed me. "Whoa."

Were all doormen stoners? I grabbed his *Spy*, draped it over my rig, and stalked back upstairs.

If this had happened to me now, after all I've been through, I would've been tough enough to handle it on my own. But back then, the old habits were still stronger than I was; I called Fraulein. I had barely got the President's name out when she cut me off.

"I can't talk to you right now," she said. "The ocelot's eating Princess Hapsepsut."

"The ocelot?" As a rule my wife doesn't do well with anything she can't sue. "What the hell are you—"

"No, Kiki! NO!" Katrinka said. "Oh, she's ripping it!"

Princess Hapsepsut was a mummy Katrinka had bought in 1977. One of her spiritual advisors (I think it was the fat one with the tiara) had said it was der Fraulein in a previous life, "a beautiful young princess carried away by scrofula." After we bought it, we sent it to Columbia and they said it was some middle-aged dude who hadn't even been Pharoah. But Katrinka's faith is unshakable when that is required. "They just wanted it for themselves—hand me that chisel!" She hacked open the case and took the mummy out, which promptly turned black and started to smell. Unable to find a penis, she declared victory and left it for Bettina to clean up.

By the time I 'died,' the sarcophagus had become a $125,000 hat stand, and we had to send the Princess out six times a year to get dry cleaned, just to keep the mold down. From the sounds coming out of the phone, the mummy's decay was being helped along by a large feline. "It's all your fault!" my wife said.

"How is it *my* fault?"

"You told me cats hate the spray bottle! She doesn't even notice! KIKI!"

"Go fill up a bucket and throw it on 'im," I said. "But call me back, it's important."

"STOP! Spit that out right now! It's my previous—" The phone fell into its cradle.

"You'll never guess how I fixed it," Fraulein said, moments later. "I got so frustrated, I grabbed that mummy, and threw it out the window. The cat went right after it!" She lit a Benson and Hedges triumphantly. "Stupid ocelot."

We lived on the seventh floor. "Fraulein, what are you doing with something like that in the house? You hate animals."

"Don't you know, Tom? I'm hurt. I read all your clippings. You should read mine." This was quite unfair, since I was dead and no longer generated much gossip. Anyway, Fraulein had attended a party out in the Hamptons, and one of the guests had brought a tame panther.

"Gaviota Henshaw always upstages me," Fraulein said. "So I thought,

'Next time, I'll bring a lion!' But there were no tame lions available, so then it hit me: a baby tiger! There are tigers on my family crest so I thought we'd have, you know, a connection. And we did! It was uncanny. We ate chicken together. But it ate the inside of the limo too, so I thought, I should get a small one, first, learn how to control that. But now what am I going to do?" she said sadly. "There are only three weeks until Labor Day."

"Fraulein," I said. "I have to talk you to about something important."

"This *is* important," she said. "When someone upstages me, they're upstaging your memory."

"My memory can take it. When I was shot, did you ever hear anything? Any rumors about who might've—"

"Oh, here we go. Me, me, me. *My* memory, *my* shooting. It's all about you, it's always about you. I don't have anything. I am destitute! Abandoned! Alone! Except for my ocelot." Fraulein had a tear in her voice. "And now she's *dead*!"

"Fraulein, for God's sake. Get a hold of—listen: I was just in my tank and guess who showed up? Uncle Milty Crouk."

"Oh, bullshit. You were hallucinating," she said. "I remember you living in there for three days, then jumping out and announcing you were a single-celled organism. The cable people still won't come back."

"I wasn't hallucinating. I saw him. I chased him."

"But Tom, why would you chase Crouk? The Sixties are over. We won."

"Speak for yourself," I said acidly. "I chased him because, in addition to apologizing for trying to get me deported, he said that I was killed by a conspiracy."

"Really. He used those words."

"Well, not those words, it was a Latin phrase—"

"Two weeks of Learning Annex sorcery classes and he thinks he knows Latin." Fraulein exhaled. "It wasn't a conspiracy. Thigg shot you. Take it from someone who wasn't in Stage Four shock."

"You didn't see anything fishy?"

"No. We were walking in the door, you were complaining about something as usual, and that crazy man started shooting at us."

"Just me, I think."

"Then the doorman grabbed the gun—"

"Wish he'd done that before the guy started shooting."

"—and Sam went over to see if you were alive. One person, one gun. I'll never forget it."

"But what if there was more to it?"

"People always say that. People are idiots." Fraulein said. "I hope you're not getting any ideas. I hope you're not planning on digging all that stuff up again."

"But Crouk said there was a conspiracy."

"Crouk lies, he's famous for lying," Fraulein said. "So, okay, who did Mr. Always Truthful Milton Crouk say did it?"

"He didn't know. He heard rumors."

"Let me make one thing perfectly clear: Crouk's fucking with you. He hates you. He's always hated you. Don't you see, Tom? He's trying to drive you crazy."

"Fraulein, if there's nothing to it, what's the harm in making sure?"

"You know if you get exposed, you know who everyone will blame? Me," Fraulein said. "They always blame me. You could be standing there next to a dead body, holding a smoking gun with a bloody knife taped to the handle, and all you'd have to do was point and say, '*She* did it.' And your idiotic zombie army would tear me to pieces."

That stung, so I changed tactics. "But if the killers are still out there, they could find out I'm still alive, and try to kill me."

"What good would that do them? I've already made you into a saint," Fraulein said. "It wasn't easy, let me tell you, not with all the people you insulted. Killing a martyr is like having sex with someone who's pregnant. You can do it, but why?"

I shuddered at the memory; those nine dry months had driven me into the arms of Bella Abzug. "No offense, but I'd like to avoid getting shot again."

"Then I would forget about Dick Crouk," Fraulein said. "Tell yourself it was a hallucination. Do whatever you need to. Let sleeping dolls lie."

Fraulein's mangled idioms usually amused me, but not this time. "But if I'm still in danger, aren't you and Jasper still in danger?"

"Not if I have a big fierce tiger!" Fraulein said.

Having gotten no help from Fraulein, I naturally swung to my old life's other pole: Clive. He was in excellent spirits. "We just broke ground on a theatre. I have great plans." Once an impresario, always an impresario. "When are you coming for another visit? Christmas, perhaps?"

"Not for a while, I'm afraid."

"Really? Forgive me but I always assume your schedule is rather…open. Anything the matter?"

"Actually, yes." I told him of my encounter with "Guilty Milty" Crouk.

"Your life simply will not settle down, will it?"

"Karma's a bitch."

"I'd send that karma back to the dealer. What did Katrinka say?"

"'Let sleeping dolls lie.'"

Clive chuckled. "She has a point, you know."

"I suppose, but if it wasn't simply a lone nut—if a group was after me, and they find out I'm alive, they could try again. I can't live like that, wondering if every day will be my last."

"Isn't that how it goes anyway?"

"Spare me the repartee, I'm paying a buck a minute."

"Tom, you have a good life now, yes?"

"Sure. It's fine."

"'Fine' is nothing to sneeze at. In the grand scheme of things, 'fine' is quite a lot. It's only the rock star in you that thinks you need more," Clive said. "But you are who you are, and I'm sure you've already decided to investigate."

"Correct."

"And I also know that nothing I can say is going to change your mind."

"Also correct."

"Do you think Crouk might be manipulating you? Setting you up?"

"It's possible. But why now?"

"Maybe Henry put a flea in his ear, after you insulted him."

My silence signaled that the matter was closed. Clive sighed. "Before we go any deeper into this—before *you* go deeper—you might not like what you find, are you all right with that? Will the truth be enough for you, no matter what applecarts go over?"

"Clive: Has that ever bothered me?" Then I uttered some famous last words. "I just feel I need to do…*something*."

The first thing I needed to do was establish a list of suspects, and Clive was very helpful with that. Once to pass the time on tour, we both did a personality test; he came out a "systematic/enabler," whereas I was 'didactic/intuitive.' This meant that, when confronted with a problem, Clive would make a list, then analyze it. Whereas I would push on my eyes and insist the colors meant something.

"Crouk kept repeating a phrase," I said. "'Cui bono.'"

"Thank Jove for schoolboy Latin. So who benefited from your death, Tom? You talk and I'll write."

"Well, the government was pissed at me for our political experiments. The Bathe-In, all that."

"Yes, Tom. You can do a lot of things, but having a tub in the middle of Times Square, that cannot be forgiven."

"What's that supposed to mean?"

"Nothing. I merely think you might be overestimating your impact on world events, that's all."

"It doesn't matter if you think I was a threat, Clive. It only matters what they thought."

"'They' meaning…?"

"CIA, FBI, NSA, RSPCA…"

Clive laughed. "'They' should've simply ignored you. In two weeks, you would've been on to ayurvedic macramé."

"Every government's mental health sinks to the level of the least sane person in it."

"I could say the same thing about rock groups. Who else?"

"After I got shot, my album sold like mad. So that's the label, the producer, maybe a rogue publicist. And of course all The Ravins shit began selling again, too."

"It's not like they had stopped, Tom. I find it difficult—"

"Everyone is a suspect!" I spat. "Everyone! Everybody at our old label, all the sycophants and hangers-on there, Nigel Bigglesby—"

"Honestly, Tom? You really suspect 'Nod-Off' of hiring a hitman? I wouldn't think he'd have the initiative."

Nod-Off Bigglesby was a schoolchum who had been with us from the beginning. We originally hired him to get at his narcolepsy meds, and forgot to sack him after. Now he ran our label, Mandala Records. "I suspect everyone, Clive, even the other three."

"Oh, come on, Tom."

"You of all people know what Ollie's like—"

"Oliver's main goal in life is to be liked. You don't get that by snuffing the other half of the most popular duo since bangers and mash."

"I turned him from Picasso to Norman Rockwell. If I was Ollie I'd kill me. Why are you fighting me on this?"

"Oliver is nothing if not smart, and if he had paid somebody to kill you—which I don't believe for a second—he would've known that you'd become a saint in the process. He wanted you to stay alive, to show he was the real talent."

"Or woo me back to the group…"

"Now you're proving my point."

"Yeah, well, that doesn't exclude the others. Harry was angry at me in 1980."

"Being angry and hiring a hitman are two different things. And Buck—"

"Buck didn't do it," I said. "When the whole world was against me and

Fraulein, Buck stuck by us."

"Speaking of Buck," Clive said, "what about that bloke he replaced?"

"God, I haven't thought of Bevin in years." As every Ravins fan knows, two weeks before we struck gold, we replaced our old drummer Bevin Fudd with Buck. (We told Bevin his name sounded too poncey.) But Bevin got something out of it; he married Miss Litherland 1962 before fading into oblivion. "Read back the list."

"The military industrial complex, everybody who worked for your solo label; everybody who worked for Mandala; the other Ravins; and Bevin Fudd."

"Still think his name is poncey."

"And yet 'Clive Solomon' isn't, somehow."

"Keep telling yourself that...Don't forget the Jesus freaks, they hated me."

"Along with the followers of the various gurus you embraced, then denounced."

"I always wanted to bring people together."

"There's your first wife Carol, your daughter from that marriage, any of the spouses and lovers you cuckolded while on tour, and all your connections, too. Maybe you burned somebody. When you got busted in '68, did you give any names?"

"I can't remember. I was high." There was a random burst of transatlantic cable weirdness. "God, this is depressing. There's millions."

"You had a talent," Clive said. "Remember when you went on Huntley-Brinkley and said the Hell's Angels were 'obviously compensating for something'? That livened up the tour."

"Can I help it if the world can't take a joke? I should've been a monk."

"Why are you panting? Am I on speaker?"

"I'm doing yoga. Talking about this is very stressful."

"Perhaps we're going about this the wrong way. Who *didn't* want to kill you?"

"Aunt Harriet. She'd prefer to see me suffer. And Katrinka's in the clear, too."

"Are you sure?"

"A couple of years before, '77 or '78, I signed everything over to her," I said. "There was no reason for her to kill me for my money, because she already had it."

"Money's not the only reason people kill. We've forgotten one person. Thigg."

"What did he ever get? Except three hots and a cot?"

"Immortality," Clive said. "It's quite attractive to those of us who don't have it, Tom."

"It's overrated. Do mere mortals have half the world hating them? The Buddhists believe that the more you act in this plane of existence, the more resistance you will recreate."

"The Buddhists didn't grow up in Greasby," Clive said. "You've got some interesting leads here, but before I spent a minute chasing anything, I'd go see Thigg. Maybe it was just a lone nut, as they say."

"I hope so."

"Meantime, if there's anything I can do to help, just ask. And *be careful*, Tom. You're the only you I've got."

CHAPTER FIVE

Did you know I was one of the first people in England to have an answering machine? Ironic given how much I hate them. You seldom get good news—people wait to tell you that in person—and then there's the nightmare of leaving messages.

"Uh, hello, Fraulein, this is Tom, the love of your life...I need you to get me the police file on my shooting. Surely someone in our employ could sneak into the Tombs and root around in their Dead Rock Star Division. I need the ballistics, the autopsy—did they do an autopsy? Guess I'd be the last to know..."

I heaved leaden nonchalance into the ether, hoping that Fraulein was screening her calls. "Any psychological workups, photos, obviously, even the gross stuff, I can take it...Hope you're doing okay. Please call me back. By the way, I saw the article about Jasper's Science Fair project, with the scorpions and the toddlers. You must be very proud."

Now for the *coup de grace*. "If you can't manage it, don't worry, I'll find the files somehow. Clive's helping."

Fraulein picked up. "I'll call Sam Wisnewski." And then she was gone.

It was basic psychology: my wife hated the idea of my poking around, but even worse was the notion that she'd be replaced by Clive. I kept trying to tell her, nobody controls me, her or my old manager, but she wouldn't listen. In fact, she wouldn't even let me finish the sentence. "Somebody's always controlling you, Tom. You just don't know it."

Hearing stuff like that makes you paranoid, and I didn't need any bummers the day I met our ex-security man. We were, after all, asking him to steal documents—and Wisnewski was just enough of a straight-arrow to try to teach me a lesson. He might even blow my cover.

Getting to Wisnewski turned out to be easy. He was semi-retired and living in Santa Ana. Like everyone else in Orange County, most of his time was taken up bitching about taxes and cultivating melanoma. Until, that is, Fraulein dangled some extra zeroes in front of him.

Do I have to mention that Wisnewski hated me? Guys like him always did. First, there was the old "never worked a day in his life" canard. If I had a nickel for everybody who thought I lucked into it all, I really wouldn't have had to work a day in my life. Second, before going into private security he'd worked in Narcotics for the NYPD, and saw me, quite rightly, as the opposition. In Wisnewski's eyes, the only difference between me and some scabby junkie sprawled in a doorway was a bank account stuffed with kids' lunch money. That offended him.

I could give a fuck. I didn't like Wisnewski either. Short, ill-dressed, and with a face like a bag of rolls, he wore too much aftershave and bit his fingernails, the most disgusting nervous habit known to man. Still and all, when he was working for us, I tried to be friendly. You know, human. I once asked him, just to make conversation, if he'd ever heard one of my tunes.

"Only as Muzak," he said.

Wisnewski was utterly humorless, so it was fun to make jokes he didn't get, like when I called him "Agent L-7." But what truly galled me was how Wisnewski walked around like *he* was the boss. Do you know, he actually came into my music room one morning? Nobody did that, not even Fraulein.

At the time of the outrage, I was under the piano looking for a roach clip. A fan had stolen it from an archeological site; apparently it had once used by the Emperor Elagabalus. I didn't know about that, but the cats had been playing with it earlier and I didn't want them to knock it down the heat register. I was arse-in-air peering along the baseboard when Wisnewski sauntered in. He didn't see me on account of the thirty strobe candles going, so I just sat tight. I wanted to test the supersleuth's powers of observation.

I loved my music room. Now it's cold storage for Fraulein's furs, but back then, it was my clubhouse. There was a suit of armor and my collection of Carnival masks, drawings I'd done at school, a moose head and a whole wall made of broken mirrors. Opposite that, for encouragement we'd hung this big poster, the infamous naked portrait of *moi* Lord Snowdon did for that BBC documentary, the one that called me "The Father of the Sixties." I caught Wisnewski staring at it. For one horrible second I thought he was going to have a wank. Then I heard him mutter. "No wonder that was such an ugly decade."

That comment wasn't why I sacked him, but things like it were; both our lives might've turned out a lot different, if he hadn't been such an arsehole. Certainly Fraulein liked him; the only bad word she'd ever say was that "he eats with hatred towards his food." And he'd done a decent job with our security—apart from the obvious, which he wasn't responsible for, having been let go the week before. I knew for sure he was doing me a favor today by delivering the files on my shooting, so I was prepared to be nice.

We were meeting at dusk, at a Fifties-themed diner in West Hollywood, right on Santa Monica Boulevard. I drove there. I had an old Roller that was built like a tank, a good thing since I tended to leave dinged body panels in my wake. I was an excellent driver, when other cars didn't get in my way. The Roller was sky-blue, with clouds painted on it. It broke all the Brigadoon rules—everybody noticed it cruising down the boulevard, kids especially—but I ask you: what was the point of staying alive if I couldn't really *live?*

I'd passed by the diner before, on the way to my urologist. That gave me a nice perspective on the evening; whatever happened, at least I wouldn't get a finger up my arse.

I was early, so I ordered a milkshake and looked at the flair-crammed walls. Every minute or so I had to peel the backs of my thighs off the red vinyl booth. I'd just done it for the fortieth time when I noticed a guy sitting a couple of booths away. I only saw him from the back, but recognized the style immediately. Here, in this ersatz Fifties diner, was an ersatz Teddy Boy.

I don't know what you'd call it in America—the Fonzie look, something like that. This guy dressed just like we did back in high school, or how we wished we could have, if we'd had the dough. Leather jacket, shades, drainpipe trousers, this dude even had the pompadour—clearly his pride and joy, given how he was always combing it. He had one of those switchblade combs, and every five minutes or so, he'd pull it out of his jacket, cock his wrist to the side—thwick!—then drag the comb around his noggin. Oh, he was cool. Part of me wanted to go over there to genuflect. Then I realized I couldn't; the leather jacket around my shoulders was from The Gap. The best I could hope for was to shoot him a meaningful look when he walked out, something like, "I get it. I know I *look* square, but you and me, we're brothers."

I was perusing the menu, looking for meatless options, when Wisnewski walked in. The years had not treated him well; he might eat with hatred, but it looked like he drank with real affection. He was still squat and solid, like a Marshall stack, but it wasn't muscle anymore. He was as soft as a Twinkie, and the bags under his eyes were large enough for a long vacation. And yet he had hair. How is that fucking fair, I ask you?

I expected the old, gruff Wisnewski to mention my baldness, lash out with something insulting and insipid, but he didn't. Instead, he greeted me like a long, lost friend. When we hugged, I smelled that sweetish scent that a lot of alcoholics have. Suddenly I was eight again, and my Uncle Philip was chasing me with a belt.

He noticed my stiffness. "I can't hug the guy who paid for my retirement?"

"That was Katrinka, actually."

We slid into the red vinyl booth, across the formica table. "Thanks for meeting me here," he said. "I love this place. Reminds me of when I was a kid."

"Me, too."

"Really?"

"Well, teenager. And the fifties were a little different in England."

"Better, no doubt." There was the needle. Once a cock, always a cock.

"Are you kidding? To us, America was Heaven." I pointed at a photo of Elvis two feet above the fry station. "I had that photo next to my mirror. I used to practice all the time." I sneered and Wisnewski laughed.

"I have a hard time imagining you as a teenager."

"You don't have to imagine. I looked just like him." I pointed at Pompadour.

"Oh, a tough guy."

"In my mind, at least." There was a mini jukebox at every table. "Do you mind if I play a few?"

"You'll be disappointed. All pre-Larkin."

"Precisely," I said. "I dig these tunes more than anything we did. Lucky for me, the rest of the world disagrees."

Wisnewski opened a menu. "So what looks good?"

"I'm not going to eat."

"Come on, I haven't seen you in four years. This is an occasion."

I keyed in "Hound Dog." "Okay, what's with the act?"

"What do you mean?"

"Being nice. You don't like me, you never have."

"Tom, you were my biggest failure. You sitting there, alive—it's like a second chance." He looked down at the menu again. "The mushroom cheddar burger is good. Would your appetite improve if I said I was buying?"

"Okay, if you insist." I can't resist something for nothing. It's the Scottish in me.

It took protracted negotiations with the waitress to find something without meat. "Come on, dear, act like you care," Wisnewski said in a patronizing tone of voice.

"I don't."

"Let me guess," the ex-cop said, "you're just doing this until your acting takes off."

She nodded.

"Then act, *bimbo*. It's the one role you'll actually get paid for."

At least Wisnewski was an equal-opportunity jerk. Embarrassed, I finally settled on macaroni and cheese. For some reason they put tomatoes on top, which I had to pick off

"'Smatter, didn't they have macaroni and cheese in England?"

"Not in Greasby," I said. "Too exotic."

Wisnewski laughed. "Listen—I don't know what to call you."

I provided that season's name: "Jerry. Jerry Atrick."

"C'mon, guy, you can't use a joke name."

"Why not?"

"Tom, Jerry, whatever, this is serious stuff. Plots and conspiracies and guns going off in the night. Why are you poking around, anyway?"

I gave him the short answer; it seemed safer. "Curiosity."

"Really? That's all? How many people know you're alive?"

"Just a few. When somebody shoots at you, you get a burning desire to know why."

"What makes you think it was any different than what the cops said?"

"Nothing," I said. "That's probably exactly what happened. If it's not, though, they might come after me again."

"Oh, I doubt it. Maybe *they're* dead, did you think of that?"

"My fondest dream."

"If you're concerned about them coming after you, doesn't snooping around make that more likely?"

"Did Katrinka give you a script, or something?"

"I'm just concerned. Once a client, always a client. You ask me, I think you oughta leave it alone."

What would get him to help me? The possibility of more money. So I said, "If I get to the bottom of it, who knows? Maybe I'll make a comeback."

Some of Wisnewski's cherry Coke went down the wrong tube. When the danger of imminent asphyxiation had passed, I cut to the chase. "Enough bullshitting. Do you have the files?"

"Right here," the ex-cop said, his voice still scratchy. "I'll hand it to you inside a menu, under the table."

"Why?"

"Uh, Tom, what I did is a federal offense," Wisnewski said. "Which means..."

"...that it's going to cost me a shedload." Soak the rich guy, America's national pastime. "What's the damage, anyway? Can I write you a check? I'll put 'stolen documents' in the memo line."

"You don't have to. It's free."

"Wisnewski, if I still drank, I'd swear you said 'it's free.'"

"This one's on the house. But don't thank me until you've read it. There's not much there."

I grabbed the plasticized menu. It was very light.

"See what I mean? Thigg pled guilty. No trial."

"That was against his lawyers' advice, wasn't it?"

"Obviously."

"So why did he do it?"

"Why did Thigg do anything? Craziness. He said God told him to plead guilty."

"But if it's insane not to plead insanity, doesn't that mean that if he pled insanity, he'd be sane? And vice-versa?"

"I let the judges handle that shit. Check through. Should be four files there. Report, ballistics, autopsy, and interviews."

I glimpsed something gory and whipped my head away. "Oh, that's me all right."

"And photos, forgot those. Everything there?"

I counted. "One...two...three."

"There should be five."

"Yeah. Report—"

"Don't show 'em around!"

"Sorry." I brought the file back to my lap. "There's the report from the scene, the ballistics, and one from the morgue." I saw another photo, and almost puked. "And photos."

"Shit, I left the interviews out in the car. Those're important, they've got the psych evaluation, too. We'll get it after dessert."

"Suddenly I'm not very hungry."

I was dying to take off, to go back to my apartment and get to reading, but Wisnewski kept on talking. I gritted my teeth and let him, on the off-chance I could buy more help down the road.

"My Dad met you once."

"Mm-hmm?"

"Cop in the Bronx, did security on one of your tours. Sixty-five, -six, somewhere around there."

"That would make sense." Clive always hired off-duty cops to help us out. They welcomed the extra money, and having a bunch of cops on the payroll helped whenever something heavy came down, which happened more frequently than anyone ever suspected.

"At the time, Pop would never tell me the details—my sister Doris wouldn't let him." Wisnewski smiled at the memory. "She adored you guys. She got all those teen magazines, and a whole wall of her bedroom was covered with little Ravin heads she'd snipped from photos. She'd play those records until they *wore out*.

"Dad finally spilled the beans—at Dorie's wake, of all places."

"What did she die of?" I always like to know what to watch out for.

Either Wisnewski didn't hear the question, or he ignored it. "Dad sure had some stories. Once he walked in the wrong door, and caught you and Dylan, spliffs in hand. He could've busted you, but your manager, what's-his-face..."

"Clive Solomon."

"Right, Clive offered Dad $1000 cash on the spot. He was torn, he said. If you knew Dad, you'd understand—a real straight arrow. But a lot of guys on the force did security, and needed the extra money. So he let it go, and distributed the cash between everybody. I know he felt guilty later, though."

"Why? We were adults, it was harmless."

"If he had busted you, do you think the Sixties would've happened?"

"Probably. Trust me, Wisnewski, you would've done the same thing. Anybody would've, it's human nature."

"You really think that?" he said. "You think anybody would've pushed a bunch of new Caddys into the Hudson?"

"Oh shit, I remember that!" I laughed, half at the memory and half that there was a memory—precious few had made it.

"Seventy-five thousand bucks worth," Wisnewski said, smiling. "But that was nothing compared to after the show. Dad said you were the main instigator. There were these girls spread-eagled—"

I held up a hand. "Please, Wisnewski. Let's not let the past get in the way."

"Do you mind if I ask you a question?"

"If it will end this conversation."

"You were young, handsome, famous, rich as hell, drowning in trim—"

I made the "get on with it" gesture. I found it all vaguely embarrassing.

"—what was your fucking problem?"

"If I knew that, Wisnewski, I wouldn't be farting about here with you. I'd be running a high-priced sanatorium for aged rock stars."

"A bright guy like you, you must've thought about it. Were you abused as a kid or something?"

I took a sip of coffee. "Is this organic?" Wisnewski didn't answer. He was going to look at me until I said something. Even the parts I could remember—and the gaps were vast, believe me—were almost impossible to explain. So I just began talking.

"From the time I was twenty, everyone stared at me. But they never *saw* me. They saw what they'd been told I was, good or bad, or what they wanted me to be. The image. I didn't exist.

"I didn't mind the people who hated us, it was the people who loved us that were the problem. Absolute adoration corrupts absolutely. Why do you think Roman Emperors fucked infants and shit like that? And people still turned them into gods! Can you imagine the impotence, the frustration? Caligula knew it was wrong, that's why he did it. *That's* why we drove the cars into the River. In America, then, that felt like the wrongest thing we could do."

Wisnewski wore a bland expression. As I talked, he sneaked a small bottle of brandy out of his shorts pocket, and tipped some into his coffee.

"All of us wanted it to end...Well, we did and we didn't, but we knew things were out of control. I remember asking Harry, 'Do you think I've ever killed anybody?' And he said, 'Does it matter?'

"It didn't matter, not by the time your father was involved. The only thing anybody ever objected to was my insulting God. Can you believe that? 'You can corrupt and destroy everything in your path, and we'll cover for you—we'll even help you do it. But don't say a word against the invisible man in the sky.' I thought they were going to lynch me. And I was looking forward to it! Go ahead! Fucking kill me! Maybe then you'll *see*." I stopped. "Is any of this getting through?"

The ex-cop put down his coffee, lips tight as the brandy burned his throat. "Sure it is."

"I am an arsehole. And yet nobody has called me an arsehole since 1962. God knows I tried to force their hands."

"You're an asshole."

"God bless ya," I said.

"Don't mention it."

"I never did break through the image, not even after death. Fraulein's seen to that."

"She's a little...weird," Wisnewski offered tentatively.

I shrugged. "When you can have any flavor of ice cream you want, you go for the most unique one."

"If you say so. Maybe I judged you too harshly, 'way back when. I have a tendency to do that, I guess."

"So do I, Agent L-7."

"Call me Sam." He slid a menu my way. "Have some dessert."

Thanks to Sam's earlier performance, the actress was even snippier this time around. But my cherry pie made it to our table more or less intact, and I found that the soul-baring had stimulated my appetite. Then my companion said, "Better check it for spit," which stifled my enthusiasm.

"We'll settle up, then you can come out to the car and I'll give you that file." He signaled the actress. "You leave first, then I'll follow. Go now."

I got up, and walked briskly down the aisle, happening to pass my friend Pompadour along the way. I glanced at him in a Ballantine Beer mirror as I walked by, wondering what kind of guy dressed like that. Answer: an old one, and he immediately changed in my mind from hip to has-been.

I walked outside into the cool desert night. A moment or two later, Pompadour did the same, bumping into a rack full of *LA Weekly*; such was the price for wearing sunglasses in the dark. He took them off and stumbled across the street, snarling traffic in both directions. His car was parked opposite the restaurant and I noticed it was just as sweet as his outfit. This guy might be a schlemiel, I thought, but he does know how to accessorize. After he got in, Pompadour did something surprising; he didn't drive away. He just sat there, listening to the radio. Over the din of traffic, I made out the familiar strains of "The Twist."

Sam walked outside and saw me twisting. "Get serious!" he growled. He was tense now, totally different than he'd been in the restaurant. Which made *me* tense.

"Is that guy from the restaurant looking at us?" I whispered.

"Where?"

"Across the street, in the old Fleetwood."

The ex-cop swore under his breath. "We're made. Don't come with me to the car."

"Who is he?"

"I don't know, and I don't want to find out."

"Are you packing?"

"Yes, I have a gun. I always have a gun."

"So fuck 'im, let's go get that file."

"What do you think this is, the OK Corral? I'll mail it to you." He walked away, and sat down on a concrete bus bench.

"Wait, Sam, if you could've just mailed this shit to me, why did we—"

"Don't come over—don't even look. Stay there!" His right hand was in his pocket. "Just walk to your car."

"All right," I mumbled. "I'll call you when the other stuff comes."

Sam didn't answer. I wasn't used to this kind of tension; it took me four tries to get the key into the Roller's lock. As I opened the door, I sneaked a glance over at Pompadour. He hadn't moved.

"Anything for Room 1404? I'm expecting—"

"—a package, sir. We know. Nothing's come in."

"Well, laddie, there'll be a bright gold shilling for whoever gets it to me, so look sharp." Over the next few weeks, I checked at the front desk so often it became a running joke, but no files were ever delivered. Fraulein couldn't get Sam on the phone, either, which is the deepest insult anyone can pay her. "His number's been disconnected," she said wearily. "You should have paid him."

"I wanted to," I said for the hundredth time. "He wouldn't take it."

"Guy gets kicked off the NYPD for corruption, but with you he's an angel. It doesn't make sense. He could've grabbed you by the ankles and shaken out a million. Why not?"

"I think we're friends?"

Fraulein didn't believe it; I wasn't sure I believed myself. "You probably stiffed him. You're so cheap."

"I prefer to think of myself as frugal," I said. "It's the Scottish in me."

"It's the *arschloch* in you. Now, Tom: are you going to quit this nonsense?"

"Probably," I said, but that was just to keep her from yelling at me. It was a funny thing: When I thought about what happened that night at the diner, the hitman in the Fleetwood watching my every move, I didn't feel scared anymore. I felt excited. It was the same feeling I'd gotten watching the riots in 1968. That had turned out all right; maybe this would too?

I decided that I didn't need Sam's interview file and psych evaluations. It was a free country, if you had my kind of money. I would go interview my assassin myself.

CHAPTER SIX

Since 1981, Eric Curtis Thigg had been incarcerated in upstate New York, rotting away in a grim concrete canker called Tannersville State Mental Hospital. If I wanted to question him, I had two options: get myself committed, or get creative. Not wanting to tempt my wife, I called TSMH posing as a reporter.

"I'm sorry, Mr—" The woman paused. She had a backwoods country accent, so I decided to play it exotic.

"Funkquist. Toge Funkquist," Clive's Army photo glared, but small-town Americans love to help foreigners. At least ones lighter than ecru.

"I'm super sorry, Mr. Funkquist, but Mr. Thigg never gives interviews."

"Ree-ally?" I continued my Swedish sing-song. "Didn't he do it to get faa-mous?"

"Guess not," she said. "Turns down fifty a year. But even if he wanted to, we have regulations of our own. If you were a doctor, or doing research... You could fax Warden Meisterammer some questions and *he* could answer them, would that be all right?"

"Afraid not," I sighed, then teed up a joke. The flack would either laugh, and we'd become friends, or get flustered, and that was just as good. "My editor is insisting I give him fellatio. You know, 'the nut's-eye view.'"

Silence. Then: "Don't know what to say to that..."

"I've offended you, I am sorry. We Scandanavians can be rather frank, it comes from attending school naked."

That did it. Desperate to get off the phone, the flack told me to send a tear-sheet when the story appeared, "for the Warden's scrapbook." I thanked her and hung up, knowing I had my man.

Clive made a morning's worth of phone calls for me, posing as the Larkin family attorney. He found a professor at Cornell, a Dr. Tarble, who was willing to ask Thigg some questions on our behalf.

"Splendid," Clive told her. "There's just one thing: The family would like a representative there. Would that be possible?"

"Probably not, given the sensitivity of this particular case."

"Who would make that decision? The warden, I assume?"

"I assume."

"Excellent." I'd told him about the warden's liking for publicity, and he knew that as soon as he said "Tom Larkin's cousin" the poor fucker would get stars in his eyes and agree to anything.

That left Thigg. None of us had any leverage on him. All we could do was ask, and hope the voices in his head were on our side.

Clive called me two days later. "They just asked him. Would you like to know what he said?"

"Will I want to strangle him?"

Clive read from notes. "'Since it's for his family, I guess it's okay. It's the least I can do…Do you think it will help me remember? They say I shot him, but I don't remember—if I could remember, maybe I could understand.'" Clive paused. "To have killed a man, and ruined your own life, and not even know why. Must be bloody awful."

"Yeah." And bloody convenient. But for whom?

I met Susan Tarble in the lobby of the Embassy Suites. By her handshake, I sensed she was both straightforward and persistent, qualities which pleased and frightened me in equal measure. I'd better be very careful with her.

"Zoltar Larkin, pleased to meet you."

"And you." She was a nice-looking black chick, short hair, glasses, around

35.

"Aren't you a bit young to be a professor?" I asked as we walked to the parking lot.

"I'm smart," she said matter-of-factly.

"And I'm rich. Let's get together and take over the world." The professor seemed lesbian, which I liked; it gave us something in common. "Here's my rental." I pushed the fob and the red Testarossa chirped to life. The guy at the rental place said he bought it at a police auction; it used to belong to Tannersville's only drug dealer.

"Nice."

"That's all, 'nice'? You spend a lot of time in Ferraris?"

"No, you?"

"Yeah, ever since Tommy died." I wanted to curry favor with her, and since my masculine charms were inoperative, I tossed her the keys. "You drive."

Big mistake. Dr. Tarble might have been smart, but she was a terrible driver. Don't get me wrong, I'm no Nigel Mansell, but she was disemboweling $250,000 of Italian perfection with every gear change.

Thankfully it wasn't far, and I distracted myself by telling her about my family. "We weren't much interested in Tom when he was alive," I said, "but once he left us a pile, we got interested. He became the family business, so to speak."

"So why are you talking to Thigg? To thank him?"

"Droll, Susan, very droll…Actually, we're writing the official story of Tom's life, for the Larkin Museum we're putting up in his hometown. Somebody's got to do this part, and well, I drew the short straw. How did you get interested in hypnosis?"

"It's an understudied area of psychiatry. I'm interested in all types of altered states. Hypnosis, dreams, psychedelics…"

"I'm a bit of an expert on those."

"So am I. My undergrad was at the University of Wisconsin." When Dr. Tarble smiled, she showed a lot of gum.

“Tell me, doc: could you hypnotize someone to do something, then forget they’d done it?”

“Sure. Easily.”

“But you can’t make people do stuff they wouldn’t normally do, right?”

“That’s an old wives’ tale. It’s not difficult to manipulate a subject—immoral, but not difficult.”

“How?”

“When they’re in the suggestible state, you place the act in a larger context. Say it must be done for the greater good, to protect the weak, to save a child. Once they’ve been convinced of that, they’ll do it.”

“Come on, Doc, really?”

The gearbox made a horrible sound, like a blender full of washers. “Every time there’s a war,” Dr. Tarble shouted, “millions of decent, moral, normally nonviolent people willingly slaughter each other, and they’re not even hypnotized. They convince themselves that killing means something, and because of what it means, it’s an exception to the rule. Of course, it isn’t, and afterwards they feel guilt, remorse…A hypnoprogrammed person has it a lot easier: they don’t have memories to suppress.”

“Do you think Thigg was hypnoprogrammed?”

“I won’t have an opinion until I examine him. Have you been inside one of these places before?”

“No.”

“Are you nervous?”

“Should I be?”

“Not really. It will be pretty straightforward. We’ll get processed—empty our pockets, get a day pass, you put that around your neck. Then a guard will escort us to a waiting room. Once he gets a signal on the walkie-talkie, he’ll bring us to the interview room.”

“Will a guard be with us all the time?”

“Outside,” Dr. Tarble said. “Planning on taking a swing?”

She’d read my face; I’d better be very careful with her. “Why would I do that? He’s my lottery ticket. Maybe I’ll kiss him.”

"That I'd like to see." The clutch screamed. "Let's review your questions."

Thigg didn't look much like the guy I remembered; I hoped to Christ he felt the same way about me. On December 23rd, 1980, he had been a chunky, anorak-wearing 17-year-old with smoked glasses and a shitty complexion. Now, my assassin was slim, clear-eyed, and polite, very much the Southern Army brat he'd been raised. Thigg smiled a lot; it was almost as if he was having fun.

I dislike touching people under the best of circumstances, but Thigg insisted on shaking my hand. This made my skin crawl. "I'm very sorry for your loss," he smarmed. "I really wish Tom Larkin were alive today."

Dr. Tarble noticed my discomfort. "Eric, we should get started, we haven't much time."

"Okay." Thigg was wearing a red white and blue necktie. He saw me looking at it. "This is my special occasion tie," he said, running his fingers across it. "Someone sent it to me. I wish I could write back and thank them."

"Why can't you?" Dr. Tarble asked.

"That's my punishment to myself. Complete isolation, like a monk. The only reason I'm doing this is because it's Tom's family." Thigg looked at me. "You look an awful lot like him, did you know that?"

"It's the nose," I bluffed. "We've all got it."

"Hey, I have a question for you, do you mind?"

"Ask and I'll see."

"Did you ever meet Peter Frampton? What's he like?" Thigg imitated Frampton's talking guitar, then returned to his tie. "The silhouettes are of all the Presidents, Washington to Senokot."

"So you're patriotic, then?" Dr. Tarble had told me that it was important to establish good rapport with the subject.

"Of course, aren't you?" Thigg asked. "This is the greatest country in the world. The next time there's a war, I'm going to ask them to send me on a suicide mission. It's the least I can do. Any other place, I would've been executed. But Americans are kind. Don't you agree?"

"To a fault," I said.

"Okay, Eric, I think we're ready to start." Dr. Tarble nodded at me, and I turned on my tape recorder. "I know you've signed the forms, but I want to ask you a last time, you're all right with us putting you into a hypnotic state? You've given your consent, is that correct?"

"Absolutely," he said. "I'm as interested as you are. I don't remember a thing."

"Well, we'll try to help with that. Now close your eyes and relax. Just listen to the sound of my voice..."

Thigg went under quickly, and achieved a deep state almost immediately; Later, Dr. Tarble told me this was a good indicator of being hypnotized previously. "Eric, your left hand is completely numb. It feels like it's packed in ice. It's cold, but not uncomfortable. You cannot feel any sensations in your left hand, do you understand?"

"Yes."

"Good."

She took out a safety pin and pricked the big vein on the top of his hand, until the blood flowed. I watched in fascination as Thigg didn't move.

"Amazing."

"Shh," Dr. Tarble wrote on her yellow pad. "That's nothing, watch this."

"Eric, I want you to get up on the table and sing the national anthem. Just climb up on the table, and start singing. I'll tell you when to stop."

"My country, 'tis of thee, sweet land of—"

"That's enough, thank you. Now come back down."

After a series of simple questions to establish the subject's state and basic truthfulness, the professor got down to business.

"Eric, did anyone pay you to kill Tom Larkin?"

Eric sighed, but didn't answer, so Dr. Tarble asked again.

"Eric, answer my question. Did anyone pay you to kill Tom Larkin?"

There was a pause, then: "No."

"None of Larkin's family, or friends, or any of Tom Larkin's associates paid you to kill him?"

"No."

"And no one from the United States government, either?"

Another pause. "No."

"You thought it up completely on your own?"

Another pause. "Yes."

"Why did you do it, Eric? Why did you kill Tom Larkin?"

"Because he was a hypocrite."

"Really? Is that the only reason why? Think harder. Why did you kill Larkin?"

Thigg spoke quickly, with one reason rushing into the next. "Because I wanted to get famous because he was my father because I wanted to commit suicide because I wanted people to read it…"

There was another pause, so Dr. Tarble pressed him. "What did you want people to read?"

"The *Reader's Digest*."

"Load of old bollocks," I mumbled.

"What?" Thigg asked.

"It's nothing." The professor shot me a "shut up" look. "All right, Eric. I'm going talk about some other things, now." She asked the assassin a long series of questions, meaningless stuff about his childhood, what life was like for him now, bullshit like that. Meanwhile, I was getting more and more pissed off; this guy was telling us nothing.

"This is bullshit," I said hotly. "How about this, Doc? You ask him about his pet goldfish, and I'll punch him in his fucking eye!"

"Mr. Larkin, *please*. Eric, you didn't hear that."

I'm sure he didn't, yet something seemed to change when Thigg heard my name. It was like he flinched, under his skin. The professor scribbled angrily, "SHUT UP OR YOU WILL HAVE TO GO." "Eric, I'm going to ask you again: did anyone ask you to kill Tom Larkin?"

"No one paid me to kill Tom Larkin."

"I didn't ask that. I asked did anyone *ask* you to kill him?"

There was a long pause. I was just about to swear a blue streak when Eric mumbled something. "What did you say, Eric? I can't hear you."

"George."

"George told you to kill Tom Larkin? George who?"

"George...Washington."

"I see. And what did George Washington look like?"

"He was round."

"I see. You're saying he was fat?"

"No. Skinny."

"Round and skinny, Eric? That doesn't make any...""They used a quarter..." the professor wrote.

"Aha," I said, forgetting.

"Who's that?" Thigg said. "I think somebody's in here."

The professor reached over and put her hand on Thigg's. "It's all right. We're alone. You're perfectly safe." Then she wrote, "I think you'd better go. I'll ask my questions and be out in 5 minutes."

I nodded. Dispirited, I got up and walked over to the door. The guard saw me through the trivet-sized window, and let me out.

"She's got a few final questions for some research she's doing."

The guard and I stood uncomfortably close in the small, brightly lit corridor, avoiding each other's gaze. I leaned against the door with my hands in my pockets, he stood picking his cuticles. Ten minutes of this, then I felt a small knock between my shoulderblades.

"Excuse me," the guard said, reaching for the knob.

Dr. Tarble emerged, carrying her portfolio. The guard went into the room, and brought Eric out. We scrunched ourselves against the wall as the two men walked past, the assassin in handcuffs, the guard's beefy hand locked securely around Thigg's upper arm.

"Nice to meet you, sir, ma'am," Thigg said, looking back. "I still don't remember anything, but I hope I was helpful." I noticed that the area around his right eye was red; after they were out of sight, I caught Dr. Tarble's attention and gestured at my own eye.

"They cry sometimes," she whispered.

By the time we got back to the Ferrari, I was the one who felt like crying, out of sheer frustration. I'd screwed up my courage, met my assassin face-to-face, and for what? To see that he was a nice person, when he wasn't shooting people? That he seemed to be having fun in prison? This had been a huge waste of time and money, a risk for nothing, and I wanted it to be concluded as soon as possible. "I'm driving," I grumbled.

"Great, I want to take some notes."

Ten miles out of Tannersville, Dr. Tarble slapped her notebook shut. "Well," she said brightly, "you must be pleased."

"How do you mean? He still didn't remember doing it, and gave the same old daft reasons he always does."

"We learned he's been hypnotized before."

"Maybe he did it to himself, the git."

"Impossible. You remember those pauses, whenever we'd ask an important question? That's blocking. You don't get those from reading comic books or whatever the police file said. Someone has to put those in."

"Cut to the chase, professor."

"It's my professional opinion that someone—a person of the highest ability, with plenty of time—hypnotized him to assassinate you."

"Not me, Doctor. My cousin."

"Come off it, Tom. I told you I was smart."

This pissed me off for some reason. "If you're so smart, why can't you drive?"

"I'd never driven stick."

"So you decided to learn on a Ferrari?"

"What do you care? It's a rental. Besides, you can afford it."

"You won't tell anyone, will you?"

"And risk thirty years of membership in the Ravins Fan Club? I joined the night after you guys were on Jack Paar. I was eight," Dr. Tarble said. "I may make fun of the beard, however. Where did you get that, summer stock?"

"Don't fuck with me. Of course you'll sell me out. Everybody has their price."

"'Love's Not for Sale,' Tom."

"That was one of Oliver's. And he doesn't believe it, by the way."

"Don't shatter my illusions, it's all we Ravins Mavens have left. I still love those records. The solo stuff, not so much." She saw that deflated me, so she said, "Thanks for standing in front of the window. I only wish I could've given him one in the balls."

"Wha-at?" I laughed. "Great, I'm gonna get sued by the guy who killed me."

"Don't worry," Dr. Tarble said. "He won't remember."

Her violence pleased me greatly; I'm not Gandhi, I just played him on TV. It wasn't totally fair—Thigg was a tool—but since you can't punch the CIA directly, he would have to do.

The professor's words bounced around in my head uncomfortably. According to her—and she would know—Eric Curtis Thigg had been specially trained to kill me. That idea was to paranoia what inorganic coffee was to caffeine. Very few groups had the money and expertise to pull off something like that, and as far as I knew, they all ended with "overnment."

Clive disagreed. "Governments change," he said. "Correct me if I'm wrong, but four years after Crouk was bugging your phones, Charlie Priestly invited you to his inauguration. Why the devil would President Senokot risk getting off on the wrong foot, just to be rid of you? And don't say he was scared of another Bathe-In."

I didn't buy it. I made the hotel switch my room, then I made them put "Electrical Closet" on my front door. It wasn't much, but I had to do something. By day I read about Manchurian Candidates, MKULTRA, Nielsen and Hardup, Sirhan Sirhan. At night I slept as best I could, dreaming of faceless men whose pistols laughed when they pulled the trigger.

A week later, Dr. Tarble's report arrived, twenty or so pages, single-spaced. In the same envelope was a copy of the tape from our session, which promised to be the rancid cherry on top of my misery sundae.

I called Sam Wisnewski and asked him to meet me at the Starbucks six blocks away, on Hill and Main. It was public, and far enough from my digs to calm my heebie jeebies. Very few people knew where I lived, and that decision was looking smarter all the time.

"Man, it's hot. I can never get used to hot Octobers." Sam saw the tape deck in front of me. "Working on some new tunes?"

I looked around nervously. "Why would I, a graphic designer with no connection to the music business..."

Sam interrupted my alibi. "I brought that file. Sorry I never got back to you. I was on vacation. A buddy of mine has a place in Costa Rica."

"Must be nice." We made an odd couple, to say the least, but I forced myself to trust the ex-cop. Things were getting weird inside my head, and I needed a buddy. "Don't worry about the file; I don't need them anymore."

"Why not? What are you fiddling with?"

I finished untangling the earpiece. "Stick this in your ear."

"Can I get a coffee first?"

"After." I put another button in my ear so I could listen along, then pushed "play."

Sam recognized the voice immediately, Thigg's lazy-tongued affectless drawl. "Holy shit, how'd you get to him?"

"I said I was doing a family history. The chick you hear is the psychiatrist helping."

The first part of the tape, I'd been present for, but now I got to hear what she'd asked after I'd left the room. "Eric, who is George Washington?"

"George Washington is the father of our country. He cannot tell a lie."

"So he's a person."

"No. He's more powerful than that. He's a spirit."

"A god?"

"No—just below Jesus. Like, an angel."

"Where did you meet him?"

"I found him."

"Where?"

"In my pocket."

"Okay. After you found him, what did George Washington say to you?"

"He said, 'Tom Larkin is a hypocrite. Tom Larkin talks about love, but that's a lie. He teaches children to hate their parents, people to hate their government, foreigners to hate this country.'"

"Holy shit," Sam said loudly. The student two tables away shot us a glance over his PowerBook.

"Learning Italian," I explained.

Thigg droned on, quoting Washington. "…'I am the Father of this Country and I have a right to protect my offspring, the most basic right of all. But I can't do it alone, I need your help. You are the one person who can set things right, the only person. You have a special mission: For the sake of this country, you must kill Tom Larkin.'"

I shivered. How flat and earnest Thigg's voice was. I remember the way he looked under hypnosis, calm, blank. Like a doll. Dr. Tarble spoke. "Did *you* want to kill Tom Larkin, Eric?"

"Not at first, no. I liked his music. I thought he was funny. But George talked me into it. He said it was important…George talked to me so many times."

"How many times?"

"Hundreds. Maybe thousands. He'd call me on the phone, late at night, again and again. It wouldn't stop for hours. George Washington was in a lot of pain. You can understand why I wanted to help him. Anyone would. He told me he'd talked to my father, and that he was counting on me to help."

"Your father is dead, right?"

"Yes," Thigg said.

"What else did he say?"

"'You must kill Tom Larkin before January 15th, before he becomes a U.S. citizen. He must not become part of the family.' He said—"

Wisnewski slapped the off button. "Christ, how depressing. What did you do when you heard all this shit?"

"It's the first I've heard it," I said. "When the doctor said my name to

Thigg—something happened. Inside. She thought he might've recognized me. So I left."

"Were you afraid he'd go after you again?"

"No." I pushed Dr. Tarble's report towards him. "This says if Thigg discovered I was still alive, there might be more programming in there to keep him from talking. A 'self-destruct' mechanism."

"Great, I'm all for it."

"Not me, at least not until I figure out who put him up to it. Fuck, Sam, when he wasn't hypnotized, he was like…him." I pointed at a clean-cut guy in a baseball cap and chinos. "Then she'd put him under, and he'd vomit up all this dark shit. It makes you suspect everyone."

"Can I have the rest of your muffin?"

I nodded. Plots against me tend to kill my appetite.

"How do we find out who scrambled his brains?"

"Susan says she might be able to find it," I said, "and I'm happy to pay for it. But it's going to take months, if not years…" I put my head in my hands, miserable. "Fuck," I moaned. "This is *exactly* why I stopped reading books about the Kennedy assassination."

"What are you going to do now?"

"Cry? Piss myself? The government tried to kill me. How do you fight that?"

"I don't think it was the government. I'm with Crouk. I think it was somebody with something to gain from your death."

"Who just happened to know how to control people's minds. Get real."

"You get real. By '80, there were hundreds of ex-spies looking around for work. President Priestly threw hundreds of people out on their ear. Real experts, people who'd been spies for twenty years. They'd send me resumes. Shit, anybody with money to spend could've set up their own little CIA."

"Did you ever interview anybody who could've done this?"

"Not that I remember."

"Did you just make a joke? Did you actually just say something funny?"

"I blame you," Sam said, then dug something out of his back pocket.

"Luckily, I found another lead."

I took the paper. It was creased and slightly sweaty, and I tried not to think of the germs living on it. It was a color Xerox of me, an old publicity photo—1974, I could tell by the newsboy cap and muttonchops. "MEET HIM AGAIN," it read at the top, then "SÉANCE @ THE CORONADO," across the bottom. I flipped the paper over. Someone had stamped various things, in different colored inks:

"Two mediums—hundreds of participants!"

"Friday, October 15th, 1985 8:00 pm at the Coronado."

"Special Guest: Rufus Byrd"

"HE'LL be there—will YOU?"

Rufus Byrd was a piano player, he'd played with us back in Marseille, then later on that horrible album we all hated, the one where we all had beards and grudges. More recently, he'd been in and out of jail (coke), then found God, which is where he'd started from, belting out gospel in Watts. "What's this Coronado like?"

"Falling apart. I'd be surprised if it's still there six months from now. It used to be a regular theater, then it went porno. Now, they rent it out for all sorts of bullshit. No offense," Sam said. "I was on the way to my smog check and saw your name. Which reminds me, I gotta go pick up my car." He heaved to his feet.

I handed back the flyer. "Thanks, but no. My crazy tank is full."

Sam sat back down. "Really? You're not going to check it out? Tom, somebody's making money on this. Benefitting. Plus, even if it's a dead end, it's the only place in the world where you actually have an alibi. Poke around. See who's behind it."

I took the flyer back. If Rufus was doing this, he was clearly scuffling. Maybe I could figure out a way to make some money materialize in his pocket. "Fine, I'll go."

"Then what?"

I mimed zipping my lips shut.

Sam laughed. "You're learning!"

CHAPTER SEVEN

When it came to the séance at the Coronado, my goals were simple. First, I'd find out who was throwing the party, then I'd make sure it wouldn't be repeated. The Friday traffic heading east on Pico gave me plenty of time to concoct a plan, but I decided not to overthink things. I'd simply find an unauthorized use of my name or image, pop it into the monthly courier bag to New York, and let Katrinka and Hitler take care of the rest.

I used to think Larkin-worship was creepy but harmless—whatever misgivings I had were drowned out by the sound of cash registers. Sometime after the first bullet, my opinion began to darken. In my present condition, such fervor was even less welcome. The last thing I wanted were people who believed "Larkin Lives!"

I parked the Roller across the street and down a little, so that I could keep an eye on the entrance without attracting attention. Rufus' brown scalp gleamed in the dusk, making me feel a little better about my own dearth of follicles. Plus, he'd gained a lot of weight. Rufus had always liked to eat. I remember wasting an entire night with him walking around Marseille looking for barbeque. He and another man, about 6'6" with a Tintin-like swoop of white hair and a plum-colored velvet tunic, were greeting people as they came in. It was a good turn-out. Every so often, the guy would be replaced by a dumpy woman in black wearing a beret and a necklace so ugly it had to be magical. He carried a cane, she used a cigarette holder.

They were either mediums, or drama students.

I ate some Raisinets and listened to Rufus laugh. He was always jolly, even before he'd gotten fat. I watched my old friend sign autographs and pose for pictures, and calculate the fees for each in his head. God knows the fans could afford it; they were all aging hippies, or that generation's kids who felt they'd missed something. All lily-white of course. Too bad the Sixties utopia never made it out of the suburbs—who knows what we might've accomplished otherwise.

I put the empty box in the plastic bag I keep for car trash, then closed my eyes for a few minutes, waiting for it to get dark. Around eight, the leonine medium checked his watch. Seeing nobody on the street, he kicked the stop out of the door and ushered Rufus inside.

After allowing a decent interval for stragglers, I got out of the car and walked across Pico to the entrance. Acting casual, perusing the poster, I glanced through the glass doors and saw that there was no one in the lobby. The fewer people I encountered here, the better. I walked in.

The theater was quite dire, with peeling maroon paint on the walls, and hand-lettered posters hawking old events nobody had thought to remove. A few tatty yellow drapes hung here and there, covering water stains and earthquake cracks. To my right was a fly-specked candy counter, which for the occasion had been loaded with Larkin knickknackery. I bent to get a closer look, hoping to find the tell-tale shoddiness of graymarket goods. Bumper stickers, patches, a poster or two. One shirt made me look constipated, the other Chinese.

"What, no Ravins maxipads?" I mumbled.

"Sorry."

I nearly leapt out of my skin. "Where the hell did you come from?"

"Tying my shoe." She was about eighteen, with long blonde hair and glasses. "Can I get you anything?"

"Yeah, the constipated one. In black." It had to be a knock-off. If it wasn't, Katrinka and I were going to have words. "Large."

"Okay…That's $42 all together."

"You're kidding."

"Nope. Shirt is $17, ticket's $25."

$25 to commiserate with my own spirit seemed a little steep, but I dug out my wallet anyway. I saw a sign: "Support PEACE!" The silly sods were so mixed up they could no longer distinguish a prayer from a profit. I looked forward to throwing the money-changers out of my temple, as soon as I found out who they were.

As she stamped my hand I saw the girl was staring at me. Fuck. "Can I have my hand back?"

"Sorry. You know, you look a lot like him. Are you related?"

I had two choices: run, or improvise. "Can you keep a secret?"

"Sure."

I leaned over. "Plastic surgery. Is it all right?"

"Oh, it's great."

"Good. I'm not even that big a fan, it's just"—I pointed to a poster of *Eraserhead*—"I used to look like him."

The girl laughed, and my crisis was over. I peered over her shoulder for signs of an office, but there were just stacks of boxes, and an unsafe-looking popcorn maker.

"The doors are right down there."

"Great." Through them I could hear Rufus going through his spiel "…if he's in your heart, you'll see him everywhere. And once you see Tom, he'll start making you see other things. Love. Commitment. How to make a better world."

I snorted. I couldn't even make beans on toast. That's why we went looking for barbeque.

"Can you point me to the lav, luv?"

"The what? Oh. Upstairs. But you should hurry. I think it's about to start."

"Tom'll wait until I have a wee."

As I climbed, Rufus kept talking. "I was aware of Tom's divinity even during his lifetime. When we started our tour, they were The Ravins, and we were Blind Rufus Byrd and the Blackbyrds. By the end of the tour, they were still The Ravins, but we were just The Blackbyrds. Tom had cured my blindness. Thanks to him, I could see."

"Oh, you fucking liar," I said over the applause. I remember exactly how that had happened, how he'd stomped into the dressing room waving a copy of *Billboard*. "Who the fuck is Little Stevie Wonder? He just stole my act!"

Around the corner at the top of the stairs there were restrooms, one in each flavor, and past them at the end of a little hallway, a door marked "Projectionist." That had to be the office, there was no place else for it to go. I listened at the door—nothing—then tried the knob. It was locked, so I opened it using a credit card. Sam had just taught me that trick, and when the door opened, I was chuffed. (Take that, Harriet.)

I turned on the light, and was greeted by a rather Spartan arrangement. In the middle of the room, there was a large projector aimed at a square hole that was shuttered for the evening. Behind that, in the corner, was a desk. There were a few racks with film canisters on them, a clipboard, an empty Coke can. The whole place was very dusty, and there were enough cobwebs to remind me that I didn't like spiders. The walls were in even worse shape up here; it doesn't rain much in West LA, but every drop had left its mark. The Coronado was demolishing itself.

I sat down in the ripped pleather chair and tried to open the desk drawer. It wouldn't budge, which was bad news; Sam hadn't shown me how to pick that kind of lock yet. I gave one more yank, and it came free with a screech. Luck was with me tonight.

I began sorting through the files, the Coronado's booking records over the last couple of years. There wasn't much, this place was really dying on the vine. From downstairs I could hear the mediums—named Theobald and, improbably, Betty Sue—getting everyone properly spooked up.

"Please dim the house lights," Theobald said. "We must all clasp hands."

Betty Sue had a really high voice. "The power of all of our psychic energy will increase our chances of making a connection. Now we must be very quiet." They milked the silence. To the audience's credit, somebody laughed.

Twenty seconds in, I found the invoice I needed. The outfit behind tonight's festivities was called Orange Sunshine, LLC, with an address on Sunset Boulevard. I copied that down in my Filofax, then replaced the paper.

"Tom Larkin," I heard Theobald say over the PA, "we ask you to speak with us. We implore you."

"We *command* you," Betty Sue squeaked.

I laughed, but apparently somebody was listening. "Hello," a voice said. "This is Tom Larkin speakin' to you from the other side..."

The crowd gave a sharp intake of breath just loud enough to mask my groan. Christ, is there anything more painful than a bad Scouse? He sounded like our old cartoons. (Those were Clive's second-worst idea, after the maxipads.)

"What are you doing now, Tom?"

"Havin' a cuppa and a facon sarnie."

"So you eat?"

"Only for a larf...It's macrobiotic fake bacon, y'know."

I turned off the lights, ready to walk out, when I heard Theobald ask earnestly, "Are you in any pain?"

I leaned over and slid the projection hole open a few inches. "After that impression? *Yes.*"

The actor they'd hired saw his fee disappearing. "Who is that? I'll—"

"Be quiet, Steve!" Theobald said.

"Yeah, Steve!" I yelled. "Shut your trap."

The crowd began buzzing. They recognized the real thing. I heard a girl's voice. "Is it really him, Dad?"

"Yeah," I said. "By the way, your dead hamster says hello."

"*Really?* What's her name?"

"Look, kid, we aren't close, she just asked me to tell you the dog ate her."

"I knew it!" the girl piped. "Your dumb dog, Dad!"

"Uh, what do I do?" Steve said over the P.A. Nobody answered.

"I think it's really happening!" Theobald said to no one in particular.

"Doesn't it always?" Rufus asked.

Betty Sue began hyperventilating. Her hands fluttered like a pair of parakeets. "I shouldn't do this! I shouldn't be here! I'm a Catholic!"

"Mistress Betty, you must not break the chain."

"Hey Rufus," I said crossly, "you still owe me fourteen francs. We were in Marseille, folks, see, and there was this sax player who just happened to be a she-male—" Theobald interrupted me. "Is this *true*, Rufus? Was there a she-male?"

Rufus nodded, looking like he'd swallowed something square. That sent Betty Sue over the edge. She stumbled off the stage and up the leftmost aisle.

"Betty Sue—"

"Fuck off!" She turned to the audience, pointing. "His name isn't Theobald. It's Jerome." Then she ran out the fire exit. The door slammed.

Jerome allowed the crowd to settle, then asked, "Tom, why have you come tonight?"

"I could never resist a crowd, *Jerome*."

With every syllable, the excitement and terror in the crowd was growing. "We love you, Tom!" someone shouted. "We all love you!"

"Heard that before," I said.

"Sorry!"

"Yeh, Tom, sorry!"

"He was a jerk!"

"What's Heaven like?"

"Who said I went to Heaven?" I let that percolate for a sec, then continued. "It's quite nice, actually. Mostly sunny. The beach is a little rocky. Rufus, you remember that island we almost bought?"

"I'm sorry, people, I got to go!" Rufus ran off the stage and up the aisle. See, that's the problem with being brought up religious, it can mess with your mind.

"Who else is there?" Jerome asked.

"Greeks, mostly. I think my ticket got messed up."

"Are there any other rock stars there?"

"What are you doing right now?"

I heard Rufus run outside, calling my name to the heavens. "Tom! It's me, Rufus!"

"Right…I don't have much time, so listen," I said. "The next time someone you admire kicks the bucket, here's what you need to do—"

Rufus was in the lobby now. "I'll give you your money! Just tell me the exchange rate!"

"Do whatever you think that person would've done. A million people doing one good act—it's as if your hero lived many lifetimes. That'll drive the bad guys barmy. They'll learn that violence doesn't work. But the best thing is, you'll have done it *yourself*. You didn't wait for Mommy or Daddy to make things better. Be your own hero. That's what I want you to do. That's what they're afraid of."

"Who are 'they,' Tom?" Jerome asked. "The people that killed you?"

"Did the government kill you?"

"Still figuring that out. They'll get what's coming to them, don't worry…" I heard Rufus running up the stairs. "I have to go."

"Wait!" Jerome yelled. "I command thee!"

I laughed. "Easy there, Jerome."

Rufus was at the door to the projection booth. The knob shook as he tried it.

"Wait, Tom!"

"Tom, how do we achieve world peace?"

Rufus was pounding on the door; I couldn't let this go much longer. Even the actor on the PA asked a question. "Will I ever get a sitcom?"

"What's the secret to life?" Jerome asked.

"What, and spoil the surprise? G'night!" I slapped the switches on, bathing the theater in light. General pandemonium reigned. It was *fantastic*.

"Who's in there?" Rufus demanded.

I threw open the door. "Boo," I said. Did you know black people can turn white? (At least Rufus can.)

"Aiggh! *He's here!*" Rufus turned and ran, screaming. I followed right behind him, galumphing down the stairs, poking him occasionally. When Rufus got to the front door, he pushed instead of pulled.

"Pull, Rufus, it says pull!" When he looked back, I said, "Oooga-booga!"

He screamed again and ran outside.

The girl at the candy counter was too mesmerized to move. "Thanks for the shirt," I waved, and walked out.

By the time the audience got themselves together, I was in the backseat of my Roller, nestled under my reflective window screen, watching everyone freak. I was laughing so hard I thought I'd burst a vessel. Being dead wasn't easy, but it sure had its moments.

When I got home that night, there was a message on my machine. It was Rufus.

"You ofay bastard!" he yelled. "I just called Katrinka and—I'm gonna *kill* you!"

"Take a number." I looked at Glucosamine and Chondroitin circling my feet. "Not even a chuckle? Tough crowd."

Washing their food bowl, I happened to look outside. A vintage Caddy was parked across the street. I immediately thought of my friend from the diner, Pompadour. But I couldn't see inside the car, my angle was too steep.

I reached over and flicked off the kitchen light, rendering my suite completely dark. Then I waited, watching, until the car started up, pulled out of the space, and glided away.

I had trouble sleeping after that, so I got up at the crack of dawn. I went for a walk over to a newsstand on the Third Street Promenade, where I knew there'd be witnesses—I mean, people—and picked up my usual armload of newspapers. The morning light, and some organic coffee, slowly began to erode my paranoia. Fifteen minutes later I was back home at the Marisol, ensconced in my usual breakfast spot, in the restaurant just off the lobby. I read all morning, and my stomach slowly descended to its normal position. Sitting by the window, facing the entrance, surrounded by friendly staff and a world's worth of newspapers, I actually began to feel normal again. Until I read a small item in *The New York Times*. Most days I would've missed it. Part of me wishes I had.

Late yesterday afternoon, while I was staking out the Coronado, something strange had happened at Tannersville State Mental Hospital. A guard had discovered Eric Curtis Thigg in his cell, wearing his special occasion tie. The other end, unfortunately, was wrapped around a steampipe.

CHAPTER EIGHT

All this shit was beginning to take its toll. I started losing sleep, which I personally need more than oxygen. As the days passed, I felt like I was suffocating bit by bit, dying by degrees inside a husk of stiffening skin. I was so miserable I even considered writing a song…until Fraulein set me straight.

"Don't you dare," she snapped. "Music is what got you into this mess."

Speaking of the mess, I didn't tell her about Thigg or Pompadour. I didn't want her to worry. "No, dear, what got me into this mess was someone telling me my bodyguard was too paranoid."

"I was hiring Sam back that very night, Tom. If you had just come inside instead of craving those rabbit pellets—"

"Do *not* insult my candy."

"Fine, fine. If you're so upset, why don't you listen to your tapes?"

Der Fraulein was big into self-improvement, and when I say self-improvement, I mean improving me. She'd gotten me a whole stack of cassettes years ago, the "You CAN!" series. Not the greatest anniversary present, but then again, she'd just caught me in a broom closet with Germaine Greer. I tried a couple—"You CAN Stop Smoking!," "You CAN Kick Drugs!," "You CAN Stop Having Sex with Germaine Greer!"—and they worked.

But around 1975, I had a thought: "If I stop any more things, I'll have nothing to do all day. Am I becoming boring?" So I dropped 'em, except for

"You CAN Have a Perfect Marriage!" That one I listened to, right up until the day I got shot.

"Oh those," I said, trying to sound casual. "I gave those tapes to Goodwill."

"You *what?*" Fraulein shrieked. "Tom, those were—I had them specially made. It's cutting-edge science! That woman is the Dalai Lama's therapist!"

"I didn't like her," I admitted, even though honesty was getting me nowhere. "Her voice sounded like Edith Ann."

"Who's that? One of your California hussies?" Lately my wife had become convinced that I was schtupping everything in sight. In my condition? Not likely. "No, dear, it's a comedian, her name is—"

"Her name? I don't want to know her name, it's bad enough you're screwing her. Call me back when you can keep it in your pants!"

"Don't you mean 'You CAN Keep It In Your Pants!'?...Hello?"

She'd hung up.

Just to pour oil on the waters, I walked over to the Goodwill on Sixth and Santa Monica, to see if they still had the tapes. Underneath all the Hall and Oates, there were only two left: You CAN Be Taller!, and You CAN Achieve Total Control! I only took the latter; I didn't want to have to buy new clothes.

What you're supposed to do is listen to the tape on headphones while you're sleeping, so it gets into your subconscious. But I improved on that. I put my Walkman on "auto-reverse" so it would keep going all night, and I also used "scan" mode, so it played twice as fast. The voice was all speeded-up and weird, but that way I got a week's worth of listening every eight hours.

After three or four nights of this, I felt one hundred percent better. I called up Fraulein and left her a message: "You are the most brilliant, beautiful woman in the world, and I am fantastically lucky to be your husband. I have achieved total control." It was nice. I no longer needed to write any songs. I even knew what to do about the case.

I realized that I couldn't outgun or outrun whoever wanted me dead. If they had the kind of money to turn Thigg into a robot, no amount of hired beef could save me. However many goons I pried out of Fraulein's black budget, the bad guys could just hire more. Pompadour was only the first, maybe not even that—maybe there were others, and I simply hadn't noticed them yet. The point was, I needed to outthink my enemy. I needed *information*. If I knew more than they did, I might be able to stay alive, find the head, then strike back.

My first thought was to call Clive, but then I didn't feel like it for some reason. Clive had circulated in some pretty seedy circles, back in his day. But his day had been decades ago, and my needs went well beyond zippered masks and amyl nitrate. What I needed was somebody loyal to me, who gathered information for a living, fresh information. Somebody like Warren Darden, the founder and publisher of *Roogalator*.

Warren knew everybody in showbiz, and had dirt on most. Even better, he'd been rich long enough to have cultivated people in DC, big swinging dicks from both parties. He could be my eyes and ears, and if things got really bad, had heavy friends I could hide behind, übercapitalists like Ted Turner, or that English guy, the one with the beard and a thing for balloons.

We'd been close once, as close as I ever got in those days, and I knew Warren would be delighted to discover I was still alive. On the other hand, he could add measurably to his vast personal pile by outing me to the world. How much was our friendship worth? Millions? Billions? I was going to find out.

Time was, anybody could see Warren Darden. All it took was an entertaining rap about Castenada or some Peruvian flake, and you were in. The first time I stumbled into his office, he even didn't know it was me, thanks to some new specs and a Biblical beard. I was just another freek smelling of herb and patchouli, tracking mud on his carpet and babbling about "El Topo."

That was a different world, Ravins Mavens, and one that I surely could've used, because getting to Warren wasn't going to be enough. He also had to *believe*. Whatever I did, I'd only get one shot before his security people would become aware of "that guy who thinks he's Tom Larkin" and all avenues would be closed forever. Thanks, Thigg, for everything.

I wracked my brain for a way to get in touch without blowing my cover. I decided not to ask Fraulein for help. Somehow I didn't think she'd approve of my contacting the proprietor of Rock's main gossip-sheet. Then one evening, coming in from a late-night walkabout, I saw the Marisol's night concierge, Maria Elena. She was sitting at her station, knitting a sweater. That gave me an idea.

Like everybody else, Warren spent most of the late Seventies giving up smoking. To help him over the hump, his psychiatrist had recommended knitting, "to give him something to do with his hands." Even though it didn't work as a smoking cure, Warren took to this new hobby with a passion. In addition to making everybody socks for Christmas, he embarked on the knitter's equivalent of Chartres: a multi-story woolen wrap for his townhouse on Bank Street.

"Warren's condom-inium" I quipped to the *Voice*, but inwardly I was impressed. I knew Art when I saw it. By the time I switched identities, the piebald, rainbow covering had become a downtown landmark. By the time Warren finished it, in August of '85, Mayor Koch had given him "The Needles to the City."

What I did was simple: first, I bought a shedload of yarn, subtle colors and rare blends that I thought would get Warren's attention. Then, I hired the night concierge to knit something.

"I don't care what colors you use," I told Maria Elena, "I just need it as soon as possible. Call in sick. I'll make it worth your while."

"What do you want it to say, again?"

"For a good time, call—" then I gave her my number. As soon as she was done, I overnighted the whole thing to New York, and crossed my fingers.

I expected to get a call from Warren himself. In fact, the whole plan hinged on it. This was a reasonable assumption—in the Seventies, everybody at the magazine was more or less *non compos mentis*. While this kept them in perfect tune with their readers, it also meant that Warren couldn't delegate, because for that you needed short-term memory, and at the *Roog* that was rarer than Republicans.

Only trouble was, it wasn't the Seventies anymore. It was 1985.

"Good afternoon," the caller said with the lazy mouth of a Yuppie. "I'm looking for the person who sent the yarn. This is—" I didn't even let him finish. I knew exactly who it was: Darryl Renton, Warren's nightmarish right-hand man.

The rumor was, "Drent" was a piece of white trash who'd started out as one of Warhol's superstars, then moved over when that scene—or more likely his looks—had started to fade. That might have been true; or he could've simply been an ambitious rent-boy with a knack for palace intrigue. Back in the day, our paths had crossed once or twice, always unpleasantly. Fraulein and I had gone to a party at Warren's place on Montauk, and this tweaked Trimalchio had seated us in Siberia, simply because I hadn't had a hit in a few years. Self-esteem at a low ebb, I wasn't going to complain, but Fraulein marched right up to Warren and demanded satisfaction. Warren apologized profusely, then gave Drent a soul-curdling glare. "Drent, switch places with Tom and Katrinka."

This is all a long way of saying, if Drent knew for a second that I was alive—if he had the merest ticklish suspicion of it—I was fucked.

"*Número equivocado*," I said, and hung up.

I was back to square one. How the hell was I going to get to Warren? Send a fax? My handwriting alone wouldn't prove anything; examples could be found in any Ravins book. I tried writing Warren a letter, with information only he and I knew, but stopped halfway through. A letter from Tom Larkin? I might as well send the guy a tortilla with the Virgin Mary on it. I tossed it to save him the carpal tunnel.

My only chance was to try something in-person, and that was incredibly dangerous. See, your ribs do more than fill out your shirt, they also protect all sorts of essential glop, and I'd left half of my ribs in a medical waste bin at Roosevelt Hospital. I wore a sort of corset, but that was for support, not protection. A punch in the wrong place, and I'd be back on the sidewalk bleeding out. Only this time as the crazy fan, not the beloved celebrity, with no one particularly anxious to make sure I lived to tell the tale.

It was the last week in October. I knew that Warren would be in LA, making the rounds at various record companies, giving one last push for ads before closing the issues for Christmas. If I hung around the right building, and luck was with me, our paths might cross. I picked our old label, hoping the context might help Warren recognize me. It's that bit of Hollywood stunt architecture, the high-rise that looks like a stack of 45s. Someday soon they'll have to tear it down and put up a building that looks like an iPod.

For two days, I loitered with a book and a sack lunch, but there was no sign of my friend. On the third day, security finally noticed me, and after an unpleasant exchange (high point: "Where were you arsebags when Tom Larkin got shot?"), I realized I needed an excuse to be there. So I bought a pretzel cart.

I'd hardly been set up an hour when a cop pulled up and told me I was breaking the law. "I can see from here you don't have any licenses."

"I didn't realize." I was beginning to feel a bit persecuted.

"Uh-huh. From the City. County and State, too."

"Okay, well, what if I don't let anybody buy anything?"

The cop frowned. "I'm confused," he said.

"News flash, Officer: white flour is poison." Or was it sugar?

"Doesn't matter," he said. "Get the licenses, or I'll run you in."

That night, I called Katrinka. "Why do you need a pretzel vendor's license?"

"The guerrilla must move among the people as a fish swims in the sea," I said.

"Oh, for God's sake, Tom, the Sixties are not a toy," she huffed. "On second thought, don't tell me what you're planning, I want to be able to deny it. I'll call the Scrivener"—that was the name of our counterfeiter—"if you promise me one thing."

"Name it."

"That you won't actually sell any pretzels. I don't want that on my karma."

"Are you kidding?" I said. "White sugar is poison."

"You're thinking of salt," Fraulein said.

It wasn't always easy to keep my promise to my wife, but I am a man of my word. Anybody who asked, I said I was out of 'em. Anybody who asked about the pretzel hanging in the case, I told 'em it was fake. "Plastic. From Japan."

Every day, I'd park my cart in the same place, over my star on the Walk of Fame. I guess that's what made me think a lot about my glory days, something I'd largely trained myself not to do. Warren and I had been friends, the kind of friends that used each other, which was the only kind of friends I had. Believe me, it was more honest than most relationships. I needed his magazine to sell my records, and he needed my line of bullshit to sell *Roogalator*. Most people thought the way to my heart was to pretend that they didn't want what I could give. That made me into a very suspicious person--exactly the wrong person to try to kill.

But even if Warren believed that the beaky git squawking at him was Tom Larkin, I needed some leverage, an insurance policy. At first I thought of Brigadoon, but didn't want to unleash the Wrath of Clive. Then I remembered something I'd overheard Fraulein say before, something she'd threatened him with the night I got shot, when she was chewing him out on the phone. That would make him stand up straight. It might not be true, but it would have to do.

I waited outside the building for three more weeks, plowing through Proust and lecturing nonplussed customers on the evils of processed foods. The consumerist sheeple thought a pretzel vendor who didn't sell pretzels was quite amusing, and yuppies started showing up on their lunch hour, bringing their friends. That led to somebody from Channel Seven coming round.

"Leave me alone," I said. "Go find some real news."

"Don't you want to be famous?" the guy asked. He looked like a bloody mannequin, all those TV people do.

"Fuck off."

"Just three minutes—it's either you or a pregnant narwhal down at the aquarium. C'mon. It's B-roll."

I was preparing to plant my foot in the middle of his B-roll when Warren's limo pulled up. I was trapped. If I did anything interesting, I'd end up on the nine o'clock news. That would be the end of Mission: Incognito. Helpless, I watched my quarry walk into the building.

As soon as Warren was out of view, I turned on the TV folk. German is the best language for swearing, so I let out my inner Kraut, making sure not a second was clean enough to broadcast. The news van actually burned rubber; I could see the two Latinas working in the lobby pointing and laughing. I flipped them off too, just for good measure.

When Warren came out, I was ready. "Mr. Darden, wait! Mr. Darden, I've got to talk to you!" Proust went into the bushes, and I took off across Vine. Unfortunately, my trick knee locked up and I went sprawling.

Unlike certain people, Warren had bodyguards, and a vast man in a blue suit emerged from the limo. He walked over to where I was. As I struggled to rise, he leaned down, pressing a meaty hand on my shoulder. "Stay there, old-timer. You're gonna get hit."

One, two, three, the heavy car doors slammed, my opportunity closing with them. The limo was so close I could almost touch it. When the goon pinning me was distracted by oncoming traffic, I lunged for the doorhandle—and got it. I hauled myself up.

"Buzz!" I yelled, rapping on the tinted glass. "It's me!"

The goon grabbed my arm, folded it neatly behind me, and slammed me against the car. This hurt, but it turned out to be the best thing he could've done; my face was pressed on the tinted glass, giving Warren a good gander at my mug. The angry goon was pressing me so hard that when the window rolled down, I nearly fell in.

"How do you know that name?"

"You told me once," I said, details pouring out as fast as I could think of them. "In 1970. In New York. During the interview. We were eating Katrinka's bran schnitzel, the stuff that made us all so sick. You said your dad used to call you Buzz. Before he left."

I kept talking, trying to give him more time to recognize me. "Your father was the inventor of the Darden bombsight," I said breathlessly. "The Allies used it in World War II. This was kept secret so he wouldn't get kidnapped by the Nasties. He felt guilty about Dresden, but that didn't stop him from taking a pile of money from the government. The day after Hiroshima, he left you and your mom, and only showed up after you made it big. My dad did the same thing to me. We used to argue about which one was the bigger shitheel, Warren. It's me, Tom."

A security guard trotted out from the building, looking to impress the rich guy. "He's been lurking around here, Mr. Darden. Want me to call the cops?"

One magic word, and my whole life would collapse. In twelve hours, I'd be on the cover of every newspaper in the world—and that was if Katrinka claimed me. She might not. She might let me rot in a fucking cell, just to teach me a lesson. What a stupid plan! What did I think would happen?

"Please don't—" I looked at Warren, but he wasn't looking at me. He was looking down, at a place where my shirt had gapped open, at the scars.

"What's that, on your chest?"

"What the hell do you think?" I groaned. "Call off your goon. I don't have any bloody ribs!"

"All right, get in," Warren said. "You're either legit, or I'm hiring you for our Christmas party."

I provided details for six blocks. I let him look in my mouth, at the tooth I'd chipped in '74 when we went rollerskating. I named his favorite flavor of ice cream. Then Warren offered me a cigarette. "I don't smoke," I said, then asked for a match.

"Jesus Christ. It really is you, Tom."

I was confused—but too relieved to question it. I let Warren hug me again and again. He even kissed me. I didn't mind. Even if he wasn't my type—a bit too *zaftig*—Warren had all his shots, and if you're going to be in showbiz, it's helpful if everyone likes you. Clive Solomon was just one of the many. It's flattering, and you feel like, "Well, if this doesn't work out, there's always that," but at the same time it's hard to take seriously if you don't feel it yourself.

"This is the happiest day of my life," Warren kept repeating. Then he'd take a hit off his asthma inhaler, and hug me again.

"Please stop," I said after he reached double digits. "I may start bleeding."

"Oh shit, do we need to take you to Cedars? And your cart! I'll send someone back for it. Why are you selling pretzels? Are you broke? Do you need money?" Warren was actually tearing up. "I can't believe you're alive. Who else knows?"

"Katrinka, the other Ravins, and you. Oh, and Rufus Byrd." I'd keep Clive to myself for the time being. There was no telling how much temptation Warren could take. "Warren, I need your help."

"Of course, whatever you want."

"Could you close the partition? What your driver doesn't know won't kill me."

"Jesus! Is it that serious?"

"I think so."

Warren listened intently, occasionally taking hits off his inhaler, as I told him my story, and my discoveries so far. When I was finished he said, "What does Katrinka think about all this?"

"The part she knows about? She thinks I'm nuts. Not wrong, mind you. Just crazy."

"But you think—"

"I think somebody hypnotized Thigg to shoot me, then forget about it. You know that old movie with Frank Sinatra, where the guy becomes a zombie every time his mother says, 'How would you like to look at my chest?'"

"I think you've garbled it a bit but, yeah," Warren laughed. "But, Tom, c'mon. Fans get weird, you know that. When I saw you lurching towards me ten minutes ago, I didn't think: 'Hey, look, a Manchurian Candidate coming to kill me. I thought, 'Eww. Pretzel creep.'"

"Which is perfectly rational, until the pretzel creep shoots you."

"All I'm saying is, maybe Thigg was what he appeared to be. Maybe it was a crime of passion."

"Then there's no harm in investigating it, is there? Anyway Thigg wasn't passionate about me. You know who he was passionate about? Peter Frampton." I didn't blame Warren for fighting the idea. I fought it, too. "Stop thinking rationally. A rational person does not kill rock stars. He pans their albums and lets them kill themselves."

"I resent that."

"Thigg was made into a robot. That takes lots of money and time and science. Now he gets suicided, right as I'm investigating the case."

"Suicided?"

"If I killed you, but arranged it to look like you killed yourself, I would've 'suicided' you."

Warren exhaled. "Tom, these all seem like excellent reasons to take up gardening."

"Until they kill me again."

"With all due respect, who would kill you now? Someone who wanted your pretzel territory?"

I ignored his feeble joke. "The same folks who'd kill me in 1980. Warren, my record *wasn't selling*. That's not what motivated them. It's what I could've done that they were afraid of, and as long as I'm alive, I could still do it."

"So do you want me to help with protection?"

"No. Anyone powerful enough to do this could squash me like a bug. What I need is information, first to find out who's behind it, and then to get something on them that'll...I want mutually assured destruction. If I die, then the papers find out they're pedophiles, something like that."

"So you want me to—"

"—talk to your friends. Ask 'em what they know, if they heard anything then, or since. Somebody talked, somebody bragged to a squash buddy or a prostitute. I don't have a lot of time. Talk to your reporters. If I find somebody I want to interview, maybe you could hire a freelancer to do it, just to cover me. I need you to be my eyes and ears."

Warren thought for a second. "Okay," he said.

"Thank you. Seriously. I mean it."

"If you change your mind about the bodyguards..."

I waved Warren off. "What about you? Did you hear anything then, when it happened? Have you heard anything since?"

"What I heard was—" Warren shook his inhaler, and gave himself another shot.

"Since when do you have asthma?"

"Since they learned how to put THC in these things. Makes the day go by quicker."

"I'll bet."

"Fuck, Tom, don't do this. I don't know much, but what I do know—I'm asking you to stop. As your friend."

"A friend would help me."

"No, a friend would tell you, 'You're alive, thank God, go put on a fake beard and let's go out to dinner.' You're wagering *everything*."

"So what? What do you think The Ravins was? There was no Plan B. It's the only thing I know how to do. You used to admire that." Warren used to be genuinely radical—not in that silly "man the barricades" way, but in how he respected freedom, and gave freedom to his writers, and told his readers that freedom was possible, and to be valued, and not to be given away lightly. But then the drugs took hold, and kilo by kilo, he hocked his ideals to pay for his habit. A lot of us faced that kind of choice.

Warren was looking away from me, out the window at the grimy permanent circus rolling by. "Stubborn bastard..." he mumbled, then turned. "Of course I'll help you. I may regret it, but—anything you want."

"And you won't expose me, just to sell magazines?"

Warren's face crumpled. "Christ, Tom. You don't even know what you're asking, and now you—" He took a hit from his inhaler. "You know why people let you down? Because you always expect them to."

"Sorry."

Warren raised his hips and got his wallet out of his back pocket. I was afraid he was going to give me some money—did I really look that scruffy? It was a $1000 bill. I was just about to decline it when Warren tore off a corner, and put it on his tongue.

"You rascal. Getting a little sparkle while you're in with the suits."

"We all keep the Sixties alive in our own way."

He offered me some, but I declined. "I don't want to spend the next six hours telling tourists and runaways I'm Jesus."

Warren smiled. "Those were the days. Everybody was Jesus."

"Yeah," I said. "Even the chicks."

Warren put the rest of the bill back in his wallet. As the limo pulled into a parking space, he came in for a final hug.

"Please—no—"

"Sorry, I forgot…I shouldn't let you out of my sight."

"I'll be fine. As long as you don't compress my internal organs."

Warren gave his hair a quick check in the partition. "I'll go into this meeting, then there's a reception I have to go to, but after dinner, I'll start making calls. We'll find out who's in back of this, Tom. We're running things now, our generation. Then we can have lunch tomorrow, before I fly back to New York. I'm staying at the Chateau Marmont. We'll eat by the pool."

My Spidey-sense went off. "No. Too high-class."

"Just fyi, the Buddha says poverty is unnecessary."

"How convenient for you. Unfortunately, 'hiding' isn't."

We got out of the limo. "Meet me at the Chateau at one, and we'll drive over to Canter's. The booths are deep. Your secrets will be safe there."

"I hope so, because Warren," I said, "if you told my secret, I'd have to tell yours."

"That I drop acid?" Warren laughed. "Shit, please tell everybody. It'll help us with the 16-to-34s."

"Fraulein told me that *Roogalator*'s start-up money came from the Agency."

Warren's smile fled again. "Jesus Christ, what a terrible thing to say."

"Is it true?"

"You better hope so. We're going to need all the friends we can get."

I am prompt, but when I was famous I always made people wait. Promptness is a form of submission. That's why I got to the Chateau Marmont an hour early, but didn't go in. I needed to stay in control of the relationship, so I spent an hour sitting on a bench opposite the driveway.

The more I thought, the more plausible a CIA/*Roogalator* connection seemed. Of course the bad guys wanted to control rock and roll. They knew the same thing we did, that it was a Trojan Horse, a conduit straight into fifty million teenage brains. Not to mention a clear and present danger to the status quo. By the time The *Roog* showed up in '67 (the same week we released Ollie's "masterpiece" *Cabinet of Curiosities*) pop had become rock, and pleasure had become political. *Roogalator* was our *Time*, *Life*, and *Saturday Evening Post* all rolled up in one. If the spooks hadn't tried to subvert that, they were bigger fools than we thought they were.

So maybe Warren had been duped, but he was no narc. He wasn't a difficult mark, either. When you're young and broke and chasing a dream, you don't have time to track every dollar back to its source. Once their money had been accepted, all the spooks had to do was wait. Then when the moment was right—say, six months before Crouk's re-election in '72—a couple of clean-cut gentlemen in suits might've showed up at *Roogalator*, told Warren in dispassionate tones what had happened, and put the poor publisher in their pocket, forever.

As I walked across the street and up the Chateau's winding drive, I wondered how I might verify this theory. There'd be no paper trail, the amounts weren't big enough, and naturally nobody would ever admit it. Shit, it could still be going on today. Now that was a depressing thought.

Roogalator pumped out three million copies per week, moving the culture, telling people what to think about and what to ignore. That might explain why so many kids *liked* President Senokot, even as he ruined their world.

A beautiful old car rumbled by, parting my grim gloom like an angel in a packing plant. It was a Chevy convertible, a '57 or thereabouts, black with lots of chrome. "Nice ride," I yelled, but I don't think the driver heard me. He was going pretty fast.

I walked in and presented myself at the desk. "Could you ring Warren Darden's room? He's expecting me."

The weak-chinned clerk raked his eyes over me insolently. Luckily I wore my leather jacket, which was just expensive enough to be owned by a mid-level Industry type or slumming celebrity. "Certainly, sir. Room 617. What's your name?"

"Tell him the Turnip Farmer is here..." The clerk frowned—maybe I wasn't acceptable after all. "Sorry. Inside joke."

Back in the early Seventies, when Fraulein and I were being harassed by the Feds and thought we might be "suicided" ourselves, we had an arrangement with Warren. Every week, we'd put an ad in *Roogalator*'s Classifieds: "Turnips are in season." If two weeks ever went by without the ad being placed, Warren was supposed to start investigating. That way Freek Nation would know something had happened to us. We did it for a couple of weeks, then Harry Nilsson came through New York with some very potent hash oil, and we forgot all about it.

We saw Warren at a party about six months later and he said, "Wasn't I supposed to do something for you?"

"Well, see, Nilsson had this hash oil—"

"Oh, don't talk to me about Nilsson and his hash oil," Warren laughed. "The magazine almost went out of business!"

Back at the front desk, the clerk put down the phone. "I'm sorry, sir, there's no answer." Mr. Officious had decided I wasn't worthy. Well, fuck him.

"Okay," I said. "I'll wait in the bar. Thank you."

When I was out of sight, I did not go to the bar; I went to the service elevator, scooping up a suitcase along the way. If anybody asked, I was a lost guest.

The old elevator heaved to life, and the floors clicked by. Warren and I had really bonded during that long interview I gave back in '70, the one where I'd said all those shitty things about Clive, and Oliver, and everybody else I ever knew. After that, whatever chance The Ravins had of getting back together was kaput. Wait…had Warren been working for the CIA when we'd done that? Was he trying to make sure that The Ravins would never reunite, so we'd lose our influence on the world's kids? Christ, once you started thinking like this…I wondered if Fraulein could get me a new tape, "You CAN Stop Being Paranoid!" The other one was helping; I felt in control, mostly. My wife certainly was a beautiful, brilliant woman.

Room 617 was down at the other end of the hall, near the front stairs. I gave his door a business-like knock.

There was no answer. "Warren, it's me." The hall was spic-and-span, but still smelled dusty, like older buildings sometimes do.

Another knock. "Open up you fucker. It's time for lunch."

The hall was empty, silent. Muffled TV came from one direction, muffled Spanish from another. I rummaged around my leather jacket and found my switchblade. It's strictly ornamental, but occasionally it comes in handy.

I slid the knife-blade into the crack, and was able to push the bolt back with only minor damage to the frame. There were footsteps from down the hall. I jumped into Warren's suite and closed the door behind me.

"Warren!" I whispered. "Are you high again?" I felt a bubble of happiness under my sternum, maybe from the tiny triumph of my B&E—or maybe I was happy to see Warren. This new life was such a lonely one, I had almost forgotten the pleasure of being with an old friend. And my burden was no longer only my own. We'd investigate together. "Rise and shine, you—"

I stopped mid-word, hearing laughter and rolling suitcases in the hall outside, then slipped off my loafers, for silence's sake. I padded around the suite, looking for any sign of my host. It was furnished in the Chateau's signature retro cool. The stars of my generation had a weakness for Hollywood of the 30s and 40s. Those people knew how to be icons. They had style, and training, and more forgiving drugs.

I paused at the bedroom door, which was closed, and listened for snoring or screwing. I heard neither. The door was unlocked and fell open with a breeze. Warren's suit carrier lay stretched across the unmade bed. Items were stuffed in it clumsily, carelessly. No way to treat a $5,000 Armani, I thought.

There was the sound of running water. I was far enough from the front door to use my normal tone, so I said heartily, "Have you passed out in the tub, you daft bugger?"

No answer. It was a joke, but certainly within the realm of possibility, so I decided to stick my head in to make sure he was all right. I'd want him to do the same, if situations were reversed. Seeing Warren naked wouldn't be a thrill for me, but perhaps he would enjoy it, and it was better to be safe than sorry.

The bathroom door was slightly open. I moved it further with my elbow, just enough to look inside. I'll regret what I saw for the rest of my life.

Warren's naked body lay in the bathtub, his knees, belly and head protruding white out of the deep red water. His eyes were open. He wore a expectant expression, like a Ravins fan between screams. An arm dangled limply against the tub, and I could see deep ragged gashes all up and down its soft inner side. There was blood all over the floor. "Oh shit," I gasped—then my legs gave way.

I wasn't out for long, but when I came to, I yelled. Then I realized my hand had fallen into a sticky, viscous pool of my friend's blood, and yelled again. I scrambled to my feet, and felt wetness against my own wrist; the sleeve of my jacket was soaked.

The room began to swim again, and I leaned against the wall for support—leaving a nice, clear palmprint. "Oh, fuck." I'd watched enough TV to know that I'd just turned the investigation from suicide to homicide.

Not that it wasn't already suspicious. Warren seemed upbeat. He and I had made plans. If there was a note, I didn't see one. And those marks on his arms, nobody could do that to themselves—it would hurt too much. If he was high enough not to feel it, he'd be too uncoordinated to pull it off.

The drain on the tub hadn't been closed, so the water had collected very slowly. Even so, it was nearly at the top, so I took a washcloth and turned off the tap, lest an overflow bring investigating parties from below.

I stood there for a second, in shock. Then someone on the other side of the wall walked into their bathroom, asking about the Dodgers' score, and I was jolted into action. I needed to get the hell out of there. My prints were all over the place, that was a lost cause. Then I saw my knife laying there on the tile, a perfect murder weapon. It must've fallen out of my pocket; I picked it up and stuffed it back in.

I padded across the suite to the guest bathroom and washed the blood out of my sleeve. It was still dripping when I finished, but rosé would have to do—the longer I stayed here, the more dangerous it became. A forced door, a switchblade covered in blood, a butchered body, and several witnesses to testify I'd been with him the day before?

I sidled up to the front door and pressed my ear against it. As quiet as the hall had been when I'd sneaked in, it was now bustling—I guess at a rock-and-roll hangout, the morning cleaning schedule had to be shifted accordingly. I stood there forever, waiting for things to grow still again... until there was a knock on the door, an inch away from my temple.

"Housekeeping."

I couldn't tell them not to come in, and I was too slow with the chain, so I did the only thing I could: flattened myself against the wall as the door swung open. Peering through the crack, trying not to breathe, I saw a slim, brick-colored woman walk in pushing a cart. "Hello?" She walked towards the bedroom.

I braced myself, but the scream still took me by surprise. Three seconds later, I saw the maid scurry out of the room, ashen-faced, crying.

This was my only chance. I leaped out into the hall and ran for the stairs.

It was a close thing. If Warren's suite had been at the other end of the hall, I would've been seen. Luck stayed with me all the way down. Not only did my trick knee hold, the stairwells were empty. I was able to get to the lobby without blowing it.

"Calm down, Larkin, you've seen dead people before." I said quietly, slipping on my shoes. But this was different, and horrible. My head was spinning. I had no idea what to do next, so I started walking. Every step I expected to hear a cop yell, "Stop!" but it never happened.

I held it together for seven blocks, until I got to my car. Sliding behind the wheel, I realized how much I'd been looking forward to showing Warren my freaky paint job. Believe it or not, I started to cry.

Fuck emotions! Fuck primal scream therapy, and being sensitive, and being alive! Who could function with *any* of this shit? I beat my fists against the wheel, then laid my head down, still blubbering. My cheek hit the horn, and the sound shocked me silent.

A smudgy little kid was standing ten feet away, chewing on a small metal car.

"Never have emotions," I said, wiping my eyes. "They suck."

"*You* suck."

I grabbed my little bottle of hand sanitizer and threw it at him. It hit him in the ear. He burst into tears, and took off, looking for comfort, sympathy, safety. He's probably still looking. I know I am.

CHAPTER NINE

When I got back to my place, I took off my clothes and, after a long shower, burned them—not so much to destroy evidence (all of it led back to a dead man), as to remove all traces of what I'd seen and felt.

It didn't work.

Before dropping the jacket into the Weber kettle, I cleaned out the pockets and found the switchblades. Both of them.

"Nice going, Tom. You picked up the fucking murder weapon." I touched the button, expecting to see a blade crusted with Warren's blood. Instead, out flicked a comb.

That decided me. Even though I was pretty sure I'd left the Chateau Marmont unseen, I was also confused, so I got the hell out of town just to be safe. I put water on the grill, threw some things into a KCRW gym bag, and pointed the Roller north. The plan was to head up to the wine country, check into a quaint little B&B, and monitor the news coverage with a six-hour head start, in the slim chance that I needed one. Unfortunately, the Roller crapped out ten miles north of Pismo Beach. Vintage cars do have their flaws.

The guy from the garage said it was the carburetor. "I gotta order it," he said. "Should be here in forty-eight hours, give or take."

I flung down *Soldier of Fortune*. "What the hell am I supposed to do until then? Camp?"

"I wouldn't, unless you want to get robbed. You could see if the Hang

Seven's got a room. It's over by the water."

By the water sounded good. "Okay, drop me there."

Folks, I've stayed in a lot of shithole places over the years: drafty Welsh hostels with compulsory morning prayers, bunker-like complexes surrounded by 10,000 Jap paramilitaries, Marseille attics so smelly Jews refused to hide in them; but the Hang Seven took the urinal cake. Imagine the Bates Motel, without the possibility of being put out of your misery.

The Hang Seven was a surfer's crashpad, which meant that people only used it for two things: sleeping, and bonking crab-infested strange they picked up on the beach. The proprietor was a surly old stoner who'd lost three toes to a thresher shark (hence "Hang Seven") and kept a taser under the front desk. I could've used one myself, and a shower cap to ward off ringworm. The shag carpet in my room was so filthy it crunched when you walked on it. I took to sleeping in the tub—after scrubbing it, of course.

Still, the place was not without its advantages, the first and biggest being that nobody would ever think to look for me there. The second was that Carlo's, the seedy package store across the street, had a surprisingly good selection of newspapers. Those, plus CNN, meant I could track the aftermath of Warren's death easily, if not exactly in comfort.

When someone famous dies, everybody goes a little mad. It's not just voyeurism, it's also grief-by-proxy, an opportunity to express emotions usually too frightening to be endured. And there's that high, hysterical, slightly shameful feeling of escape that comes whenever you survive a person you know. Since we all think we know celebrities, we get domesticated grief, release without consequence, and a delicious little jolt of schadenfreude.

The media outdid themselves with Warren. The consensus was that this was rock's biggest story since Live Aid, or maybe even the exit of yours truly. That was perhaps a little much, but people could be forgiven for thinking so. *Roogalator* was particularly frenzied in its morbid sentimentality, mourning all the way to the bank.

I didn't give a shit about all that. Warren was my friend. I missed him, and

I felt guilty. Sure, he could have been killed for something entirely unrelated to our conversation, but what were the odds? My guess was that he'd done exactly what he'd promised: made some phone calls, asked some questions. Then he asked the wrong person the wrong thing, and by noon the next day, Death had come, wearing rubber gloves and carrying a hypodermic, or a taser, or a cosh. The how was immaterial; bodies are fragile, and the tiny spark of life cowering beneath our breastbone can be doused a million different ways. Maybe Warren had been tipped off—his half-packed bag said so—or maybe he had just put two and two together and decided to run for it. He was a brilliant guy and, whether or not my CIA theory was correct, knew all manner of things happened in the shadows. He respected that fact.

You didn't get to be Warren Darden without knowing that every person is like an iceberg. There's a clean, white tip you can see, and a darker, sharper, much more dangerous portion hidden underneath. It's the part under the water that can send you to the bottom, and the higher-profile someone is, the bigger and deadlier that part becomes. That's why it's unlikely a celebrity death will be investigated very thoroughly; once you start looking under the water, there's no telling what you'll find. Some heir has to smell dough in it, and none of Warren's heirs felt that way. They just wanted "closure," their pet name for Warren's money.

The good news was, the LAPD was calling it a suicide, so the police weren't looking for anyone, including *moi*. The bad news was, they weren't looking for the person who had actually done it. He or she was still "at large," as they say. At large and determined to add me to a grim collection of Greatest Hits.

That did not help my mood. In a moment of particularly heavy freak-out, I called Wisnewski.

"How did the séance go?" he asked. "D'ja find anything out?"

"Let's just say I gave everybody their money's worth."

"I swear, Tom, sometimes I think you want people to discover you. Am I on speaker?"

"Yeah."

"Are you shitting?"

I dislike crude people. "No, I'm in the bathtub. Long story."

"Hear about Thigg?"

"Yeah."

"Is that why you're calling?"

"No." I didn't tell him about Warren. There's trusting someone, and then there's confiding you crashed the scene of a murder. "Listen, Sam, I think I'm being followed."

"By who? The AARP?"

"Get stuffed."

"Love talking to you, it's like watching 'The Two Ronnies.' Okay, so who's following you?"

"The guy from the diner. Pompadour."

Sam chuckled. "Highly unlikely."

"Yeah? Then explain the vintage cars I've been seeing."

"You mean, like the one you drive? Tom, use your nut: if you spotted him, he's probably nobody to worry about." Wisnewski sneezed. The fall burning was going strong and there was a lot of junk in the air. "Why are you so spooked? What happened?"

"Nothing."

"Then why are you calling me from the 805?" Fuck! Hadn't thought of that. "Why don't you let me handle the investigation for a while? Stay up there, I'll come meet you, we can hang out."

"No thanks."

"You don't want me to protect you?"

"No, Sam. The last time you did that, things didn't work out very well."

"Fuck you for that. So why the hell did you call, wacko? Are you stoned?"

"No!" What could I say? That I wanted to hear another voice? That I needed to talk to the one person who might understand what I was up against? There was a click. "That's my other line. See ya."

"WACKO!"

It was the mechanic, telling me my carburetor had arrived. Glory hallelujah. My whole body ached from sleeping on porcelain, but at least my pubes remained uncolonized. As I was checking out, someone called in a bomb threat. "Bring it on," growled the owner. I wished them all the luck in the world.

One tank of gas and an In-N-Out milkshake later, I was on the road back to LA. Both my car and my relaxation tape were going double-speed—I needed Total Control. As Edith Ann talked, my fear subsided and was replaced by determination; I began to make plans. I had to keep going, to find out what this was all about. Warren had died for it. I wasn't seeking private justice anymore, but justice for us both.

The tape sounded weird. I turned up the volume; there seemed to be a kind of whooshing sound in the background. Wait…was that a voice? It *was.* It said "Tom, you must"—then a bunch of shit I couldn't make out.

I rewound it and listened again, and again, letting my musician's ears chew it over. The fourth time through, I remembered a radio program I once heard, Mae Brussell, Art Bell, someone like that. Apparently ghosts try to communicate with us via the background noise on cassettes. But of course—my mum Helena was trying to help me with the case! I fiddled with the bass and treble, the balance and EQ, then turned it up even more.

I pulled up to a stoplight, tape blasting, then felt someone's eyes on me and looked over. A tough-looking kid in a hoopty was giving me the once-over.

"TAKE A DEEP BREATH, AND FEEL THE HEALING ENERGY," the player boomed. I made eye contact with the kid, then breathed in emphatically.

"NOW LET IT OUT." I blew out.

The light changed. "Fucking hippie," the kid said, pulling away.

"At least I don't have a neck tattoo!" I yelled back.

Before the words were even out of my mouth, the player ate my cassette—*fuck!* Now I'd never discover what Mum was trying to tell me. But it was my own fault; when you put negative energy out into the Universe, it always comes back. That's guaranteed.

I knew what I had to do: As soon as I got into Santa Monica, I went to the Goodwill and took one more look through their bins, just to be sure. I even looked behind the Harold Robbins section, just in case one had fallen back behind. There were Carpenters, Stray Cats, Falco—but no more "Yes You CAN!"

I walked out. I was standing on the corner being pissed off when a Goodwill employee touched me on the arm.

"Hey, can I bum a cigarette?"

"Sorry, I quit," I said, exhaling deeply.

"Yeah, so did I," she said, taking one from the pack. "Best thing I ever did." Her lighter wouldn't work, so I gave her mine. "I tried everything. Nothing worked until I found that tape."

"What was it called?"

"You CAN Stop Smoking!"

"That was mine! I gave you the whole series, I was just inside, looking to buy 'em back."

"Oh, those have been gone for months, the staff snapped them up. They're amazing. I stopped smoking, another girl did 'You CAN Be Taller!'—she's eight foot five now. At least I think she is. She quit her job. People say she never leaves her bedroom. She just sits around watching TV."

"You're sure there aren't any more of 'em? Like, in the back?"

"If there were, I wouldn't tell you!" she said. "Do you know how much money I could make if I could *fly?*"

She walked off. I dropped the thing in my fingers and crushed it under my foot. I guess I'd have to see if Fraulein could get me a replacement set. If anybody could, it was her—she really was a brilliant, beautiful woman. A genius. In the meantime, I had a bold new plan. I'd go see the other Ravins, one by one, and ask them straight up: Did you do it? Did you sic Thigg on me?

They might lie—or worse—but at least no more innocent bystanders would die for it.

If anybody had benefited from my demise, it was my three former co-workers, Oliver, Harry and Buck. They each had a classic reason to want me dead: money.

It's common knowledge that Clive was out of his depth in certain areas. A gentleman in no business for gentlemen, he shackled us with the shittiest deals in the history of rock and roll. The Delta bluesmen who started it all might disagree, but then again, they never had to pay 98% British tax. Fact was, we had to sell a fantastic number of records to stay afloat, and for eight years, that's precisely what we did. In the process, the four of us got used to a certain standard of living. If you're looking for a root of all evil, that's as good a candidate as I've ever met.

After the break up, Buck and Harry were screwed. They'd always gotten less—Harry'd famously called them "the Ravins who fly coach"—but by 1980, they were looking has-beenery right in the face. For Ollie's part, songwriting insured that he would never starve, but survival wasn't nearly enough. He was a pop star, and he compulsively judged himself against the latest big thing, a hell of a standard in a young man's game. But that's just Ollie's nature.

My nature, however, made a reunion about as appealing as eating a ten-year-old sandwich. Back then, reuniting for a concert seemed like showbiz at its schmaltziest. Doing an album seemed like a public admission that breaking up had been a mistake, and since I was the one who'd forced that, well…As the offers got bigger and bigger, the meetings got so nasty I started sending Fraulein (and Hitler) in my stead. Meanwhile, Ollie's record sales began to tail off, Buck's session work dried up, and Harry's castle in Oxfordshire was crumbling under his feet. The pressure was mounting on them. I suspect it was Ollie who had the idea; he's always had a knack for marketing. A reunion would sell one new album, but a tragedy, that could sell twenty old ones. "…and that bastard Larkin would get his just desserts, to boot!"

For me they were gunshots, but for others, the knock of opportunity.

The day after I "died," a fresh herd of gently baa-ing teenagers presented themselves, and The Ravins became the ultimate crossover product, old *and* new, cool *and* hot, comforting *and* relevant. For ten years I'd fought the whole bullshit fairy tale, and now it was back with an irresistible tearjerker ending, and I was shut up for good.

Do you see? Now do you see, how it could've been them? We always said we were brothers, the four of us and Clive, and we loved each other, there's no doubt about that. We knew we were the keys to each others' lives, the only people who could really understand. But love can turn into murder, if conditions are right. One day on Brigadoon, I was reading a book called *Why You Hate Everybody*, a Twelve Step thing on alcoholic families. The book said that these families often assign a specific role to each child, so that the parent can continue to be sick. There's the caretaker, and the scapegoat, and the hero, and the lost child, and the clown. Or, if you prefer: Clive, and me, and Ollie, and Harry, and Buck...So the fairy tale was right: we *were* brothers, we *were* a family. We were just really fucked up. How fucked up? I'll tell you.

When I survived, I didn't contact the other three—but they didn't ask, either, and that's on them. I suppose I should've told them what happened, or about Clive at least. Looking back, that would've been kinder. But my life felt complicated enough and, to be brutally honest, sometimes it's cool being dead. You get to hear what people really think.

But I paid the price for my silence. The summer before I had my visit from President Crouk, some lawyers at our mutual Frankenstein, Mandala Records, had gotten their knickers in a twist over my bootlegging. I can't say I blamed them—I'd sneaked out a ton of material in a very short period of time: all the outtakes, the BBC shows, the stuff we did in disguise for Radio Caroline. What I did resent, however, was them involving Interpol. There was no call for that. What I was doing, it wasn't serious cops and robbers. Yet there I was, hanging from a drainpipe, waiting for the sniffer dogs to leave.

That was a real moment of clarity, three stories up: "This is ridiculous.

Either this gets sorted, or I'm gonna get killed." So I climbed back in the window, and called London.

I asked to speak with ol' Nod-Off, the school chum who ran Mandala (I use the term loosely). Of course he didn't believe it was really me, so I did the only thing I could: started telling rude stories only he and I knew. By the time I got to him supergluing that Kraut hooker's tits together, Nigel was convinced. And having a coronary. Luckily his secretary knew CPR, so he survived.

Twenty-four hours later, I was sitting in our headquarters in Knightsbridge, picking macadamia nuts out of my teeth and waiting for the other three who were, predictably, sprinkled about the globe. The cover story was that I was an actor, hired as a double for some sort of photo shoot, and Ollie, Harry and Buck were coming in to see if I passed muster.

Everyone at Mandala was very nice, and much more efficient than I remember, and because I was incognito there was none of the embarrassing bowing and scraping that would've accompanied a visit from The Founder Himself. Actually the atmosphere was a bit too irreverent, if you ask me. As I was waiting, I noticed a printed sheet tacked up in the lounge. "It has come to my attention," Nod-Off had written, "that some employees are in the habit of referring to a certain individual as 'Cruella DeVil.' Regardless of said individual's rather quirky and demanding personality, I expect all Mandala employees to conduct themselves in a businesslike manner. The jokes, songs, cartoons, limericks, *et cetera*, while possessing undeniable therapeutic value, must be curtailed. In the interest of harmony with the Larkin estate, as well as respect for Tom's memory, I'd ask that..."

I was writing "BLOODY SEXIST BASTARDS" in the margin when the guys walked in. They entered as a group, like they were too frightened to encounter me one-on-one. Maybe they thought I was a ghost. Maybe I was.

Buck was the first to speak. "Is it really you?"

"Five years to think about it, and that's what you come up with?" I teased, and hugged him.

I saw Harry and started a wisecrack, but my old lead guitarist commanded silence. Then with a look of concentration, he put his tongue on my third eye. Those of us who knew Harry were used to shit like this. Then he pulled back, smacking his lips. "It's him," he said.

"The taste of an old generation," I said.

"I was RIGHT!" Ollie said. "I *knew* you were having us on!" I don't know which made him happier, seeing me, or guessing correctly. Being right was always very important to Oliver, particularly where I was concerned.

"Maybe he did die," Buck said. "After all, he is Jesus."

Harry mimicked my nasal sing-song. "I have an important announcement. I, the entity you knew as Thomas Dunkirk Van Weltanshuung Larkin, am in reality the reincarnation of our Lord and Savior—"

Now I cut *him* off. "Sixty-nine was a hell of a year."

We all sat down around the glossy black conference table. Nobody said anything—how to start? Finally Buck mumbled, "Someone bringing us lunch?" He picked up the phone.

"Macrobiotic for me," I said.

"I'm ovo-lacto," Ollie said.

"I require nothing but air," Harry said.

Buck conveyed everyone's order, then added, "...steak and kidneys for me, double portions." He put down the phone. "Fifteen minutes. Can you make it that long Granddad?" It was true, I looked significantly older than the other three; that's what a near-death experience will do for you.

"If you don't eat me, Fatty," I said to Buck. "Don't you realize rich guys can have plastic surgery? Or has Ollie used up the entire Ravins' allotment?"

Oliver ignored the barb. "So, Tom. We hear you've been selling a few records out of your van."

"You're going to have to knock that off." Harry pointed at Oliver. "He'll sue you again."

We all shared an uncomfortable smile. Only Buck was allowed to say stuff like that, not Harry.

"We've been over this a million times," Ollie whined, "I had to do it, so Ackbar Musselman wouldn't take all our money."

"Impossible," Harry quipped. "Mandala was already doing that."

"Musselman wasn't so bad," I said.

"Yes, he was. You gotta be pretty low to steal from lepers!" In '73, Harry did a big benefit, *Let's Give 'Em A Hand*. Six months later, Musselman was living in the Caymans.

"Ah yes, the ol' three-and-a-half-finger discount."

"Shut your mouth! You didn't even do me the courtesy of showing up."

I smiled acidly. "It's a good thing you're so spiritual Harry. I'd hate to think you sat around harboring resentments."

"Look, lads, let's not fight," Ollie said.

"Yeah," Buck added. "Let's address Tom's profound baldness."

Harry rounded on Ollie. "Did you just call us 'lads'? I'm forty-three fucking—"

"Oh, I didn't mean anything by it. You're so bloody sensitive."

"I'm going to check on lunch." That was Buck-speak for "fuck this."

"Quit treating me like your little brother," Harry growled. Ollie ignored him, desperate to keep things civil. "So, how've you been for the past, erm, five years? Write any tunes?"

I brought my two ex-bandmates up to speed. After I had finished, Oliver had only one comment: "It was *her* idea, wasn't it?"

"Actually," Harry said, "I think that's a very sound strategy. I've a mind to try it myself."

I thought about telling them about Clive and Brigadoon, but thought better of it. (I told them later, after we did the documentary.)

Buck came back. "They're bringing it up. Harry, I got you a thermos of damp air."

"Mighty white of you," Harry said, and it was. Buck lived to eat, so our time with Swami Roger the breatharian had been the darkest two months of his life.

There was another throat-tightening silence. "So..." Oliver said, "who here thinks Tom should stop ripping us off?" They raised their hands. "Three against one, mate. No more bootlegging."

Harry stood up. "Now that's settled, I'd like to go back to my regularly scheduled life."

Buck looked hurt. "Aren't you going to stay for lunch? I got you the air…"

"Wait, Harry," I said. "I got a proposition…"

"I tasted it in your aura, you wanna restart the band! Well, fuck that, Tom. I waited ten years—I make movies now, that's who Harry Thompson is *today*. I gave my entire youth to that insanity, and—"

"That 'insanity' paid for everything you've got," Oliver pointed out. "You might show a little gratitude."

"To who? You?"

As ever, Buck poured oil on the waters. "Do we have to dig all this shit up? I wanted to come in, visit with Tom, celebrate the fact he's not dead—"

"I don't wanna restart the band," I interjected. "Not in 1980, and certainly not now. I just want us to release all our old stuff."

"I don't see the point," Oliver said. "They've got all the original albums."

"Yeah," Buck said, "that should be enough to relive the childhood of their youth."

Harry smiled. "He still does it. The Yogi Berra of rock and roll."

"The only Yogi Harry hasn't followed," Ollie said.

"Sod off."

I wedged past the sibling rivalry. "All I'm saying is, why let the bootleggers make the money? We'll do a couple new tunes. The fans would love it."

"You of all people—" Harry said. "The fans are *berserk*. If we did what the fans wanted, we'd be playing the Sands twice nightly." He popped some Nicorette. So *that* was why he was so grouchy.

"You should try these tapes I know," I said. "The Dalai Lama's therapist—"

Buck raised his hand. "Serious question: How can we do new tunes when you're dead?"

Oliver twiddled his pen. "That's why he's 'the practical Ravin.'"

"I'll get Fraulein to send over some demos, and you three can vamp."

Ollie made a face. "Sounds a bit tatty."

"Oh, it'll be all right. It's not Mozart."

There was a knock on the door. "Thank Christ," Buck said. "I'm about to eat my shoe."

Harry got up again. "Tom, I'm delighted to see you're no longer dead. You should come visit me. Where are you living?"

"Santa Monica."

Oliver pointed to himself "Bel-Air. Harry's in Holmby Hills. It's just like '57."

"Only warmer." I turned to Buck. "What's your problem, wack? Didn't you get the memo?"

"Nouveau riche throwin' their money about, makes me sick," Buck joked. His neighbors on Bermuda were a Rothschild, Sir John Templeton, and the Duchess of Kent. (According to Buck, she cut her own grass.)

A cadre of absurdly young employees scurried about, putting down plates and tea. Harry waved them away. "Fine, Tom. You and I can spend Chanukah in Santa Monica. However: I am not interested in reliving the past in any way, shape or form. The Ravins were, in case you don't remember, a colossal drag—"

"A bit of a broad brush," Buck said, cutting his food up into little bites.

"You just want to be the boss again, Tom. And Ollie wants to be on Top of the Pops, and Buck—I don't know why *he'd* subject himself to the madness—"

"I want a hovercraft." He held his knife parallel to the table. "Goes on top of the water."

"Cool," Oliver said.

"Much safer for mermaids," I said.

"But the only way I'd ever dig up that corpse is if I needed the money desperately. So if I'm ever broke, you might get a phone call. Until then, include me out," Harry snorted.

"Be reasonable," Oliver said. "We can't do anything without you. It wouldn't be The Ravins."

"Well then, I guess the decision is made. Breathe easily." And with that, he walked out.

Buck belched. "I thought meditation was supposed to make you *happy*."

I thought about that meeting a lot in the days before I approached the other guys again. What kept bouncing 'round my head was this: If that had been my big homecoming—rivalries and resentments back before we'd even said "hello"—how would my mates react when I accused them each of murder?

CHAPTER TEN

The day I went to see Oliver, I was nervous, and not just because he might've had me killed. Having someone know me too well always makes me feel ill at ease, like they'll use it against me, like I'm at a disadvantage. Funny thing was, perhaps Ollie felt the same way.

When you're 14, getting famous with your mates is the coolest thing imaginable. Then after it's happened you think, "Who invited those arseholes?" The world may worship you, but those guys, those three fuckers, they remember everything. Every boil, every ugly shirt, every bird who stood you up. They make you feel like a fraud merely by existing, and knowing *they're* frauds too doesn't help. It's fucking insulting. That's why I had to break us up.

"Break up" doesn't really cover it; it was more like a five-year brawl between guys too rich to fight. We dragged each other through the courts, slagged each other in the press, wrote nasty songs back and forth. The cover of Oliver's first solo album—inventively titled "Oliver"—has a secret dig at me written right across the front. No, I'm not going to tell you what it says. I'm not going to dignify it. He knows it, and I know it, and that's enough. You have to squint, and look at it from an angle under black light, but trust me, it's *there*. Once Fraulein showed me, it was obvious. I'm amazed they let him print it.

Surprised? Not if you knew Oliver like I did. He was sneaky. When we were in the group together, he'd always do something shitty, then when you'd confront him, he'd deny it. He'd say, "You're paranoid," or "That's the DMT talking" or "No, I'm not going to call you 'the Christ.'"

Even under the best of circumstances, creative partnerships are half-love match and half fight to the death: Me and Oliver, Gilbert and Sullivan, Leopold and Loeb. The very similarities that allow you to work together, make a bad ending almost inevitable. You begin by waltzing, but end with knuckles white, hands clamped around each other's throat.

Oliver was the heartthrob, even Clive admitted it. Ollie's face was a baby's face, big eyes, tiny nose and chin, rosebud of a mouth—disgusting. It cried out for mothering, which is why the females of the world made such fools of themselves over it. As a result, Oliver developed an unshakable belief in his own charm, and that gets tiresome, you know, after a decade.

He was always trying to upstage me. Subtly, in ways no one else would notice. Waving when I was singing, so the screams would drown me out, or working on his signature so that it looked more artistic than mine. I'd write a hit, and he would have to write a bigger one. I'd fuck somebody, so Oliver would have to fuck her *and* her sister. (He drew the line at boys, though. Ollie's nothing if not middle-class.)

Don't misunderstand; it wasn't the competition that bothered me, it was how Oliver went about it. Christ, if I'd wanted a regular job...Then he started beating me, which was completely out of line.

Ollie's two years younger, so he was a bit behind at the beginning; but after '65 or so—that folkie album we did, *Plaster Caster* or whatever it was called—he was as good a songwriter as I was. I had to make a choice: either start working as hard as Oliver, or start taking enough drugs that it didn't matter. For a layabout like me, that was no choice at all.

If Oliver was half as nice as he wants everybody to think he is, he would've gotten the hint, quit writing songs, and started dropping acid with the rest of us. But he didn't. He actually wrote more, the conniving little shit, which shows you what his *real* game was.

This bothered me intensely. After a certain point, every time I'd come into the studio, Oliver'd lay some monster hit on me, or like fourteen songs he'd written over the weekend. It was bloody intolerable.

"See here, fucker—what's the meaning of all this?"

"What do you mean?"

"These...songs. This work."

"I thought you'd be pleased."

"Why? I know what you're up to, I know exactly what you're trying to do. You're trying to show me up in front of the others."

"Show you up? It was rainy, there was a piano..."

"You want to take over the group."

"Does that mean you *like* the song?"

"Snake in the grass."

"You don't like the song?"

"You disgust me."

"Honestly, Tom—I just have a lot of ideas."

"Oh, like I don't? I have a million ideas. Great ones! You know that recording I made, the one in the monkeyhouse? That's real music. That should be our next single, not more of your teeny-bopper bullshit. Wakey-wakey, Ollie—the future is now!"

"Okay."

"And for the B-side, we'll record us throwing a piano off the roof. It's time for The Ravins, to make a statement."

"Like, 'Look out below'?"

"What's that supposed to mean?"

"Nothing."

"Nothing you say means nothing. Not even 'nothing.' Even 'nothing' means something."

"I think I lost you there."

"Yeah, well, maybe you should expand your mind a bit, eh? Instead of writing another bloody top of the pops. Maybe you should open your mind up a little."

"Maybe I should...Does Harry have any tunes?"

"Very funny. 'Does Harry have any tunes?' Fucking hilarious. 'Better ask

Harry, because Tom's off his rocker again. Obviously Tom's a huge fucking nutter—even though he's the one that started the bloody group! I'd like to see where you'd be without me!"

"I don't know. Teaching school?"

"You could never live my life—you couldn't hack it! I work my arse off. First, you have to find the chemicals, which is fucking impossible, because most of them are illegal. Then you have to prepare them, which takes brains, science. Then after going through all that *shit*, you still have to take them…I've seen Death, man! God and the Devil, six o'clock in the morning, before you've even had your soft-boiled egg! You remember that, the next time you're working on a bloody pop song!"

"You're panting, Tom. Are you okay? Do you need to lie down?"

"What? No! Why—I can't—Yes. Yes, I think I should…"

That was how it went with Oliver. The calmer he was, the crazier I got, and the crazier I got, the calmer he became. He was always so reasonable. Right up until the point he arranged to have you killed.

That night in November of '85 when I confronted Oliver, we were sitting in the back garden of his pad in Bel-Air. It was nighttime, but there were no crickets—they couldn't afford the neighborhood. He'd sent the staff home early, then fed me a delicious vegetarian meal. Now, security system armed, I could accuse him of murder in complete privacy.

"What's this terribly important matter we have to discuss?" Ollie sat a few feet away, working on something as usual. He was designing a combination art gallery/orphanage/desalination plant.

"Oliver," I said coldly, "I know you had me shot."

"I what?"

"Don't worry, I won't press charges. All I need to know is: are you going to let me live in peace?"

"I should ask you the same bloody thing," he said under his breath. "Are you high?"

"No. I might need to run for it."

"You might need to run for it…" Oliver put down his compass. "Tell me, how did you come to this brilliant conclusion? Was it during dinner, where I didn't poison you?"

"Here's how I figure it went down." I let my eyes play over Ollie's latest piece of modern art, a neon map of the London Tube set into the back hedge. "It's 1980. You're getting older, the hits are coming harder. The punks make fun of you, the new wavers don't even bother. So you have an idea, 'We'll get the group back together. Then I'll be on top again.' But *I* wouldn't let that happen, so you despised me. Do you deny it?"

"So I was cheesed off, so what?"

"So one day somebody calls you up and says, 'We can do this, you know, if you ever wanted us to…'"

"And when you say 'do this,' Miss Marple, you mean 'pay someone to kill my ex-songwriting partner'?"

"'Pay someone to *hypnotize someone* to kill your ex-songwriting partner.'" The Tube stops blinked randomly; I squinted, trying to control them with my mind.

"And why would I do this?"

"Money."

I expounded on my theory, how he was desperate to keep up with the Joneses. "Slip a million to some government loony-trainer, get fifty million back. It's a sound investment."

"But your estate has made as much as I have," Ollie said. "More, even! How do I know it wasn't some daft 'experiment' of your wife's?"

"Watch it," I warned. He and Katrinka had never gotten along. She saw through all his games, and that drove him crazy, the sexist bastard.

"Tom, I don't know if you've noticed, but I don't need more money. Not in 1980, not now."

"Bullshit. Everybody needs more money."

"That's your wife talking."

"I didn't come here to be insulted—"

"Only to insult me," Oliver said. "Look, if I had you murdered, it wouldn't have been for money. I would've done it for revenge. The Ravins was what I was born to do. You took that from me—for no good reason I've ever been able to discover. You were angry; you wanted to hurt me, that's all. But you ended up hurting yourself more."

"That's bullshit."

"You can psychoanalyze, but I can't? Whatever, man. The fact is, I didn't have anything to do with your getting shot."

"But you admit you were angry at me."

"Of course I was angry at you, I was always angry at you. Everybody was always angry at you. Tom, I don't know if you realize this, but you're an arsehole!"

"I'd like to think that I've gotten a bit better now that I'm unfamous."

"Sure, instead of calling me 'Captain Boring' in *Roogalator*, you come over, eat my food, then accuse me of murder. Less public, still beastly. But—and I'd like to bring this to your attention—I have not killed you tonight."

"Yet."

"The day you died was the unluckiest day of my life. Do you think I'd be designing this thing if you were still alive, making me look sane?" Oliver took off the light strapped around his head, and rubbed his eyes. "Sorry, I don't mean to snap at you, it's just—I've been up since six. I haven't been to a party since 1983."

"Got you beat."

"Yes, but you're *dead*," he said. "I'm supposed to be relaxing, enjoying the fruits of success. Instead, I'm working harder than ever, and people still think you were the genius."

I laughed.

"I'm sorry, but I don't think it's funny."

"Do you remember when I chased you around Regent's Park with a hand-drill?"

"As I recall, you wanted to put a hole in my skull."

"Just a little one. So the evil spirits could come out."

"Nobody remembers your lunatic moments. They only remember the great humanitarian. The bloke who hated people—that's for me and Harry and Buck to cherish."

"I didn't hate—"

Oliver looked over his reading glasses. "Atlanta."

"Oh. Right." Once, when we were on tour I spent an entire week plotting to get a nuclear warhead so I could blow up Atlanta. I forget why. "Okay, then, you didn't kill me for the money," I said. "But you killed me for turning you into Norman Rockwell." My Gandhi-on-acid thing had really fucked Oliver—by the end, he was doing our albums almost single-handedly, and I was the one people admired. "Don't feel bad. If our situations had been reversed, I would've rubbed you out."

"I don't doubt it," Oliver said. "Do you know that last year, I sold three million records, wrote two symphonies, published a memoir, and endowed a school for the blind? But you, the guy I saw vomit *at* stewardesses—gets our hometown airport named after him. Imagine what they'd say about me if I actually had killed you? It ain't worth the risk." Then Oliver got a funny little smile. "'Course, now that you're dead, I could do anything I wanted. Nobody would be the wiser."

I grabbed the armrests, ready to spring from my chair. Ollie's old drooly cat Carnaby leapt off my lap.

"Relax. Tom, as you are so fond of saying, I'm bourgeois. Among my tribe murder is frowned upon. Then there's the whole prison thing, which I don't think I'd enjoy."

"Okay," I said. "You weren't trying to kill me, I believe that. You were trying to kill Fraulein, but the assassin missed—"

Oliver sighed. "Tom, if you and your insanity will excuse me, the delegation will be here in"—he checked his watch—"seven hours. I have a lot of work to do. I have to stress-test the model."

At the door, I told Oliver I was going to see Harry next, then Buck.

"Should I call them? So they can get their stories straight?"

"I'm glad you find my murder so amusing."

"I don't. I find the way you're investigating it amusing."

"Do you think either of them could've done it?"

"Come on," Ollie said.

"But they needed money. Do you remember those slasher flicks Buck acted in? And Harry's memoir?"

Ollie gave a rueful laugh. "Harry's the only person in the world who would write a tell-all that didn't tell anything. That house he had, I'm surprised he wasn't out hawking plasma. Smartest thing he ever did, by the way, selling that pile to Bono. By the way, what do you think of them?"

"About time Ireland got a group," I said. In '85, U2 was everywhere. "But it's not like back in the old days, me lad. Back then it took more than a cheap delay pedal and a Christ complex to get on the charts. Back then, it took talent!" Bit over, I asked Oliver his opinion.

"Who cares? According to the *Roog*, I'm an 'elder statesman of rock.'"

"Well fuck them very much." We hugged, and my skin didn't crawl. As I walked to the car, I thought that maybe Ollie wasn't such a bad fellow after all. I tried not to think about what that made me.

Oliver had a right to hate me; I'd screwed him out of the best job in show biz. Harry, on the other hand, was a bus driver's son who'd only wanted to play music—what did he have to be angry about? The fact was, it didn't matter. It had only taken me three decades worth of the morning paper to learn that human beings don't need a reason for murder. Especially when those humans can pay for it.

Harry avoided publicity, but I'd been able to find out a few recent developments courtesy of the Santa Monica public library. According to a fourteen-line interview in *Lute Enthusiast*, he'd downsized considerably since 1980. Gone were the sports cars, the collection of Edgar Cayce memorabilia, the castle. Of this last he said, "I got tired of it. It took a barrowful of hundreds just to keep the chill off."

However, as I drove up to Harry's mansion in the Hills—the old Fatty Arbuckle spread, if you know that bit of Hollywood Babylon—my ex-bandmate's life didn't seem particularly frugal. Maybe his early 80s fire-sale had a different purpose entirely. Like paying some high-priced professionals for a certain expensive job of work.

Harry Thompson was a complex person. On the one side was all his mystical argy bargy, which he pursued with admirable, annoying devotion. He was the one who introduced us to Swami Roger the breatharian, and after we fucked off, he stuck with it. Breatharians believe that the body can be sustained solely by breathing (and the occasional large donation). The sect that Harry hooked up with took this even further, and tried to hold its breath. Eventually you passed out, but it was said that through complete body control you could make that time last longer and longer stretching, theoretically at least, into immortality.

This played into the other side of Harry's character, his thing about money. He was always worried that he didn't have enough, that it would run out—a reasonable concern, if you were shooting for Methuselah's record. Don't underestimate the fear at work here: For a poor kid who's made it big, the ultimate nightmare isn't death. It's falling back to earth. And that, Ravins Mavens, might just be why Harry had me shot.

Walking up to the front gate, I tried not to hold it against him. Oliver and I never let Harry have more than one or two cuts per album. Over thirteen LPs, that added up to tens of millions of dollars in lost royalties. Shit, if anybody'd done that to me, I'd have killed them myself. And I wouldn't have waited until 1980 to do it.

On the gate, there was a picture of Harry, a publicity snap from several years before, I could tell by the feathered hair. It was sun-bleached and the tape was peeling. I pushed down the corners, just to be helpful. Under the picture was a small, gray speaker, with a white call button. Underneath the speaker, someone had made a little sign using a label maker:

"ATTENTION ALL FANS

Please go away. I don't care where you're from, or how long it's taken you to get here. I cannot cure your disease, sign your tits, or read your mind, and I certainly don't want to hear your song. Please get the fuck away from my home. Your pal, Harry."

Smiling, I pushed the button. That was very much the Greasby sense of humor. You could never tell if someone was joking, or about to hit you.

"Hello?" All of Harry's flunkies sounded holy, which pissed me off.

"Could you tell Harry that Artemis Heliotrope is here to see him?"

The flunky put down the phone, and I stood there for a long while. He probably thought I was some kid having him on, but that was one of the names we used to register at hotels, back in the days when our real ones caused riots. Harry would remember.

When the flunky picked the phone up again, he said, "You can come up, but it'll be a while. Sri Thompson is in the maze."

Sri Thompson, eh? We used to call him 'Stinky.' The gate buzzed and I walked through.

Harry's estate was even larger than it appeared from the outside; my guess was five acres, maybe more. I shuddered to think what it cost, and what he'd be willing to do to keep it. When I got to the main house, a neat Spanish number surrounded by outbuildings, one of Harry's red-robed assistants was waiting.

"Please come with me." He didn't allow me to come inside—something about "subtle conflicts of energy"—but ushered me straight into the garden. The man was dressed in flowing garments and had a sun-flushed shaved head that made me grateful for my panama.

"Did you say something about a maze?"

"For a time each day, Sri Thompson wanders the labyrinth. It's part of his spiritual practice. "

"Uh-huh. Is there anything that's not part of Harry's spiritual practice?"

The monk pursed his lips. "The sacred scriptures have a name for people like you. Would you like to hear it?"

"Nope."

"You are wiser than you look."

"You don't know the half of it."

"What's that supposed to mean?"

I give him a little smile. "Those who speak, do not know. Those who know, do not speak."

More sour-face. He didn't like the taste of his own medicine. Mystic-types never do.

We arrived at a small gazebo. I saw it and burst out laughing. It was just like the one off Greasby Common, where Harry, Ollie and I used to smoke handrolleds and wait for the bus when we were kids. Scratch that, it was the one off Greasby Common—there were the letters I'd scratched in 1957! (F-U-C; never got to the K.) Harry must've bribed the city fathers and had it shipped over, stick by stick. Turns out he was as nostalgic as the rest of us, he just preferred to hide it.

"Wait here," the monk said.

"Do you know how long it might be?"

"The point of the maze is to become lost, then wander until you reach the exit. There is no time limit. That is the point of the maze."

"I see."

What I saw was that there was no way I was going to sit there doing nothing. Given what I planned to ask "Sri Thompson," I was pretty keyed-up. I made sure the flunky was out of sight, then picked a direction and started walking.

The grounds were crawling with men in cardinal robes, sporting shaved heads and unfocused eyes, all tending the greenery. In exchange for opening his home to Swami Roger, the Swami's followers handled the upkeep. (The Swami himself was back in India, evading some very unspiritual back taxes.) An army of glazed gardeners would be very helpful in burying a body, I thought glumly.

I stopped a monk pushing a wheelbarrow full of peat moss.

"Excuse me, could you point me to the maze?"

"Follow your nose," the monk said. "The exhaust. From the bikes."

"Ah." Clasping my hands, I gave him a blessing. *"Embuego fantoni."* No, it doesn't mean anything, but it was the thought that counted.

When he wasn't holding his breath in the lotus position, Harry was on a motorcycle. He'd always been nuts for them. In fact, Zimmerman's famous crash, the one that almost killed him, happened because he and Harry had been racing. (Harry made sure he won, then took Bob to the hospital.) For such a spiritual guy, Harry was really quite competitive. 'Course, I'm one to talk. I gave der Fraulein the silent treatment for most of 1977, after we held a séance and she turned out to be Joan of Arc, and I was just a slave.

I crested a hill, and the great green maze hove into view. It was amazing how huge the hedge was, and how lush. Harry claimed that he never watered it, even in this dry climate. Instead every fifteen feet, a monk sat atop the hedge, meditating, falling over, waking up and meditating some more. "Water isn't necessary," Harry had told *Prana Collector*. "It's nourished by their energy." Yeah, plants grow well in bullshit, I thought.

The serene, immaculate landscape was filled with the sound and smell of dirtbikes. There was no way to tell where it was coming from, so I picked an entrance at random. I walked; the minutes mounted. I started to worry—say Harry had done it, and when I confronted him, he tried to finish the job. I'd be trapped in this bloody hedge! He'd know the layout, I wouldn't. I wouldn't be able to escape. Perspiring freely, I fondled the pepper spray I'd bought at a 7-11 on the drive over.

Another dead end. This was hopeless. I looked up at the nearest monk. "Where the hell is Harry? And don't you dare say 'Everywhere.'"

He just smiled, and then fell over.

On and on I tromped, tripping occasionally over ground churned uneven by motorcycles. My bad knee was killing me. This was so like Harry; he was always making me jump through hoops, as if I had to prove, or pay for, something. It was one thing to be the "lost child" playing hard-to-get, it was another thing to be a git.

When I got tired of hating Harry, I switched to Swami Roger. I hadn't been lying to that monk, I knew all the dirt on "the Blessed One." When we'd gone to India, one of the first things Fraulein ever did for me was send a file on the Swami, you know, to keep me from making a fool of myself in public. That didn't work, but I was amused to discover that Roger was a ex-Coldstream Guardsman with a slight criminal record who used to run a psychedelic merkin shop on the King's Road. (It was called "The Electric Bush.") When I went to confront Swami Roger with his sordid past, I found he wasn't a creature of pure energy, either. He was sitting on the loo! I never told Harry that.

But I could've now—there Harry stood, in racing leathers, astride his bike. "You bastard," I said, out of breath. "You were driving away from me, weren't you?"

"I thought you could use the exercise." There was that Greasby sense of humor again, reminding me why I left.

I leaned on my knees and tried to keep my lungs in their proper place, behind my throat. "Some of us have been shot, fuckwit."

Flipping down the kickstand, he pulled off his helmet and shook out his hair. Harry's long face grew more and more mournful as the years passed—he looked like an undertaker too tenderhearted for the job. "Your arms are red. You should get out of the sun."

"Thanks, Timothy White. I have a quick question for you, then I will." I pulled the "Maps of the Stars" out of my back pocket and fanned myself. Then I asked, casually, so as not to detonate Harry's prodigious temper, "I'm investigating my murder. Tell me, man to man: did you try to have me killed?"

Harry laughed. "You're just finding out about this now?"

"Finding out about what?"

"Everybody's known for years. It was in that horrible biography of you, the one that said you were a poof."

"Wait wait wait wait—what?"

"Swami Roger, blessed be his soul, asked me to 'have you removed.' He said you were hurting the movement."

"Wow." Asking the question and getting the answer were two totally different feelings. "I can't believe it. You really had me shot in 1980?"

"1980? No! This was in '69, after you said the Blessed One was 'full of shit,'" Harry said. "I begged off. I told him that everybody from our hometown has a weird sense of humor. You *were* kidding, weren't you?"

"Oh, yeah," I lied. "Just popping off, you know how I do."

"People who go on David Frost can't just 'pop off.' You never learned that." Harry slapped his helmet back on. "I can't believe you'd think I'd actually kill you."

"Then I won't tell you about the pepper spray in my pocket."

"See how happy wealth and fame makes everyone?" He kickstarted his bike. "You know the way out."

"No! No!" I shouted. "I can't take any more walking! I'll die in here." He shut the engine off again. "Please don't be offended, Harry. I'm asking everybody."

"And what is everybody saying?"

"That I'm crazy. But Thigg *was* hypnotized—"

"Did you talk to Ollie? What did he say?"

"He thinks you did it." A little lie, to give Harry one last chance to confess.

Harry snorted. "You two deserve each other. The wind blows and you both think somebody pushed you." He started the bike. "Get on."

Back at the house, Harry and I cleared the air over iced tea made of tofu. I drank it. He just took deep breaths.

"What's your beef with me, anyway, Harry? I made you rich."

"You were the one that wanted to be rich, Tom. I just wanted to get laid. Actually, I didn't even know what I wanted. But it wasn't what I got.

"Then when I met Swami Roger, blessed be his name"—Harry blew a kiss to the portrait on the wall, there was one in every room—"I realized that the things of this world were merely distractions. Wealth, power, the love of woman, all these appetites must be overcome if the soul is to be purified. Thanks to you and your little rock band, I live in a world of endless temptation."

I held up my thumb and forefinger.

"What's that?"

"World's smallest sitar, playing the saddest raga in the world. So give it all away."

Harry shook his head. "Even then I'd still be famous, lusted after…"

"Not *that* lusted after."

My ex-bandmate pointed at some monks digging a flowerbed. "Those blokes've got it easy, they don't know what they're missing. I did hate you, Tom, for the gilded cage you led me into."

"I'm still waiting for the part where you convince me you didn't have me shot."

"Haven't you been listening? What's the point of purifying my soul if…" He paused, then: "I *couldn't* have you killed, Tom. My karma couldn't take it."

Had anyone else said that to me, I would've considered it a pretty weak alibi. But since it was Sri Thompson, I believed it. I swirled the ice in my drink. "Well, Harry, I'm certainly sorry for what I did to you. Next life around, I promise to get Clapton."

Harry laughed. A monk appeared and Harry stood up. "Sorry, Tom. Time for my shiatsu."

"I didn't think you breatharians had to bother with that."

"Very funny. Would you like to stay for dinner? Fellini is coming over. He wants to do *Autobiography of a Yogi*."

"That is tempting." I liked the movies Harry produced, when they weren't too preachy.

"If you're worried, I think he can keep a secret."

I poked a forearm; it went white, then flushed angry pink. "Some other time. When I'm not parbroiled."

Harry walked me through the cool, dark house. When we got to the front door, he asked, "Are you going to ask Buck?"

"Of course," I said. "I wouldn't want to hurt his feelings. Do you think he could've done it?"

"Doubt it," Harry said. "The only time Buck ever gets mad is last call. But you know how it is in the mystery books. The person you least suspect, is always the one."

"Shit," I said. "I was hoping you could save me plane fare."

"There are worse places to go than Bermuda. When you get back, come and see me. I'll make Ayurvedic pizza and we'll watch some rushes."

"If Buck doesn't kill me, sure."

"Don't even joke."

"Who's joking?"

Buck still lived in the house he'd bought twenty years before with the proceeds from our first movie. Like most drummers, he was a simple man. But like most successful drummers, Buck's life had become quite complicated.

For one thing, where did Derek Richmond end and Bucky Rich begin? I used to know, or think I did, but not anymore; you can only inhabit an image for so long before it starts changing places with your soul. Another complication was three ex-wives, perhaps four by now. Paying all of them, plus the children sired along the way, kept Buck scrambling a bit. But he handled it all with calm good humor—he called the alimony "rich guy tax" and didn't take it out on the children. Except in rare cases, Buck didn't take things personally. Consequently, he'd stayed out of court better than the rest of us.

People complained about Buck's musicianship, as if that had been the point. You want perfect time, go buy a fucking metronome. Without Buck, there might not have been a Ravins. It was Buck—steady, encouraging, gently deflating, easy to laugh, always a friend—who'd been the common ground. Whatever was going on between Ollie, Harry and I, the path to Buck was always open, and through him, you could reach the others. Buck starred in most of my fondest memories. Buck was the one I had the most fun with, and that held true even on this grim errand.

We were sitting in the basement of his mansion outside Hamilton, in the room he'd had made into a snug. In the corner was a jukebox full of rockabilly 45s, and memorabilia all over the walls. It was lovely, the kind of macho hideaway Fraulein would never let me have. "Sure I can't interest you in a pint?"

"No thanks, Derek. Like I said, I don't drink anymore."

"Mind if I have another?"

"Certainly not." Buck worked the pump behind the bar. Was that five or six? I'd lost count. Buck being buzzed might make my question go down easier—or it might turn things ugly. You never knew with booze. I felt in my jacket pocket. Had I brought that pepper spray?

Buck saw me groping around and accused me of having crabs. "Remember that *fille* in Marseille? The one whose knickers came down by themselves?"

"It was like a bloody flea circus," I grumbled warmly.

"Cost about the same." Buck came back around and sat beside me. Perched on my stool, I looked about the room, remembering the time when to have your own pub, in the basement of your own house, had been our idea of Nirvana. Buck had christened it The Tom and Snare, for obvious reasons—but I had insisted that the painted sign above the bar show a cat hanging by a rope. Buck and I had wordplay in common. I did it on command, whereas he got transmissions from some distant, oblong planet.

"So why aren't you imbibing anymore?"

"Only half a liver," I said. "I have to make it last."

"I'd lend you some of mine but you don't want it," Buck joked. "Half a liver, is that from your...accident?"

"Nothing accidental about it. Matter of fact, it's looking less and less accidental every day." I told him about Thigg, and the séance, and Warren.

"And you're investigating it? Shit, I'd be running in the other direction." He studied his pint glumly. "But people like me don't have to worry about things like that."

"Thank Christ you don't."

"Easy for you to say, Mr. Father-of-the-Sixties."

"Are you serious? Really? Let me show you exactly what you missed." I pulled up my shirt, and showed Buck my corset. "See this? I wear it to keep my guts from falling out. Want to see what's underneath?"

"No."

"Good, because it's uglier than the Devil's nethers, you tit."

Buck didn't say anything. I suddenly remembered his melancholy side.

It always surprised me, how quickly he could turn morose. When we'd first made it, some Lunchtime O'Booze had described him as looking like "the illegitimate offspring of a Baronet and a basset hound." That stuck in Buck's head for some reason, and it took a mountain of Aussie minge to put him right.

"Put your shirt down before I vomit," he said. "I didn't mean to belittle what you've gone through, Tom. It's hard to be the World's Luckiest Man. Sometimes I get fed up."

"Fed up enough to have me shot?"

I saw Buck's pint slip before he caught it. "Who told you that? Carol?"

"Nobody told me anything." Buck wasn't looking at me, but I slid off my stool, just to be safe. "What would my ex-wife tell me, Derek?"

"I called some gangsters once."

"Fuckin' hell! You called a gangster to have me shot?"

"Nothing came of it."

"Oh, that's all right then!"

Buck looked up. "I'm sorry, Tom."

I didn't say anything. I walked over to where Buck's O.B.E. was hanging; it was closer to the door. "I'm telling the Queen on you," I said. What a nest of vipers my band had turned out to be. That's the thing about great wealth; it magnifies all of you, not just the good parts. "I just talked to Harry, and he said Smarmi Roger wanted me dead in 1969."

"I thought about it in '68. Remember when I left the group?"

I did—those sessions were a bitch. We couldn't even agree on what to name the LP, so we called it "Untitled" and made up an excuse after.

"I was sick of everybody telling me I couldn't drum, that I'd gotten everything off you and Ollie."

"Did I say that?"

"You didn't have to," Buck said, the hurt surprisingly fresh in his voice. "I remember doing two hundred and fifty takes of some bullshit heroin song of yours. Then when I went to move my car, you let Katrinka have a bash. On *my* kit! She couldn't even hold the sticks, and you called her a 'genius.'"

"I was in love, mate."

"Yeah, at my expense!" Buck said. "What did I ever do to deserve that?"

I didn't know what to say.

"I got drunk and called up one of the Kray brothers, Ronnie I think, or Gareth. Was there a Gareth Kray? Doesn't seem very gangster-y, does it? Maybe he was compensating."

"What happened after that?"

"Nothing. The guy just laughed at me. 'Sleep it off, Derek,'" Buck said bitterly. "Then I came back, and you all treated me like a king. Baba au rhums, carton of Rothmans, an Iso Griffo, the works. But believe me, Tom. I was serious. I would've done it."

"I can tell." I was poleaxed. Ollie, sure, Harry, maybe, but Buck—I never would've guessed. "Were you ever going to say anything?"

"It's a bit embarrassing." Buck took another swig. "I was going to kill Ollie, too, if that makes you feel any better."

"Well, no one can say you're not thorough." I moved back to my stool, strangely reassured. "But that was '68, right? The thing in 1980 with Thigg, you had nothing to do with that?"

"Oh, no. I give you my word. I don't have the money to hire hitmen. With what I pay every month to the Three Witches?" The alcohol gave Buck a delayed regret. "I shouldn't call them that," he sighed. "They're the only expenses I've ever loved."

The jukebox let out a yodel. It was The Fendermen doing "Muleskinner Blues." Suddenly, Buck and I were laughing, like we always did.

"I'm sorry, Tom. Forgive me?"

"Sure." We hugged, awkwardly but sincerely, like a couple of dancing bears. Northern men are like that. Maybe things are better now, less repressed. As it was, Buck could only take a couple of seconds. Pushing me away he said, "Fancy a game of Aunt Sally? Or pinball? I have some fruit machines, too."

"Anything you want." We played the games for a bit, trying to restore equilibrium. Then we prodded at the jukebox, which had just come back from the shop. “I had to send it all the way to California.”

“Pity, I could’ve delivered it to you.” I looked over the selection. “I see you have both kinds of music, country and western.”

“Bloody Townshend wrecked it.” Buck did his impression: “‘Where’s Roy Acuff? I demand Roy Acuff!’ Peter Dennis Blandford Townshend and brandy do not mix.”

We went back to the bar. As Buck poured himself another, I swiped a pickled egg.

“Nice one,” Buck said, sitting down. “Did the bartender see you?”

“Nah.” I gave him a piece.

“Ta, mate.”

We sat on our stools, listening to Hank Williams. Buck chewed. “This isn’t so bloody awful, is it? I never understood what everybody’s problem was with it.”

“With what?

“Getting the band back together. Why did you leave, anyway?”

“Wasn’t meant to be permanent, just wanted to knock Ollie down a peg. Then…one thing led to another.”

“Story of life.” Buck said. He looked around. “Why do we always come here?”

I laughed again, thinking he was joking, but he wasn’t.

“Don’t like this poncey place…” Buck growled, then his face lit up. “Hey,” he whispered. “Let’s pinch summat.”

“All right,” I said, sliding off my stool. “Time for Derek to go beddy-bye.”

“Nah, nah, nah—” He stood up. “Whoa. I *am* pissed.” We started to walk. “You know what I would do if I were you?”

“Lean on me so you don’t fall over.”

“The séance people. They’re the cooley boners.”

“The cooley boners? Oh right,” I said. “Already ahead of you. I’m checking them, first thing when I get back.”

Buck stumbled into the doorjamb, then apologized to it. “Where are the séance people?”

"Skulking round LA somewhere. Along with all the other nutty religions."

"'S decent of 'em," Buck said.

"Huh?"

"If they kill you, at least you won't have to travel for the funeral."

CHAPTER ELEVEN

I didn't sleep on the flight back west. Ever since I'd been shot, I felt like flying was tempting Fate. Intellectually I knew that if anything were to happen thirty thousand feet up, there's no reason being awake would be better. But somehow I couldn't bear the idea of being asleep if it did.

I wasn't always such a nervous flyer—just the opposite, in fact. I remember one night, Harry and I were standing on this tiny little airstrip, like the ones drug dealers use, only there weren't any of those in East Bumfuck, Iowa, in 1965. Ollie and Buck were off in the corn, finishing a joint we'd started. It was night, and cold, and we were huddled next to this beat-up Cessna, which didn't look like it could fly ten feet, much less the 450 miles between us and our next gig. Without thinking Harry leaned against the plane, and some piece of it broke off in his hand. We fell about laughing. After we were airborne, we threw it in Buck's lap, and everybody got the cruelies again. Part of that was the pot, but part was—back then, the four of us lived in a nimbus of luck, and knew it, and took it for granted. We were fucking invulnerable, invincible, inevitable. That's how we could do what we did. But things were different in 1985. Whatever else Thigg meant—and I was starting to think he meant plenty—he was proof positive that God no longer took special care of Ravins.

So when I saw that my front door was open, my first impulse was to run. Then I spied the bulbous black Ford lurking across the street. It looked old—old enough to be Pompadour? I wasn't sure, so I stayed put. I slid my leather carryon to the floor silently, and listened.

How the hell had they found me? Before going to see Buck, I'd gotten these new digs, a sublet off Main Street. I still had my rooms at the Marisol, and two weeks before that, had hired some at the Georgian, too. All fake names, all done through New York. The plan was to use these three addresses more or less randomly. Now I was blown.

Or was I? Over the pulse pounding in my ears, I heard a faint rustling, then a muffled profanity. If the voice had been low, I think I would've turned tail and taken my chances with the Ford, but because it was higher register, I decided to investigate. "Sexist from birth," as Fraulein might say.

I crept inside, closing the door softly behind me; if the intruder had friends, I didn't want them sneaking up from the rear. Then I walked through the living room, doorway to doorway, timing my movements to the sounds. The tinny shriek of a cheap metal clothes hanger told me that the intruder was rifling through my stuff.

"Thank god," I thought. "It's only a robber." That's how bizarre my life had become: anything less than a bona-fide assassin, and I felt ahead of the game. On my way through the den, I grabbed a samurai sword out of my elephant's foot umbrella stand. Since we couldn't go out, we bought all manner of daft shit on tour, and Japan had been especially bad on both counts. The sword still had a nick on the end, where I'd attempted to perform *seppuku* on my Rickenbacker.

I held the three-foot blade out in front of me, trying not to feel stupid. Passing my priceless Duchamp ready-made (the robber clearly didn't know art), I stepped into the bedroom. The sounds were coming from inside my walk-in closet, and the painted bamboo curtain shimmied incriminatingly. As I was thinking of something suitably tough to say, one of my motorcycle boots came flying out. I knocked it aside with the sword, feeling my inner Mifune—then the other one clocked me right in the noggin, and I got pissed off.

"Come out of there right now and you won't get hurt!"

The intruder screamed, and pulled a clothes rack down trying to get up.

With the tip of the sword I pushed the curtain open.

My daughter Helen swam up from under a pile of Hawaiian shirts. "Dad! What the *fuck?*"

"I thought you were a burglar."

"I mean with the shirts. Go to a lot of luaus?"

"Tacky throws people off. Let me help you up."

Brushing herself off, Helen emerged from the closet in a headscarf, some ancient jeans of mine, and my old WABC "Good Guys" sweatshirt.

"Smart," I said. "Burgle in the victim's clothes, so you don't leave evidence."

"If I was a burglar, I'd just take the Duchamp." I didn't doubt it; Helen was 23, and slowly but surely working her way through the Edinburgh College of Art. I probably should've mentioned our relationship before now, but what can I say? I'm a self-obsessed 45-year-old crispy-brained rockstar and, though I'd never say so to Helen, she does tend to slip my mind now and then. And when I say "now and then," I mean "about 85% of the time." It was nothing personal, but I couldn't blame her for feeling like it was.

"Where have you been?" she demanded. "My plane got in at ten. I waited there for an hour, then came here and picked the lock."

Bloody boarding schools, I thought. "I don't know whether to be proud or appalled. What are you doing in my closet?"

"Exercising *droit de fille.* Can I have this?" Helen dug into the pile and pulled out a heavy beaded jacket.

"That's Buck's actually. He wore it during a TV show." Not just any TV show: the first-ever worldwide satellite hookup, and the last Ravins session before Clive disappeared and everything went to shit. "*This is a Love Song for the World,*" I sang. "*It's easy as breathing if you want it to be.*"

"I should probably give it back to him," I said.

"Please?"

"Oh, all right." I couldn't say no to Helen, not after saying nothing but no for twenty years. But I'd have to grow a pair quickly, because the last thing I needed right then was a houseguest. I itched to get back on the hunt, and had a vague feeling my time was running out. "Helen, don't take this the wrong way, but why are you here?"

"You don't know? Really? For fuck's sake!" She threw the jacket on to the bed. "It's my birthday week, Dad. We talked about this months ago."

"Oh, right." Months ago was pre-Crouk, pre-Warren, pre- all of this. "Sorry."

"Jerk."

Not only had I stepped in it, I'd lost whatever small chance there'd been to send her home with our relationship intact. "Helen, I've had a lot on my mind."

"What? Retirement? *Knots Landing*?"

"Don't be cheeky."

"It's this mysterious thing you're doing. The 'project.'"

My silence was assent.

"I don't think it's good for you, Dad. I wish you'd tell me about it. Let me help."

"Absolutely not." Even the idea made me want to vomit. If I told her it was dangerous, she'd freak, but if I told her it was boring, she'd be offended. So I did the only thing I knew how to do: I threw money at the problem. "Let's not talk about that now. How did you know I was living here?"

"I called Ollie."

"Ah, right." She and Ollie had always been buddies. "I need you to scram for an hour, while I check on some birthday arrangements."

"Don't lie," Helen scoffed. "There are no arrangements. You totally forgot."

"I'm not lying," I lied, pulling her off the bed. "Go on, there's a coffeeshop just up the road."

"I don't drink coffee."

"And you call yourself an art student. Tea, then." I launched her towards the door; it was like pushing a noodle.

"Can't believe this," Helen pouted. "You weren't at the airport, I waited for you all day, and as soon as you come home, you throw me out."

"I'm not throwing you out. It will be worth your while, I promise." I peeled off a ludicrous amount of money and stuffed it into her paint-stained pink palm. "Now give me a hug." We hugged and she left. Ten seconds later, I stuck my head out the window. "Are you wearing sunscreen?"

"Yes, Dad," she lied.

"Fine, learn the hard way, like I did. And get me a quintuple shot. But make sure it's organic!"

Two minutes later, I flipped open an *LA Times*, and seven minutes after that, had purchased a largeish sailboat, okay a yacht really, from the classifieds. Some bond trader had had a bad month and I got it for cheap. Well, not that cheap—but I'd think of something to tell Fraulein. I'd tell her I'd had a butt-tuck. That would please her actually. She'd always thought I had a dumpy rear-end.

When Helen came back, she announced that instead of coffee or tea, she'd gotten a tattoo. Not for the first time I thanked God Helen's mother didn't know I was alive. "Carol's going to love that," I said.

"Could be worse. Now she doesn't have to worry about my becoming an Orthodox Jew."

"Was that a possibility?"

"I'm your daughter," Helen said, kissing my bald pate. "*Everything* is a possibility."

Did I ever tell you why the tabloids decided I was Thigg's long-lost pop? The chords in his dopey little song. Somebody looking for a story noticed they spelled out "B-A-D D-A-D." Thigg read that and thought, "Yeah, *that's* why I did it. I guess. Maybe?"

Ever since then I've had a bit of a complex. Billions of shitty fathers in the world, and I'm the one who gets shot for it. How is that fair? Mind you, Thigg was right. I was a "bad dad," but not to him, or Jasper—to Helen.

When I was a young guy, before I became a mythological beast, I married a local girl, as young guys in my world did. And as nature forces nurture, Carol and I had a kid. We named her after my mother Helena, minus Mum's scarlet "A." Two weeks after Helen was born, however, The Ravins notched our first American number one. Fantastic for my career, not so great for my family.

My whole life, I'd wanted to get out of Greasby. I got my wish—at the price of a wife and kid trailing after me like toilet paper on my shoe. A bad situation all around, but as usual the kid suffered most. Carol could get her own back in all the classic ways: criticism, withholding sex, buying couture. Helen couldn't do anything but cry and wonder why Dada was such a foul-mouthed, evil-tempered git.

And I was—you'd think the world's adoration would be enough, but you'd be wrong. I needed my wife to be totally focused on me, as well. Maybe it was because my mum left when I was small. Maybe it was because I tend towards arseholism. Whatever the reason, I'm not proud of it.

Helen was six when I split and moved in with Katrinka. Every once in a while, I'd try to talk with her, but it would feel awkward so I'd quit. Even at my most bloated and syncophant-encrusted, I knew this wasn't fair to Helen, and I felt bad, which made me avoid her, which compounded the hurt…What a cock-up. I wouldn't have even tried to reconnect if Jasper hadn't brushed me off first. But my new life was lonely. I needed someone. I needed family.

So in 1983, when I was still holed up on Brigadoon, I dialed Helen for the first time in five years. I know, calling's a bit cold and strange, but I couldn't do it in person. For one thing, I didn't want Carol to know I was alive. Katrinka was convinced my ex-wife would blow my cover out of spite. I wasn't so sure, but security wasn't the only reason I used the phone. I'm not good with emotions, especially when I'm in the wrong. If Helen started yelling at me, I could hang up or run into another room or something.

"Hello, Helen, this is your father. I'm alive, and I want to know you again."

"Whoever this is, I don't find it funny."

"I'm not joking. It's really me. I love you, don't you love me?"

Silence.

"How can I prove it's really me, Helen? What can I do?"

"Calling up out of the blue expecting adoration is a bloody wonderful start. Only you would be so arrogant. But you're still dead, Dad. You've been dead since 1969." In other words, since I'd married Katrinka. Katrinka had insisted on as little contact as possible—my wife slightly resents that I existed before she came along. She considers it impudent. "Does Queen Beryl even know you're calling me?" "Queen Beryl" was Helen's nickname for der Fraulein.

"No."

"So you've finally escaped the Negaverse then. Good for you."

"I hate it when you say stuff I don't understand. Comic books have rotted your mind."

"Now you're telling me what to do. This just gets better and better."

"Ahh, fuck, I'm sorry, Helen," I said. "I'm sorry for everything."

"Prove it."

So that's what I did. I wooed her for *years*, writing her letters, sending her things I thought she'd like. The first couple were awful (A bat house? Omaha steaks? What was I thinking?), but I got better at it as time passed. I began to learn who she really was—not as a six-year-old, or a reflection of me, but as herself. My gifts got more extravagant as I zeroed in, and this caused a few problems. The Christmas before I discovered Helen in my closet, I got her a car.

"It's lovely, Dad. But what do I tell Mum?"

"Come clean," I said. "Admit you're a drug dealer." My ex needed to loosen up. She was so tense she used to get hair-aches. "Tell her you need *help*. That ought to be good for a week's worth of pampering, at least."

Helen laughed. "Don't ever tell Mum you're alive, okay? I want to keep you to myself."

That's why I couldn't send Helen home, no matter how much I wanted to move forward with the case. For the first time ever, we were actually *friends*. A month before Crouk showed up, we were talking about her getting a place in LA—that's what this trip was really about. Now my investigation made that level of contact hazardous to Helen's health. How the fuck could I explain that, without explaining everything? I tried not to think about it.

The morning of Helen's 24th birthday, I took her out to breakfast at Cora's Coffee Shop, which she liked. Then I drove her down to Chace Park, in Marina del Rey. I played it cool, like we were just seeing the sights. She and I were walking along the slip, cataloguing the daft things people name their boats, when I stopped and pointed. "Now there's a pretty craft. As fine as any in the Auld Reekie."

"Which?"

"The one with the blue stripe. 'Knot Me.'"

"Don't much like the name," Helen said.

"So change it."

"What do you mean?"

"It's yours. You own it, if you want it."

Helen's mouth fell open. "Wow, Dad. I don't know what to say."

"You don't like it."

"It's very generous. But what am I supposed to do, park it in the Firth of Forth?"

"Artists don't need school."

"I don't know how to sail."

"That's the best part—I do!" I'd started learning in my previous life, and learned more on Brigadoon, the better to annoy all the fishermen. "I'll teach you. Then we can sail around together, just you and me."

"Really?" Helen and I hugged. When she did it, it never hurt.

"Really. As soon as I finish this project."

I felt my daughter crumple in my arms. "I know I've said that before—"

"A million times!"

"This time it's important, Helen. It's not some career bullshit."

"But you won't tell me about it."

Because I don't want you to end up like Warren. "I'll tell you the whole story when it's over, promise…If you don't like the boat, I'll sell it. I've outfitted it so you can sleep aboard while you're here, to get a feel. We can sail it together, or I can teach you and you can go off by yourself. You can be totally free." I wondered if she heard the envy in my voice.

Helen put on a figuring expression, the same look she used the first time Carol had given her spaghetti. "If I lived on it, I could stay near you, without blowing your cover. There'd be nothing fishy about that, a spoiled daughter of a dead rock star living on a yacht. Throwing wild parties, waggling her titties at paparazzi…"

"Since when are you spoiled?"

"Are you kidding?" Helen said. "First a car, now a boat—at this rate, I'll be in rehab by Christmas."

I laughed. "I see your point. I guess it would be okay. Except for the titties part."

"Prude."

Driving back to Main Street to get her stuff, I discovered what had been my motivation all along. If Pompadour or someone like him came for me, my daughter would be two miles away, safe as houses, someplace only she and I knew about. It was brilliant. My subconscious has always been much smarter than I am.

Helen stayed for the rest of that week, and for most of her visit, it was almost as if my life was normal again. Every shadow stopped looking like a hitman; classic cars stopped prowling my dreams. I suddenly realized how wonderful my quiet little pre-Crouk existence had been. A melancholy thought, under the circumstances. I tried not to show it, though.

Helen and I made the rounds of the local galleries and museums: Bergamot Station, the Getty, the Huntington, the Hammer. She'd heard about a bit of inspired madness called the Museum of Jurassic Technology, and we enjoyed that afternoon immensely. We watched movies and sat on the beach and went to dinner. She told me about men she was seeing, and I told her about books I was reading.

We had a lovely visit—but it wasn't always easy. For one thing, Helen was a little heavier than I thought was strictly healthy, and for another, she didn't wash her hands nearly enough. Then there was her haircut. I tried not to stare, but one morning she caught me.

"Honestly, you of all people have no right to get exercised."

"Who's exercised?" It was completely absurd, all jagged edges, two-toned with an irritating flop of chestnut bang slouching over one eye. "I haven't said a word."

"You don't have to. You're cocking your nostrils."

"I'm what?"

She shot me a look full of ill-hidden disdain.

I felt my features, rearranging them into an alibi. "Paranoia runs in the family," I carped into my paper.

Helen walked over, and before I knew what was happening, I was in excruciating pain. "Ow! Let go of my ear!"

"Say it, you big hypocrite. Mr. Honesty, Mr. Truth-to-Power."

"Those are just bloody songs—OW!" After a final twist, she released me. I rubbed the raw appendage and grumbled, "Hair is wasted on the young."

In case you're wondering, Helen and I looked alike, but not so much that either of us was in danger (or so I told myself). She had that beaky Larkin nose, the price of admission, but it was modulated by her mother's soft, kind eyes and more determined chin. She was a better-looking version of me. I realize all fathers think that, but every time we went outside together, the men of Southern California ogled their unanimous agreement. As a result, we both traveled incognito, me in my usual get up of Hawaiian shirts, chinos and a panama hat, her in a kerchief and big sunglasses.

"*Trés* LA," I said.

"We try," she said.

Her penultimate day, we were walking down the Venice boardwalk, dining *al fresco* on Jody Maroni's sausages. The weather was beautiful, the people just as, and I was in such a mellow mood that I suspected a contact high.

"Nah," Helen said, "it's just the pork fat."

"Me, eating sausages. Fraulein would shit."

Helen laughed. "Exactly why you should. She needs to loosen up. Besides, the fat lubricates your insides."

A middle-aged blonde heading in the other direction suddenly reached out and grabbed Helen's arm. I wish fans wouldn't do that.

"I know you!" she said, in a thick Aussie accent. "You're Helen Larkin, aren't you? Tom's daughter?"

Helen shot me a look: Seem okay? I gave a tiny nod.

"Guilty as charged," my daughter said.

"I knew it!" She looked at her husband. "He didn't believe me. We know who the brains are in this family, don't we?"

The blonde's husband stood there uselessly. When our eyes met, he smiled please-excuse-my-wife. I could only spare him a fraction of a second. I was reading the situation, ready to go.

"So what are you doing in L.A., Helen? Soaking up the sunshine?"

"A bit, yeah. And I got a tattoo." She pulled up her pants leg, to show the circle of barbed wire around her calf. (When I expressed dismay at the commonness of the motif, Helen informed me that, on her, it was meant ironically.)

"Barbed wire, isn't that nice?" The woman didn't like it—but who was she to disagree with celebrity spawn? "We're only here for two days, then on to Vegas for Peter's convention. I hope you won't mind my saying, but it was such a terrible shame about your father. I still think about him."

Heartfelt message delivered, she noticed me "Who's your friend, here? Oh, don't tell me, you look so familiar—"

"I'm David Bowie," I said.

"Of course!" She hit me on the arm, playfully. "I told you not to tell. Peter, hand me my purse." Receiving it, she rooted around, telling Helen in a commanding voice, "You stay right there. Don't move."

More rooting—then the sun glinted off a short metal tube. I saw it sticking out of the woman's hand. It was pointing towards Helen's face. Instinctively, I lunged, seizing the fan's wrist. The woman stumbled backwards, shocked, and the object fell to the ground. It was a lipstick.

Her husband grabbed my shoulders and shoved me back. "Are you barmy, David? What's the idea of grabbin' on my wife?"

"I'm really very sorry. I—"

"You think just because you're a big star, you can push people around?"

The blonde massaged her paw. "That hurt. I've a mind to sue you!"

"Please don't," I said weakly, imagining the hell that would break loose. One wrong move, and here I was at the whim of a couple of tourists. "Please. I didn't mean any harm." A few people were stopping now. I think the legal term is "witnesses."

Just as things looked ready to spin out of control, Helen stepped in. "Please forgive David," she said. "He's taking some medication that make him impulsive. Plus"—she leaned in to share a secret—"he's a little overprotective of me, after what happened to my father."

"He thought—how ridiculous—do I look like…?"

Helen smiled sweetly, and kept smiling until the Aussies' indignation cooled. A few autographs did wonders for the woman's injury, much to the dismay of the human seagulls that had been drawn by the commotion.

As Helen played to her public, I quick-stepped away, darting into a bar directly to our right, then walking through to Speedway Street on the other side. I walked about a block north, then headed back left, towards the boardwalk. I went into a sunglass shop, which opened on both sides of a corner, then hid behind a pile of novelty boogieboards, waiting for my daughter to walk by. When she did, I sauntered out and matched her stride, as if nothing had happened.

"You handled that well," I said.

"It's the genes. Why Bowie of all people?"

"Old, English, rocker…But I could've said Abraham Lincoln. Fans get flustered."

"They're not the only ones, apparently. Are you okay? Want to go home?"

"Why would I want to go home?"

"It's all right, Dad. I'm not judging."

I stepped in some warm bubblegum. After I finished swearing, I said, "You think you can read people, and then you're wrong one time, and you jump at shadows for the rest of your life."

"Don't be so hard on yourself."

"No," I said firmly, "I'm going to be, and you should be, too. Remember, Helen, the key is to move. Always keep moving, and trust your instincts. That's how Thigg…I couldn't get a read on him. He wasn't like normal fans. He was cold, like a reptile, like a robot."

"What do you mean?"

"Ah, shit, forget I said it."

"I *thought* that's what this project was. So it wasn't a crazy fan after all?"

"No comment."

"You sure I can't help?"

"Positive."

"All right Secret Squirrel. Be super-careful, yeah?"

"Let's talk about something else. I want to enjoy our last 24 hours together."

We walked on. My daughter bought sunglasses, and I bought some SPF 45, which I forced her to use. At Charly Tremmel's we got two ice creams. A pack of women in bikinis strolled across our field of vision, followed by a guy on roller skates playing a Stratocaster.

"You remember that time you came to visit me here, back when I was famous?" I asked. "How old were you then? Nine? Ten?"

"Twelve. That was the same year Ollie got me the cockatiel. Lasted two weeks before Mum's dog killed it."

I laughed. Carol was always taking in nasty-tempered beasts. "Maybe we should go visit Ollie in Bel-Air. Shit!" Some of my hazelnut ice cream bounced off my leg and onto the blacktop. "Can we sit? I'm not coordinated enough to eat and walk at the same time."

"Is that from your injuries?"

"No, it's from my forty-fiveness."

Helen and I sat and watched the world go by, or a version of the world at least. The scene at the Venice boardwalk is pretty unbuttoned. "I think we sat on this very bench, back then."

"Yeah?" Helen said. "All I remember is a guy snorted coke right in front of me."

"Ah, 1974. Did I get you the hell out of there, like any sane parent would have?"

"No. You just made a joke. You spread your arms out like this, and said, 'Someday, Helen, all this will be yours.' Then we went to see the Smothers Brothers at The Troubadour."

"God, it's hard to be old. You see all your flaws and have to keep living anyway."

"Oh, you're not *so* flawed," Helen smiled. "Nobody died."

CHAPTER TWELVE

The next day, Helen's last, I showed up at the Knot Me around 8 a.m. I got exactly the reception I expected, which is why I'd brought coffee.

"Now I understand why you drink this swill," my daughter mumbled, her bunk belowdecks a tangle of sheets. "You get up too bloody early."

"Stop complaining and drink your octoshot."

Helen's flight left LAX at 4:30. One part of me longed to break all the clocks in the world. Another part wanted to drive her to the airport immediately, and handcuff her to her gate. That way, she'd be safe and I could get back to work. "What's the matter, didn't you sleep well? The sound of the waves hits me like a knock-out drop."

"So you sleep here." Helen put down her blue paper cup. "I want to know what's going on. What have you discovered?"

"Please, Helen, I can't."

"It's the same old relationship, then. You get to do whatever you like, and I pop in occasionally to make you feel good."

"It's not the same and you know it."

"If you get killed, they'll have won. If you tell me, I can keep fighting."

I tidied and didn't say anything.

"Put down that wastebasket and listen. They can't kill us all. That's all I want to know—who are they?"

I sighed. "I can't tell you."

"Fuck you, Dad!"

"No, I would tell you, but I don't know. All I know is that Thigg was under somebody's control. He had to be." I told Helen about Crouk's visit, and she, like Fraulein, was dubious. So then I told her about the interview, and the tape.

"Maybe he hypnotized himself," Helen said. "You said you used to do that, by looking in a mirror."

"But I didn't go out and plug Elvis did I? If everybody acted like Thigg, there'd be no celebrities left."

"All that means is Thigg was one in a million."

"Try a billion."

"My point is, freaks exist. People become ax murderers. The Yorkshire Ripper."

I shook my head. "Not the same. With serial killers, there's a sexual motive. It's the same basic drive we all have, only twisted. And there's a logic that persists over time. They build up to it. It's a pattern, not just one event.

"None of the motives Thigg gave justifies murder to a normal person, so he had to be really crazy, right? But that kind of ga-ga craziness wasn't present in his behavior, before or after. Before, he had a job, a wife, a life. After, he was a model inmate. Thigg was only insane for that one moment, leading to that one outcome. An outcome that didn't benefit him. People don't work like that, dear." I held up some socks. "Clean or dirty?"

"Dirty. Then who did it? The government?"

"Or someone trained by them, some spook on the dole. All you need is a working telephone and a wheelbarrow of money."

Helen made a quick calculation. "You don't think one of my Uncles did it?" (That was her nickname for the other Ravins.)

"Don't worry, you can still accept their Christmas presents. That's where I was last Friday." I shook out the rag rug at the foot of her bed. Helen coughed. "At the risk of ruining an otherwise pleasant visit, what about Queen Beryl?"

"No motive," I said calmly. "She already had my money, and I was willing to share everything else." I could tell Helen wasn't convinced. "Look, I'm trying to be logical. Just because you don't like her—"

"Skip it. If it wasn't someone who knew you, why do it? You were a rock star, not the President."

"Freaks exist," I said. "Why tap my phones? Why have me watched, or try to get me thrown out of the country?"

"All that's loads different from having you shot."

"Is it? Just a different number on the exchange." I ran the liquid soap under hot water, to get the crust off the squirter tube.

"Come on. Murder? It's a lot riskier."

"Tell me, Helen: who got fired when JFC got shot? Or King, or any of 'em? It's always one crazy person, couldn't have been helped—and everybody gets to keep their job."

"And so...?"

"When somebody shoots me, I take it personally. I've suffered. Somebody is going to suffer back."

"Great, Dad. Risk your life over revenge. That always works out well."

"It's not revenge, it's self-preservation. Remind me to get Windex."

"Say you find the bad guys. What then?"

"I don't know, but maybe if people feel some consequences for doing shit like this, it'll finally stop. Get off the bed and let me make it." I pulled the sheets off, then put them back on, tucking in the corners. Just smoothing them like people do is unhealthy. It traps germs. "We gotta quit assuming that there are places the bad guys won't go. We gotta stop thinking they're dumber than we are, or play by our rules, or want what they want *less* than we do, simply because we can't handle the alternative." I threw the pillow back on the bed.

"Have you ever considered working in a hotel?"

"Blame Harriet. Shall we go into the sunlight?"

My daughter trooped up the steps. "Dark life you lead, Pop."

"Not for the last week."

"Occasionally it's not so bad when the condom breaks, eh?"

My head dropped. I once told the readers of *Roogalator* that the only reason Helen existed was a substandard prophylactic. "I am really sorry I said that, Helen. Really, really, very sorry."

She squirted SPF 45 on her arm. "Here's how you can make it up to me: Let's spend today working on the case."

"Aw, Helen, haven't you been listening? These people—they probably *want* to kill you."

"Then I have a right to help, don't I?"

"Helen…"

"I have a *right*, Dad."

I couldn't argue. I could only think of something harmless, boring even. "Okay," I said. "We're going to the library."

The fuzz-faced biddy broadcast a sour little smile. "I'm sorry, sir, only UCLA students are allowed to use the facilities."

"But I—"

"Sorry, sir. That's the policy." Resistance was futile; under that cardigan lurked a whim of iron. I thanked her, and walked back to where Helen was defacing a copy of *ArtForum*. "Guess it's my day to be pushed around by females," I griped.

"Don't lump me in with her," Helen said, scowling faintly. "I bet she wears Old Spice. What's the problem?"

"You have to go here to use the microfilm readers." Why must they make it so hard? Didn't they know I had a thing about authority? No solutions came to mind, other than burning the place down, and that would be a somewhat Pyrrhic victory. "Okay, screw it. Investigation over, let's go get some fro-yo and laugh at the shit in the Hammer." We'd hated the exhibits at the Hammer, but my daughter enjoyed looking at art she despised. It gave her confidence for her own stuff.

"No. Wait here. And no matter what happens, stay cool."

"Wait, what? 'Stay cool'? What are you about to do? Helen—I'm talking to you—"

Helen walked along the outer edge of the room, where cases of reference books alternated with tall, sun-filled windows. When she was far enough away that I would have to shout, she slowed, dragging her finger across some spines with casual focus. What was she doing?

I found out when a student got up and walked away from her stuff. Helen plucked a book from the shelf, then walked the five steps to the vacant seat. Opening the book, she propped it upright, concealing her hands as well as the student's pink LeSportsac. Fifteen seconds later, she got up, put the book back on its shelf, then walked over to where I stood. Cool as could be, she leaned over to tie her shoe. As she did so, she slipped the girl's ID under my left Reebok.

I knelt down, and retrieved the plastic rectangle. "I've sired an arch-fiend."

"Oh stop. What am I looking for?"

"Anything that mentions 'Orange Sunshine LLC.'" Patting her hand, I handed back the ID. "But what if the HMS Bint over there notices you're not LoShandra Jessop?"

"Then, we run."

Sticky-fingers Larkin printed out a whole stack of research before we had to hoof it, but one article in *Fortune* told me all I needed to know. It had been published about eighteen months earlier, and was titled, "Ex-Radical Turns Righteous—and a Profit."

Back in the Sixties, Robbie Illadro had been almost as famous as I was. God knows he worked at it; Robbie would crash anything from a riot to a mildly countercultural briss, as long as there was a camera present. In those days, his rap was revolution (whose wasn't?) but everybody who got close saw that his only real passion was himself. Robbie was to our side what Mayor Daley was to law and order: a walking argument for the alternative. We never liked each other, and when I slugged him backstage at Woodstock, the Sixties were officially over. Sorry. I held off for as long as I could.

Robbie was a twerp—no, he was more dangerous than that. He was a follower pretending to be a leader. Whatever was hip, he became: Free Speech turned into overthrowing the government, overthrowing the government became EST, which turned into health food, which turned into a ponzi scheme called Hempcleanse, and so on. There was a hole where Robbie's self should've been, and he filled it with whatever the media told him to. That's why they loved each other so much.

I thought I had gotten rid of Robbie after leaving my knuckleprints on his neck, but the *Fortune* article told me different. I read it five times, just to be sure: "After Hempclease ran afoul of the FDA in 1979, Illadro poured his profits into a fledgling record label, Titanic Records."

What a coincidence: Titanic had funded my last album.

When Fraulein and I decided to do *Romance, Redux*, we had a lot of trouble finding someone to back us. I was coming off my "extended holiday," but at least I was capital-T Tom capital-L Larkin. Katrinka, on the other hand, was a capital-G genius, but record companies don't want genius, they want Ollie O'Connell, so we were forced to take whatever we could get. I remember when Katrinka called me with Titanic's offer.

"We're going to be King and Queen of a new label, isn't that great?" She was over the moon—I hadn't heard her so happy since they smashed the Red Army Faction. So I didn't ask who was behind it, I did what any good husband would do: "Yes, dear, lovely. Where do I sign?"

The *Fortune* article made Robbie Illadro number one with a bullet, as far as suspects were concerned. *Cui bono?* Him. I'd always known that Titanic had made good money on that last album, but *wow*. It hadn't been selling until I got shot; then it went from nothing to album of the year. The news-driven sales—and a hefty life insurance policy taken out only three weeks before—had made Robbie a very rich man. Too bad it all went up his nose.

So how did this character get into the séance business? After spending a few years in rehab Robbie experienced, in his words, "a spiritual awakening." He founded Grok and Roll, "a diversified concern positioned at the heady nexus of pop culture and religion." Grok and Roll's first subsidiary was

Orange Sunshine, LLC, which, according to *Fortune*, "spreads the good news of the Sixties via spooky evenings with dead rock stars."

"My generation doesn't believe in religion," he told the reporter. "We know that's all fairy tales. What we do believe in is marketing. If you want the values to survive, they have to be embodied in a name brand. Every religion in history proves the way to a profit is a prophet. *Our* prophets are rock musicians who, conveniently for me, all happen to be dead."

Not all of them, Robbie. Inconveniently for you.

Helen and I ate lunch at a Persian joint on Westwood. I was extracting a promise that she would stop living on curry-flavored crisps when she rather abruptly changed the subject. "I thought Robbie Illadro was dead."

"Nope. Nobody is."

"That's a shame. People like him should have an expiration date. Is he friend or foe?"

"Remains to be seen," I said, underplaying my anxiety. "I know he made a pile when I died. And after." I told her about crashing the séance.

"Shit, if this meeting'll be half as fun as that, count me in."

"Do you mind not coming? I'm nervous enough."

"Nervous, like 'danger' nervous?"

"No, nervous like 'Robbie is a creep' nervous. If you walk in the door, he'll find some way to make money off you," I said. "Do me a favor and walk around the neighborhood. I promise to tell you all about it. Don't bite your nails, it's repulsive."

Helen whipped her hand to her lap. "Where is it?"

"On Sunset. There's an Amoeba right across the street."

"You're sure you'll be okay?"

"Yeah. I'll bring my pepper spray."

"Then I'll buy you some decent bloody music." "No more Bing Crosby!" had been Helen's lament throughout the entire visit. What can I say? I have an addictive personality.

After lunch, we got in my car. As we drove through Beverly Hills, I could tell that Helen was chewing on more than just her fingernails. "I know what I can do while you're having your powwow."

"What happened to hanging out at the record store?"

"I've got a better idea. And I'm not letting you go in there without backup."

"Robbie's a shrimp. He grew up eating wheat paste and Spartacist pamphlets. But if he does try anything, I expect you to run like hell, and call my friend Sam."

"Who's Sam?"

"He used to handle security for me and Queen Beryl."

"In other words, the guy who got you shot!"

"Now, now, Sam's all right, my little Amazon," I said. "He's loyal. Trust me, I have good instincts about people."

Helen grunted.

"Did you just grunt at me?"

She grunted again. To coax her back into words I asked, "All right, what's this scheme of yours?"

"It's a project I've been working on. I put a £100 note on the end of a fishing pole, then I went up to the roof of a building, and dangled the money. I trailed it along the sidewalk, trying to get people to chase it."

"Did they?"

"Oh yeah! They'd knock each other down, old ladies would go all aggro and start scrapping—but when they caught the money, they'd always look up and say, 'thank you.' I call it 'fishing for compliments.'"

I laughed. "And you were given credit for this?"

"Hell yes." Helen scratched her nose, which was peeling.

"That sounds like something Fraulein would do. It's a shame you two don't get along."

"It's a shame she's a—"

"Spare me."

"You go compare acid flashbacks, and I'll be up on the roof, exploring the tension between material desires and social conditioning." Before I had a chance to dissuade my daughter, Helen pointed out the window. "Dad, stop! There's a sporting goods store!"

Illadro's office was right down from the Cinerama Dome, a place I hadn't been for thirty years. That's where we'd celebrated Buck's 25th birthday, with a night of home movies projected in 7000 millimeter. For a while, Buck had harbored ambitions of becoming a film director...I wonder what became of that? Being around Ollie and I—or as Harry now calls us, "Celebrity Deathmatch"—probably wasn't good for Buck's self-esteem. Shit, it wasn't even good for mine.

Helen and I sauntered through the lobby and into the elevator unmolested; in this building, security was strictly ornamental. After the doors closed, I affixed a fake beard. "Purely precautionary," I explained. "Everybody knows I'm dead." As I was about to get off, Helen tugged at my chin.

"It was a little crooked."

"Isn't everybody?" I joked. "Don't fall off the roof."

"You worry too much." I used to say the same thing to Harriet.

Grok and Roll, Inc. was at the end of a musty-smelling corridor on a floor of fly-specked suites which could've been in a million buildings in a million different cities. Buzzy fluorescent lights, chipping acoustic tile, rough low-pile industrial carpet, the atmosphere was as utilitarian and tired as a working girl without her makeup. Inside, the reception area reminded me of a dentist's office, as did the bland, sharp-faced blonde sitting at a desk in the corner.

"I'm here to see Mr. Illadro," I said.

"Do you have an appointment?"

"No."

Her smile-covered scorn was pure Hollywood, as native as cactus. "Sir, I'm sorry, we can't—"

I drew a cassette from my pocket. "I have a song he'd like to hear."

"We're not looking for original material." She didn't like me.

"I didn't write it, you ninny. Tom Larkin did."

She liked me even less now, but the magic name was too powerful to ignore. "I'll tell him. Go sit over there."

There were a couple of brown naugahyde couches squatting on either side of a cheap metal coffee table. Plopping down, I held up a three-year-old *National Geographic*. "First tits I ever saw."

"Thanks for sharing."

I laughed, loud enough for her to hear. After all the fucking I've done, chilliness from women amuses me.

Muzak, wood paneling, abstract art that looked like a chimpanzee fight; the whole set-up made my teeth ache. Robbie had the scratch to afford a better place, but was simply too cheap to shell out for it. The only item of any interest was a framed tie-dye shirt, with holes in it and a bit of supposed blood. (Memo to Robbie: blood dries brown, not red.) I went over and examined the label. "Worn at the 1968 Democratic Convention." It always amazes me when ex-hippies celebrate Chicago. Robbie had a right; he got famous. The rest of us got Milton Crouk.

The minutes dragged by like clubbed demonstrators. At one o'clock, the receptionist buzzed her boss. "I'm going to my audition," she told him. "Want me to pick you up something?…Skooby's special…no peppers, no chili on the fries, got it." She hung up and grabbed her purse. On her way out she tossed over her shoulder, "Mr. Illadro'll see you now. Don't take too long, this is his naptime."

A nap sounded good. Seeing Helen had been great, but restful it was not. I went to the door and knocked.

"Come in."

Robbie looked like a million bucks. Actually $2.5 million: that's how much the *Variety* in his waiting room had said he'd snagged for the pay-per-view on his next séance. My chinstrap beard was working; he didn't recognize me. "Have a seat."

Robbie's desk was big enough for a complicated phone, a daybook, a rolodex, and even a few awards—nothing notable, just the sharp-edged Plexiglas shit that guys in suits are forever lobbing back and forth. Clean-shaven with cropped curls, clad in Italy's best pinstripes, the yippie had become a yuppie so thoroughly that I caught myself wondering: which side had he been on, back then? Had *anybody* been what they had seemed?

My plan, such as I had one, was to give Illadro a shock, to reveal myself suddenly and conclusively. How he reacted would tell me all I needed to know. I looked around the office. It was filled with framed pictures of Robbie and I. He must've finagled a photo literally every time we'd met.

"Took that one myself," he lied, pointing at a portrait from the day I got shot. God, I looked like shit. The coke-burn was painful. "Tom and I were close. He told me, 'If anything ever happens to me, promise you'll carry on my work.' I've kept my promise."

I couldn't help but laugh at his unctuousness and presumption, then turned it into a cough with extreme difficulty. "Can I have a glass of water?"

"There's a fountain in the lobby downstairs. What's this about a song?"

I fished the tape from my pocket. Robbie took it and read the label: *13/10/68—Experiment in Peace (Final Edit).* He frowned. "How do I know it's genuine?"

"That's Katrinka Van Weltanschauung's handwriting."

"I doubt it," Robbie said.

Shit—I never thought he wouldn't believe me. I didn't even remember what song it was. I'd just asked Fraulein to send me something unreleased, whatever she thought was appropriate. "So play it," I said. "Do you have a tape deck?"

Robbie rummaged around in his desk and found a small tape player. He popped out a cassette. "I'm learning Mandarin," he said. "I expected the Chinese to keep me out—they've had some bad experiences with Western religions in the past. But they're all for Larkinism, as long as they get to manufacture the t-shirts."

He put the cassette in, and three seconds later, we heard my young voice. "This is called 'A Experiment in Peace.'"

"How much are you asking?"

Before I could answer, the room was filled with car horns and lowing cattle, table saws, church bells, explosions and the sound of broken glass.

Singable? It was the kind of thing that makes sheep sterile. Robbie snapped off the tape player.

"Genuine, right?"

"Yeah," he snarled. "Genuine shit. Look, I don't know where you got this, but it's not *our* Larkin. We want the sappy utopian stuff."

"You're just trying to lower my price."

He took the tape out, then put it in his desk drawer. "Your price is zero. Bye."

"What the fuck, man? That's my tape!"

"No, it's property of the Larkin estate, and obviously stolen. In fact, you're lucky I don't call a cop right now."

"You're a real prick, Robbie. You've always been a prick."

"Okay." Robbie picked up the phone. "I'm calling the cops now. Here's me, calling the cops. You just sit right there like a good little thief."

"You don't wanna do that."

"Why not?"

"Because I'm Tom Larkin." My beard pulled as I stripped it off. "Ow!" I threw it at him.

"Fifth one this week," Robbie said, unimpressed. "Hello, officer, this is—"

I lifted up my shirt. He saw my corset, and the wounds peeking out over the top.

Robbie hung up the phone. "Holy shit."

"Not easy to look at what you did, is it?"

"*I* did? What do you mean? Are you going to punch me again, because this time I will sue."

"Sue? I'm the one who should sue."

"For what?"

"So you're denying you had me killed?"

"What?" Robbie was a good actor, I'd give him that. "It was that fan, what's his name? Thigg."

"I heard different."

"Oh yeah? From whom? Geraldo?"

If I said "Crouk" we'd never get back to the original conversation. Crouk hated Illadro even more than he hated me, and the feeling was mutual.
"Come on, Robbie, 'fess up. Me getting shot was the best thing that's ever happened to you."

"Agreed, but that doesn't mean…I wasn't involved in it. Fuck, Tom, I was out of my mind on cocaine."

"And we know that nobody makes any crazy decisions on drugs."

"Look," Robbie said in a put-upon tone, "if I hired a murderer, it would've been a professional. Not some busstop-mumbler like Thigg."

I didn't know what to say to that, so Robbie filled the space.

"What are you, some kind of detective? You're not very good at it."

"Fuck off! And stop doing séances off me!"

"No thanks, they're quite profitable—and we've got to honor the agreement with your wife. I did appreciate your showing up at the Coronado back in October. Seems like everything you do makes me a little richer," Robbie said, chuckling. "Sorry if you expected me to be shocked, Tom, but it's totally like you to show up, selfish bastard. You're not planning on a comeback, are you?"

"I ought to, just to fuck you."

"I wouldn't. I bet you think everybody'd be happy to see you. I bet you think people'd welcome you back with open arms. Well, they wouldn't. They'll feel played with, used. Do everybody a favor, yourself included—stay the fuck dead."

"You should know about using people. This guy you're getting everyone to worship, he's a fraud," I said. "You're taking advantage of them. And me."

"How?" Robbie scoffed. "It's a fun evening out."

"No it's not. It's snake-oil. Normally I wouldn't care, but my name happens to be on the bottle."

"So what? I'm giving people hope."

"*I'm* giving them hope," I said. "*You're* taking their money."

Robbie waved as if to say, "We could argue about this all day." "What's your game, Tom? I didn't kill you. If anything, you should've killed me."

"Why?"

"Let's just say, I had Katrinka wrapped around my finger."

"She doesn't control me."

Robbie laughed. "Whatever, dude. Sure, I made some money when you died, but I lost a lot more. I could've gotten every album you ever did, for a pittance. All I had to do was flatter your wife. You know, there's nobody easier to con than a cynic."

I sat there, unsure of what to do next. I desperately wanted it to be Robbie, because it was so comfortable hating him, but I had to admit he was making sense. "Do you know who was behind it, then? The murder?"

"Was there a murder? Or was it another stunt of yours and Katrinka's?" Robbie asked. "Who's the snake-oil salesman? You couldn't sell records anymore, but you still wanted one last moment in the sun…"

I stood up, ready to re-imprint Robbie's neck.

"Sit the fuck down, old man. Nobody has to put up with your shit anymore…I'll tell you what I know, just to get you out of my office so I can take a nap."

Robbie rose and walked over to a large black filing cabinet. He opened a drawer and extracted a folder. "Before I set up Orange Sunshine, I had to do some due diligence. You can't start a religion and then find out somebody's faking. And with your tendency towards put-ons, well…" The thick file hit his desk with a thud. "I did what you're doing—only more competently, of course. I was shocked when I found out it was real, that you'd really eaten pavement. Up until ten minutes ago, I happily thought Tom Larkin was dead."

"So who was behind it?"

Robbie shrugged. "As soon as I confirmed your demise, I rapidly lost interest."

"How much do you want for that file?"

"Sorry, Tommy," he laughed. "I like my life more than your money. I give this to you, you go bother them, and I've got a problem. Not worth it."

"Name your price."

"Not. Worth. It."

"Why?"

"Somebody powerful wanted you 'neutralized.' That's the word they always used." He opened the folder, and slid out a single sheet. "Apparently there was a operation, codenamed SITAR—"

"That was Harry's instrument, not mine."

"Weren't big Ravins fans. Obviously." Wearing reading glasses, Robbie looked like a college professor who seduced freshmen.

"Who were they? CIA? FBI? Contractors?"

"They didn't leave W-2s. Does it matter? Guys with guns."

"Can I see that sheet?"

"Ah, what the hell, won't do you much good." Robbie was right; it was heavily redacted. "I figured since they'd gotten what they'd come for—you on a slab—I was fairly safe. But I didn't push it, either."

"Thank you. Will you please stop the séances and shit? It's insulting."

"Nothing insulting about a profit." Robbie picked up a stress ball and played with it. "I'll make you a deal: when I have as much money as you do, I'll stop."

"I don't have any money. I gave it all to Katrinka."

"You'd better be nice to her then." He stopped squeezing for a second. "Are you going to tell me how much you want to stay quiet, or do I have to guess?"

"I don't want your money. I just want to be left alone."

"Then maybe you should pay me to keep quiet."

"This is a waste of time." I got up.

"Where are you going?"

"I asked you if you killed me. You said you didn't and I believe you. But you better believe I'll be telling Katrinka about our little talk, and if I die again, expect a visit."

"What's that supposed to mean?"

"You're a smart guy, Robbie, you figure it out. We're not friends. I asked you to stop your bogus religion, you won't. I don't like that, but I've got bigger fish to fry. You've told me what you know, so—

"So, what?" Robbie said. "You think I'm going to let you stroll out of here?"

"That was my thought, yes," I said. "Oh, and give me my tape back."

Robbie opened the drawer. Instead of the tape, he pulled out a gun. It was little as guns go, but nasty and definitely looking at me.

I began to tremble and sweat. "Not funny, Robbie."

"Am I laughing?" he said, cocking the pistol and making sure the silencer was screwed on tight. "I have a business to run, shareholders to protect. I can't have my blesséd martyr running around alive."

"I know you're not a killer," I said, more optimistically than I felt. "What can I give you? The tape?"

"That piece of shit? *Please.*"

"Okay, then, let's work something out. Surely I've got something you could use."

"Yes, I think you have. I could use your corpse. Chop it up, sell it as relics, that would work."

I saw something dance behind Robbie's head. The wind gusted and it swooped into view again. It was a $1000 bill, fluttering on the end of Helen's line.

"What are you looking at?" Robbie said, gun still pointed at what was left of my innards. He turned and saw the bill. "Don't move." Robbie walked over to the window as the bill dropped out of sight.

"It's my daughter Helen, she's just—"

He fiddled with the window, then slid it open and stuck his head out. "There's a crowd down there. What the fuck is she doing?"

"It's an experiment. She dangles money and people chase it."

"So it's genetic," Robbie grumbled. "All Larkins are annoying." He grabbed the line and gave it a yank. "Sorry, folks, party's over!"

I heard a group of distant voices groan and swear. "Hey, give that back!"

"I own this building! I'm liable if anybody gets hurt!"

Robbie had placed the gun on the windowsill, so he could wind the line with both hands. His back was to me; I began walking towards him.

"Hey!" I heard Helen yell, "Watch it, you pillock! That's art!"

"Stop pulling on the line, little bitch." While Robbie was occupied, I grabbed the gun.

"Don't move. And don't call my daughter a bitch."

Robbie dropped the $1000 bill, and it fluttered down, eventually causing a scuffle. "Thank you!" someone yelled upwards.

"Step inside."

"Tom—"

"Shut up and turn around," I said. "Look out the window."

"What are you going to do?" Tom mumbled nervously. "Shoot me? That tell-all book was right, Tom, you really are a psych—"

I brought the gunbutt down hard on Robbie's noggin. The impact was louder and more solid than I'd expected, and for a few horrible moments I'd thought I had killed him. When I heard him still breathing, I heaved a sigh of relief. I was no murderer. I couldn't make him stop his religion, but he couldn't bother me either—mutually assured destruction. It worked for the Cold War, might work for us, too. Even so, time was of the essence; that horrible receptionist wouldn't appreciate the subtlety of our arrangement. I looked at the clock: 1:40. I'd better get a move-on.

I dragged my unconscious nemesis from the window to his office couch, then threw a blanket over him. With a bit of manhandling his posture looked normal. If anybody happened to look in his office, they'd think he was napping. By the time he stumbled out with a headache and a dazed expression, I'd be long gone. I grabbed the file off his desk, and walked out of the room.

Removing the bullets, I laid the gun in the secretary's in-box. Maybe that would let her know what kind of malevolent bastard she was working for. Then again, maybe she knew already and got off on it; there was no accounting for taste. While I was waiting for the elevator, I fed the bullets down the old-time mail tube. I rode downstairs with two guys from an accounting firm one floor up. They seemed none the wiser.

Helen was waiting for me in the lobby.

"What the fuck was that guy's problem?" she said.

"Some people can't appreciate art," I said.

"Dad, I want to stay with you." Helen braced her arm in the doorway of the cab. "Things are getting dangerous."

"That's exactly why you're going to the airport. Now."

"But—"

"Don't argue," I said, feeling like a proper parent for once. "This isn't curry-flavored crisps. Clive's meeting you in Athens. Stay with him for at least six weeks. Then you can go home."

"Home here? Or Auld Reekie?"

"Here. If it's over."

"Please be careful."

"I will." We hugged, and she got into the taxi. As it pulled away, Helen stuck her head out. "Love you! And for the love of God, please stop smoking!"

I smiled at her surrealist humor. We were so much alike, my daughter and I.

As the taxi headed towards the PCH, I noticed that there was a two-toned '52 Plymouth parked three car-lengths away—totally restored, completely sweet. What were the odds? Long enough for me to worry.

I saw no one behind the wheel, which was more bad news. The driver was out and about. I looked up and down the street, expecting to find Pompadour stepping out of a doorway, silencer rising to head-level. Could I make it to my door? Should I run?

Squatting down to tie my shoe, I sneaked another glance in the direction of the Plymouth. An old lady bobbed into view. She'd dropped her compact, and was now applying face-powder in the rear-view mirror.

I stood up and laughed in relief. The woman noticed, and gave me a dirty look.

"It's not you..." I said too weakly for her to hear, then caught a glimpse of myself reflected in the window of a Taurus. I looked old, tired, wild-eyed. "I gotta get outta here."

True, but to where? I needed to find someplace safe, someplace where I could keep working, keep putting things together, but someplace where I could see the bad guys coming. I saw a seagull, and knew what I had to do.

CHAPTER THIRTEEN

Six hours later, Rufus Byrd and I were a mile out in the Pacific, on the deck of the Knot Me. I stood at the wheel; making sure we didn't hit anything; that far out, it wasn't difficult. The sun was setting, the gulls were wheeling, and Rufus was apologizing for bringing a bottle of wine.

"Dumb of me," he said. "I should've guessed. Everybody from the old days is in a Twelve Step program."

"What Step is getting shot?" I joked. "My liver hasn't been the same since it tried to pass a bullet. You enjoy your wine, though."

"I shall, it's a saucy little Australian, a shiraz. The guy at Wally's practically shot his wad."

I laughed. It didn't surprise me that Rufus was a wine connoisseur. The reason we'd become friends, all those years ago, wasn't his piano playing, excellent though it was, but his intellect. There aren't a lot of *readers* in rock-and-roll, so when I caught him backstage cracking open Nietzsche (and an asthma inhaler), I made an effort. Neither of us had been much for school, but we both considered ourselves cum laude graduates of the University of Marseille. "Majoring in fucking, and minoring in rock and roll."

As the wind picked up and the sun went down, Rufus relaxed, and I relaxed too. Out here, I could see anyone coming. "This is the good life," he said. "Thanks for calling."

"My pleasure. I felt crummy about the séance." Guilt wasn't the only reason. Sailing alone can be dangerous; you can fall overboard—or be pushed—and disappear, plop! without a trace. I'd taken every precaution to insure that my pal Pompadour hadn't seen us leave the slip, but if he had, taking on myself and Rufus would be quite a task. Buzzed or not, Rufus was a big man, and a good friend. I'd seen first hand what he could do in a fight.

"You should've felt bad," Rufus said. "Scaring me like that. After I saved your life?" My friend was referring to a night in 1961, when I was four steps in front of an irate husband waving a butcher knife. Rufus happened to be leaving a whorehouse at a propitious moment; he stuck his big foot out and tripped my pursuer. When the guy wouldn't leave off, Rufus broke his arm in three places.

"It's your own fault," I said. "You should've known it would take more than a few bullets to get rid of me."

"Don't get cocky, Tom. You never know when your number's up. Did you hear about Robbie?"

My heart jumped into my mouth. "Robbie who?"

"Illadro, your old sparring partner. It was on the radio when I was driving down. He got hit by a car. Right there on Sunset, a random hit-and-run."

"Ah fuck." I made a snap decision to let Rufus into my nightmare. "Nothing random about it, Rufus."

"How do you know? Were you driving?"

"Ha ha. I was with Robbie this afternoon, before I called you."

"Why? I thought you hated him."

"Yeah, I paid him a visit, to see if the feeling was mutual. I'm investigating my murder."

"What's there to investigate?" Rufus asked. "I thought that crazy fan did it."

"You know better than to believe the newspapers," I said. "I don't know who was behind it. But if somebody bumped off Robbie, I'm obviously getting close." I spent the next fifteen minutes bringing Rufus up to speed.

"I need another drink." My friend refilled his wineglass. "Who's the leading candidate?"

"It *was* Robbie. Now I'm back to the CIA, I guess."

"Oh come on. The sixties are over, man."

"No, you come on. Why is it that Uncle Sam can do all sorts of nasty shit to me, but when I suggest that they might've, you know, gone a little farther still, everybody thinks I'm a nutter? It's fucking childish."

"You're misunderstanding. I think the CIA is perfectly capable of trying to ice you. Maybe they did. But most murderers are somebody the victim knows. That's where my money would be, if I was a betting man."

"Which you are."

"You have your Twelve Steps, and I have mine," Rufus said with a rueful smile. "Ever heard of Occam's razor? In cases like this, the simplest solution is the best."

"Except that everybody knows about Occam's razor, so they add a little complexity to cover their arses—just enough to make the truth seem unlikely. But it's still the truth."

"I wish there was some way I could help."

"Not at the moment," I said. "Unless you can magically uncensor some CIA files."

"How'd you get those?"

"From Illadro."

"Shit, I'm glad we're out here, away from everybody."

"Me too." I had a horrible thought. "Unless…"

"Unless what?"

"Unless they fucked with the boat."

Rufus threw his head back and laughed. That's the good part of being religious, I guess. Not having that kind of faith, I swung the boat around and gunned us towards shore. "Rufus, if we die out here, I'm sorry. I am the world's worst detective."

"You have other talents," my friend said. "What was Robbie doing with a CIA file on your murder?"

"Before he started the company, he checked to see if I was really dead."

"Robbie always was thorough. Except when it came to cutting checks."

Rufus shook the last drops of wine from the bottle. "Now I'll never get paid for that dog-and-pony show! You got the file here?"

"Yeah. I think if I could just read one specific page, I'd be able to get somewhere. But it's all blacked-out, like they do."

"Is it an original?"

"No idea," I said. "I assume it's a Xerox."

"Can I see it?"

"Why?"

"Just humor me."

"Hold the wheel. I'll be back in a second." I went below decks, ferreted around a bit, then reemerged sheet-in-hand. Rufus stuck out a massive paw, fingers twittering. "Gimme."

Just as I handed it to him, a gust of wind whipped it out of my grasp. "No!" I yelled, and scrambled after it. The document swooped and dove, and just as it went over the edge into the open ocean, I grabbed it. I slumped against the railing, heart pounding.

When my blood pressure subsided, I toddled over the rolling deck to Rufus. "Use both hands," I commanded. He took the sheet, and I took the wheel.

"Hot damn!" Rufus yelled. "It's an original!"

"So?"

"Back then, originals were done on typewriters. Typewriters leave impressions. Impressions can be felt—if you've got sensitive fingers. "

"Can you do it?"

"I'll try. I haven't pretended to be blind since 1962."

"Maybe it's like riding a bike."

Rufus paused. "You'll have to buy me dinner."

"Blackmail's a dirty game, Mr. Ellis."

"I pick the place. The last time you paid, we went to a gas station. No microwave burritos."

"Since when is it a crime to be frugal?"

"You're not frugal, you're—"

"Yeah, yeah, yeah. Can you feel anything?"

"I'm trying...could you turn off the light? It helps."

"Okay." I switched off the console light.

"Also don't talk."

"Okay."

"Now unzip my fly..."

"Shut up and feel, *arschloch*."

We sat there in the dark. I listened to the waves lapping against the boat, and the scratching of Rufus's pen as he wrote down notes. I became terrified that a big wave, a rogue, would hit us and sweep us both out to sea, just as we discovered the answer. I'm also the kind of person who can't listen to his own heartbeat, in case I might jinx it. It other words, just as superstitious as Rufus, only there's no God watching out for me. How did that become the thinking man's stance?

Rufus ripped a page from the mini legal pad and handed it over. I locked the wheel and dropped anchor. "Let's go below decks. It's getting a bit chilly up here."

In the golden light of the galley, Rufus and I pieced together the fragments and codenames that told the story of Operation SITAR. My friend wasn't simply writing down what he felt, but writing it on the page where he felt it—"Official Memorandum" was on the left at the top, and someone had stamped it "Top Secret." The memo had been routed to a list of people; this copy was from initials JAB.

"JAB should fire his housekeeper," I said.

"Or pay them more."

```
7/16/80: Subject announces return to public life.
7/18/80: JM/LIBERTY agrees to move subject from KU/
HEADPHONE to MH/SITAR.
```

"It never stopped," I mumbled. "I was being watched even before President Senokot got elected."

"I thought Priestly was a friend of yours."

"Seems not. Or maybe he didn't know about it."

> 8/2/80: MK/FREEZER opened: ICE CREAM, POPSICLE and TVDINNER. Defrosting process begun by JOKER for possible use.
> 10/80: Subject releases album. REBEL promotes it heavily, but unenthusiastic reviews increase the likelihood of political activism to maintain cultural profile [see Psychological Review prepared 7/4/71, Appendix C attached].

"I wonder whether CIA thought I was crazy?" I mused.

"You're lucky they didn't ask me," Rufus said. "Remember the time you glued that hooker's—"

"That was Nod-Off. Come on, less talking and more feeling."

> 11/20/80: Provocative statements by subject are carried in several major newspapers. Interview in *Corriere Della Sera* attacks President Senokot's character, intelligence, fitness for office, et cetera. At weekly check-in, REBEL assures JM/LIBERTY that this is "just marketing."
> 11/22/80: JM/LIBERTY activates HORTON, asking for confirmation of subject's political intentions. Interview is planned for late December.

"I bet JM/LIBERTY is the New York City station." Rufus gave me a puzzled look. "The CIA office for Manhattan."

"Who's this EINSTEIN, or REBEL? Or JOKER?"

"No clue. Codenames are supposed to be random. Sometimes they're not, like me calling a piano player 'Magic Fingers,' but unless you already know the context, it's a waste of time."

He tore off another page and handed it over. "Next time, bring bigger sheets of paper," Rufus complained.

```
12/7/80: Subject announces plans for world tour in
Spring 1981, plans to march in Argentinean farmers'
rights rally, 1/1/81. BI/GAUCHO requests assistance
from JM/LIBERTY. MH/SITAR now "highest priority."
12/8/80: JOKER contacts TVDINNER and initiates
activation routine Argus-Delta.
12/17/80: Argus-Delta confirmed. TVDINNER moved into
position at safehouse CLOISTER.
```

"TVDINNER is Thigg, it's got to be."

"How do you know?"

"Tracks with his movements. He was living in Phoenix, had a job and a wife. In August, all of the sudden, he quit Dairy Queen. Why?"

"Tom, man, you do not need a reason to quit a job like that."

"From August to December, he sits around watching TV."

"So what? You did that for five years."

"Then he gets on a 'health kick.' He meditates all day long, and never sleeps. One time his wife caught him 'working out'—know what he was doing?"

"Something creepy?"

"Sitting in the lotus position saying over and over, 'Tell me what to do, God, tell me what to do.'" I pointed to an item. "They told him all right. The they brought him to New York in December, one week before. That hostel up near Columbia must've been a safehouse."

```
12/19/80: EINSTEIN contacts JM/LIBERTY, asking
about increase in surveillance. EINSTEIN is told it
is due to subject's greater public profile and is
for his protection.
12/20/80: HORTON contacts JM/LIBERTY with
```

> information regards subject's statement of 12/7. Says that subject is "all talk." HORTON's friendship with subject is well-known, and his information is filtered accordingly.
> 12/21/80: JM/LIBERTY authorized to initiate final stage of SITAR pending confirmation. Target's name is released to TVDINNER for lock-on. Autodialer calls, random meetings, reinforce TVDINNER's progress.
> 12/23/80: Political activities of subject confirmed in interview.

"Knew that reporter was a prick," I mumbled. Rufus handed me another sheet. As I read it, I found myself telling the subject—me—to run, hide, stop promoting the record, anything to derail what I knew was going to happen. But he didn't. I felt a chill when I got to the end.

> 12/23/80: JOKER confirms subject terminated. TVDINNER apprehended by police.
> 12/24/80: JOKER intiates disconnection sequence for TVDINNER.
> 12/25/80: ICECREAM, POPISCLE returned to MK/FREEZER.
> 12/28/80: SITAR closed, mission status: unsuccessful. JOKER lodges formal protest with JM/LIBERTY.

Finished, Rufus now read over my shoulder. "Unsuccessful? I don't get it. They shot you, you 'died,' everybody went home."

"It means they realized I survived," I said bleakly. "Robbie assumed from all the redaction that the operation had been a success. But it wasn't. They fucked it up, and they knew it."

"That's fantastic," Rufus said. "If that's true, they don't care you're still alive!"

"Tell that to Robbie Illadro."

"Could've been bad luck."

"Warren Darden wasn't. I didn't wanna get into this, but…" I told him about the Chateau Marmont. "And it gets worse. There's a guy following me."

"A hitman?"

"Presumably."

"God*damn*, Tom. What are you going to do?"

I exhaled. "JOKER ran the operation, then lodged a formal protest. That means he wanted to go after me again. He's obviously the guy trying to kill me now."

"So avoid him!"

"He'll get me sooner or later. I'm an amateur; my only chance is to do something he doesn't expect. Like show up at his house with a gun."

"You'd really do that?"

"It's him or me." Hearing the words made it real, and my stomach quivered. I'd better toughen up.

"How do you find somebody like that?"

"Maybe I'll look 'im up in the phone book," I growled.

Rufus let me have my tough-guy fantasy; I think he could see I needed it. Neither of us said much on the ride back in. When my friend got off the boat, he turned. "You know what's worse than being paranoid, Tom? Being paranoid, and being right."

I felt my wallet lightening the moment Rufus and I walked into Annelida, his choice to complete our agreement. It was a hot new place in Beverly Hills, one of those hotel restaurants with a star chef, serving up nouvelle-this or regional-that. I honestly had no idea what it served. I couldn't bear to look. The appetizer prices alone made me black out.

"Wouldn't you rather go to Pink's?" I said plaintively.

"Oh, no you don't. I deciphered that document, and now you're gonna pay."

"But I'm dangerous company these days. What if you get shot?"

"Then I'll die happy. *Garçon!*"

Rufus still ate like a man unsure of his next meal. Course after course arrived and I grew more and more glum. After a while it wasn't the money as much as the boredom. Okay, it was the money—but it was also boring. Annelida wasn't macrobiotic, so I sat there drinking ice-water, watching Rufus shovel.

"Rufus, do you even know what you're eating?"

"Nope, and I don't care. It tastes good."

My eyelids were closing when a waiter touched my arm. "Hm?"

"Message for you, sir." He handed me the folded note.

"So nice that you're still alive," the note read. "Come see me. Room 1425. Tootles." There was no name, but I didn't need it—I recognized the handwriting immediately. I guess she'd been sitting in the famous people's section; every restaurant in Los Angeles has one.

Rufus paused momentarily in his decimation of my monthly budget. "Who's it from?"

"American Heart Association," I lied. "They want to stage an intervention. Don't you have any food at home?"

"I will after this." Rufus grabbed a passing waiter. "Could I wrap this up, and look at a dessert menu?" Then he pointed. "Is that the chef? I'd like to pay my compliments."

"And I'd like to pay her mortgage," I mumbled.

The chef, a tense-looking woman with a rather severe bun, came to bask in Rufus' honeyed tones. "Wonderful experience," he burbled. "Really interesting flavors. So complex."

"Thank you, I'm glad you liked it."

I looked her over; the chef wasn't conventionally attractive, but I've always had a thing for women who are really good at what they do. And everybody looks pretty when they smile. So I tried to strike a spark. "Can you tell me what kind of meat was in the entrée?"

"Yes," Rufus said, "it was such a unique texture."

"Let's see..." The chef ticked it off on skinny fingers. "The appetizer was roundworms, the soup earthworms, and the entrée, that was leech."

"I thought so," I said. (I'd seen a documentary.)

Apparently seeing his friend's ghost wasn't the only thing that turned Rufus white. "Did you say—leech? Like, bloodsucking..."

"Yes," the chef said. "They're a source of protein throughout the Third World. Everything on our menu comes from the family Annelida—" Rufus continued his fade to taupe as she spoke, but the chef didn't seem to notice; I expect she was used to it. "Thank you for joining us tonight. Now, if you'll excuse me..." She glided away.

"Oh God," Rufus whispered, laying his head on the table.

I leaned over. "Can I ask you a question? Do you feel them...squirming?"

"I have to go." He got up quickly, staggering in the direction of the W.C.

Rufus' early departure was wise. The note was from Victoria Callaway O'Croesus, and whenever she was involved, things tended to get weird. Not for the faint of heart, or weak of stomach.

I first got to know Vickie in 1965, during our second tour of the States. Those big tours were the draggingest drags in the history of dragdom, and we were forced to come up with a million little things to keep from going crackers. One of my favorites was a game, a holdover from the Marseille days called "That's a Bet." It combined gambling and boasting, which made it the perfect male pastime.

That's a Bet went like this: someone would set a pot, then state a boast. Then the next person would add to the pot, trying to top that boast if they could. The money would increase, turn by turn, but wherever it stopped, the boast became a bet. If you made good on the boast, you got the pot. If you didn't, you had to pay out the pot three times over. There was a lot of risk, a lot of reward, and as you might imagine, That's a Bet got us into a lot of trouble. I adored it.

En route to New York, thirty thousand feet over the Atlantic, Buck started us off. "For £100: between today, August 13th, 1965, and the end of the tour,

I'll pull twenty-five birds."

Ollie didn't even look up from *Melody Maker*. "£150, forty-five."

The total increased relentlessly until it had reached two hundred women, or roughly fourteen a day. This was the group record, set by Ollie in Australia over a year ago, and was widely considered unbeatable. It was Harry's turn.

"So, Harry?" I teased. "Been taking your vitamins?"

Here's where the skill came in: you could change the boast, but only slightly, and it still had to be more difficult than its predecessor. Harry was particularly good at shifting parameters like this; he was always coming up with tasks that we thought were dreadful, but played to his strengths. It was a game of That's a Bet that got him to India the first time, "to drink out of the Ganges River while someone within my sight is having a slash in it." He came back with intestinal worms and £6000.

Harry knew that Ollie was a thoroughbred of fucking, with an iron prostate and a libido to match. So he redefined the bet. "For £2700, I will shag the daughter of a mayor." That started another round, which spiraled rather predictably—town size first, then mayor to governor to senator, then from daughter to wife—until it got to me.

"Well, Larkin?" Ollie said. "Wilting under pressure?"

I paused dramatically, letting the catcalls build, then delivered the knockout punch: "For £3200, I will fuck Vickie Callaway."

"That's a bet!" Buck cried. Vickie was the recent widow of the American President, practically sacred ground. I might as well have said I'd pull the Virgin Mary.

Ollie smiled. "I'd like my money now, please, so I can change it into dollars when we land."

I ignored him. "Standard rules apply?"—the tag from a pair of knickers.

"Under the circumstances," Harry said, "we'll need more than that."

"A photo," Ollie demanded.

"You got it," I said. "Destroyable upon receipt."

Buck crunched the ice from his rum and Coke. "He's too agreeable. I smell a set-up."

I rubbed my hands together evilly. "As well you should, dearie." We called No-Doze over and got him to write down the terms.

"All right," Buck said, "next bet. For £100…" And so it began again. I forget where that one ended up, but it probably had something to do with crashing all those Cadillacs.

What the guys didn't know was that three months before, in May of '65, I'd been to dinner at the satirist Jonathan Crake's house. Vickie had also been there, squired by some horrible washed-out looking bastard from the Home Office. .During the meal, the former First Lady and I had been seated opposite one another, but only exchanged a few words. I was a bit shy if you can believe it, and everyone was too busy listening to Jonathan, who was doling out jewel-like anecdotes he'd polished during a long run on Broadway. At certain lulls, I could've sworn Vickie's foot brushed against mine. With intent.

After all the other guests had left and his then-wife had gone upstairs to bed, Jon and I were sampling brandies in his study. "Am I mad? Could she have been coming on to me?"

"Either that or she's slightly spastic," Jon said. "I slept with Vickie, you know."

Jon's grotesque ramblings were so funny it always seemed a shame to disbelieve them. *"Really?"*

"Really. In Washington."

"Well, that's nothing," I countered. "I had it off with Khrushchev. In Moscow."

"No, no. I'm serious. What's more, something very alarming happened. Since she was married to Mr. Callaway at the time, I thought I'd triggered World War III. As you know, I never kiss and tell—"

"What's this, then?"

"A friendly warning," he laughed. "Tom, if you ever cross swords with Vick, it'll happen to you, and you'll be prepared for it."

From that moment on, I was a man possessed. What was her secret? I had to have her! Remember, this was less than two years after Omaha, so that was like declaring, "I shall fuck the Statue of Liberty!" And when I say "fuck," that's what I mean—the dirtier and more outrageous the better, because I was a macho Northern guy back then, and I believed her image in the press. As far as I knew, Vickie was the trophy wife, the ice queen, the ultimate deb. Little did I realize…I mean, I should've guessed. People are never like how they're portrayed. For example, I know for a fact that Bert Russell was functionally retarded, I helped him tie his shoes before an Embassy party in 1964. And Hefner and Rock Hudson lived together for years. I have a guest towel with their twined initials.

Everybody talks about our concert at Yankee Stadium, but for me the strongest memory of that tour came the night before, with Vickie Callaway. Clive had set up a *tete a tete* at Vickie's apartment over by the U.N., and after that, we were supposed to go to Le Cirque. I say, "Supposed to," because we never got there. She greeted me at the door in a long leather trench, and as soon as I walked in, she opened it.

"What are you trying to tell me, Vick? Would you like to shave before we go out?"

Vickie didn't say anything, she just made that back-of-the-throat sound a cat does when it sees a bird. Then she grabbed my arm and yanked me forward. "Come inside."

For the first inch, I thought, "Bloody hell—this is the President's widow" and then the floor dropped out. Vickie was like a circus ride that was breaking as you rode it. There was nothing flattering or tender about it, and you had to be super-aware every single moment, for fear she'd accidentally choke you or rip your rig off.

I don't know, maybe she was still, uh, grieving, but Vickie Callaway was—let's just say I realized why the kids were sent away for school. People call women "insatiable," and you think, hmm, that'd be nice, but it wasn't. It was actually quite terrifying. The speaking in tongues, the ululating…And the shit she had me do—she didn't have sex like somebody who was grieving.

She had sex like an insane person. I mean, like someone who was literally *insane.* Like "I don't know what sex is, I'm just going to have you stick it somewhere and then we'll grind and howl and I'll beat against the wall so hard there'll be little fistmarks in the plaster." Vickie had very small hands.

More than once somebody came to the door to ask if everything was all right. I was shitting myself, thinking of the headlines, but Vickie would just roll over, or undo the straps, or wash off the minstrel paint or whatever, and traipse to the door. "No, everything's fine, we're just watching a film on television. I'll turn it down." They must've known what was going on; God knows how much Clive had to pay to keep the whole thing quiet. At least he could split the costs with the Callaways.

There was bondage, there were costumes, there were quasi-religious rites, I had to be her ex-husband, I had to be a girl, I had to be the element Antimony...Listen, I'd done it with whores, and I'd done it with groupies, and none of them, not even the old Vichy clap-wagons I grappled with back in Marseille, none were as thoroughly bonkers as Vickie Callaway. And who could blame her? The whole country—shit, the world—wanted her to be this untouchable widow, beautiful and celibate until death. Vickie was rejecting that. She'd seen death, she'd practically worn it. Now she was celebrating life, celebrating it whenever and however and whoever she could, like a piece of out-of-control construction equipment. There's something admirable in that.

But she did make me cry. When the car came to pick me up in the morning, I was in the corner, literally in the corner, cowering, *begging.* "Please don't touch me. I can't take it." I was so unmanned I forgot to get a picture, and lost £9600.

I didn't care; Vickie had been worth it. After all the sex I'd had, I wasn't looking for orgasms, I was hunting an experience. Vickie was certainly that. I'm convinced that's why O'Croesus married her a couple of years later. He was in the same position I was. He could have anyone, so he wanted flavor.

The day after, she wrote me a very nice note, in that super-loopy handwriting of hers, something like, "Thanks for a nice quiet evening." It's still around somewhere, unless Fraulein decided to sell it.

When I got back to England, I called up Jonathan Crake.

"So?" he asked. "Did she do it?"

"What the hell didn't she do? That woman should come with a bloody warning label. Did she make you do the motorcade?"

"That must be new. I had to dress as Marilyn and lick the bottom of her shoe."

"You got off easy."

"What did you do when she passed out? I remember pacing around the Lincoln Bedroom horrified. 'What if people think it was the Russians?'"

"Oh that," I said. Fuck, a night of toe-curling existential terror, and I hadn't even made her come! I guess Vickie enjoyed herself, though, because when we came through New York the next year, she took me to dinner, then to a party at George Plimpton's, where I hit James Baldwin with Truman Capote. Afterwards, she wanted to start another round, but I begged off. Or, more accurately, when the limo was at a stoplight, I yanked open the door and ran.

I hoped Vickie wouldn't hold that against me now.

I went up to Room 1425 quickly, before I could talk myself out of it. Seeing Vickie was a definite risk: with the delightful woman came her battering-ram of a pelvis, and frankly, I didn't know how much blunt-force trauma I could take in my weakened condition. On the other hand, Vickie knew everybody, which made it entirely plausible she could help me with the case.

I knocked. Right as my knuckles touched the paint, I felt doom flash up my spine: What if this was a set-up? What if she was in on everything? Why hadn't I thought of this before?

The door opened, and there stood Vickie. Still slim, raven-haired, and obviously unarmed.

"Tom—"

I covered her mouth with my hand, determined to enter silently—then tripped on the carpet. Trying not to fall down with me, Vickie grabbed at a cart full of room service, and that toppled too.

"So much for quiet," I laughed, shaking vase-water off my sleeve.

Vickie helped me to my feet like one of her arthritic Labrador retrievers. "It's fantastic to see you, Tom. I so hoped you weren't dead." Vickie wasn't whispering, her voice was naturally like that. Like she was saving it for the ululations.

"How did you know it was me?" I said.

"You always fall asleep at restaurants. You did before the party at Plimpton's, too."

"I don't remember that. All I remember is throwing Truman at Warhol, and hitting Baldwin instead." (I *still* say I invented dwarf-tossing.)

"That was quite an evening. George still talks about it." She was blotting me with a napkin. "As I recall, he had the bad form to put on a jazz record, and all the sudden, guests started flying."

"I hated jazz back then."

"Yes, you did!" she laughed. "It was like a barfight in an old Western. Thank goodness Mayor Lindsay had his bright idea."

"Thank goodness for forced-air heating." Lindsay sent a cop to get a kilo of pot out of evidence, turned Plimpton's furnace on and threw it in. Everyone stripped and got mellow. I remember getting a backrub from U Thant.

Vickie straightened my collar. "There." It was almost maternal.

"Stop it, you're turning me on."

She didn't stop. "I can't wait to hear all your news."

"Then, allow me to fill you in."

Age had slowed us both, thank Christ. I think I suffered a bit of internal bleeding, but this time, I'm pleased to say, Vickie passed out. More than once.

After she came to, we talked about Clive and his island.

"What a fabulous idea," she said. "I should retire there myself." Then her face darkened. "My second husband isn't there, is he?"

"No," I said. "Not nearly fabulous enough." Then I told her about the search I was on, and my current brick wall. "His codename was 'JOKER,' but that's all I know."

"It's funny," Vickie said without a hint of a smile, "wherever you dig these days, you eventually hit a spy. Didn't used to be like that."

"Can you help me find him? Do you have any friends at CIA?"

"Oh, I have friends there. I have friends all over DC. After the President died, it was Open Season on me."

"What do you mean?"

"Lots of them had been cuckolded, and they wanted payback. I didn't mind. I just adopted their attitude about it, what else could I do?" Vickie said. "I think I turned a couple of them queer. Crouk, for example."

"Don't even mention that fucker. He's the bloody start of it all." I told her what had happened in the tank.

"Milton Crouk was a bastard, and I hope he and Roy Cohn are swapping anal warts in Hell." As I digested that image, Vickie continued. "But Tom, if Crouk had said the same thing to me about the President's murder, I wouldn't be investigating it, I'd be trying to forget it."

"I'm the one they shot at, Vick. I can forget all I want, until somebody decides to remind me."

"Good point. I guess it can't hurt call a few old friends, and see what turns up."

"Do you think you'll be able to find out who JOKER is? Be honest—I don't want to get my hopes up."

Vickie smiled. "You know what they say, Tom. It's a man's world. Which means that a beautiful woman can do *anything*."

Not qualifying on either count, all I could do was sit on the Knot Me reading John le Carré while Vickie worked her magic. It's funny, I never read hard-edged spy stuff like that before the investigation. Now, I couldn't get enough. I guess I was looking for an advantage. When Helen had found a copy of *Soldier of Fortune* on my coffee table, I told her, "Don't worry, I only read it for the articles."

A week of spy-pulps later, a man from FedEx came galumphing down the slip. He had that look a lot of Americans have, like livestock in a baseball hat.

"You B.A. Ware?"

"About bloody time," I said, signing for it greedily.

"We do our best, sir." He paused.

"Well, go on," I waved him away. "It's personal." After he'd gone, I stuck my hand in so fast I got a paper cut.

It was only a single sheet. From her day job running the American branch of Gallimard, Vickie had sent a fax, to the 202 area code. "My darling Stephen: 'Joker', Active 70s/80s??? Thx, V."

Under her typed question, someone had written, ".JOKER: Joseph Alan Bronstein, Office of Naval Intelligence 1943-73; contractor 73-81. Do you have a date for Shuck Carlson's thing?"

And under that, Vickie had written me, in red felt-tip. "He wishes. I'm going with you—we might be able to find out more at the party. Call me when you get to DC on Friday and my car will pick you up. Hope this helps, Vickie.

P.S.—You *do* have a tux, don't you?"

Bronstein, Joe Bronstein...I'd heard that name before. But where?

CHAPTER FOURTEEN

I knew who Shuck Carlson was, everybody did. S. Charles Carlson ran for President in 1984, not well but omnipresently, as a sort of corn-pone comic relief to the usual two stiffs. Before that, he was a "can do"-oozing Indiana businessman who'd made a pile with a bunch of High Street shops selling spy gear to the public. That's progress, I guess—first we got a chicken for every pot, then a car for every garage, and finally, a bug for every phone. Shuck's store had the ominous name of "Wetwork" and I knew it well. Der Fraulein got the catalogue.

In addition to funding a whole array of disgusting right-wing causes, over the years Shuck had amassed the world's largest private collection of espionage memorabilia. Through government connections, monomania and a three-pound checkbook, Shuck now possessed everything from Ian Fleming's *Beano* night-light to a plate of exploding spinach penne made from green plastique. To curry favor with the Senokot Administration, Shuck had established a program whereby recently retired intelligence officers could tell their life stories in exchange for a small honorarium. These manuscripts would then be placed in a private, restricted-access library established and maintained by Shuck. Tonight was the grand opening of the library, which was in a renovated, climate-controlled brownstone in Georgetown. Naturally Vickie was on the guest list; she and Shuck were already batting about a book deal.

"It's a bit of a shot in the dark," Vickie admitted in the limo from the airport. "Shuck's working his way down the chain-of-command. I don't know if our boy Bronstein is important enough to have made it in yet."

"Don't be ridiculous," I sniffed. "My assassin has his own *wing*."

Vickie laughed. I was her date, a wealthy book collector named "Gugliemo Rigatoni." On the flight from LAX, I'd changed into my new tux, memorized my ID, and put a pint of V05 in what little hair I had left. I didn't know a word of Italian, but if necessary I could unlimber my usual gibberish and call it dialect. I looked eminently respectable—from the ankles up at least. Instead of tuxedo slippers I wore motorcycle boots, just to show everyone who was boss.

It was a mob scene, an utter crush. Shuck was one of those people for whom nothing existed unless everyone knew about it, so every friend and rival had been invited. Vickie was in her element; alabaster-skinned, big-eyed, beautiful. When we got out of the limo, I told her she looked like Marianne at a Bastille Day party.

"As long as I don't end up Marie Antoinette." She had a dark sense of humor, understandable given the husbands that had been shot out from under her.

Attending an affair with Vickie was like having a friend with X-ray eyes. She knew how Washington worked, who had power and who'd lost it, the whole hidden constellation of debits and credits. After Shuck had led us in compulsory prayer, I stood there in the back of the packed ballroom, listening to Vick's fascinating play-by-play.

"Look at that dress, she must be in her manic phase again. You couldn't *pay* me to be on the Supreme Court with her...See those two? They're neighbors. His dog keeps pooping on her lawn, and that's why the healthcare bill always dies in committee...I see Buzz made it."

"Buzz?"

She indicated a sweet-looking old man with a prominent nose. "That was my husband's nickname for him. Ex-Joint Chiefs, I forget which branch. He's obsessed with bees."

"The insect?"

"Uh-huh. Tried to launch a nuclear war to get rid of them, 'Operation Fumigate.' Jack said no. Buzz never forgave him."

"How bizarre," I mumbled.

"Not if you met his first wife. Her name was Honey."

I realized how terrifying it was to know the inner workings of power, and another piece of Vickie fell into place. I took a deep swig of mineral water and tried to concentrate on Shuck's prepared remarks, hoping they'd anesthetize me

"—in a completely secure, climate-controlled environment," our host twanged. "Then, upon my death, the material will be donated in its entirety to the Library of Congress."

"Until then," Vickie whispered, "those files mean Shuck's got everybody by the short and curlies." She gave my arm a tug. "Let's go, Gug."

"Go where?"

Vickie got a mischievous glint.

I knew that glint. My nether regions throbbed in alarm. Vickie's penchant for semi-public sex was well known; it had taken all of my cunning (and most of my limited upper-body strength) to keep her clothed on the way in from Dulles. But here? Up the very bunghole of the people who'd tried to kill me? I trotted after, terrified. "Vickie, you know I love you, but—"

"Oh, don't be such a spoilsport."

We got to the elevator. Vickie looked to see if anybody was watching, then swiped a key card and the door opened.

"Where'd you get that?"

"Hugging can be useful." Vickie was the most touchy-feely WASP I'd ever met, and now I knew why. She pulled me into the elevator. As soon as the doors closed, her mouth was on my neck, getting lipstick on my tuxedo shirt.

"Leave off!"

"Bok-bok-bok..."

"I'm not chicken. I'm focused. We're here to find out more about Bronstein."

"That may be why *you're* here..."

Oh God, she was playing with my fly. I tried to wriggle free—and no, *not* like you think. "Come on, Vick!"

The doors opened with a cheery ding. Vickie stuck her head out. "Honestly, if I'd known you were going to be such a wet noodle..." She walked ahead quickly, like she knew where she was going. "Anybody asks, you're looking for the john."

I put my flute of mineral water down by the elevator, just in case there might be running involved. "I hardly think that not wanting to shag in front of all those creeps is—"

"So you've gone queer. Fine with me, they all do sooner or later." She was standing in front of a nondescript door. The black plastic label on the jamb read "203: Processing."

Vickie swiped her card; nothing happened. She did it again, swearing softly, and this time the door unlocked with a vacuumy click. Vickie grabbed the handle and leaned. The heavy door swung to.

Fluorescent lights flicked on automatically, revealing a room ringed floor-to-ceiling with file cabinets. In the middle stood a large formica table. I paused in the doorway. "What if somebody finds us?"

She pulled me inside, and the door shut with a clang. "They'll think we're canoodling. That's what we used to call it at Miss Porter's."

"So you're fiddling with my belt simply to further the illusion?"

"Do you always *talk* so much?"

Trying to ignore the former First Lady, I slid open a file cabinet, and saw reams and reams of reports, each in pale-beige acid-free folders. On the tab was a name, last name first: I saw a character from my spy novels—*ANGLETON, James Jesus*—but fought the urge to grab it. I didn't have time; Vickie was stepping out of her underwear, so I trotted away, peering at the little white labels on the handle of each cabinet...A-An, Ao-Be, Bf-Br...I yanked the drawer open, its hinges squeaking in protest.

"Aren't you even going to take off your jacket?" Vickie said.

"Ah, *fuck*! Come on, man!" *BRONSTEIN, Joseph* wasn't there.

I tore open the next drawer, and the next, hoping it was in the wrong place, then went back to the original spot and looked again. Every moment was precious; what if somebody saw us? There had to be cameras in this joint, of all libraries, this one would have cameras.

"I'm waiting, lover..."

"Found it!" It had been slightly misfiled. "Shuck needs to learn the bloody alphabet." It wasn't thick, maybe I could photocopy the lot and we could get back downstairs. "Is there a Xerox machine? Vick, do you see—"

"All I see is five foot ten inches of hot *homo sapiens*."

I flipped open the file. "1943: US Navy; 1944: dishonorable discharge (homosexuality), transferred to the Office of Naval Intelligence."

"Tom, it's cold in here, don't you think? Aren't you cold?" I kept ignoring her, which was the wrong thing to do. She came over and started fondling me.

I read furiously. After the War, Bronstein had been sent to Hollywood, to keep tabs on Reds. Then ONI had him infiltrate the jazz scene, to get at the blacks. They kept sending him deeper, into seedier and seedier places. He picked up a habit with a capital H. At least we had that in common.

"Quit it, Vickie, I'm trying to focus." The file was fascinating, but I couldn't help myself—Vickie was talented.

"Goodbye *homo sapiens*, hello *homo erectus*."

I took off my jacket and laid it on the floor. "All right, look," I said testily, undoing my cuffs and rolling up my sleeves, "if we do this, will you leave me in peace?"

"You don't mean that," she said, suddenly hurt.

"I meant, so I can read this file." She was really quite vulnerable, when you got down to it. And sweet. A bit damaged, but aren't we all?

"Yes, I promise."

So we got right down to it. The floor was hard, so I took off my boots and she kneeled on them. I laid the report on her back, and tried to keep my head steady enough to read. Usually I'd never do something like that, not after Women's Lib, but this was a special circumstance.

Bronstein's life unrolled before me. He married a stripper, and—"Holy fuck," I mumbled.

"What?"

"Nothin', dear. Just think of England."

"Joseph Bronstein" performed under the stage name "Joey Browne"! *That* Joey Browne. Dirty Joey, the one who transformed comedy. The one who OD'd at 41. And the one who wrote his bosses at ONI: "[T]he government will never control domestic dissent by fighting it directly. Those being manipulated must mistake the means of control as their *own free will*—cf. the mass hysteria of Fascism. However, America's diversity and competitive ethic makes 'national identity' a weaker force; we are a nation of individualists, of rebels, so the means of control *must* be framed in those terms. If we were to introduce illegal drugs into the mainstream, their use on a mass scale would give us the leverage necessary to repel the Communist threat. If dissenters use illegal drugs, they criminalize themselves. If we control the supply, they pay us for the privilege. Put simply, if we want to win the Cold War, we must make illegal drugs America's national pastime."

My head swam. Father of the Sixties, nothing—I'd been cuckolded, and was holding the proof in my hands! Plus, the cold linoleum was doing nothing for my bad knee; fucking outside of bed was definitely a young man's sport. I shifted my weight painfully. "Vick, dear, would you mind if—"

"No, shut up! *Faster!*"

Ah well. At least I had something good to read. After getting the thumbs-up from his superiors, Bronstein had worked tirelessly for a decade, "turning on" opinion leaders, showbiz folk mostly, but socialites too, pitching drugs as a gesture of rebellion and personal freedom. The list of contacts was impressive. Most of my friends were on it. How many of them were in on the plot, and how many were just having fun? The cunning thing was, it didn't matter. I skipped down.

By '67, Bronstein had done all he could as Joey Browne, so it was decided he should overdose. The hope was that "dissenters" would begin to see

ODing as the ultimate act of revolution, a sort of final fuck-you by souls too sensitive and brilliant to live. Bronstein's file called it "implanting a self-destruct mechanism in the New Left." Postmortem, Bronstein relocated to DC, where the ONI got him cover at the Bureau of Weights and Measures. The spy retired in 1981, but he'd saved the best for last. My assassination was his final operation.

As fascinating as this was, it was also, uh, softening. Vickie responded by bucking like a show-pony. The paper was shaking too much. "Slow down, Vick!" The words jiggled distractingly, and I expected someone to burst in at any moment.

"What's wrong?"

"Don't you expect someone to burst in at any moment?"

"Yeah!" Vickie said, flushed. "Isn't it great?"

There was nothing left for me to do but bring it home. I put the report aside, and began to mete out twenty of the best. I got to four, when the door opened.

A jowly old man in a trenchcoat stood there. "Okay kids," he said not unkindly, "party's over."

I was frozen with embarrassment. Vickie wasn't. "Do you *mind?*" She's the only person I know who can sound imperious on her hands and knees.

"Nobody has more respect for your late husbands than I do, Mrs. O'Croesus, but I really have to insist. Everybody's coming up for a tour of the facilities."

Sullenly, Vickie disengaged. When I was dressed, I walked over to where the man was standing, back towards us. "Do you work for the library? In case you're worried, we didn't get anything on—"

"I'm Joe Bronstein." He took the file from my hands and replaced it. I never would've recognized him, for the same reason nobody ever recognizes me. I expected him to be hipper, or scarier, something other than ordinary. In his rumpled trench this guy looked worn and greasy, like a six-by-three grocery bag. . "*Buago fenolli, signore*. I'm—"

"Cut the crap." Joe pushed up his large, square bifocals. "You know who

I am, I know who you are."

"Oh yeah?" Years of living incognito made me a bit belligerent about it.

"Thomas Dunkirk Van Weltanschuung Larkin—"

"Oh yeah?"

"—born June 6th, 1940, Greasby England, died December 23rd, 1980 New York—"

"OH YEAH?"

"—or so I thought until I saw you eating canapés downstairs." Joe rubbed his baggy eyes. "I know you, all right. I never forget a failure."

We each retreated to the appropriate bathroom, and when the guestly herd arrived moments later, the three of us joined them seamlessly. Then we slipped downstairs.

"So Joe," I said gruffly, "since you're such a mastermind, why the fuck did you try to kill me?"

"Not in front of the lady."

"Oh please," Vickie said, still pissed over our *coitus interruptus*. "I've lived harsher shit than both of you lightweights put together." That was the great unspoken, the public horror that Vick had suffered through. She'd held it together, God knows how, and preserved a fantasy people *needed*. Gratitude was why everybody respected her, and kept her secrets, and let her prance around like a horny teen. She'd play the role for the public, but in her heart Vickie refused to be tragic. Death's breath had been on her cheek, we all saw it. Next to that, what was a little canoodling, as they used to say at Miss Porter's? She was probably the only sane one among us.

"I've made the match, Tom," Vick said. "Keep fighting, if you want to, but try not to get killed. You're good when you put your mind to it. And you"—she turned to Joe—"you're responsible for him tonight. If I hear that you've pulled any spooky bullshit, you will find out what clandestine power really is. Got it?"

"Lady, I never wanted to kill him in the first place."

"Fucking liar," I growled.

"G'night, boys," Vickie said, waving.

"We'll talk in the car," Joe started walking away.

"Are you crazy?" I said. "I'm not getting in a car with you. I read a whole *book* about Chappaquiddick."

"You wanna know what I know?"

"Fuck yeah."

"Then come with me."

My likely final resting place was a bird-spattered late-model shit-brown Olds with sprung seats and a cracking dash. Looking at the coffee-stains and the Boogeymonger wrappers, I suddenly realized why spies sell secrets—they're fucking broke. "Where are we going?" I demanded.

"That's top secret," Joe said. "Put on your seatbelt."

"Why? Me going through the windshield would probably make your night."

"The plan wasn't to kill you," Joe said as we turned on to Wisconsin Avenue, heading north. He was driving fast, so I buckled up. "We wanted to scare you, that's why there were blanks in the gun. You'd freak out, retire again, and everything would be hunky-dory."

"Blanks, huh? The three holes in my chest say that's bullshit."

"You don't have to tell me. I was there."

"You were?"

Joe nodded, then said, "Please don't."

"Don't what?"

"Smoke in my car. It kills the resale value."

What a nutter. "That's some bloody nerve. I'll do what I like, 'Joker.' You owe me."

"I owe you? You ruined my beautiful op!" Joe shouted above the din of his open window. "That little stunt you pulled got me fired. It got all of us fired. Thanks for dying, Tom. I *should* fucking kill you!"

We cut a corner so close I was sure we'd hit the mailbox. "Slow down, man. Jesus!"

"Uh-uh. We gotta get to Bethesda by 10:30." Brakelights lit up in front of us. "Fuck!" Joe wrenched the wheel right and we shot onto a side street.

"Who gave the order?"

"Civilians always ask that," Joe said with a rueful smirk. "I don't know. It wasn't my job to know…I saw everything that night, Thigg, the shots, you dropping. I was across the street. In Central Park, behind the wall. Watching my pension vanish into thin air."

"So what the fuck happened?"

"I don't know that either."

"You don't know either?" I yelled. "Fuck, Joe—I go through all this shit, and now *you* don't know? Was there another shooter?"

"No, I would've seen him. And I would've shot 'im myself."

"Okay, so Thigg shot me. Somebody took your blanks out, and put real bullets in."

"Doesn't make sense. No professional would've risked that."

"Why not?"

"I assume you've met Thigg? People like him are used as distractions, not as assassins. Everybody's looking at Fruity McLoop, meanwhile there's a pro in the bushes."

"Seems overcomplicated."

"But necessary. The hypno stuff had glitches, back then at least. It's probably fixed by now. Back in '80, people like Thigg weren't 100% reliable. You saw it yourself—five hours before, you walked right by him, remember? You signed his album and he didn't give you so much as a rude look, much less shoot at you."

"It's tough to find decent help."

"Forgive me if I don't find that funny."

"Me, either. Joe, where the fuck are you taking me?"

"I'm not going to tell you. You might run for it."

We were on Wisconsin again, a busy street. "I might run for it anyway."

"Not if I don't go below thirty." He floored it, and we ran a red light. I screamed.

"Joe, cut the shit! Are you going to kill me? Yes or no!"

"I hope so!" he yelled back. "But not the way you think!"

Fifteen minutes later, after the crotch of my tux had dried, I understood what Joe meant. On the lower rungs of the comedy biz, performers are required to bring a guest to pay the cover and swell the bar tab, otherwise they can't get on stage. That's why Joe hadn't wanted me to run off; he needed me.

The Ha-Ha Hut was a tired-looking joint, but the parking lot was impressively full, especially for a Thursday night. When we walked in, I said, "I'll watch your act, but afterwards you're going to answer every goddamn question I can think of."

"That's fair," he said. "Hold this." Joe handed me his trench, then disappeared.

I found a table in the back—it wobbled—and ordered two Cokes, the minimum. I drank one and poured another into a potted plant.

"And now, someone you all know, he's a regular here at The Ha Ha Hut, ladies and gentlemen, Mr. Sonny Fontaine."

So many names, so many roles, so many secrets. Joe ambled over, shaking the emcee's hand and taking the mic. Then he turned to the audience.

"Oh, don't clap," he said. "I haven't said anything yet—you keep your *pro forma* applause. I don't need charity from the likes of you." Joe's voice rose an octave. "'Look, Janet, look at this schmucky guy, let's give him a little something for the effort...Whaddaya mean, he doesn't know he's a schmuck'? Of course he knows, he's got mirrors in his house. But still he goes up there. Good for you, you schmuck! Striking a blow for the schmucky guys everywhere, for schmucks yet unborn!"

Bit over, Joe paced for a second, then said, "I used to work for the Bureau of Weights and Measures—you know us: the people who *didn't* bring you the Metric System. It was a crazy gig. We'd just say 'the Bureau' you know, to impress chicks. People assumed we meant the FBI." Hand on his hip, Joe became an ogling floozy.

"'I wonder if he's packing?'

"Yeah—a scale!" Joe mimed a gunfighter pulling out an ungainly object, and the audience laughed. It was a decent crowd, probably fifty.

"I worked for them for forty years. I used to wake up and think, 'How the fuck did this happen?' That's when you know you're an adult, Jack—when you find yourself in the middle of an entire life, with no idea how you got there. 'Wha—where am I?'

"I don't care where you're from, not even kids *in DC* grow up thinking, 'I wanna work for the Bureau of Weights and Measures.' Not that there's anything wrong with that. Things must be weighed, and also measured, and it is important that such functions be done accurately. I see that—I just don't know how I got stuck doing it: The last thing I remember, I was in the Navy. That was 1943. Things just sorta snowballed.

"It started back in the War, the Second World War, you remember that one. People knew how to throw a war back then. Sure, you were gonna die, but at least it was the big event, Your Show of Shows. I feel sorry for the guys who died in Grenada. What do you say to them? 'Sorry, kid—we just couldn't line up the sponsors!'

"I joined up like most people did, to get laid. That should be on every tombstone in Arlington. 'He just wanted to get laid.'

"I decided on the Navy after looking at a globe. All that ocean? The Japs would never find me. And it woulda worked, too, only the captain had a hangup. He put the needs of the Navy over his own. 'Oh, I'll go here and help. Oh, they need me over there.' Today, they'd call him codependent, give him some Prozacs, *sei gesunt*. Back then, they were less enlightened. They gave him a battleship.

"When I first got in, I was gung-ho. That's how you could tell I was underage. I was two tons of patriotism in a 120-pound bag. I memorized the Constitution. I knew all my Presidents. I was determined to be a part of history. Yeah. What I didn't realize is this: History is what you tell your parents.

"Say you're coming home from a date, and your mother is sitting there at the kitchen table with a glass of milk.

"She asks you, 'Did you and Sally have fun? What did you do?'

"You don't say, 'I picked Sally up, we necked a little in the car, then we went to the park and put down a blanket and so forth.' You don't tell the truth, even though your mother knows exactly what you did. Your mother invented sex, that's the only reason you're here. But you don't tell her the truth, you don't really connect with her like you would a human being, because she doesn't want to hear that. That's disgusting! What kind of monster says that to his mother? Next thing you know, you'll be admitting what you do in the bathroom when the door's locked. Where does it end? So instead you say, "Ah, nothing. We went to the movies."

"And how was the movie?"

"GR-R-REAT!"

Joe waited for the laughter to subside, then added, "By the way, you could always tell when I'd gotten lucky. I'd reek of Ivory soap. When you're a kid, any bodily secretions—they're like nuclear waste, man. I was terrified that my Mom would smell the girl on me. I'd walk in, sweating, because *I* could still smell it—or maybe the memory was just so strong. In my fantasy, there Mom would be, with a glass of milk, sniffing the air like a little Jewish bloodhound.

"'What's that? What's that? Could it be...PUSSY?"

Joe shoved the mic into his mouth for the last word, so that it sounded like the voice of God. That got the crowd, myself included. Then he continued. "I think that's good advice, just generally, for life: If you wanna know who's got something to hide, find out who smells like Ivory soap. 99 and 44/100 percent pure...pure bullshit.

"And that brings us back to History. History is a way for us all to wash our hands. Some of us wash heavy like Pilate or Lady Macbeth, others like horny sixteen-year-olds, but we're all grateful for the opportunity. We gather all that shit together, all those lies and half-truths and polite blank spaces, and we make some of the people in the story seem clean and good, and some of the people seem dirty and bad, and we put it into books for children to memorize.

"And people love it. You know why? It gives a pleasant place to live. Charlie Parker once said, 'If we heard all the sounds in the world, we'd surely go mad.' And I say, if we knew all the things that happened in the world—the truth in full, all the stuff that is really going on—right now, and now, and now—we'd go mad from that, too. To keep sane, we play roles, make events into a story. We gotta turn reality into a place we can *live*, and the only way to do this, is to lie.

"People know this. They know it from their own lives and the little lies they tell to keep comfortable, in spite of all the pregnancies and affairs and embarrassing diseases and African-Americans in the woodpile. But I ask you, and this is a serious question: if we can't be honest with ourselves, with the people who love us, why should we expect honesty anywhere else? See, dishonesty is an addiction, man. It starts out at the kitchen table with your *mama* and *tateh*, and one morning you wake up, and it's taken over your life. I'm not Sonny Fontaine, and that doesn't matter. But you're not who you say you are, either, and that might."

People weren't laughing at Joe now, they were just listening. He was a smart dude. I was glad we'd put him on the cover of one of our albums.

"In this world, anybody can get away with anything—all you have to do is make the truth too uncomfortable for people. Make it a reality in which they will not live. Then they'll hide it for you. The cover story doesn't matter, it can be any old bullshit. Really. As long as their world stays the way they like it, they'll believe. Shit, they'll improve on it in ways you never could. They'll never give it up, even under pain of death.

"Take the polar ice caps. I read yesterday that the polar ice caps are melting because of too many cars. Now I have no reason to doubt this. It was a reputable source, and I don't know the first thing about pollution, climatology, whatever the relevant discipline might be. But as soon as I read that, I felt a little push against it, you know, just a little push. That was me, weighing the options. On the one hand, there's my convenience. On the other, all life on planet Earth. And life was coming out behind! Can you believe that?

"If things stay as they are and the caps melt, I'm going to suffer, I know this—I'm going to lose my vacation house on the shore, and maybe this whole city will be flooded, and fuck, maybe civilization as we know it will collapse, which, most days, I'm against. But on the other hand, I *like* to drive. So I think, "Ahh, what do scientists know? They could be wrong. People are wrong all the time. I'll just keep driving and see what happens. All this global warming shit, that'll be a little secret between me and my car."

We all laughed, in spite of ourselves.

"It's a lie of convenience. It seems like a small thing, a small price to pay. Tell that to the fucking polar bears, Jack. They know the truth: a lot of little prices add up to one big one. One big, dishonest, fucked-up world."

"I'm not putting myself above you on this. Here's another truth that's too uncomfortable for me, an even more immediate one." Joe held up a pack of cigarettes. "These are a little secret between me and my lungs. Bethesda may or may not be underwater in a hundred years, but these little bastards will definitely kill me. Knowing this, I would rather live in a comfortable fantasy—even at a clear and present danger to my life—than with an uncomfortable truth. Most people would. When you find somebody who will risk everything just to know the truth, you gotta give them great respect." Joe was looking at me. "Took me a lifetime of lying to learn that.

He took a deep breath, and continued, the audience following him with stunned, unwavering eyes. "The lies of convenience never stop, even when we're dead. Someday, if you go out to Arlington to check out my tombstone it won't read, 'He died for a comfortable lie.' Which is the whole problem. Until we start addressing the real problem—until we start replacing the secrets and lies with honesty and truth—we'll never fix any of this shit. And it's all fixable, I believe that, in my heart. Reality could be better than any fantasy. This place could be heaven. We could make it that. And then all the tombstones would say, "He ate and drank and learned and loved and once in a while, when everything lined up right, he even got laid, and what could be better than that?'"

The audience sat in stunned silence. Joe threw his hands up in a big Vegas-style send off.

"Thanks, you've been a great audience. Good night."

He left the stage to the lonely fizz-whoosh of a bartender filling a highball glass with the soda gun.

CHAPTER FIFTEEN

An hour later, I was sitting at a card table in the basement of Joe's house. He lived just north of Bethesda, with hundreds of framed photos of his pretty dead wife and two wiener dogs. When we pulled into the attached garage, he called his pad "Squaresville," and I was inclined to agree. A boxy little bungalow clad in vinyl siding, it was the epitome of pre-Ravins America. Even in the dark, I could tell the lawn was perfectly mowed, winter-brown but waiting for Spring.

Joe took me straight down to the basement, to his den. It was a "safe room." "That's been my business after '80. But of course you know that."

"Didn't get that far," I admitted. "I was a little distracted."

"You were a little rascal is what you were. How far did you read?"

"Far enough to not believe a word you say."

"I can tell the truth now. I'm retired."

"So who did it? Who shot me, and why?"

"I don't know, Tom, honest to shit. All I know is what I did. Somebody high up wanted to scare you back into your cave—my money'd be on Casey, he was full of stupid-ass ideas. So I got a phone call, a timetable, and a budget. I did what I was asked to do. After that, I'm as mystified as you are."

We'd argued all the way from the club. Joe said there *had* to be a second shooter, but when I pressed him on details, he admitted he had none. I stuck with switched bullets. Occam's razor and all that.

Joe cracked open another bottle of scotch. He drank it like water. Some ex-junkies do. "Sure you don't want one?"

I shook my head. "I'm clean, no thanks to you."

"Withdrawal builds character."

"Fuck that." I yawned. "Der Fraulein gave me some tapes."

Joe sat back down. There were cards and chips piled between us, from last Monday's poker night. "Der who?"

"My wife." I played with a blue chip.

"Oh yeah, right. It's been fifteen years since I read your file."

"Listen, do you have any organic coffee?"

"At midnight?" Joe laughed. "You're not totally clean, Mr. Caffeine."

"It's not addictive if—" Fuck it, I didn't want to get into *that*. "It's a damn sight better than what you were pushing."

"We never pushed anything, Tom. That was the beauty of it."

"That's your guilty conscience talking. A lot of people died—

"—and a lot more didn't," he interrupted, taking another gulp of booze. "We were the good guys, Tom. It was either us, or the Cro-Magnons, *schtarkers* like LeMay. Shit, at least I have a conscience. Those guys are *blank*. No sense of proportion, or fallibility. They wanted full-on nuclear war, with a martial law chaser."

Joe leaned in, warming to his topic. "They used force; we used pleasure. We gave people what they wanted—and we were doing it for their own good! What do you think would've happened with the Panthers, if we hadn't nullified them? Add in all those GIs rotating back from 'Nam, trained in weapons and tactics? There would've been fighting in the fucking streets. That's what the Cro-Magnons *wanted*. They wanted paramilitary groups killing each other, and civilians crying out for law and order. That's how things like the Nazis happen, man."

"But they didn't."

"No they didn't. Because our group saw it coming. We flooded the country with cheap, strong heroin. The ghettos burned, and some vets got hooked, but the rest of society survived, more or less." Joe sucked some ice, and topped himself off. "Trust me, Tom, we were the good guys. And we won."

"What about the assassinations, all that shit?"

"Knuckle-draggers again. In '63, we had Vickie's husband dropping acid *in the White House*. Our plan was working, so they popped him. They'd always resort to violence, when they saw they were losing…Maybe that's what happened with you."

"Really?"

"Maybe someone on the other side fucked with the op. It happens. All I know is, the equipment I provided had blanks in it."

"No offense, but I don't believe you."

"Only one way to be sure."

Joe got up, and walked past me, into a dank room. There was a clicky, springy sound as he turned on the light; I smelled mildew and saw a washer and dryer through the doorway. "One sec." He rummaged around some metal storage shelves. "Don't you dare slip lysergic into my drink."

"Are you joking?"

"Yes."

Joe returned with a sealed yellow bag in his hand. It had an NYPD symbol on it, with names and dates scrawled in Sharpie. He put it down with a clunk. "Here 'tis. The gun I provided, the one Thigg fired. Open it."

"I'd prefer not to."

"Jeez, it won't bite you." Joe tore the plastic open with his teeth, then widened it with his fingers, so that the gun could slide out. I stared at it, squatting there like a poisonous toad.

"Never fired since that night. Unbroken chain of possession from then to now."

"How'd you get it?"

"Once there wasn't going to be a trial—that part of Thigg's programming worked, thank Christ—it was just taking up storage space."

I shivered. "All right, show and tell's over, Joe. Put it away."

"No, I want you to shoot me with it."

"I'm not going to fucking shoot you with it. I can't even look at it."

"In the hand or foot or something," he said, pushing it toward me.

"You're mad."

"Perhaps, but it's the only way you'll ever believe me."

"I believe you."

"No you fucking don't, and I wouldn't either. I'm a spy, I spent my whole life lying. That's why it's important to me that you know I'm telling the truth."

I picked it up gingerly. "What if you're wrong?"

Joe smiled. "My punishment for fucking up the op. And you'd be getting revenge—isn't that what you want?"

"At this point? Answers are enough, and peace."

"Whatever. You'd be doing me a solid. My wife's dead, and the ciggies are closing in," Joe said. "Come on, either I'm right, or it'll be deliciously ironic. You'll make the *Book of Lists*."

"I'm already in the *Book of Lists*."

Joe looked over his glasses at me until I relented.

"All right," I said. "I can't believe I'm doing this." I pointed the gun in his general direction.

"Tom, I appreciate it."

"You spy fuckers are crackers, you know that?"

Joe rolled up his sleeve, then stood sideways, like a matador "Actually, no. That's bullshit." He presented his chest. "A man should commit to what he believes in." He scratched an itch, then said, "Fire when ready, Griddley."

I aimed…"Fuck, Joe, I can't do this. I have all your old LPs."

"That's *my* line!" he laughed.

Strangely, the laughing made it easier. I re-aimed and fired.

The report was loud, and a tongue of orange flame leaped out of the muzzle. But Joe didn't move. He opened his eyes and smiled broadly. "Either those are blanks, or I'm Superjew."

Joe was elated—his professional honor had been restored. I was depressed, because I was no closer to the truth than before. We sat in his basement, him losing steam, me spinning theories. "But I've checked the personal angle," I said, tired and angry. "Why couldn't the second gun have been someone else in the government? The Cro-Magnons—that's what you said an hour ago."

"I was spitballing. Like, 'Maybe Clara Peller did it,'" Joe said. "Two operations working simultaneously? No offense, but I don't think anybody would spend that kinda dough. Shit, I couldn't even expense your last LP."

Joe chuckled; I didn't. "Maybe it wasn't official. Say some spook got wind of your plan, and thought, 'Scared's good, so dead's gotta be better.' A keenie, bucking for a promotion."

Joe sighed. "DC's a small town, I would've heard something. And I'd like to think a friend would've piped up when I was getting shitcanned."

"What about the people who programmed Thigg to shoot me?" I said. "Might they know something?"

"Nope. I compartmentalize my ops, Tom. And just for the sake of correctness," Joe continued, "we didn't program Thigg to shoot you. That's not how it's done. We programmed him to hypnotize himself. Then when he'd gotten to the suggestible point, we provided your name, and Thigg did the rest."

"What's the difference?"

"Functionally, none. But it's infinitely harder to trace back after the fact. It looks like Thigg hypnotized himself into a murderous rage—because that's what he did. And why did he pick Tom Larkin? 'Who knows, he's crazy! For God's sake, he sits around hypnotizing himself!' If you give people an open-and-shut case, they usually take it."

I laid my head on the table and whimpered.

"Meanwhile, nobody thinks to ask the real question, which is, 'Who taught him how to do it?' If it was that easy to hypnotize yourself into murder, people would be dropping like flies. But they aren't, because it's something you have to be taught."

I pounded my fist against the side of my head. "God! I just want this to be over!"

"So give up. Go back to your comfortable anonymous life. If they haven't killed you by now—"

"It's only a matter of time." I told him about Warren, and Thigg, and Robbie, and how I'd been followed by Pompadour.

Joe shrugged at Thigg. Then he said, "Warren and Robbie, they were both assets, you know that, right?"

"I guessed with Warren."

"Robbie's even easier. Clue #1: he travels to Cuba in '64. Cuba, our sworn enemy, the place we'd nearly gone nuclear over. Clue #2: we let him back in. It's like Oswald and Russia, nonsense if you think about it. Clue #3: As soon as we let him back in, he gets political."

"So..."

"So we painted him Red, man! Then we used him to control you guys. It wasn't my op, but from what I heard it was a mindfuck, part of keeping the hippies away from the blacks. While they were getting shot and lynched, people like Robbie were trying to levitate the Pentagon." Joe traced a water ring on the table. "SCLC, SNCC—those people were the real revolutionaries. I admired them. Still do.'

"Yeah, right. All you spooks just loved Martin Luther King."

"Some of us did. We kept him safe for as long as we could," Joe said, taking another sip of scotch. "What, did you think he was lucky?"

"Joe, come on—you honestly expect me to believe you people planned out the Sixties?"

"As much as we could. It was our job. Forty hours a week, fifty weeks a year."

"But King got shot. Did that happen during vacation?"

"We weren't omnipotent, Tom. As you well know. Just well-funded, and organized, and dedicated to what we believed in. Which was probably closer to what you believed in than you ever realized."

I looked at the sagging, burping, old fart in front of me. "Amazing."

"No, not amazing. Just how stuff gets done. What's amazing is how the clues were right there, in front of people's faces, and how they refused to see it. They still won't. Because they don't want to live in that reality. They prefer a fantasy of randomness and emotion." Joe looked at his watch; it was getting late. "Anyway, I don't weep for Warren or Robbie. They lived the life. They knew the rules. If they were civilians, I'd say it's likely they were killed because they met with you. But since they were spooks, who can say? Could've been something twenty years old, something totally unrelated."

"Fuck!" I yelled, but it came out weak. "You're the spy, what would you do?"

"I'd go see your wife, where is she now? New York, still?"

"Yeah."

"Go up to New York, and make sure that she and Jason—"

"Jasper."

"—Jasper have enough protection. That's the first thing," Joe moved to the couch. "Then, I'd get some protection for you. Three bodyguards ought to do it, working in eight-hour shifts. Bulletproof vest, obviously. And no unnecessary trips."

"For how long?"

"Until you kick off for real," Joe laughed. "Or you could go public."

"You mean be Tom Larkin again?"

"Yeah. The publicity would be so huge, it'd be hard to get to you."

"Until someone did."

"Yeah. That's the risk."

I shook my head. "I can't do that…I made a commitment to Katrinka I would stay hidden."

"And that's non-negotiable?"

"Utterly."

"Then I'd get out of the private eye business. Is there someone you can hire to investigate for you? Someone you can trust?"

I thought of Sam. "Yeah."

"Let them take over. And the first guy I'd have them hunt down is Pompadomp."

"Pompadour. His name is pompadour. Well, that's not really his name..."

"Whatever. But first, go see Kristina, and do it without anybody knowing."

"Katrinka."

"Sorry. It's beddy-bye time for me." Joe got up. "Sleep here tonight, and tomorrow morning, I'll drive you to the airport. I'll go get some blankets."

I was bone-tired, but couldn't sleep—any number of reasons suggested themselves. First, I still didn't know who had tried to kill me, which meant I was still in danger. Second, my new best friend Joe, who had lived in spook-world for decades, thought Katrinka and Jasper might be in danger. And third, tomorrow morning I had to drive to Dulles with Mr. Vehicular Manslaughter.

I lay under the blankets, itchy and hot, for two more hours. When I heard the clock strike three, and my eyes were still open, I swore loudly and threw back the covers.

I didn't want to leave the house—Joe had mentioned all sorts of security—but my lighter was in the pocket of my tuxedo jacket, and that was in the front seat of Joe's car. I couldn't say exactly why I wanted my lighter, but I wanted it. So I slipped on my shoes, and walked quietly upstairs, walking slowly to minimize creaking. The clock on the oven ticked impossibly loud as I tiptoed through the kitchen and out to the garage.

I flicked on the light, hoping that Joe's mania for security didn't extend to locking the car doors. To my relief the driver's side opened. I leaned inside, stretching over to grab my jacket. I'd begun rifling through the pockets when I felt something cold and hard press behind my right ear.

"Don't move," an oddly familiar voice said.

"Can I piss myself?" I glanced into the rearview mirror. It was Pompadour.

CHAPTER SIXTEEN

Up close, Pompadour looked a lot rougher than he had in the diner. His face had the kind of puffiness that made me think of fried food and lager. His hair was streaked with gray, and his nose looked like something overripe and ready to fall off the end of a branch.

"What are you gawping at?" Pompadour grabbed an old deli wrapper, and threw it into the front. "Write him a note," he said. "I don't want him tailing us."

"I don't have a pen."

He tossed one at me; it hit my head and caromed onto the seat. "No need to be violent," I said.

"I'll be the judge of that."

"What would you like me to write?"

"You, at a loss for words? That's a first." Pompadour dictated testily. "'Couldn't sleep, so I took off early. Thanks for everything.'"

I wrote it.

"Now add something funny, so he doesn't suspect." When I paused, Pompadour got impatient. "Forget it, we haven't time for the mood to strike. Come on!"

I stood up, handing back the pen. Pompadour got behind me, gun in my back. "We'll go out the side door."

"After you," I said.

"Don't be cheeky."

Pompadour seemed nervous, so I wasn't sure whether I was rooting for Joe's alarm system or not. At any loud noise, my captor might startle and pull the trigger. I knew what that felt like and had no interest in reliving it. I closed my eyes and turned the knob.

Nothing happened. "Bloody drunk," I mumbled.

"Keep quiet," Pompadour ordered, nudging me forward. "Car's down the street."

"I always like your cars," I said once we were away from the house.

"They're just rentals. Not everybody has the lolly for the real thing. I sure as hell don't. Thanks to you."

"Thanks to me? We've never even met."

"Come on," my captor said, "after all these years, you don't recognize me?"

"I'm nearsighted," I said lamely.

"And poverty ages a man. But adding insult to injury isn't smart, given that I've got a pistol in your ribs."

"I haven't any ribs. If you let me turn around—Ow!"

"I'll give you a clue." Pompadour's breath was hot in the cool night air, and smelled of cheap beer. 'Duke, duke, duke/Duke of Earl, earl, earl/Duke of Earl, earl, earl/Duke of Earl, earl, earl…'"

The beer, the voice, and the song all congealed instantly into a memory. "Bevin? Bevin Fudd?"

"You were expecting Ollie O'Connell? Keep walkin'."

The Ravins started out as me, Ollie, Harry, my artsy friend Gilgamesh, and Bevin Fudd. Bevin was our drummer, mainly because he was the only kid in Greasby who owned a proper kit. Still, he went to Marseille with us, got the same VD, suffered through the same shitty gigs, and even after Gilgamesh quit to become a sculptor, Bevin stuck in there drumming, not well, but certainly loudly. The girls liked him, too, especially when he did his star-turn, that old Gene Chandler number I'd just heard.

He expected me to grovel, so I did the unexpected. "Bevin, did you shoot me?"

"Not yet."

"I mean back in '80? Were you the second gun?"

Bevin snorted. "Bloody typical. One assassin's not good enough for Tom bleeding Larkin. There have to be two, or four—how about a bloody brigade? How could I shoot you, *I* had to work," Bevin said. "In '80, I was bolting side-mirrors onto Morris Marinas. What a shitbox. I swore then that the moment I got some money I'd—"

"Yeah, yeah, Bev, but did you do it?"

"I didn't have the time or the money to go jetting around the world offing high school chums...But I had every right to, didn't I? I should've shot you, you and Ollie both, after what you did."

I couldn't disagree. Right after our first session with EMI, we gave Bevin the sack. Buck was a better drummer, but it was still a shitty break.

"You didn't even have the balls to fire me yourself—you sent that smarmy ponce to do it for you. But he got what he deserved, didn't he?"

I resolved not to tell Bevin about Brigadoon.

"And so did you, you bastard. But not from me. I didn't have that pleasure. Here we are."

A jab stopped me in front of an MGB two-seater. I resolved to butter Bevin up. "Wow, that's beautiful. I can't tell, is it black or dark red?"

Keeping the gun on me, Bevin extracted his keys from a tight pair of jeans, then opened the boot. "Get in."

"I'll never fit in there."

"Make yourself fit."

"Fuck you. I'll yell. I'll run." I pointed at Bevin's shoes. "Those winkle-pickers aren't built for speed."

"But bullets are." He waggled the gun towards the small boot.

I hoisted in a leg. "Would it matter if I told you this tux was a rental?"

"Christ, I'd forgotten how annoying you are."

"Just imagine how you'd feel if I was kidnapping you." Bevin closed the trunk lid. "Thanks for taking out the spare," I grumbled.

"Now stay quiet," he said. "We have a long drive ahead, and if you make noise, I'm going to have to take back roads, and if I have to take back roads, by the time we get there, you could suffocate. So none of your Blarney Stone bullshit, okay Tom?"

I heard Bevin walk around to the front, get in the driver's seat, and start the car. When the engine noise seemed loud enough, I began testing the lock, and the lid. There was no play in either, so I resolved to conserve my energy. I was deeply weary; maybe a solution would come to me in a dream? Trying not to think of what lay ahead for me—or for Katrinka and Jasper—I reluctantly allowed myself to asleep.

Three or four hours later, judging by the daylight leaking through the edges of the lid, I felt the car stop.

"Yeah, I'd like an Egg McMuffin, a black coffee, and three cherry pies." Bevin still had his sweet tooth.

About fifteen minutes later, Bevin pulled off the side of the road, walked around to the rear of the MGB, and opened the trunk.

"Here's a pie." He tossed it at me.

"Can I have a slash?" I said, squinting into the morning light.

"Use this." He threw me his empty coffee cup.

"How? I'll pee on myself."

"Not my problem."

I looked at the cup. "It's too small."

"Give it back then."

"NO!" I said, and after he'd closed the lid, I'd licked it thoroughly, greedily, harvesting the stray drops that clung to the Styrofoam.

The trunk opened again, mid-lick.

"Tom, what the fuck are you doing? Why are making those noises?"

"Get back!" I hissed, clutching the cup close to me. He'd have to kill me first.

"Fucking weirdo." Bevin flung in some photos, and a pen. "Sign these."

After we'd gotten back on the road, I found that Bevin and I could hear each other if we spoke loudly. "Bevin, I'm really sorry Ollie kicked you—"

"It was Ollie who did it, eh? You're such a coward. Do you know, you never even told me why?"

It was simple; Bevin didn't fit inside our little dysfunctional family, Buck did. But I couldn't say that. So I said, "It's complicated—"

"I'm sure it was, Tom. Very complicated. You know what wasn't complicated? Watching you three fuckers get fantastically rich and famous. That wasn't complicated at all."

"Bevin, are you going to kill me, like you did Warren Darden?"

"You mean the bloke in the tub? Struth, that took a year off my life. I didn't kill him. I threw up on him, though. He was like that when I come in."

"You didn't kill Warren? Did you run over Robbie?"

"You daft git. You don't rent a flashy old car then go hit someone with it. Cost you thousands, *and* get you caught."

"I'd think better if you let me sit up front. All the blood's pooling in my arse."

Bevin ignored that woeful fact. "You never helped me," he whined. "You wouldn't even blurb my book."

"You sent me a book?" I was genuinely surprised. "Oh...my wife must've screened it. She was handling all my affairs."

"Likely bloody story," Bevin said. "I remember how you used to treat birds. All that househusband crap—what a load of bollocks."

"Tell you what, Bevin, I'll help you now, all right?"

"Sure you will; sign those photos yet?"

"Yes," I lied.

"You're a bad liar, Tom. Now shut up, we're coming to a toll."

Angry at being caught out, I signed the photos—then dated them, so that they'd be obvious forgeries. Mid-chuckle, I had a very troubling thought; the reason my thinky-parts were sputtering wasn't lack of coffee or the blood pooling in my arse, it was because the old exhaust system probably had a leak in it. Carbon dioxide was building up in the boot. If I didn't get out of there soon, I'd be dead.

Asking Bevin to let me out hadn't worked, I'd have to find another way. The good news was, between the noise of the engine and the doo-wop cassette Bevin had put in the tape-player, I could let off a small bomb without him noticing. The bad news was, I'd left my small bomb in my other tuxedo.

I felt for a trunk release cable; there wasn't one, the car was too old. Was there a tire iron, something like that? Perhaps I could bash out the rear light, and hope we got pulled over. Unfortunately, Bevin had removed anything that could be used as a weapon; he knew how I could brawl. That left the trunk latch, I'd have to try to pry it loose. But with what? The contents of my pockets were on the card table back in Bethesda; all I had was the silver Cross pen that Bevin kept throwing at me. It was metal, and had felt solid enough hitting my head. I hoped it would hold; if it broke, I was fucked.

Carefully I wedged the pen between the latch and the lid, and gave a tentative downwards pull. The lid budged, but only just. I sighed; this was going to be difficult. I wiggled, and levered, and got it some distance—but then the pen snapped, spilling ink all over my tuxedo shirt.

And with that, Ravins Mavens, I was done. The great Tom Larkin, Father of the Sixties, was going to die trapped in the boot of a classic car, carried aloft by Bevin's cheesy doo-wop cassette. If it hadn't been for Milton Crouk—or my own damn stubbornness—I could've been wasting that morning over a nice breakfast at the Casa Marisol. So what if someone eventually shot me? There were worse ways to die—I was doing one of them. And the worst bloody part was, I never even figured out who did it! What a waste of a second chance. I'd never see Katrinka again, or Jasper, or Helen. Is it still feeling sorry for yourself when you are actually fucked?

Between bogey-sniffles, I felt the car slowing. I heard the gritty asphalt of an old access road, then the crunch of gravel. Where were we heading? Was this where he planned to dump my body? The adrenaline started to pump, washing away all that self-pity. We pulled into someplace and stopped. A series of annoying electronic beeps told me we were in a filling station.

I sat in perfect silence, listening as the nozzle was inserted and the tank began to fill. Bevin's footsteps came around. "I'm getting a burrito, do you want one?"

I feigned weakness. "Only it doesn't have meat." I wanted to occupy Bevin for as long as I could, reading ingredients. I waited for my captor's footsteps to fade. When the door jingled open, I counted five and made my move.

Putting my foot against the trunk—and really thanking God I'd worn motorcycle boots—I kicked. And again. And again. Finally, the lid gave way. I scrambled out, blinking, sucking in the cold December air. My palms hit the pavement; after six hours in the fetal position, my body was totally asleep.

A woman using the pump next door stared blankly. Her dark green SUV was crawling with kids; life was complicated enough without engaging whatever I was involved in. I gave her a reason anyway.

"Bachelor party." I looked over and saw Bevin at the burrito counter, talking to the cashier. "That's my best man in there. I'm gonna get back at him. Don't say anything, okay?" I grabbed the squeegee from the container of blue goo it was soaking in; in three steps I was shoving it through the handles of the door.

The terrier-faced cashier saw me first. "Hey!"

"Bachelor party," I said. "He locked me in the trunk, I'm just getting him back."

Bevin glared at me. "Ha ha, Tom. *Tres amusant.*"

I flipped him off. The tank was full, so I unhooked the pump. Smiling now, the woman was still pumping; her SUV had quite a tank. The kids were pointing and laughing as Bevin shook the doors and swore at me. "Wait ten seconds, then let 'em out," I said. "I just wanna piss him off a bit."

The SUV's radio was playing a Ravins song, one of mine. "You like that song?" I asked the nine-year-old in the passenger seat.

"Yeah."

"Then play it loud!"

We both smiled as I drove away, leaving my past in the dust.

CHAPTER SEVENTEEN

Bevin had been heading north towards Manhattan, towards Katrinka and Jasper. As I continued his trajectory (in his car) I consoled myself that he would find them harder targets than I had been. After what had gone down in 1980, Katrinka had installed the full panoply of celebrity security, from bodyguards, to motion-detectors, to a guy trotting behind her with a hazmat suit, just in case of bio-chemical attack. For a second I considered holing up someplace *gemutlicht* and letting Bevin hurl himself kamikaze-like against the best precautions money could buy. But that was a risk, and if the drummer-turned-hitman made it through the pickets, I'd never forgive myself. Whatever else happened, I had to reach my wife and child before he did.

The question was, how? I could call Katrinka, but it would be at least 72 hours before I heard back; she was deeply committed to isolation as a lifestyle. My wife was a lanky blonde island, a 6'1" country unto herself, so meeting her face-to-face was going to take real planning. Predictable stratagems—porn movie gambits of cable guy, pizza guy, plumber, or gigolo—these all melted in the awesome force-field of her brain. I spent the first twelve hours in New York trying to think of a better idea, and waiting for some luck. Twelve hours after that, I got both.

I was eating breakfast at a Viand on 68th, across the street from where I used to send my bedclothes to get dry cleaned. Two bites from the end of my shreddly wheat, I spied a man attempting to wheel a large crate into the cleaners. Halfway through this highly entertaining ordeal—the crate was at least seven feet tall, and it looked heavy, too—the man's hat fell off, and I saw that it was an assistant of Fraulein's, a luckless schmo I remembered from the old days, Gabe or Dave or something. He must be a real go-getter, I thought, to still be working for us five years later; I knew what Fraulein considered a salary.

My eyesight has never been very good, so I slapped down a ten and walked outside to get a closer look. I wrapped my scarf around my face, more for concealment than warmth; New York at Christmastime is cold, but not that cold. Someone had set up a table with coverless paperbacks on the sidewalk, and browsing those blackmarket wares gave me ample excuse to cast sidelong looks through the plate-glass window. As Gabe/Dave read typed instructions to the nonplussed Korean lady behind the counter, the item he'd brought slid off the dolly a fraction, and the front lid opened for a moment. Gold flashed through the excelsior, and I saw my opportunity: It was time for Princess Hapsepsut's bimonthly mold treatment.

Gabe/Dave concluded his business, then returned to the mothership. I didn't go directly to the cleaners'—there was no rush; the Princess was in before eight, so she'd be back after four. Instead I turned and walked across the park to the Metropolitan Museum of Art. I can spend hours at that museum, and I did. In the afternoon, I walked back across the park, to a men's clothing store where I bought a pair of hideous gabardine pants. At 4:15 I presented myself to the dumpling-shaped laundress, who was watching a soap on a small black-and-white TV. (It was the same soap Bettina used to watch.)

"Excuse me, do you do alterations? I need these pants hemmed."

"Turn inside out." She put down her Diet Pepsi, and walked past me to some drapes that cordoned off a space the size of a phone booth. "In here."

"Thanks." I closed the drapes, waited ten seconds, then exclaimed: "Bloody hell!" I stuck my head out. "I just realized I forgot to feed the meter. Could you do me a favor and put these quarters in? I can't really, in my condition." I stuck out a hairy, skinny leg.

She laughed. "Sure. What kind car?"

"Silver Mercedes wagon. Just down the block." I'd noticed it on my walk from the pants shop. "Thanks."

I heard the bells on the door tinkle, and stepped back into my pants, leaving the hideous gabardines as a tip. Then I made a beeline for the backroom. The crate was there, towering like a monolith, surrounded by piles of worshipful laundry and clothes on racks. I opened it, and saw the Princess' gleaming golden container. The sarcophagus had a small latch just in front of the ear, which I undid.

"Excuse me, dear," I said shifting the desiccated royal heap to one side. "Don't mean to be fresh." I sniffed her. "You're certainly not." I got as comfortable as I could, then shut the lid and waited.

I must've fallen asleep, because the next thing I remember was the flunky's voice. "Oh my shit, the front panel's loose!" Gabe/Dave said. "Thank god nobody stole it!"

"Turd in golden box still turd."

"I'd better check inside, to make sure the mummy's okay."

Oh, shit, don't do that, I thought. I was preparing to leap out and run like hell, when the proprietress came to my rescue.

"No way," she said. "You not opening that here. Place still stink."

"All right—but if anything's missing, you'll hear from our lawyers."

"Eh," the lady shrugged. Such threats came with the neighborhood.

I was tipped backwards. "Seems heavier."

"You weak," the proprietress said. I liked her.

The flunky took me outside, and I began my trip down Memory Lane. The stoner doorman was still there, only now he dispensed stock tips. Our upstairs neighbor Gloria Swanson was out walking her pair of eczema-ravaged Dobermans. They barked like mad when we rolled past; they'd always hated me, because I wouldn't feed them our cats. When they stopped, I even heard Drummer Dan's bongos, wafting past me on the wind.

We were off the street and in the service entrance, around the corner before I could get really homesick. I heard Gabe/Dave swear as the heavy door knocked into the crate, nearly dislodging it. I scratched my leg, where the mummy was rubbing it, and decided that I'd had just about enough of confined spaces, thank you.

We sat down in the loading dock for five minutes, until Gabe/Dave got fed up and called upstairs. "Do you still want the Princess sent to the warehouse?"

Oh fuck, I hadn't thought of that. We maintained a refrigerated warehouse in Brooklyn, and my wife was always cycling belongings back and forth. I'd freeze to death in there, and if I didn't freeze, I'd starve. And I had to pee!

Silence; maybe only twenty seconds' worth, but it felt like forever.

"Okay." Gabe/Dave hung up the phone.

I briefly pondered escape plans; maybe if I acted strangely enough, he would think I was a hallucination. Did our assistants still get stoned? Of course they did; but was he now?

Gabe/Dave tipped me backwards again and we began rolling towards my doom. I took a deep breath and pushed against the lid—it wouldn't budge! To my horror, I remembered that it was always difficult to open the sarcophagus, owing to the pine tar or duck resin or whatever it was they had used to seal it 2,000 years before. I tried again, mumbling eternal fealty to the ancient wog gods, but the lid remained stuck. Cursing them now, I decided to be done with the whole charade. Being unmasked was better than becoming a Larkin-sicle. One good yell ought to do it. I took a deep breath, and—

The metal gate of the Oneida's ancient service elevator gnashed open. "What floor?"

"Eight," Gabe/Dave said.

Ancient wog gods, I owe you one.

Fifteen minutes later, I heard my wife dressing down the Columbia work study kid in charge of her hazmat suit. "Go ahead, quit," she snapped. "The last one liked being paid in coupons!" She went through a couple of students a month; it was a good experience for them. Der Fraulein's the type of person who teaches lessons without even realizing it. That's what "bodhisattva" means.

The front door slammed, and I heard the rough rhythmic scrapes of my wife trying to light a cigarette. Uttering a pungent word, she gave up and hurled the lighter. Hearing it bounce on the carpet in front of me, I readied myself. When the grumbling grew close, I threw all my weight against the lid. Praise Osiris, the ancient gumminess cracked and the door swung to.

"Ta-DAAA!" I flung my arms wide, like a stripper emerging from a cake.

"Schisse!" Fraulein staggered backwards, knocking over a sacred Magna Mater statuette, the one I always thought looked like a dildo. A person couldn't turn around in our Treasure Room without breaking something priceless, so we learned not to care. Besides, everything is "priceless" until you try to have it fixed, then it's price-full.

"What's wrong, aren't you glad to see me?" I said. "Why are you clutching your heart like that?" I stepped out of the sarcophagus as nimble as Peter Pan—then it was my turn to clutch. Next to my wife stood Bevin Fudd.

We must've looked like right idiots the pair of us, gaping and gasping and toppling magical bric-a-brac. But you couldn't have told by Bevin. He munched an apple, cool as you please. "Right, he's here," Bevin said. "Time to pay up."

At the mention of money, Fraulein sprang back to full power. "Oh, no, that wasn't the deal. I hired you to bring him from DC, not lose him in Delaware and have him wander in himself."

"Hired…him?" I croaked.

"Yeh," Bevin sniggered. "I was s'posed to keep an eye on you, Sherlock." He put the apple down, and started switch-combing his hair. "Make sure you didn't hurt yourself."

"Don't leave your apple there!" Fraulein hissed. "That table's from Atlantis."

"You—he—" I felt my face turning colors. *"We will talk about this later!"*

"What's there to talk about? Bevin saw you shoot a guy in Washington. He called me and I told him to bring you in. You're showing a pattern of escalating violence. Have you been listening to your tapes?"

"They broke."

"Well that explains a lot. I think you might be turning into a psychopath."

"I've been scared out of my mind by Bevvy No-Mates here," I said defensively. "Did he tell you the gun had blanks? Or that the guy asked me to shoot him?"

"Spare me your delusionary mechanisms," Fraulein said with a wave. "I was against this from the very beginning, you know. It was obvious that you'd crack under the strain, but you wouldn't listen. You had to be nosy, you couldn't leave—"

"I hate to interrupt this heartwarming moment," Bevin said, "but there is the matter of $50,000..."

I whipped my head around. "FIFTY THOUSAND—" An ancient Aboriginal battle digeridoo leaned next to the sarcophagus; I grabbed it and charged. My first swipe missed Bevin's shimmying quiff by inches. I didn't get a second swipe; my ex-bandmate was even quicker than Milton Crouk. I chased him through the apartment, out of the service entrance in the kitchen, and to the edge of the back stairs. The prospect of tromping down eight flights cooled my anger.

"You'll be hearing from my solicitors!" Bevin yelled up at me.

"And you'll be hearing from Classic Car Rental," I said. I'd dumped his MGB in the Hudson.

Bevin scurried away; I had protected my home and hearth. Proud of myself, I strutted back to the service entrance, digeridoo in hand. The door looked like shit, it's brown paint scratched off by Swanson's pair of crusty dobies. I tried the knob. It didn't move.

"I see you still haven't fixed this," I called to my wife, trying to sound non-psychotic. "Let me in."

There was no answer.

"Dear, we haven't time for an experiment right now. We have to talk, I discovered a plot. You and Jasper might be in danger."

Gloria Swanson yelled down the stairwell. "Whoever that is, quiet!"

"Shut up, you old bint!" I yelled, then turned to the door and murmured sweetly, "Let me in, dear!"

Swanson grumbled, "I knew you were too annoying to die, you degenerate."

"I could say the same thing about—HEY!" A rotten half-grapefruit hit me on the back of the neck. Ever classy, Swanson had started throwing garbage.

"Hophead! Pervert!"

Under heavy fire, I whipped out my wallet, and began jimmying the door with my Macy's card.

"I don't want your AIDSy money, dirty hippie!"

An eternity later, the lock clicked. "You *will* clean this up!" I shouted at her as it swung to. I didn't hear what Swanson said next, but the racket continued for a while. Never fight with an old person; they have nothing better to do.

The kitchen was empty. I walked through the hall into the Treasure Room, and replaced the digeridoo. "Katrinka," I called, "come out. We have to talk, I know the whole story. Well, sort of. Anyway, you and Jasper need bodyguards."

I peered into each room: the maid's quarters, the study, the parlor, the solarium, my wife's office, her dressing room, my wife's auxiliary office, the fur-freezer, and her bedroom. Katrinka was nowhere to be seen—then, suddenly, her voice was everywhere.

"Go away, Tom," it boomed at me over the sound system. "Go back to California. We have nothing to discuss."

"Are you mad?" I said. "There was a whole plot against me."

"I'm warning you, Tom. If you don't leave, I'm going to call the police."

"But why?" I walked into the living room. "You and the boy might be in danger."

"I'm well aware of that, that's why I'm calling the police."

"Have you gone insane?" I said, looking at a new Diebenkorn on the mantle. "The fuzz are the last—"

"Yes, hi, this is Katrinka Larkin at 5 West 68th, There's an intruder in my home. I believe he's wanted for the murder of three people."

"WHAT THE FUCK?" I dropped the print, and the frame shattered. "Where are you?"

Fraulein hung up. "Why should I tell you? So you can kill me like Warren and Robbie—and now that fellow down in Washington, too? You're a maniac, admit it. That's the first step to getting better."

"I'm not the only one," I mumbled, then heard a small creaking sound to my left.

My wife's ocelot Kiki had not died after jumping out of the window. Instead, she'd hit a windowbox halfway down, and had become partially paralyzed. Her useless hind legs were held in a little cart fastened to her belly with a strap. "Kill, Kiki, kill!" Katrinka hectored. "Go on, bite him! You can do it!"

Kiki licked my hand, and I tried to steer her away from the broken glass. "Katrinka, darling," I said to the nearest speaker, "you've got it all wrong. Warren was my friend. He was cut to ribbons then left to die. Do you honestly think I could do something like that?"

"I remember what you did to the Cuisinart. It wasn't working so you took a hammer and you smashed it."

I sighed. "Love, that was the Seventies. People did a lot of embarrassing things."

"Go do embarrassing things in California. Kill more people for all I care. Just leave."

I sat down on the couch. "Nope," I said. "I'm not moving."

"Fine, get arrested."

"Fine, I will, and when I do, I'll tell them the whole sordid tale."

There was a knock on the door.

"Better run, Tom."

"Oh no. Not me. I'm going to say, 'Hello officer, I'm Tom Larkin. Take my fingerprints if you don't believe me.' Then I'll tell them it was all another one of your kooky experiments."

Katrinka's voice lowered. "You wouldn't dare."

"I would."

"But you promised!"

"Desperate times call for desperate measures."

More knocking. "Is everything all right in there? We got a call about an intruder."

"Just think of it, Katrinka," I said. "You'll be more popular than ever."

My wife gave a little scream of frustration, "Come here, into the laboratory. Quickly!"

I got up. Whistling, I strolled nonchalantly into the hall.

"Hurry up, *arschloch*! It's ADT, they have keys!" I broke into a trot. "Where is the lab?"

"Jasper's old music room." This back bedroom was originally intended to be our son's recording studio, but after his first single flopped, Fraulein decided he was untalented and made it into a room for her experiments.

My wife stepped from behind the one-way mirror which ran along one wall. "Hey!" I pointed at the mirror. "That used to be the butler's pantry."

She grabbed my arm and threw me into a chair. "Be quiet!"

Down the hall in the living room, the front door opened. "Mrs. Larkin?" a male voice called. "It's the police..."

Flipping on several machines, she handed me a lasso of spiral cord. "Loop this around your chest. Put this cuff around your arm. Now stick these on your head."

"Where?"

"Anywhere, just hurry!"

I'd finished sticking the last electrode on my third eye when my wife yanked my arm down. She fastened them both to the chair with large Velcro straps. "Is that really necessary?" I asked.

"It must look *real*."

Kiki ambled in, her wheels squeaking faintly. "Go!" Fraulein commanded, as the cat began to lick my hand again. "Go, you big dumb thing!" Hearing the men coming down the hall, she grabbed a clipboard. She'd just started writing when a couple of cops walked in, guns drawn. One looked young and rather bashful; the other was fatter and definitely more aggressive. "Holy shit!" the baby-faced one said. "What's that?"

"Ocelot," I said mildly.

My wife looked up from her phantom notations. "Oh, hello, officers."

"We got a call about an intruder," said the aggro cop. "Is everything all right?"

"Oh yes," my wife said. "Everything is *excellent*. Heart rate went up, breathing up, plenty of sweating—I think we can definitively say that accusing someone of murder yields a very definite, measurable physiological reaction."

The aggro one gestured at me with his pistol. "Who's he?"

"Watch where you're pointing that thing.".

Everyone ignored me. The bashful cop asked my wife. "So everything's okay?"

"Absolutely." My wife put down her clipboard. "Thank you. You've both been very helpful. And rest assured I will be writing a letter of thanks to your superiors."

"But lady," the aggressive one said, "you can't just call the police and say—"

"Nonsense," my wife said. "There's nothing one cannot do for Science." The cops looked dubious until Fraulein sealed the deal. "There's a bowl of money by the front door, please help yourself to a handful on the way out. And Merry Christmas."

When the front door slammed behind them, we both breathed a sigh of relief. "All right, Fraulein. Turn me loose."

My wife didn't say anything. Instead she grabbed my chair and turned it ninety degrees. At the far end of the narrow room sat a metal cart with a TV monitor on it. She had been working on a bunch of experiments studying the effects of Richard Simmons on heterosexuals.

"I don't want to look at Richard Simmons," I said. "Undo my arms!"

"Shut up and watch," she said, turning off the overhead light. She pointed a remote at the TV cart, turned on the set, and left.

"Come back, you nutter!"

"When it's done."

My acid retort was drowned out by the hiss of electric snow. A color bar appeared briefly on screen, with an irritating tone. The image jumped, and there was Fraulein, standing in our living room. She had on the hat and short coat she always used to wear, and was pulling on a pair of leather gloves Klaus Kinski had bought her after attacking us once in the street by mistake.

"Hello, Tom. It is October thirty-first, 1980, at"—she checked her watch—"ten fifty-seven p.m. You and Jasper are down in the Village at the Halloween Parade. You asked not to be disturbed, so I am honoring that, but I just got a call from Warren Darden. He says he has a fantastic new way to promote the album, something totally innovative and guaranteed to work. He won't tell me what it is over the phone, so I'm going to go over to Mr. Chow to meet him and Robbie Illadro. They sounded high, but whatever, it's worth a shot, right?"

As she laughed, Katrinka wound a long red scarf around her neck, which always looked so nice next to her blonde hair. "As per our agreement, I'll be filming so you can view it when you come home tonight, and we can decide." Since we'd split the album 50/50, my wife and I had agreed to make all decisions regarding it the same way. "See you at the restaurant!" Video-Fraulein leaned over to the camera and switched it off.

There was a bit of blue-screen, then an image appeared—we were a half-hour in the future, at Mr. Chow. At this point, and from then on, the camera was perched on Katrinka's shoulder. I saw Warren Darden with his old mane of hair, shoveling a forkful of General Tso's into his mouth; behind him was the cordon of empty tables we always commanded at the restaurant. He looked a little less tan than usual, from the harsh little spotlight mounted on the side of the camera. Behind him, at a table far away, another diner would occasionally point and wave.

"...took me a half-hour to get here," Fraulein said quietly.

Robbie's voice was partially masked by clinking plates. "...digging up 57th. Fucking city workers, leaning on their shovels."

Katrinka cleared her throat and took command. "Okay, we're rolling. Warren, tell Tom and I about the idea you've had."

"Wasn't mine, actually. It was Robbie's."

The camera panned, and there was Robbie, not eating, clicking a ballpoint pen nervously. "We like to stage an attempt on your husband's life."

"What do you mean, an attempt?"

"Like, a shooting."

"What?!"

"He'd be perfectly safe," Warren said.

"There'd be blanks in the gun."

My wife paused. "Even if I thought that was a good idea, it's something Tom would have to decide himself, don't you think?"

"Oh no, Tom couldn't know about it," Robbie said.

"See, Katrinka, the whole thing depends on it looking *real*."

"But why? Why can't we just keep promoting the LP the normal way?"

"Why not?" Warren continued. "It's never been tried before. Don't you want to break new ground?"

"I would imagine simply from a scientific perspective—as a matter of mass psychology—"

"Don't soft-soap me, Robbie," Katrinka growled. I smiled. I loved it when my wife busted balls.

"Think of it as street theater," Warren said, chewing an egg roll. "One thing's for sure: it will sell albums."

And magazines, I thought glumly.

"But you're sure he'll be safe?" Katrinka said.

"Absolutely," Warren said.

"I don't know. It seems quite—excessive."

"We have to do something," Robbie said. "The LPs DOA."

"What does that mean?"

"Dead on arrival," Warren said.

"It came out September one. We shipped 150,000 units. As of last week, we've already got 68,000 returns."

"Is that bad?"

"Uh, *yeah*," Robbie said, then took a big gulp of white wine.

"So we do more promotion. Warren, can we do another interview?"

The editor shook his head. "I'm maxed out. My people are accusing me of favoritism, the readers are bitching. People already say we're stuck in the 60s."

"You were!" I yelled at the screen. "I told you punk was for real, but did you listen? Noooo..."

"Don't you see, Katrinka? This will make you and Tom relevant again."

"I don't like it. It seems risky."

"I promise you, it's not," Robbie said. "We'll take every possible precaution."

I yelled again. "Like taking out a big life-insurance policy on me!"

Warren leaned over, and put his manicured paw on Katrinka's free hand; he always did that during the big sell. "I really think this is the right thing to do. Do you want to see Tom fail, in public? Because that's where it's going. Tom's proud. I know it's eating him up. Do you know where Ollie's album just debuted?"

"Where?"

"Number Seventeen."

"How high have we gotten?"

"Fifty-three," Robbie said. "And we're dropping."

At the bottom of the screen, my wife played with her spoon, a nervous habit. "You two thought of this yourselves?"

"Yeah," they lied.

"If we do it, it's got to be totally secret. If anything gets out," Katrinka said, "you know what people will think. They'll think I was behind it."

"If that happens Katrinka, I swear to you, I'll tell everyone the truth," Robbie said.

"Me, too," Warren chimed in. "After it's over, I'll tell Tom myself."

I snorted; he hadn't even told me last month. He could've saved me some trouble—if somebody hadn't killed him first.

"That's on tape. I'm going to hold you both to that... You're sure he won't be hurt?"

"Positive," Robbie said.

"He'll laugh about it, after," Warren said. "You know Tom's sense of humor."

"When were you thinking of doing it?"

"Two weeks before Christmas," Robbie said. "That'll give us maximum impact, and time in the racks."

Fraulein sighed. "Okay, but I can change my mind at any time. What do you need from me?"

"Nothing much," Warren said, smooth as butter. "We were really telling you out of respect."

"One thing would be helpful, though: could you get rid of the bodyguard?"

"But wouldn't that make it less real?"

"Not if Tom fires him," Robbie said.

"Katrinka, I know it seems weird, but it's just that we'd have to let the bodyguard in on it, and—this will only stay secret if as few people as possible are involved."

My wife paused. "All right," Katrinka said. "But I'm only doing it to save Tom's ego. He's horrible to live with when he's depressed."

"I don't doubt it," Warren said.

"As far as the bodyguard, I can't make any promises. My husband's... erratic."

"Just do what you can," Robbie said.

"And if anything goes wrong, I'm telling him. Everything."

"Of course," Warren said.

Robbie leaned back to signal a waiter. When he leaned forward again he said, "So it's decided. A toast"—he raised a glass— "to Tom's next #1 album."

The screen went blue, and the irritating tone came back. When the sound was suddenly muted, I turned and saw Katrinka kneeling, undoing the straps on my arms. Next to her was a small gray flashlight-like device.

"I needed you to watch it all," she said. "I know how you get angry."

When she had finished, she picked up the flashlight and walked out of the room. I followed, rubbing my wrists. "But why didn't you tell me? In the hospital for example?"

"Because I didn't want you getting all macho and going after them. The moment you got shot for real, obviously they became the leading suspects. Not only did they come up with the plan, they made millions off your death."

"I think somebody in Washington came up with the plan," I said. "I think they just knew a good thing when they saw it. What's with the flashlight?"

"It's a taser. In case you get any ideas."

"Are you kidding?" I'd read about those in Shuck Carlson's catalog. We got to the kitchen, and Fraulein flipped on a light. "As long as they thought you were dead, all of us were safe."

"Why didn't you kill them?"

"If I killed the one, the other would be alerted," Katrinka said. "And if I killed them both, it would raise suspicion. I didn't want to go to jail. Do you want some coffee? It's organic."

I nodded.

"When you became determined to dig it all up, I did what I could. I helped as little as possible, I hired Sam and Bevin to keep an eye on you. But I knew you'd end up finding out the truth, and killing them. And maybe, depending on what lies they told you, coming after me."

"I keep telling you, I didn't kill anybody."

"Oh yeah, they just happened to die, right after they saw you."

"Katrinka, I had no reason to kill them. Warren was going to help me. I only gave Robbie a bump on the head, and that was in self-defense. Christ," I said, "I'm practically Mohandas K. Gandhi, Nonviolent Private Eye.

"I thought the government was behind it. Then I tracked down this spy in DC. He told me a story, which I believe, that—"

My wife interrupted. "Did you ever notice, Tom, how you only believe people who lie for a living?"

"I believe you."

"Only because I insist upon it. Who did your spy say was responsible?"

"He's not *my* spy." I opened my mouth prepared to recap what went down in Joe's basement safe room, then felt exhausted at the many, many arguments it would trigger. I gave up. "Bottom line is, he didn't know."

Fraulein laughed. "You mean after all this time and money and dead bodies, you still don't know who shot you?"

"No," I said. "I don't think I care anymore, to be honest."

"That's some progress."

"But I'd like to keep Sam on the case, if you don't mind."

"Fine." She slid the cup of coffee in front of me.

"Thanks…Katrinka, I have to ask," I said, "apart from what I just watched in the lab…Sam's not going to find out anything unpleasant, is he?"

"I imagine anything he would find would be unpleasant, don't you?"

"He's not going to find out that you arranged it, is he? Used the plot as a distraction to hide an assassin firing real bullets?"

My wife straightened, as if a small electric charge had been applied to her spine. "After all I've done for you," she spat. "That is incredibly insulting."

"Now you know how it feels," I said. "Just tell me—I promise to believe you, I'm good at it. Did you hire the second gun?"

"No."

"And your proof is…?"

"Reality, *dummkopf*. Oh, sure, I had you killed, so I could spend the rest of my life tending to your legend." Der Fraulein stopped fiddling with her spoon and unwrapped a pack of cigarettes.

"I wish you wouldn't smoke, but if it'll make you feel better…You should do those tapes."

"Those tapes," Katrinka groaned. "I should get a refund. All I wanted was to make you a little easier to live with, make sure you didn't love me and leave me like all the others. Then I got trapped in this Romeo and Juliet *thing*." Fraulein lit her Benson and Hedges, snapping shut the lighter, taking a drag. "You love me more than I love you, and that makes me feel like shit. The songs, the press conferences, the erotic lithographs. Other people just *fuck*, Tom!"

"What can I say, Fraulein? I adore you."

"Do you have any idea what that's like to live with? I either feel guilty because I didn't adore you back, or shitty for not feeling guilty enough. For years I looked around and thought, 'Everybody else thinks he's great, it must be me.' Then I realized something: All those adoring fans—they didn't have to put up with you. They'd never even met you.

"Every interview, it's 'Katrinka has an IQ of 900' or how I gave Catherine Deneuve body-image issues." She slurped her coffee angrily. "I started making shit up, just to see if you'd snap out of it. Was it all a put-on for you, too? Or did you really think I could *bake a cake with my mind?*"

"Stranger things have happened."

"NO THEY HAVEN'T! God, you drive me crazy! But I did not have you shot," she said. "Absolutely, positively not."

In moments of great emotional stress, we all fall back on clichés. "Talk is cheap," I said. "Actions speak louder than words."

"How's this for action? I was in the middle of hiring Wisnewski back when you got shot. If you'd just come inside like I'd wanted instead of getting that stupid candy," she said. "As soon as you told me you wanted to investigate the case, I hired Sam again, and Bevin, too. Does that sound like someone who wanted you dead? Honestly, Tom, I did the best I could. You have to trust me."

"Right. Remind me where the taser comes in, again?"

Both of us were silent for a bit. My wife blew smoke out of her nostrils and said, "I wonder what Dr. Randlesmann would say." Dr. R. was a marriage counselor we'd seen in the late 70s.

"He'd say 'More zex! More zex!'" Randlesmann was a strict Reichian. The laughter broke the ice. "Okay, Katrinka, I'll make you a deal. If you believe that I haven't murdered anyone, I'll believe the same about you."

Katrinka smiled, and nodded, then she looked at her watch. "But you do have to go. Jasper's coming home for holiday break. I expect him any moment."

I got up from my seat, coffee in hand, and walked to the window. I looked at the snow, and the traffic passing in the night-time "It's pretty. Come see."

Fraulein got up and joined me at the window. "I've got an idea," I said. "Instead of me going, let's celebrate Christmas together," I said. "As a family, the three of us. It'll be the one we never had."

And that, Ravins Mavens, is exactly what we did.

CHAPTER EIGHTEEN

I'm here to pick up a prescription for Gnog," I said. "First name Edelweiss, middle initial V."

A girl surely much too young to be a druggist put the amber plastic bottle into a white bag, folded over the top and stapled it shut. "If you have any side effects, call your doctor."

I hadn't the heart to tell her no doctors were involved, only Clive Solomon, lay-pharmacist. So I simply smiled and handed her my credit card. I ate two Prozacs in the parking lot, then drove over to UCLA, where they were showing "Shoah." If you can't beat depression, join it.

I don't know about you, but doing the right thing always makes me feel like shit. From the moment I agreed to quit investigating and 'let sleeping dolls lie,' I fell into a funk more intense than any since the day I first heard about paraquat. I was a past master of depression—that's what all the booze and drugs had been for, at least initially—but this one was a real abyss. I'd go entire days without noticing my cock, and for a man, that's the last stage before death.

"Classic case of *shamus interruptus*," Clive said, with irritating jollity. "Should I come visit?"

"Nah." I couldn't even entertain myself, much less guests.

"In that case, have you heard of Prozac?"

One pile of forged scrip later, and I was on the road to recovery… perhaps. A pill couldn't tell me whether quitting was wisdom or cowardice.

It couldn't give me my sense of purpose back. It couldn't make me forget that the answer to Crouk's "cui bono?" had been, "Everybody but me."

I thought things would end up like they do in the movies: me squaring off against the one guy who was responsible, Tom Larkin versus his assassin, *mano a mano*, with the loser falling into Niagara Falls or something. Clean. Satisfying. Finished. But life isn't a movie, not even my life. It's messy, and just as I now accepted that washing my hands fifty times a day was probably excessive, I had to make peace with the fact that I might never know the identity of that second shooter.

And I did make peace with that. Until he showed up in my bedroom.

When I returned from *Shoah*, I asked Jermaine at the front desk if I had any messages. I was expecting Sam to update me on the case.

"Only these two," he said, handing me the slips with "Casa Marisol" written on the top.

I looked at the one on top. It was from Vickie O'Croesus, and it said, "Discovered everything! Meet me at the ferris wheel. 10:00 pm. Car #6." I glanced at the clock—it was already 9:57. So I shoved the other in my pocket and took off.

People say quitting smoking improves your wind, but that hasn't been my experience; I'm just as wheezy as when I smoked two packs of Galoises a day. By the time I got to the Pier, I was coughing so violently a homeless person made a crack about the "cords in my neck."

Still breathing hard, I got to the wheel right at the stroke of ten. The solar-powered contraption was using up its surplus in the cool night air, music playing, bulbs pulsing. The kid running it wrenched a lever, and it stopped, the bottom-most car swaying slightly as it slid into position.

He saw me hesitate. "There puke or something?"

"No, I—I have a sentimental attachment to Six."

Tugging on the neck of his yellow windbreaker—it can be quite cold at night, windy—the kid leaned on the lever and it juttered back to life. I had ridden a ferris wheel exactly one time before, and it hadn't gone well. For my sixth birthday, my Da had shown up unannounced. Telling my Auntie that he was acting on Helena's orders, he'd scooped me up and taken me to Brighton. Which made sense—if you're going to kidnap a child, it helps to take them someplace they like.

When Mum got wind of what was happening, she jumped on the next train. When she got there, the two of them staged an old-fashioned custody battle in front of hundreds of laughing witnesses. The operator stopped the ride, and I sat up at the top until Da had been carted off by a constable. Ever since then I didn't much care for heights. Or ferris wheels. Or, to be honest, fathers.

My neck began to prickle as the cars cycled past. "Do people really puke?"

"People do everything in 'em," the kid said, with a world-weariness usually reserved for soldiers. "*Everything.*"

"I'm sorry I asked." I got even sorrier when I slid into car Six; the hard plastic bench was wet. "Yuck."

I sniffed my palm, fearing the worst, but it didn't smell like anything biological. It must be dew. The car lurched forward and I gave an involuntary yell. Like I said, I didn't enjoy heights, and there was a twenty mile-per-hour crosswind which I didn't appreciate either.

The ride was nearly deserted—it was cold up there. As we climbed, I felt around on the floor for a note or a cassette or something from Vickie, and got a handful of thin, sandy muck for my trouble. I ran my fingertips under the lip of the bench, then around the low table in the middle. Nothing there either, just dried gum.

I gave the floor and edges another pass, getting more annoyed by the second. Here I was, spinning around in the dark with a wet arse, and Vickie wasn't even there to warm me up. Somebody was getting a spanking.

I had just closed my eyes to imagine it when I heard the most beautiful sound. It was barely audible over the distant hiss of the waves and the creaking of the ride, and if I hadn't had a musician's ears, I would've missed it entirely. The stars seemed to be *singing* to me. I had to concentrate quite hard to follow the tune, and I guess I had a weird expression on my face as

I passed the kid manning the controls.

"You better not puke!" he warned.

As the car vaulted upward again, the sound increased, refining itself into a weird, ghostly melody without beginning or end. Through the armature of cables, I saw a couple in another car. "The music of the spheres!" I yelled, pointing upward. "Can you hear it?" They looked at me dumbly. That's the story of my life.

Up and up I went, until the stars seemed as big as apples in front of me, liquid silver and gold, big enough to touch, pulsing in time with the rhythm of the surf below. At the wheel's apex, the car stopped, perhaps just for a moment, or perhaps much longer. It was wonderful up there, very calm and peaceful, and me finally among my kind.

Then there was a laughing scream from the roller-coaster next door, and we started to descend.

I woke up in my bedroom at the Casa Marisol, with a slight headache and a mouth that tasted like a pigeon's foot.

"What the fuck?" I tried to move, but couldn't—my arms and legs had been fastened to the bedposts with leather straps. Vickie? Not likely. For one thing, she was strictly consensual. For another, she didn't watch crap TV. The set in the room next door was blaring "The A-Team."

I blinked. My contacts felt like poker chips, and I strained to make out the digital time projected on the ceiling. 11:17—what had happened to the last hour? Obviously I'd freaked out on the ferris wheel, had a post-traumatic flashback or something, then some good Samaritan had grabbed me by the heels and dragged me home. But why had they tied me up? Easy: they thought I was going to flip out.

I was just about to call out my gratitude when I noticed something peculiar. My bedroom was a mess. There were old newspapers scattered about, brands I never read. Styrofoam oysters smeared with take-out lay atop piles of rancid underthings. The deep leather morris chair, where I liked to curl up with a book, was stained and broken as if someone had taken a sledgehammer to it. Underneath an LP-sized hole in the plaster, a Fender Tele lay dormant, broken strings angled crazily, its neck piercing the screen of a ruined amp. Inane slogans and clumsy doodles in Day Glo paint festooned the walls. And just when I thought it couldn't get any more offensive, my nose grabbed a passing smell. I traced it back to its awful source. There in the corner opposite the writing desk, under my Twombly, someone had taken a messy dump.

I was appalled. When I had left earlier this evening, the room was ready for the Aunt Harriet Seal of Approval. Now, it looked like home to a pack of angry badgers. Had *I* done this, in my blank hour? It was all very odd, and I was beginning to get worried. It was 1985, not '65—such stuff didn't happen to me any more. I gave each limb a preliminary tug, to see if there was any give in the restraints. No luck. I was able to lift the bed slightly, though, and it made a small thump. That gave me an idea: the guy who lived downstairs was not afraid to come up and complain. If I banged the bed against the floor, the finicky bachelor might come investigate. If my captor was friend, it would be a funny story; if not, it might save my life.

Before I could start, I heard footsteps approaching from the other room. To be on the safe side I pretended to be asleep.

A fat bloke with glasses and a full beard shambled past the bed to the bathroom. He looked vaguely familiar, but my main thought was not wanting to tangle with somebody that large. He could easily suffocate me with a single man-tit. So I kept playing possum.

I listened to the sound of water running. Five minutes later, a different man walked out of the bathroom, less heavy, clean-shaven, without glasses, and with lighter hair. It was Sam Wisnewski. Thank fucking Christ!

In one hand he had a tumbler full of whisky, and in the other, a can of spray paint. It made a rapid clack-clack as he shook it and started writing something on the wall.

"Sam, what the fuck are you doing?"

"Shit!" Sam turned around so fast he spilled his drink. "You should be out for six more hours!"

Never underestimate the tolerance of an ex-rock star. "Is this your idea of an early birthday present? Because I don't really do drugs anymore."

"Bullshit," the ex-cop said, a little more angrily than I expected. "The man who sold it to me called it 'Spike.' Said it made Ozzy Osbourne the man he is today."

"And you dosed me with that. Charming."

"You absorbed it through your ass," he smirked.

I jiggled my wrists. "Are these real, or am I hallucinating them? Unhook me."

"Sorry, I can't do that."

"Sam, I promise I won't go psychotic. I haven't done that since Crouk got reelected."

Wisnewski turned back and resumed spraypainting.

I squinted. "Why are you spraypainting 'BOVRIL' on my wall?"

"Seems like something a Limey rockstar would write."

The "L" continued onto a painting, and I howled. "Not on the Motherwell, you cunt!"

Sam stepped back. "I think it improves it," he said, then put the can on the desk. "Aren't you going to ask why I drugged you?"

"I don't care, just untie me, and tell me what's going on with the case."

"Well," Sam said, "you'll be happy to know I've discovered the identity of the second shooter:"

"Mr. Bella Abzug, right?"

"What? No. Me."

"Fuck off," I growled. "Sam, I can't feel my bloody hands. If you wanna get paid, you better—"

"Sorry, Charlie. Katrinka's paid me upfront, in advance. She owed me money for years. That would be enough to shoot you, but that's not why I did it."

"Sam, I was there. You didn't shoot me. You threw yourself on top of me, then—"

"Did you feel anything before then?"

"I—I don't remember."

Sam put down his tumbler full of brown liquor, then walked over to the bed, shooting his cuffs. "I threw myself on top of you…"

"Oof!" He did so, knocking the wind out of me,

"Then I told you, 'Stay down. Don't move.' And then, you felt a pain."

Sam smiled at me lupinely as he said this; then I heard the sound of greased metal, and saw a dark rod sprung out from his sleeve. He pressed it against my sternum.

"Bang," Sam said, laughing. "Sleeve gun. *Wetwork*, page 47."

"You're bloody joking."

"No sir. Then a pal and I loaded you into the squad car, where I put two more into you for good measure. Still don't know how you survived. I knew I should've given you one in the head."

"But I—you—"

"It's always somebody who knows the victim, Tom. Any cop'll tell you that. The only reason you're alive today is because Pancho hit a fucking pothole on 60th and Columbus." Wisnewski held up two fingers, a quarter-inch apart. "Missed your aorta by that much." He took the sleeve gun off. "What they don't tell you is that it's not very accurate," he said, then picked up a pistol. "I should've used this. Ah well, live and learn."

I babbled out a question, to keep a hold on reality. "Were you working for the government?"

Wisnewski gave a rueful laugh. "They didn't want to kill you. They wanted to use you, like everybody else uses you. I'm the only one who cared enough to kill you."

My mouth had been open for so long, my tongue was drying out. Sam read my surprise as scorn. Oh what the hell, maybe there was a little scorn in there, too.

"Christ, I put three slugs into you, at point blank range, and you still can't get your mind around it. You think you're so big and important that there's no way a nobody like me could—"

My sarcasm came back on line. "Spare me the 'average Joe with resentments' speech, all right? I didn't make this world, so quit blaming me for it. People like me only get famous because average Joes like you make us famous. Blame yourself."

"I never liked your music."

"Your sister, then."

Wisnewski sprang to the bed. He put his face into mine, so I could see every pock and burst vessel. "You shut your mouth about my sister. *You* of all people." He pushed off against my chest. "She was worth ten of you."

"So what's she going to think when she finds out you tried to kill me?"

"You'll see her before I will. She's dead."

I sighed. "And I suppose I'm responsible..."

"Yeah, you are. You're a Pied fucking Piper."

"Listen, Wisnewski, I didn't know your sister. She didn't know me. I was just an image in her mind—"

"Bullshit! Bullshit, Larkin! You don't even remember, you fucked her, you prick! She was seventeen. She said you were determined to deflower the security guard's daughter right under his nose. You thought it would be funny. So you two smoked some pot, and—"

"Can we skip to the back-alley abortion? Just to save time?" Maybe if I got Sam really stoked, he'd do something stupid, make some noise, attract some attention.

Sam took two steps towards me. I thought he was going to hit me, but instead he grabbed a fetid sock and jammed it in my mouth. I gagged. "Taste good? I got it special. All this stuff, I bought off a wino down by the Promenade."

My back arched and I tried to spit my mouth off my face, but no luck.

"Doris didn't get pregnant, you were just a funny story. She went to community college, wanted to be a nurse...One night in '74, her boyfriend asked her to drop off a Christmas present while he waited in the car. The guy was a dealer, the package was smack, and Doris walked right into a bust. Just like that, her life was ruined, because she trusted the wrong person." Wisnewski took a swig from his tumbler, and crunched some ice. "Can you imagine how my Dad felt, bailing her out? And me, working in Narcotics? Dorie took it even harder than we did: one night, after everybody'd gone to bed, she took a bunch of pills. And that was that.

"You screwed my life, too, Tom. The guys in my division hated me because I wouldn't take graft, so they made it look like I was dealing. They set me up, forced me to quit. Could've been worse, though; I could've gotten a .44 in the face..."

As my assassin droned on, I carefully tried each cuff, to see if I could squeeze a hand through. It was no good.

"Because of people like you, every kid with an extra $20 was turning on. Some stuck to the harmless shit, some didn't. And some people who never took anything got fucked regardless. The problem wasn't corrupt cops, or dealers, or the Mob—it was the whole society...A society you created, Mr. Father of the Sixties."

Wisnewski spat the words at me, each one a bitter little seed of hatred. Not that it would've mattered, but I wanted to tell him about Joey Browne, about plots and plans and flooding the country with heroin, but all I could do was lay there and try not to choke.

"You were one big advertisement. 'Tom Larkin came out all right, didn't he? He tried it all, had a ball, then gave it all up just like that, through true love and a macrobiotic diet.' Only you didn't give it up, did you, Tom?"

I shouted, but that simply made the sock settle itself deeper in my throat. I gagged and coughed; that bastard didn't lift a finger.

"When I met you and your lady wife, I just wanted a job, any job. I wasn't gunning for you then. I didn't like you because of Dad's stories, but you had a wife and kid. Then I saw you using—remember when I walked in on you, that morning? When you were under your piano?"

I screamed and thrashed. Wisnewski leaned over. "Okay, okay, Jesus... You're going to have to be quiet, though. Any yelling, and I'll put one in your brain." I suddenly noticed the pistol was wearing a silencer.

"I wasn't doing heroin!" I said, desperately. "I haven't used since '71—Fraulein gave me some self-hypnosis tapes. I kicked, I swear. *I'm clean!*"

Wisnewski got up and back into the bathroom next door. When he returned, he was carrying a small leather shaving kit. He showed it to me. "Yours, right?"

"Yeah." It had been a Christmas present from Jasper.

Wisnewski sorted through the contents with his stubby fingers. "Razor, styptic pencil, tweezers, hemorrhoid cream…What do we have here?" He pulled out a little foil packet, and showed it to me. "Looks like heroin." He tasted a bit. "Tastes like heroin…"

"You put that in there, just like you've trashed my apartment!"

"Bullshit. It comes in your monthly envelope, with your allowance. Believe me, I didn't expect to find it, I just wanted to make sure you would pay me when I started helping you investigate. Anyway, I didn't trash your apartment, Tom. I just made the outside look like your inside."

"Fuck you! I've been clean and sober for years."

Wisnewski laughed. "And you don't smoke cigarettes, either. Addicts lie. That's how you can tell they're addicts."

"But Fraulein gave me the tapes—"

Wisnewski stuffed the sock back into my mouth. "The tapes didn't help you quit anything, champ. What *did* they do, I wonder?" Wisnewski dropped the packet back into the dopp kit. "One for *The Weekly World News*, I guess." The ex-cop looked at his watch. "Wow. I'd better finish up. I've got a plane to catch, to Costa Rica. Permanent retirement. What I've been charging Katrinka…trust me, you don't wanna know.

"When I realized you were still using, and getting ready to warp another generation, I had no choice. I had to protect all the people who'd believe in the fairy tale, all those kids. You're a father, you know I'm right."

I gagged on the sock, trying not to think of all the *E. coli* trickling down my throat. My captor continued.

"Five years later, Katrinka calls and tells me you're alive. Bad day, Tom. But I'm not a vengeful man; I was willing to let you alone, as long as you stayed hidden. I was going to manage the investigation, make sure you didn't find anything, just to protect myself. Then I met you at the diner, and you said you were planning on a comeback. That meant I had to shoot you. I would've too, if that idiot in the Fleetwood hadn't shown up."

I was joking! I screamed into the fetid cotton. It was a joke! But all Wisnewski heard were glottal vibrations.

"There didn't have to be bloodshed. It could've ended before it began, or just with you. But you had to keep *pushing*. Every time I'd kill somebody, I think, 'He's gotta quit now.' I only killed people who encouraged others to think of you as a role model. Warren, Robbie. Now that your wife's finally paid me, I'll probably kill her, too." The ex-cop chuckled. "Hate to say it, but her cheapness was the only thing keeping her alive."

I thrashed and screamed for mercy. "Relax, relax. I'm not going to shoot you, Tom. I want your death to mean something—we all want that, right?" He took the packet out of the kit, then turned away from me, hunching over. I craned my neck but couldn't see; he filled in the blanks for me. "Don't worry, you won't feel a thing. But I gotta make sure to give you enough this time."

At the strike of a match, everything seemed to fall into place. Wisnewski triggered Thigg's self-destruct to confuse and discourage me. The ex-cop knew Robbie's greed would make him try to kill me, that's why he gave me the flyer. When I escaped, he had to kill Robbie for the same reason he'd been forced to kill Warren: one of them would've told me the original plot wasn't lethal. I would've gotten to Wisnewski sooner or later, because I kept digging, and that he couldn't allow.

Wisnewski turned back around. He was holding a syringe loaded with heroin. I moved my arms as much as the restraints would allow.

"Don't!" he snapped. "If you fight me, I'll have to switch to Plan B. That will be a lot more painful, I promise."

I gave up. What else could I do? "I knew you wanted it, deep down." He sat on the edge of the bed and searched my bare arm for a vein. "Once I'm safe, I'll sell the story—how you survived, then spent the last ten years in hiding, living in squalor, as a junkie. You'll be a warning, Tom. It won't be random. It won't be for nothing." He found his vein.

I bellowed, desperate to stretch this out as long as I could. The ex-cop paused. "Do you ever think about what kind of man you could've been, Tom, if you'd just had a little self-control?"

I felt the prick of the needle, and the rush…then my eyes drifted open. I could swear I heard a voice coming from very far away, perhaps from the other room.

"Helloooo? Anybody home?"

Sam withdrew the needle, plunger halfway down. Clive stuck his head in the bedroom, saw what was going on, and withdrew it just as quickly.

"Sorry, didn't mean to intrude. You two have fun. I'll be out here."

"Fuck," the cop said, putting the syringe down.

Clive hollered in from the kitchen. "I hope you don't mind I'm making an omelet. Would you like one, Tom's anonymous sex partner?"

Wisnewski grabbed his gun from the floor. "I'll be right back."

The cop walked out of the bedroom. Moments later, I heard the sonorous "bonk" of steel on skull. It was the most beautiful sound I'd ever heard.

Clive walked in brandishing a cast-iron pan. "Tom, are you awake?"

I was not. I was somewhere else entirely. But not dead. Not yet.

When I drifted back, Clive had undone the restraints, and left a big glass of orange juice on my bedstand, with a note reading, "Tell me when you're up."

I shuffled into the kitchenette in my complimentary bathrobe, swigging OJ. Clive was sitting at the table, reading a copy of *Variety*, and eating a bagel. With his reading glasses and gray hair, he looked like any other respectable, retired businessman. Except that Wisnewski's revolver was sitting on the table in front of him, between the butter and the lox. "I took care of your nasty little friend," he said, not looking up.

"He was no friend of mine."

"Realized that the moment I saw you two," Clive said. "As I recall, you prefer the dominant position. Except with your wife, of course."

"Get stuffed." I helped myself to a bagel. "What did you do with the body? Chop it into bits or something?"

"Who do you think I am, Meyer Lansky? He's right over there, behind the couch. I had to give him a few sleeping pills to keep him quiet. And a few other things. Mr. Man has dealable quantities of many, many things on his person. He won't be coming out for a long time."

"I never thought I'd say this, but 'thank you War on Drugs.'"

Clive snorted. "Quite."

"But what if people believe his story? That I'm alive, all that?"

"With what's in his pockets and his bloodstream, he could shit gold doubloons and they'd still think he was mad." Clive looked me up and down. "You all right?"

"I think so."

"What was he injecting you with?"

"Smack," I said.

"I thought you'd kicked that," Clive said. "You know, tied yourself to a chair, wrote a song, all that."

"I thought I had, too," I said. "But if I had, I'd be dead.

"What's the point of doing drugs if you don't remember doing them?"

"I don't know," I said, thoroughly confused. "Why don't I remember? And if I'm doing that without remembering, what else might I have done without realizing it?"

"And Inspector Hound is off on the next investigation."

"Bite your bloody tongue."

Clive dialed the police and told them to come over. When he hung up the phone, I walked over to Sam.

"They'll be here in three minutes...What are you doing?"

"Untying him."

"You're what?"

I grunted, struggling with a knot. "Do you do this...often?" Then I slapped the ex-cop until he registered semi-consciousness. He mumbled and flopped about, but I kept the gun trained on him, just in case. "Get up," I said.

"Fuck off..." he mumbled.

"But why?"

"Quiet, Clive."

I stepped back, and Sam struggled to focus his eyes. When he managed it, he saw the gun in my hand. "If you're gonna do it, do it," he slurred. "Junkie piece of shit."

That decided me. I turned the gun around, handing him the handle.

Wisnewski snatched the gun and pointed it at me. His arm wavered and Clive ducked behind the breakfast bar.

"Larkin, you're mad!"

"Relax." I fished a bullet out of my bathrobe pocket. "I've got these."

Sam pulled the trigger several times. Giving the gun a betrayed look, realizing it was useless, he swore and shoved the gun into his pocket. Or tried to. It fell to the carpet.

I handed it to him. What would the guy in my songs say? "Now go, and sin no more."

My sincerity was a little much for Sam. "You're a fucking lunatic," he said.

"Nope. Just a free man. You should try it sometime."

Wisnewski stumbled out of the suite, shaking his head, completely unglued. Clive was only slightly less confused.

"That man tried to *kill* you, Tom. Why did you let him go?"

"Everybody deserves a second chance, don't you think?" Then I added, "If the cops catch him here, they'll ask a lot of questions. This way, when they come we can say 'he went thataway' and go have brunch."

"And you're not afraid he'll come after you again?"

"I choose not to be. Now he owes me. That matters to people like him."

Clive looked dubious.

"I'm not the selfish, evil bastard he thought I was. I'm on the right side of his conscience now." And my own, I thought.

"Think that'll be enough?"

"It'll have to be. Anyway, we know the truth, don't we?"

I'd turned my back, heading for the shower, but I could tell by Clive's voice that he was smiling. "Yes, we do."

ACKNOWLEDGMENTS

It's never easy to write a book, but this one was a doozy. They say that "writing is rewriting," but that's crap. Writing is somehow resisting the urge to stab yourself in the eyeball when you realize the book you're working on kinda sucks, no it *definitely* sucks, and you have to start over—again, from scratch—a year older, a year poorer, and even less sure that this isn't your own personal Vietnam. What I'm trying to say is that any sane individual would've declared Peace With Honor sometime around January '08, slung the manuscript into a drawer marked "OK, You Win!", and spent the last 30 months pitching teen vampire dramedies to the CW. But if this project is the most difficult one I've undertaken, it's also the story I've felt the fiercest personal duty to tell; so I persevered, and am glad I did. I hope you are, too.

I could not have completed *Life After Death for Beginners* without the help and support of many friends, family, and fans. Special thanks go to my wife Kate, Jonathan Schwarz, Jerry Neufeld-Kaiser, Pete and Priscilla and all my friends at *Chez 1122*, Devin McKinney and the Dullbloggers (www.heydullblog.blogspot.com), Charlie Schroeder, Dirk Voetberg, my indefatigable agent Edward Necarsulmer, Jonathan Lyons, Ellen Geiger, Deborah Arakelian, Ellen Ryder, Tim Bent, Kate Jacobs and Jon Bieley, *Yale Record* pals far and near, my friends at The Aero, Diane Goldner and Julie Hoyle, Norbert at the Beverly Hills Cheese Shop, the guy who sells that super sourdough bread at the Wednesday Farmer's Market, Mom and Dad, David Lancaster, and of course, Aunt Mary for starting it all. Thanks for the dreams, whoever you were, they always calmed me down and broke me through—I'm taking you at your word. And I mustn't forget the fans who write me such nice emails and letters; your support is like water in the desert, and I always do my best for you. Apologies to anyone I've forgotten—if you feel you belong on this list, you probably do. I've got like, four calories in me at the moment, and a long night ahead figuring out how to upload this for Kindle.

Will there be a sequel? That would be telling. For updates on that book—and all my others, past/present/future—shoot off an email to mikesnewbooks@gmail.com. I can also be reached through my website, mikegerber.com. The more emails I get asking for a book, the more quickly it goes to the top of my To-Do List. So write!

Your time and attention is a great gift; thank you for reading.